THE TROUBLE WITH BABY GODS AND VAMPIRES

A CARY REDMOND NOVEL, BOOK 4

KAT SIMONS

PUBLISHING

To my family, for getting through this year together.

*C*ary grinned at the vampire, frankly relieved. This was what she knew how to do. And after the last week with her boyfriend's family—they'd used the spring equinox as an excuse for a full family visit—this was a lovely break.

Although, she had been dealing with a lot of vampires in the last month. Since early February actually, nearly two months. She should probably be a bit more worried about that. All these vampires defying the Master's laws was…odd.

"I'm sure you know the rules," she said to the one she faced now. He was tall and thin and preternaturally beautiful with pale skin, silver white hair cut in a short, spiky style, and a face so chiseled and perfectly symmetrical he could have graced magazine covers and underwear ads. "In this town, no feeding on the unwilling," she said. "That's the deal."

"Gabriel is changing the 'deal'," the vampire snarled.

"Not that I've heard," she said reasonably. "And, you know, I would have heard. People talk about these things."

He lifted his lip in a look that was super condescending.

Cary just smiled. "You're looking at me and thinking I'm gullible and naive and don't know anything at all. But you'll notice how I'm *looking* at you, right? In the eyes? Like, maybe there's more to me than a little human blood?"

The vampire wasn't a spring chicken. He was past the century mark at least. And his initial attempts to toss her aside had required her to stand firm because she actually felt the tug of it. That meant he was a really powerful vampire, whatever his age. That was the only time she felt a vampire's attempts to move her. The only times she had really bad reactions to those attempts were when she met a Master vampire—which was blessedly rare. The last time she'd met one, she'd nearly thrown up on his shiny shoes.

Gabriel was the current Master of Portland, and when he'd overthrown the previous Master, he'd declared he'd uphold all the laws Ariel had put into place to keep the hive safe. One of those rules—one that Cary had negotiated with Ariel personally because they'd both agreed, although likely for different reasons, that vampires shouldn't drink innocent kitten blood—was that the vampires in Portland only drank from willing people. *People*. Not kittens. Only those who could consent to the bloodletting.

Vampires didn't need to kill to live. Some liked to. All of them could. And the young ones sometimes had a hard time controlling that urge. But for the most part, they could carry on quite easily without killing anyone.

And in Portland, for the safety of everyone involved—not to mention the kittens!—vampires lived off the willing. In this town, there were more than enough willing to feed the hive.

Unless Gabriel had been allowing an increase in new vampires.

Which might explain why she'd been having to get between these guys and unwilling victims so much over the last two months.

She narrowed her eyes. "You're not making more vampires than you can support are you? Because that's not okay."

"What is it to you, human?"

"Hey, I live here too. We all need to utilize our resources, and overburdening any of them is irresponsible."

The vampire blinked at her, his jaundiced-yellow eyes iridescent. Eyes that would have been mesmerizing if not for the trembling human man Cary was protecting from being eaten.

The poor guy was not the kind that usual came into contact with vampires, that was obvious at a glance. And he wasn't even the kind of man she usually ended up protecting. To be honest, she mostly figured grown ass men should be able to take care of themselves. She had her prejudices. But in this case, the guy had just been minding his own business, locking up his fishing supply shop, and ready to head home.

"Do you think Jim here wants the waterways in the area over-fished?" she asked the vampire. "No. You know why?"

"Cause I'd go out of business," Jim muttered.

"Right," Cary said. "He'd go out of business. Overextending our resources is bad for everyone." She glanced back at Jim and nodded.

He returned the gesture, a little frantically, his eyes wide. Jim was a lanky, tall, bearded older man who looked like he was a lot more comfortable by a lake than walking around a city. He wore a flannel shirt under his heavy army surplus coat, his boots and jeans neat and clean but well worn. He had a nice, comfortable face with character wrinkles around his eyes and across his brow. She had a hard time guessing his age—because she was really bad at that—but she'd figure around his late fifties, maybe early sixty.

A far cry from the Goth kids and clueless tourists that usually fed the vampires. And the tourists were only allowed because the ones that agreed thought it was some sort of performance art specific to Portland, thanks to a little vampire mesmerism.

"So as Jim has clearly stated," she said to the vampire, who was trying to reach through her Protector shields to strangle her, "it's a really bad idea to make too many vampires. Has Gabriel been falling down on his job?"

Master vampires were supposed to keep hives under control, to sustainable numbers, and generally in line so no wars broke out. Falling down on those responsibilities usually led to another Master overthrowing the weaker one and taking over.

Cary wouldn't have thought the previous Master, Ariel, had been weaker. After their meeting, Cary had been terrified of her. Which meant Gabriel was even scarier. She really really didn't want to have to meet Gabriel if she could at all avoid it.

But if something was amiss in the hive and it was driving vampires to feed on the unwilling ordinary Jims of the city, it might fall to her to intervene. And wow did she *not* want to do that.

"You're meddling in business that doesn't concern you, woman," the vampire said, his voice very deep now.

"Yeah, you keep saying things like that, but really, if I have to keep getting between you guys and unwilling people, this is going to cut into my time. A lot. And that very much does concern me." She glanced back at Jim. His skin was very pale beneath his dark beard. "Bad guys always say stuff like that, though. I'm not sure why they can't think of more original lines. But it's always 'you're meddling in things you shouldn't' and 'this doesn't concern you' and 'you're a dead woman' and 'this isn't over, bitch'." She made a face. "I get those last two a *lot*. It's sometimes hard not to take personally."

She faced the vampire again. He was shaking his hands as if they'd gotten hurt. She frowned. "What did you just try to do? You really should stop before you catch on fire. That happens you know. Vampires try too hard to get at me and they catch on fire." To Jim, "The smell is really gross. It'd be better if he didn't do that."

"Wouldn't..." Jim swallowed audibly and lowered his voice. "Wouldn't it be bet-better if he was... You know?"

"Dead?" Cary frowned a little at the vampire. "Depends really. I don't know him." To the vampire, "Do you feed from unwilling a lot? Or is this just some new, desperate thing you've engaged in for some reason that I might have sympathy for and could therefore forgive you and send you on your way without you being dead? Again." To Jim, "Technically, he did die already. That's kind of how the vampire thing works."

"Didn't know they were real," Jim muttered.

"Yeah, that's generally better for all concerned," she said. To the vampire, "Are you going to answer my question or just keep trying to break through my shields to strangle me? I mean, I'd *rather* you didn't just randomly burn to death, but if you're determined, I guess I can't stop you."

"Gabriel will want to see you," the vampire growled, taking a few steps away from her. "After I tell him of your insolence."

She laughed. Really hard. "Me? I doubt he gives two flying fucks about me." Over her shoulder, "Sorry about the language."

"Understandable," Jim said.

"I'm an insignificant bug as far as the Master of the city is concerned," Cary said. "If you go to him complaining about a human woman preventing you from breaking *his* laws, I think it'll go worse for you than for me."

The vampire's eyes narrowed. She couldn't begin to read his expression. He was way too old for that. Outside of the anger he'd been purposefully showing her earlier—probably to try and scare her—he kept the rest of his thoughts to himself.

On the whole, she figured that was a good thing. She really didn't want to know for sure what he was thinking since it likely involved bloodletting, and specifically, her blood.

"I won't indulge you with the usual 'bad guy' parting line," the vampire said.

"You want to, though, don't you?" she said with a grin. "You are just itching to tell me 'this isn't over,' aren't you?"

He frowned, ever so slightly, and her grin widened.

"When—" he emphasized the word, "—Gabriel commands you appear before him, don't make him wait. That will go even worse for you."

"Yeah, good luck with getting him to have any interest in me at all."

"Oh, he's interested in you," the vampire assured. "Cary Redmond."

She blinked and he was gone. So fast, a breeze ruffled her hair. In the wake of his departure, her heartbeat hammered hard.

He'd known her name. He knew who she was even though she'd only said her first name aloud to Jim when trying to calm him down.

A strange vampire knew who she was, and said the Master of Portland was interested in her.

Oh boy.

2

"So they're all back home safe and sound," Cary said, trying not to reveal her relief to Deacon even though he could obviously smell it.

Deacon Jones was her mate, in his leopard shifter terminology, and her boyfriend in her human terminology. And not all that long ago, he'd told her he loved her. Mostly because she'd almost died and he was worried she would die before he said it. But still. It was nice to know. She'd yet to say it back, though. Not because the feelings weren't there. But because there were complications in their relationship that she was still dealing with.

Not least of which was his family and the fact that one day he'd be the leader of his people. Also, unlike most leopard shifters, he had magic, and if he lost control, he could rip apart another leopard shifter without having to use his hands.

Finding his mate—finding her—had upended his lifetime of control and turned him into a very dangerous man. The full depth of that danger had only become clear to her when they'd gone to stay at his family's home in January. Since that visit, she and Deacon had stuck to Portland, for everyone's sake.

And in the two months since then, with continued distance from most of his people, his control had slowly come back without him having to be a complete iceman—which he had to be if surrounded by other leopards. He'd been able to return to work. Which was great because his job was rescuing animals and Cary was all for that particular career choice.

Things had been good. Even the wizard who'd been trying to kill her had vanished. Or at least he hadn't made an attempt to kill her recently. And since he knew how to kill her, knew she was a Protector and what her vulnerabilities were, the fact that he wasn't still gunning for her was nice. Maybe? She still felt like she was waiting for the other shoe to drop. A threat she kept on constant alert for, except when she was in her own home which had a protective glamour on it so no one could find it unless she wanted them to find it.

Outside of the unresolved wizard issue, though, life had been relatively normal. For her.

The visit from Deacon's family had upended that normalcy for a full week.

"Everyone has scattered again," he assured. "Except Caitlin, obviously."

Caitlin was the sister who lived in Portland and worked with Deacon here. Cary officially adored her because she didn't take any shit from her big brother and was a fabulous person to gossip with. She'd been giving Cary a lot of good tips when it came to this shifter mate business too. Since Cary was *not* a shifter in any way shape or form, she really didn't know how to deal with being and having a "mate." There were a lot more hormonal and instinctive side effects to it all than just having an ordinary boyfriend.

Actually, she really liked all his siblings—and there were a lot of them. She particularly loved the way they gave Deacon grief but were also fiercely loyal to each other. The ones who had mates, or relationships with people not their mates but still serious enough to bring to family events, spent a lot of time coaching her on Deacon's loveable foibles and how much work relationships could take but they were worth it.

She suspected Deacon had put them up to that last bit.

Either that or his mother had.

His mother was, surprisingly, on the side of their relationship working. His father... Well, Cary and Evan had made up since their little fight a few months back, when Cary had accused Deacon's mother of maybe overusing her skills with her people. It was a sore spot for Evan that Cary had accidentally hit. And he'd accidentally, or maybe not so accidentally, hit her right in her overactive sense of guilt at not being good enough to do her job.

They'd made an effort to get back on friendly footing with each other since then, and spent a lot of time discussing pizza. Evan had learned how to make pizza in recent months and pizza was Cary's favorite food. But she was still working at being comfortable with him. She kept worrying she'd say the wrong thing, which she did a lot anyway. Usually, though, that was with bad guys and she didn't care if *they* liked her or not.

"Did everyone have a good visit?" she asked as she poured out a cup of coffee.

They were standing in her small kitchen, her three dogs arrayed on the floor around them waiting patiently for attention. Deacon stood at the counter, arms crossed over his thick chest, looking all sexy and big and delicious. His dark hair loose and in need of a trim. His golden eyes intent on her. She used to duck from that look in his eyes. She really loved it now.

"They did," he said, his voice deep. "But I'm glad they're gone."

She grinned. "Too much family at once?"

"Too little time alone with you."

"I'm okay with those feelings." She set her coffee aside—a sure sign of how she felt about him—and went into his arms for a kiss. Not an intense one, because the dogs were watching and one of them was a demon dog and one a foo lion and one just an ordinary mundane mutt, but she still got weirded out having them all watch her and Deacon kiss.

She did stay in his arms, however, to ask, "How was work today?"

"We found a good sanctuary for the monkeys, so they'll be good now."

"Oh, that's a relief." Some woman just outside Vancouver, Washington, who had no sense whatsoever, had spent an inordinate amount of money buying three wild Capuchin monkeys for pets, and they'd torn her home apart. Even with all that chaos, she'd tried to keep them, convinced they were her soul mates or something. Until one attacked her and she'd ended up in the hospital. Animal control was called in, and Jones family's animal rescue group took the monkeys in for safe-keeping and rehousing.

"I'm glad you've been able to go back to work," she said. "Caitlin is keeping you in line?"

He chuckled. "I'm not sure it was a good thing introducing you two."

"She does keep me updated on everything you're doing, you know? She's a very sweet woman."

"Yes, she is. Which is why she's better at the fundraising part of our jobs than I am."

Cary smiled but every time he mentioned fundraising in passing, it reminded her of a subject she kind of wanted to forget and yet couldn't. "How's Sasha? I was afraid to ask your mother."

"Same," Deacon said, shortly.

Sasha was an ex of Deacon's and had been his mother's assistant. It also turned out she had the wrong idea that Deacon was *her* mate and that taking over the leopards—by having his mother killed—was the only way to have him. Also, she kidnapped and tried to kill Cary, but Cary got death threats more often than was really a good thing so she was kind of used to them.

Deacon still wasn't.

Sasha had ended up cursed and Deacon's mother was still working on breaking the curse. Removing the tainted blood that had gotten into Sasha was proving a lot more difficult than they'd hoped.

But even without the curse, Sasha had tried to kill people and endangered all the leopards and so wouldn't see freedom for years. If ever.

The whole thing left Cary feeling a little sick to her stomach, for a lot of reasons.

Since Deacon obviously didn't want to talk about it, though, and she didn't really want to either, she moved on to other topics—including getting back to her coffee.

"So another vampire, huh?" Deacon said as they settled on her couch. "That's how many in the last few weeks?"

"I don't know. About six or seven. A lot more than the one every six months since Ariel set down the no-drinking-from-the-unwilling law." She leaned into him, cradling her coffee mug, her back to his solid chest, resting her head against his shoulder.

She loved Friday nights. Deacon took the weekend off, if he could, and unless her bosses needed her, she and Deacon got the night and morning to themselves. She pretended she loved the sleeping in part, but they didn't do an awful lot of sleeping.

"And," she said, "the ones that usual break that rule are young and impulsive. The ones that may or may not even survive to the century mark. This one tonight, he was old. Not a Master, not that strong, but strong enough. Poor Jim."

"Jim?"

"The man I saved from the vampire. He owns a fishing supply store. Nice guy. Did *not* know what to make of there being real vampires in the world."

Deacon kissed her on the head.

She looked up at him. "What was that for?"

"Your compassion," he said. Then shrugged. "And for the fact that you *only* feel sympathy for this Jim guy so my leopard isn't acting up."

She snorted and settled back against him again. His jealousy—instinctive and not really in his control—had been a thing since they met. She'd gotten a taste of that instinctive chemical reaction herself a few months back and she had a lot more sympathy for him now. There was still an issue between Deacon and her former mentor Jaxer, but that was because her former mentor had gotten it into his damned fool head he was in love with her. And until he could stop feeling that way about her, there would continue to be a thing between the two men.

Cary had given up trying to talk them both out of their feelings. Eventually it would work itself out.

"Have you heard anything from the vampire world?" she asked Deacon. While he did real work in the real world with mundane humans, he was a shapeshifter, a pretty powerful one at that. He did have an ear to the ground when it came to the preternatural world because it could affect his people.

"Nothing that would explain this sudden defiance of Gabriel's laws." He paused. "Unless he's changed the law."

She groaned. "I really hope he hasn't. I don't want to have to go see him and sort this all out in person." She ducked her head toward her mug, hesitating to tell Deacon this part. He was going to freak out. "Apparently, the Master knows who I am now."

"Does he know what you are?" Deacon asked in a quiet, frighteningly controlled tone.

"I'm not sure," she said, just as quietly.

As a magical Protector, Cary was impervious to the powers of others—when she was protecting someone. When she wasn't, she was vulnerable. And if someone knew the truth, that all it took to kill her was to go after her and her alone with no intended threat to anyone around her, she could be killed. The trick was that the person trying to kill her couldn't just be attempting to get her out of the way so they could kill someone else. Her powers kicked in in that circumstance.

But if she were the sole target…

That was the problem with the wizard who kept coming after her. He knew what she was, he knew how to kill her, and he'd come close to doing just that. Twice now.

If a Master vampire knew what she was and how to get around her Protector magic, she wasn't sure how she'd survive that.

"The bad guy tonight, he said Gabriel would want to see me," she said. "I wrote that off to talk at first. They all say that. But since Gabriel knows my full name, knows exactly who I am, I'm not so sure he won't try to demand a meeting now."

"Obviously, you won't go," Deacon said.

"That's easier said than done," she countered.

"Not that complicated. Just don't go into the hive."

She rolled her eyes. "And have every vampire in Portland pestering

12

me for days and weeks and months until I do. Plus, you know, they might catch me alone and not with someone around to protect."

Deacon's arm tightened around her. "I'll stay with you. Vampires love shifter blood if they can get it. You'll have me to protect."

On the one hand, Cary loved that he so easily allowed *her* to protect *him* given he was the big strong shifter—even if he only did it as a way to protect her. Somehow it worked out in her head as being a sweet and supportive gesture.

On the other hand, "You've only just gone back to work. You can't just drop everything again for my sake."

"That's what mates do," he said. "Caitlin will understand. She'd encourage it. She adores you."

"Ah, that's sweet. I adore her, too. But still, I can't keep dragging you into my stuff and away from yours."

"I dragged you into my stuff a few months ago."

"And look what that got us?"

"The loyalty of most of the leopards?"

"Oh, well that's just because I saved the kids. But I'd do that anyway. Not like that required any arm twisting." She always chose protecting kids and animals over just about anyone else, without any hesitance.

"My point," he said. "You didn't hesitate to help when I needed it. Why do you think I'd hesitate to help you?"

"It's not that. It's the upending of your life. Again. Eventually, you need to get back to normal."

He laughed. A deep chuckle that vibrated along her back. "Cary, love, nothing is ever going to be normal in my life again after meeting you." He kissed the top of her head. "And I'm very pleased with that."

She made a face. That might have been insulting except she understood. Nothing would be the same for her now either. Still, his life hadn't exactly been *normal* before her. You couldn't be a shapeshifting, magic-wielding, leader of your people and have a *normal* life. She winced. Her life hadn't exactly been what people might call normal either before Deacon. Not for the last six and a half years anyway. Really, she didn't have a lot of ground to stand on here.

"Fine. But you taking time off work again is only an emergency backup contingency. We might be worrying about nothing. Not like Gabriel has tried to summon me yet."

Deacon made a noncommittal noise in the back of his throat.

She wanted to argue more but knew it was pointless. He was a grown man who would do whatever he wanted to do and there was only so much trying to change his stubborn mind she could deal with in one night. "I've been free of wizard threats for a while now," she said to bring up a positive subject. "That's a good thing."

His shrug made her head lift and settle. "If he's given up on trying to kill you, yes, it's a good thing."

"Maybe me being constantly surrounded by shifters has changed his plans." She really had had a lot of shifters in her life lately. Mostly of the leopard variety. And mostly Deacon's family. But she'd made a few friends among his people, too, and she'd been spending time with them. As well as spending time with her best friends.

Actually, except when she was protecting people, she really wasn't alone a lot these days. Outside of occasionally being alone in her car when getting from place to place...

She hadn't really thought about that before this moment.

"I seem to have had people around me a lot," she said aloud, slowly. "Almost nonstop company." She sat up and faced him. "Any thoughts on that?"

While having people around her didn't guarantee the wizard wouldn't attack—both times he'd tried to kill her, she'd had people with her; he just hadn't been interested in killing those people, which meant he could take advantage of the loophole in her magic—it did mean there was always someone there to help if the wizard came after her.

And it was just occurring to her that that might not have been coincidence.

"Sherri and Lucas and Diana are all very interested in keeping you safe," Deacon said. "After you saved their kids. Twice."

"And the others? Caitlin? Nicky and Jillian?" In fact, Nicky and Jillian lived on the Oregon coast—and Nicky didn't much like crowds.

The fact that they kept coming into Portland to visit her really should have clued her in earlier. "Damn it, Deacon, you've got them all guarding me, don't you?"

"I didn't order them to do it," he said. "They volunteered. They *like* you." He glanced away. "And you'll be their…queen one day."

"Argh."

The mere thought of that always freaked her out. Which was why he hesitated to bring it up. She really couldn't see herself as anyone's queen and the fact that her mate would be their version of a king didn't seem to change her vision of herself in that mix. She didn't have the first clue how to be a leader of an entire people. She didn't particularly want the pressure.

But if she stayed with Deacon, there was no real way to avoid it.

"I'm supposed to be the Protector in all this," she said to avoid the subject of her status among the leopards. "I'm not supposed to have bodyguards. I do the body guarding."

"But you can't protect yourself," he said bluntly.

"Hey, I've been training hard with Lucy. I can kick ass a lot better now, thank you very much."

Lucy was one of her best friends, a martial arts expert, and her personal self-defense trainer. Actually, Lucy had been trying to teach Cary self-defense for years, but it was only since entering her test year as a Protector that Cary had started taking the training seriously. She needed *some* skills that didn't rely on magic she had no conscious control over.

"That still won't keep you alive if a wizard throws magic at you that you can't block," he said bluntly. "And none of us want to see you dead."

It was hard to be offended by that. Still… "You should have told me what was going on," she said. "Secretly surrounding me with body-guards is not a good way to engender trust."

He sighed and ran a hand through his hair, leaving it mussed and sexy looking. She resisted the urge to bury her fingers in that thick mass of beautiful black silk until later, once they'd had it out about this.

"Fine. I should have told you," he said. "Honestly, it wasn't a planned thing, though. It just sort of evolved out of their concern for you. You have only yourself to blame for being likeable."

She snorted. "Likeable? Right. Tell that to the wizard."

"So… No news I take it?" he asked. Carefully.

She made a face. "No. And no, I haven't talked to Jaxer in the last week or so."

Her faery mentor had finally started abiding by the terms of her test year and staying mostly away from her. It was her seventh year as a Protector and she was required to sink or swim on her own—either survive and come into her full powers, whatever that meant because no one would explain it to her, or die and her family would be compensated.

That last part still freaked her out if she thought about it too much.

Jaxer wasn't supposed to do anything to help her this year, unlike the constant help he'd been during the previous six years. It had taken a few months to adapt to that distance, for both of them. But since he'd revealed his feelings for her, she'd preferred things this way. She didn't return his feelings. She adored Jaxer as a friend and mentor. She missed him and the way things used to be between them. But she wasn't in love with him. And it hurt to think that being around her right now hurt him.

They both needed this distance.

She suspected having Jaxer less of a fixture in her life helped Deacon's control, too. He could scent Jaxer's feelings, and his jealousy acted up every time the two men were around each other. They'd been friends before, so this all kind of sucked in a big way. But there wasn't much they could do about it until Jaxer got over his feelings and moved on.

"No sign of Sheldon either," she said, to get her mind off the melancholy topic of her mentor. "I'm starting to wonder if he really did survive or if maybe the wizard has been disguising himself as Sheldon to throw us off."

Sheldon was a teenage wizard she'd faced last Halloween when he'd kidnapped and tried to swap bodies with Deacon. That was how she and Deacon had met. Sheldon had tossed a powerful wizard bolt at Deacon, Cary had blocked it, and it had rebound on Sheldon. They'd all thought Sheldon had been killed, except his body was never found.

And he'd been spotted alive and well a few times since.

The wizard after Cary was apparently Sheldon's teacher—*his* mentor—and this was some sort of revenge thing. Although, if Sheldon was alive, she wasn't sure why they needed revenge on her. Unless they were just being petty. Which wouldn't surprise her.

"I wouldn't be sad to hear that little shit was dead," Deacon said sourly.

She'd probably feel the same way if someone had tried to steal her body and kill her. But Sheldon had been pretty young—was still pretty young if he was alive—so she had trouble wishing him dead. She didn't want him or his teacher to succeed in killing *her*, but that was different to wanting someone dead.

"Different topic," she said. Boy, they had a lot of touchy topics of conversation to avoid. "How's Jon doing at the shelter?"

One of the people she'd had to protect not too long ago, a thirteen year old kid named Johnathon Webber, had an amazing talent for talking to animals. He could do some other things too that leaned toward scary, but he was a good kid, and they were hoping to influence him toward using his skills for the good.

Even though he was technically too young for a job, his mother had agreed to let him volunteer at one of Deacon's animal shelters. Caitlin had taken him under her wing, teaching him as much about running the shelter as about carrying for the animals in the shelter. Cary suspected Deacon's sister was training her own future assistant—or replacement.

"He's doing good," Deacon said. "Settled in and getting his hands dirty. He doesn't even mind cleaning out cages."

"Because Caitlin pays him under the table when he does?"

Deacon smiled. "And he's just mercenary enough to take the money."

"Sally's okay with this?" Sally was Jon's mother and she was very strict about the rules for her child.

"According to Caitlin, she is."

Cary grinned. Caitlin probably put it to Sally in just the right way —like it was a contribution to Jon's college fund or something. Caitlin Jones was the schmoozer and charmer in the Jones family, and she was very good at dealing with people whether it was getting them to donate their money or their time to her cause, or getting them to accept her donations when they were too proud to take charity.

Discussing Jon led them back to talk of Deacon's work which was an easier topic than her work, so Cary gratefully kept things there.

Right up until one of her bosses appeared suddenly in the middle of her living room.

Wisat was from a North American faery tribe that didn't have a name in modern times and most humans didn't know even existed as a separate group from the European Fae. They were outwardly strange and beautiful looking, they created Protectors, and they did their best to save who they could in the world. An effort which Cary respected. Even if she frequently resented the way they'd tricked her into her current job.

But they paid her to be a walking, talking Kevlar vest so that mitigated her annoyance most of the time.

"Protector," Wisat said, sounding…breathless. That wasn't normal. "You're needed. Now."

Cary launched up from the couch, heading toward her coat and keys, but Wisat raised a hand. "Not enough time for that," he said. He took her arm.

She started to ask what he intended as Deacon rose from the couch, frowning.

And then the living room vanished around her.

3

"Wait," Cary said, holding her hands up. "You want me to what?"

Wisat had brought her to a small, tree-circled grove. She didn't have the first clue where the grove *was*, but given what was happening there, she didn't have time to ask.

A man in gray slacks and a black t-shirt hugged a woman in his lap. Her head hung at a terrible angle and blood pumped from a gaping wound in her chest.

"We don't have much time," the man on the ground said. "She's dying and there's no way to save her now." His voice hitched at that last. "I failed. And we need your help to ensure we don't fail the world. This baby *has* to survive."

Liruk, Cary's other boss, stood over the man and woman in all her gold and white glory, looking as sad and uncertain as Cary had ever seen her. The Fae was typically almost too assured, too positive in the correct course of action. And positive that Cary wasn't doing as much as she should. Now, Liruk's deeply green eyes held only sorrow, and a kind of fear that made Cary's heart race.

Although, she still wasn't sure why.

"But…" Cary swallowed, her gaze settling on the dying woman. "How would this even work? It's not possible."

The woman was pregnant. And they wanted Cary to carry the fetus, only just a little over the twenty-six week mark. But they were in a grove, not a hospital, and even then, there was no way to move a living fetus between wombs. It just wasn't possible.

"Liruk and Wisat can manage the magic of the move," the man said. He nodded to the woman. "She was a surrogate, too." He pressed his lips together. "And she was mine to protect. I failed. They got to her. And unless you help us, they'll succeed in destroying a great hope for humanity."

"I have a *lot* of questions about all this," Cary said.

"Which we don't have time for now," he said.

"I get that. But I still want them all answered. Eventually." She pulled in a deep breath. "Why me?"

"I don't have a womb," the man said matter-of-factly. "And my offensive magic would interfere with the development even if I did." The man looked to Wisat. "I understand you're unique as far as Protectors go?"

"More questions," she murmured. Then also looked to Wisat.

"You have no magic to disrupt or interact with the fetus's developing magic," Wisat said. "Nothing that will interfere in the transfer either."

"And you have a womb that's not currently occupied," Liruk said.

Cary scowled at that. "By choice," she snapped. Which reminded her. "I have an IUD. A fetus and an IUD aren't compatible." And the combination could be very dangerous for her and the baby.

"We can remove the IUD when moving the fetus," Wisat said. He raised a hand when she opened her mouth. "Magically."

"This won't be permanent," the man said, dragging her attention back. "I just need to find the next surrogate. She's missing, gone into hiding after the attack. Once I can get to her, I'll bring her here and she can take over."

"So I'm not going to have to give birth or anything? Cause, I'm really really not good with that." Or ready for it. Or anything else. But even as more questions bubbled up, the bleeding woman convulsed, and even Cary with her human hearing heard the rattle of her last breath.

"Protector," Liruk said. "Cary. Please. You're the only one who can do this. We're out of time. And this is very important."

Cary closed her eyes, not sure whether to curse or panic and pretty sure she was going to do both any minute now.

"Fine," she said. "What do I have to do?" She glared at Liruk because it seemed easier to blame her for putting Cary in this horrible position than it did the dying woman or the Protector who'd failed the woman.

She looked at the man. "We will have a lot to talk about after this. Don't you dare disappear right away."

He nodded and gently set the dead woman's head on the ground. The grove was carpeted with soft grass, damp and cold in the early spring weather.

Liruk nodded to Wisat, who looked to Cary. "I will need to place my hands over your womb, Protector," Wisat said. "Is this okay?"

She liked that he was asking permission. Given the panic she could feel in that clearing, she half thought they'd just move forward doing whatever they were going to without giving her a moment to accept it all.

She nodded her approval and he stepped close. The glow of his green eyes against his bright red skin seemed deeper in the darkness under the trees. The soft red velvet covering the horn that circled his head like a halo glittered in the faint light coming from the storm lantern she could only assume they'd brought with them.

He touched her shoulder first. "Thank you, Cary. You can't know how vital this is."

"You're going to have to enlighten me once this is over," she grumbled. "You'd better hurry, though."

He glanced at Liruk who had knelt by the dead woman and had her hands hovering over the woman's stomach. Now that she was reclined, Cary could see the small bump in the woman's lower abdomen. She wanted to cry at all the blood covering the woman's t-shirt and the top of her loose skirt.

She blinked away her sadness and waited for her bosses to do their thing—whatever it was.

Liruk closed her eyes and hummed something under her breath. Her hands glowed as if from an inner light, white and sharp. A spark of light rose from the dead woman, as if drawn to the glow in Liruk's hands. The orb spun in frantic little bursts, fading and growing brighter as it hovered a few inches above the woman. It dipped back toward the woman, Liruk hummed something that was almost a song, but with a discordant note to it, and the little orb rose again. But its light faded the farther it got from the woman.

Cary's chest tightened as she waited and watched. Fear clutched at her for that little spark of potential hovering just under Liruk's glowing hands. She didn't understand the potential yet, not fully, but watching it struggle and fade made Cary sadder than she might have anticipated.

Liruk turned her hands up, creating a cradle over which the little orb hovered, almost like Liruk was holding the orb but without actually touching it. She stood, bringing the little orb to Cary. As she moved, the orb continued to fade, its light retreating into a tighter ball. Sparks danced away from it, like stars or comet dust, creating a bright wake behind it.

"What will it be?" Cary murmured. She wasn't expecting an answer yet.

But the man still kneeling beside the dead woman said, "She'll be a god. If we can ensure she survives."

Cary blinked. Her heart hammered. "A god? Like…a real god?"

Liruk angled her cupped hands toward Cary and Wisat pressed his hands gently against Cary's lower abdomen. The little orb hovered and danced in the air currents, wobbling in the space inside Liruk's hands. It had faded so much now, it looked more like a firefly than a sun spark, but it still swirled and whirled as Liruk urged it closer to Cary.

With a suddenness that startled a gasp from her, the little orb flew into her right at Wisat's hands, through the tiny gap just between his spread fingers. Cary blinked, staring at her own stomach. For a split second, her middle flashed with light. Then it faded, leaving her blinking back spots.

Her vision settled, readjusting to the fainter light of the storm lantern. She took a deep breath, waiting for…something.

Wisat removed his hands from her and looked up into her eyes.

She met his gaze and shrugged. "Did it work?"

For another moment, the only sounds in the dark grove were the rustling of leaves overhead and Cary and the other Protector's heavy breathing. Another heartbeat…

Cary spun for the edge of the clearing and unceremoniously threw up.

"It worked," she muttered, pressing a hand to a tree to keep her balance as a wave of dizziness washed over her. She ran the back of her hand over her mouth, swallowing hard and trying not to throw up again. She hated throwing up.

"Why the hell am I throwing up?" she asked no one in particular.

A gentle hand settled on the back of her shoulder. "Your body has to catch up to the appropriate stage of the pregnancy," Liruk said.

Cary frowned at her over her shoulder. Liruk was *never* this gentle with her.

"It will take a few hours to adjust," Liruk continued. "I'm afraid you'll run through all the typical morning sickness in that period of time. Some dizziness and, if your mother was prone to it, you might faint."

Cary shook her head, then had to stop as a wave of nausea crashed through her. "No," she said, pressing her teeth together so she didn't throw up again. Her gut was really churning now. Gross. "My mom and sister both had horrible morning sickness, but no fainting."

"Then you'll likely experience the same," Liruk said.

"Great," Cary muttered. She closed her eyes in a vain attempt at settling her stomach. "Why are you being so nice to me?" she asked Liruk.

Liruk's hand stilled as if she hadn't realized she was rubbing Cary's shoulder in a gentling gesture. "You've agreed to something many wouldn't, for the sake of something you don't fully understand yet," she said quietly. "I'm grateful."

Cary huffed, a sort of laugh but restrained so she didn't barf. "From the people who tricked me into being a Protector in the first place, that's unexpected. But I'll take it." She opened her eyes. "Now what?"

"Now I need to find the next surrogate," the man said from his crouch next to the previous surrogate. He was looking at the woman, not Cary.

Cary finally took a moment to study the other Protector. She'd never met any of the others before—she suspected that was on purpose but wasn't entirely sure why—and for some reason she was a bit surprised by how normal he looked. That shouldn't have surprised her given how normal she looked, and was, but she'd been starting to think she was super unusual for a Protector.

His height was hard to gage because she'd only seen him crouching so far, but he seemed pretty average. He had brown hair that wasn't too long or too short for his pleasantly round face. In the light from the storm lantern, his eyes looked very dark and his skin looked pretty pale, almost blue. But some of that might have been from his grief.

He set a hand on the woman's arm, his jaw tight, heavy creases on his forehead. He didn't cry, but Cary could almost feel the sadness.

Then he pulled in a deep breath and looked up at Wisat. "You'll ensure she's taken care of?" he asked quietly, nodding to the woman.

"Of course," Wisat said.

The man looked at Cary. "My name is Frank, by the way. Frank Schmidt. And this was Mila Juhl."

"Cary Redmond," she said. "And I'm very sorry for your loss."

He acknowledged her condolences with a nod. "The people who did this…" He looked at the ground, not at the dead woman. "They will come after you now. They're determined that the new god doesn't come into existence."

"And who are they?" Cary asked. She put a hand to her stomach when it rolled again, worried she'd throw up. The wave of nausea passed, but a terrible metallic taste coated the inside of her mouth. She swallowed hard.

"They're a group of fanatics. The Polrom. They worship a demon god—"

"Oh," Cary interrupted, raising her hand. "I fought one of those." She frowned. "Maybe two depending on if you think the son of a demon god qualifies as a demon god in his own right. Although, maybe not since the son was really eager to avoid his dad." She looked at the faces around her, all staring silently. "Sorry. Go on."

"This particular group of fanatics see the child you're now carrying as their god's downfall."

"Why?" Cary asked the obvious. "What sort of god will the baby be? Also, how many gods, like actual gods, are there running around in the world?" She looked at Wisat. "And why didn't I know there was such a thing as baby gods? Demon gods, fine. But baby gods that are good and might need protecting?" She paused. "Wait, this *will* be a good little god, right? I mean, otherwise, saving it wouldn't be so important."

"She'll be a wonder," Frank said, his tone quiet and awed.

"What *kind* of wonder. Exactly?" Since demon worshipers were unhappy with the little god's impending birth, Cary had to think it had something to do with demons—ugh, not demons again—but you never knew with fanatics. They got really weird ideas in their heads sometimes. Or a lot.

She hated fanatics.

"The full extent of her domain is still nebulous," Liruk said. "Just as she is still a nebulous potential and not a living god yet. But she represents hope."

"The god of hope?" Cary asked, initially in jest, but as she thought about it, she realized a god of hope seemed...wonderful. Hope was always a good but much needed trait in the world. "A god of hope," she repeated, in a tone filled with her wonder. "Huh."

"And since the Polrom worship a demon of despair, she's the antithesis of their god," Frank said quietly. "They don't want her to come into existence."

"And will kill the surrogates carrying her," Wisat said. He looked at Cary. "Except they can't kill you now."

She raised her brows in question.

"You're a Protector," Frank said, and nodded to her stomach. "At the moment, you're on the job every minute of the day, so your powers will be active constantly."

"You might find you get more tired than normal," Liruk added.

"Cause of the pregnancy or power use?" Cary asked.

Channeling the Protector magic didn't, in and of itself, generally make her that tired. Though she'd had some moments following an intense fight that left her pretty worn out. The time she'd accidentally used her powers offensively—and *still* had no idea how she'd managed that—had been so exhausting, she'd ended up sleeping for three days solid. But for a normal job, jumping in front of a bad guy and standing there long enough to keep the good guy alive, she didn't usually feel tired after.

"A little of both," Liruk admitted.

"Do you get tired when channeling the Protector magic?" Cary asked Frank.

"You can discuss that later," Wisat interrupted.

Which made Cary extremely suspicious.

"Frank needs to locate the missing surrogate," Liruk said. For once she came across as the gentler of the two.

That made Cary even more suspicious. She narrowed her eyes, looking at them both.

"You're virtually indestructible now," Frank said, ignoring Cary's expression. "Until I can find the new surrogate anyway. But you might find doing some of the things you're used to doing a little more physically difficult, just because of the pregnancy changes."

"Uh huh." She swallowed yet another wave of nausea and pressed a hand to her mouth. "Ugh, this taste is making it worse."

"That happened to my wife," Frank said. "Try sucking on hard candies, like ginger or peppermint. Even lemon will work. Depends on your tastes. Some women find ginger tea settles their morning sickness, but again it'll depend on you."

"I'm not crazy about ginger," Cary said. One of the few flavors of food she didn't normally gravitate to. "But my stomach didn't rebel at the thought of peppermint. I'll try that. Thanks." She frowned. "Wait, you're married? With kids?"

Frank nodded.

"You can do that as a Protector and be…fine? Is your wife more than a mundane human?"

He smiled. "She's unique, and has some powers of her own, which helps."

"I bet." Cary might have issues with being mated to a shifter who was the future leader of his people, but at least he wasn't as vulnerable to her enemies as an ordinary human might have been. "But kids? That isn't scary?"

"It is. But it would be even if I didn't have a dangerous job. If you have your own children one day, you'll see. The fear is its own thing."

"Thanks for not painting rainbows," Cary said. "My mother keeps trying to tell me my sister is exaggerating about the side effects of having kids." She pressed a hand to her stomach and breathed through her nose for a moment, hoping to settle things before she threw up again. As she did, it occurred to her, "Why isn't a Protector acting as the official surrogate? I mean, we're talking a little god here, right? Why not have someone who'd be indestructible do the job?"

Wisat and Liruk exchanged a look. Frank looked at them, frowning slightly, then at Cary with his eyes narrowed. He finally stood, though he didn't move away from Mila's side just yet.

When no one immediately answered, Cary snapped, "What?"

"You haven't told her?" Frank said. "She doesn't know?"

"It was important she enter her Seventh Year with a clear mind," Liruk said.

Cary snorted a laugh, heavy with sarcasm. "Right. That's not what's happening here, is it? Tell me what I don't know. Now."

When Wisat and Liruk still remained silent, Frank said, "Most Protectors have their own magic. Their own powers. It varies. But there currently aren't any Protectors with wombs that could carry a baby like this one without their own magic interfering and causing trouble. The results would be very unpredictable." He frowned at

Wisat. "But I understand you're unusual. That you don't have any outside powers."

He was almost asking. Like he didn't quite believe that was true. Or maybe was doubting the truth of it now.

"I don't," Cary said, turning her scowl on Wisat because she could see him easier. "I was an ordinary woman when these guys tricked me into this job."

"Tricked you? You didn't grow up knowing this was what you'd be doing?"

Frank's question made her gape at him. "You *knew* you'd be a Protector all your life?"

"We don't have time to discuss this right now," Liruk said, sounding more her usual annoyingly strident self.

Cary might have found that reassuring if she hadn't just had several bombs dropped on her. She'd known most Protectors had offensive magic, that her not having any was unusual. But discovering everyone else knew they'd be doing this job most of their lives was new. And the knowledge ratcheted up her annoyance with her bosses big time.

"Unless you want to carry the god to full term," Liruk said. "In which case, Frank doesn't have to find the next surrogate."

"No," Cary said. She pointed a finger at Liruk. "And you're using my being unprepared for that as an excuse to hide this other stuff from me for longer." She looked at Frank. "I know you have to go, but when we meet again, we need to talk." She glared at her bosses. "I get the feeling there's a *lot* I've been misinformed about. And given that I'm in the middle of this test year business, it's past time I learned the truth."

Frank glanced between the two Fae, then nodded. "Yeah, I think we'd have time for a talk after all this is over. Sounds like it might be a good idea."

Wisat actually looked down, not meeting Cary's gaze. Oh, she was really suspicious now. What the ever loving hell?

"Until then," Frank said into the heavy silence, "I do need to go. I'll be back as soon as I can manage it."

He glanced down at Mila and this time Cary saw a tear leak down his cheek. He didn't bother to wipe it away. Then he turned to a spot in the woods, made some gestures with his hands, and a very black rectangle appeared in front of him. He stepped into the blackness, disappearing completely. The rectangle collapsed into a dot and then winked out.

Whoa. "What did he just do?"

"Teleported through a space-time tunnel he can create," Wisat said quietly.

"Cool," Cary said. "I'm jealous. Teleportation has always been the superpower I wanted."

So much so, she'd actually read up on teleportation—and retained enough of the information to know there were several different ways of moving from one place to another in a short period of time that got called teleportation. Her favorite—and the one she really wanted to be able to do—was the one where the person visualized where they were going, a specific spot, and then *poof* they would be there. That seemed remarkably easy. And she could visit her sister in New York a lot more often if she could do that. Or just randomly go to Hawaii for the day.

It would help in escaping bad guys too, making her job a whole lot easier.

Which reminded her that other Protectors *knew* they were going to be Protectors from childhood.

She narrowed her eyes at her bosses. They didn't meet her gaze.

She started to say something but another punch of nausea rolled her stomach. She breathed threw her teeth. For some reason, she could *smell* everything in that clearing at the moment, the dirt, the trees, the damp air, the drying blood on poor Mila. The nature smells were fine, but the sharp metallic scent of Mila's blood and the very faint sweet smell of rotting detritus from the surrounding woods made her want to gag.

She pressed a hand to her stomach. The slightly more pronounced, and solid, bump made her start. She'd been working out enough with Lucy lately that her stomach was, relatively speaking, flat, although she wouldn't be gracing any swimsuit magazine covers. She liked her pizza and nachos way too much. The sudden feel of a much larger midsection, which wasn't soft like she'd been overdoing the pizza but firm and substantial, was a shock to the system. Her whole body suddenly felt…thicker.

Holy shit. She was pregnant.

And now she had to explain this to Deacon.

4

*A*fter Liruk gently lifted Mila's body and disappeared with her, Wisat brought Cary home. The woods faded, Cary blinked, and she was standing in her living room again.

Now that was a cool kind of teleporting. She could get used to getting around that way.

Deacon was pacing the room when they materialized. He reached her from the opposite side of the couch in a blink, with that shifter speed that was always shocking, and pulled her into his arms.

What a nice greeting.

She leaned into him carefully, not wanting to surprise him with her now very pregnant midsection until she could explain.

"Everything is okay?" he asked, his nose in her hair. Then he paused and pulled back, frowning down at her. "Why do you smell different? Why do you smell…pregnant?"

"You can smell that?" She gaped at him. "Wow." Also, she probably should have known he'd be able to tell. Her hormones had to be hoping and the pheromones she was sending out were likely all full of pregnancy chemicals.

Deacon glared at Wisat. "What the hell is going on?"

Cary let out a deep breath and glanced at her boss. "Better leave this to me. Keep me updated."

Wisat disappeared without saying a word. She wasn't sure whether that was him being wise or just rude. When she looked back at the hard, angry expression on Deacon's face, she decided Wisat had been acting with great wisdom.

"So, this is job related and temporary," she started. "Try not to freak out. I'm carrying a still developing baby god, because her original surrogate was killed by fanatics before the Protector looking after her could save her. He's pretty upset about it, and I can't blame him."

"Why you?" Deacon asked, cutting to the chase.

His tone was neutral, and he'd wrapped himself in that iceman control that had so grated on her nerves in January when they'd returned to his childhood home and been surrounded by his people. He'd had to shut down his emotions and adopt that control to keep from hurting others. She understood, but she'd still hated it.

She was not happy to see that iceman façade return. Especially not here.

"Me," she said slowly, her tone also neutral, "because I'm a Protector and can keep the growing fetus safe. I have a currently unoccupied womb. And I have no magic beyond the Protector stuff to interfere with the baby god's development. Apparently, my ordinariness came in handy in this particular circumstance."

"You're not ordinary."

"Magically speaking, I am." But the unexpected compliment forced a little smile from her. "This is temporary," she said. "There's a second surrogate in the wings, a backup, but she's in hiding from the people who murdered Mila, and Frank needs to find her."

"You're not giving birth to this…god?" he asked, still in that too controlled tone.

"That's what I've been promised. Which is good since I'm not ready for pregnancies and babies and giving birth. Not even close." She narrowed her eyes at him to make sure he understood that part.

It hadn't come up in a while, but she knew he wanted them to have kids at some stage, if they could. Because she was human and he was a shifter, they might not even be able to. But since they were still adapting to being mates, they both agreed the family planning discussions were a long ways off.

She had to survive her test year before she could even begin to think about what she wanted from her future.

"The good news," she said, "is that I'm officially in Protector mode twenty-four seven while keeping this little god safe." She waited to see if he realized what that meant. When he continued to stare at her, showing no cracks in his iceman expression, she said, "I'm virtually indestructible now. Wizards. Vampires. None of it is a threat as long as I'm carrying this potential life inside. For a few days, anyway, I'll be impossible to kill. That's a change of pace, right?"

Slowly, Deacon's expression shifted, emotion rolling back across his features. She could see the anger and disorientation and confusion all fighting with the realization she would be safe from her more persistent enemies.

"You want to be happy about this, don't you?" she asked.

He scowled. "I'm always happy when you're safe," he snapped. "I just didn't expect…"

"That my first pregnancy wouldn't have anything to do with you?" she guessed.

He had the grace to look chagrined. "Yes," he admitted. "My leopard side is jealous." He lifted a hand before she could protest. "For no good reason. I know there's no cause to be jealous. Once this all sinks in, I'll be fine. My instincts keep getting ahead of my logic with you."

She snorted. "I've noticed. Tell your leopard to chill out. This is just like when I had to keep Jon here in the house to keep him safe. Only now I need to use a slightly smaller house."

"Inside your body," Deacon said.

She shrugged.

"Is this…common?"

"You mean have I done this before? No. And I'm a little freaked out about doing it now, to be honest. I didn't expect my first pregnancy to be a sudden drop into the fourth month. By the way, I'm apparently going through all the early stages of pregnancy in fast forward so my body can catch up."

"Which means?"

"I've thrown up once already, and I may well do it again in a few minutes. Plus my sense of smell is going haywire. If this is even remotely close to your sense of smell, I don't know how you handle it."

"Practice," he said. "You're handling this all very calmly."

"Not really. I'm freaking out inside. But I didn't want to aggravate your leopard side's already jumpy reaction."

He sighed and pulled her close again. "A good idea," he said. "And I should really have thought more about how this is affecting you, rather than my own reaction."

"True. And now that you realize that, I can allow myself to freak out."

Because, oh boy, was this freaking her out. Her feelings about all this were overwhelming and complicated and she hadn't had a minute to sort through it all yet.

She wasn't really pregnant and yet she was most definitely pregnant. But since she'd ended up pregnant through magic and wasn't going to stay this way, it still felt bizarrely like she wasn't actually, technically pregnant. Just then her stomach rolled, making a joke of her complicated feelings. She lifted her lip at the weird taste in her mouth.

"I need to see if I've got any crackers. Or hard candy," she muttered.

"What's wrong?"

"Oh just morning sickness on steroids." She *felt* her eyes growing wider with each word. This was so weird.

Not exactly the way she'd expected to get pregnant for the first time. She was still a little waffly about having kids, given her job.

Frank had kids. And a wife. And a life outside of being a Protector. Superheroes managed it sometimes. There were even movies about a superhero couple and their kids. Though their kids had superpowers too. Hers might be shapeshifters if she had kids with Deacon. That would help with their safety. Maybe.

Ah! She wasn't even close to ready to think about this. She'd only been with Deacon for a few months. And while she'd gone into this whole thing knowing that, at least from his perspective, this was supposed to be a long term deal, she couldn't think long term yet because every time she did she got jumpy and itchy and remembered that she might not even survive this year.

Kids were way *way* down on the list of thinking priorities at the moment.

But being the protective womb for a baby god was bringing the topic up, and she was so not ready for it.

She pushed into the kitchen to find her little pack of dogs coming in from the mudroom, having obviously been in the backyard for a final potty break before bed.

"Hey guys," she said, "I have some weird news."

Deacon leaned against the kitchen doorframe as she rummaged through her cabinets for hard candies. She didn't have any, but she did have some saltines. Those would do in a pinch.

She studied her little pack as they sat down in a semi-circle in front of her, patiently waiting. Whether they were waiting for her to tell them her news or for their nightly treat was anyone's guess, but she was leaning toward the nighttime treat being their primary focus. Especially when the smallest—and only mundane dog—Fred licked his lips and glanced back at the mudroom where she stored their treats.

With a snort of amusement, she retrieved the bag of fake bacon and handed them each a piece while she explained her predicament. The smell of the doggie treat hit her in the face hard, but weirdly it wasn't unpleasant. She normally didn't much like the fake bacon smell. Strange it didn't bother her as much now even though it came across as a stronger scent.

"So I'm carrying around a little baby god," she said to the dogs. "A sort of pregnancy which I'm sure you can smell since you have great senses of smell just like Deacon."

Pickles glanced at Deacon while she gulped down her treat. "Woof."

Cary grinned. Pickles, the only girl in the pack, was a foo lion.

She'd chosen to take the form of a basset hound after losing her mate, though, and had pretty much stayed in that form since Cary had adopted her—or more accurately since Pickles had adopted Cary.

"I bet you do have the best sense of smell," Cary told her and handed her another bacon-flavored treat. Fred barked and jumped up, enthusiastically bouncing off Cary's thigh. "Yes, you can have a second."

Buck, the golden Labrador and also demon dog, sat patiently waiting for his second treat. These nightly treats had started because Buck's demon side had been triggered by a demon god messing around in Portland. Since adopting him, Buck hadn't really acted as anything other than a Labrador, so the incident had scared the hell out of Cary. She'd been pretty lax on the treats ever since.

She fed him his second fake bacon and said, "This pregnancy is just temporary. I'm keeping the baby god safe until her new surrogate can be found. So we're not having a new addition to the family just yet." She rubbed Buck behind his ears and he leaned his big head into her palm, his tongue hanging out.

"Woof," Pickles said.

"Yes, I am officially indestructible now," Cary said. "But only for a little while. Maybe only days. It's kind of a cool trick, though, right?"

Fred jumped up about a foot in the air because…well, terrier, and let out a loud yippy bark.

"Exactly, Fred," Cary said. She knelt down to give them all scratches and rubs. And because she was more than a little unsettled by her current state, she allowed the face licks. Then she hugged her little pack tight before standing, washing her hands, and returning to her crackers.

Strangely, the smell of dog didn't bother her either. A relief since she was noticing *everything* at the moment. Even the scent of her leftover coffee in the pot was making her stomach rebel. That wasn't good.

Hard on the heels of that realization, it hit her that she probably shouldn't drink coffee while she was carrying the baby god. Her sister swore up and down that was a myth and caffeine didn't hurt devel-

oping fetuses. Cary believed Valerie since after three successful pregnancies and two early miscarriages, she seemed to be the pregnancy
expert in the family. Still, given the way Cary's stomach reacted to the
thought of coffee, it might not be as big of a sacrifice as she'd have
assumed. The smell of the hours-old brew was really making her
queasy.

Wait, what if she couldn't stand the smell of pizza?

Ah!

"Guys," she said to the dogs, "I don't know how you handle this
hyper sense of smell thing. It's kind of horrible."

"You adapt," Deacon said. He'd waited patiently through her
exchange with her dogs. He'd gotten used to the way she was with her
pets, even liked it since he was an animal person too—outside of also
being a shapeshifter. The fact that he accepted that part of her so easily
had always been a point in his favor.

She glanced at him. "I'd rather not adapt. The smell of coffee is
upsetting my stomach and I cannot live that way forever."

His mouth twitched at one side. She could tell by his crossed arms
and lowered brow he wanted to stay upset about all this, so the mouth-
twitch of amusement was involuntary.

"According to Brigit," he said, "it doesn't last." Brigit was one of
his middle sisters. She was mated and had twins. "You'll go back to
enjoying the smell of coffee."

Her eyes widened. "Oh my god how much worse is this for a
shifter who already has a strong sense of smell?"

That sounded very unpleasant. Why had Valerie done this so often?

She pulled out a glass for some water to wash down the dry
cracker. Her stomach approved of water. It thought the saltines were
okay too, but nothing else sounded like it would stay down.

So much for pregnancy cravings.

"So what now?" Deacon asked.

"It's late. I'm exhausted—more so than I should be so I'm
assuming that's the pregnancy. And we wait for a few days until Frank
finds the right person to take over gestating a baby god. Until then, you
don't have to worry about guarding me or getting the other leopards to

follow me around. The wizard won't be an issue. Gabriel won't be an issue." She smiled. "I could get used to being indestructible. Shame it won't last."

"Shame."

His tone was strange and difficult for her to read. She wasn't sure if that was sarcasm, seriousness, anger, fear. Or some combination of all of those things.

"You okay?" she asked.

"I'm…adjusting." He let out a deep breath and finally relaxed his stance, running his hands through his hair.

She loved when he did that. He looked super sexy with his hair all mussed like that. It really was too bad neither her stomach nor her body could muster the energy for sex right now, because her mate looked very yummy in that moment.

"I'm conflicted," he said on a sigh. "And my leopard side, that instinctive refuses-to-believe-logic side…"

She smiled at that.

"It's conflicted too," he said. "There's a part of me that knows this is temporary and not a reflection on our relationship one way or another. You're not pregnant by another man or anything I need to be jealous about. Logically, this is just another job for you. And it has nothing at all to do with me."

"Very true," she said. "I'm glad you recognize that because I was starting to wonder."

His lips twitch again before he got serious once more. "But then, there's this other part of me. The part that would like…"

She narrowed her eyes when he trailed off. "Maybe you shouldn't say that out loud."

She knew what he was implying. It was there in his expression, in the softening of his mouth and eyes. They weren't ready for the discussion but he would want to have the talk one day. And the whole pregnancy job had launched them into something neither of them was ready to deal with yet.

He nodded and looked at the ground, not finishing his thought. But it hung in the air between them.

"We need a different topic." She paused and pressed a hand to her belly as some of the water didn't settle well. She let out a slow breath through her teeth so she couldn't smell anything. "I really hope this catching up part happens fast. Morning sickness sucks."

"Especially since it's not morning," he said.

"Yeah, that's a misnomer my sister spent a lot of time cursing during her first pregnancy. 'Why the hell do they call it morning sickness when it happens all fucking day?' Her words."

Deacon smiled a little at that. "I'm looking forward to meeting Valerie one day."

"She's looking forward to meeting you, too. The invitation to New York has already been extended."

"You didn't tell me," he said quietly.

"I'm not ready to take you to meet her yet," Cary said. She raised a hand. "Before you get your feelings hurt, it's not because I don't want you to meet my family eventually." While she'd met his entire family at this stage, she had yet to introduce him to her parents who lived just a few hours away up in Washington. "But..." She sighed. "But I'm stalling because I don't want to hear the nagging from my mom. Which will start the moment she lays eyes on you."

"Nagging?" He raised his brows.

"'When are you getting married?' 'What does he do for a living?' 'When do I get to meet his parents?' 'Why has it taken you so long to find a good man?'" She groaned and rolled her eyes. "My mother is a lovely woman, but she's been eager to see me married off for years now. I finally got her to stop nagging when my sister had her second kid. I've been enjoying the blissful peace. The fact that I'm seeing someone now, and have been for more than two dates, will start it all over again. So I'm pushing that out for as long as possible."

"Your sister knows about me, but your mother doesn't yet?" he asked, his tone neutral.

"Yes, and for your sake, be grateful. You think your mother is overwhelming."

"You and my mother get along really well now," he pointed out.

"She's a magical shifter queen. If I don't get along with her, I'll be in trouble."

"And how is your mother going to be any worse than that?"

"Wait," Cary said ominously. "You'll see."

He finally pushed away from the door frame and crossed to her, pulling her close. The feel of his warm solid body wrapping around her was like a little slice of heaven and she leaned into him. Even her rolling stomach settled enough for her to enjoy the sensation of being held by her mate.

And he smelled so delicious she wanted to lap him up. Maybe she wasn't too tired for sex.

"I'm looking forward to meeting her then," he said, nuzzling the top of Cary's head.

She drew in a deep breath and pressed her face into his neck. "You smell yummy," she murmured.

His hands flexed against her back, his fingers tightening in her shirt. "You're changing the subject."

"Not cynically," she promised as she kissed his pulse. "This is your distraction, not mine. You smell like the best thing ever." She rubbed against him, pressing hard into all those tight muscles and savoring the sound of his quiet groan.

"Cary."

"Hmm." She leaned back enough to look up at him. His eyes were dark golden and intent.

"Never mind," he growled. "I forgot what I wanted to say anyway."

She grinned as his mouth captured hers, his kiss fierce and hungry. Just exactly the way she loved. She'd lost track of the conversation, too. And this was better. She stretched against him, wrapping her arms around his neck and burying her fingers in his hair.

This was much, much better.

5

"Wait, you've got to say that again," Marianne said. "You're what?"

Cary sat in Angie's living room with her three best friends, drinking a bottle of water because she couldn't stomach anything else yet. "Pregnant. But not in the real I'm-going-to-have-a-baby way," she repeated.

"Yeah…" Lucy said in her little girl voice, "you're gonna have to clarify that."

"It's a job," Cary said, trying not to laugh at her friends' expressions. "I'm protecting the little fetus until her proper surrogate can be found. Her last surrogate was killed."

"That's sad," Lucy said. "But I'm still confused."

"Apparently, she's a god of some kind," Cary said, taking a sip from her bottle. "No one knows exactly what kind yet, but she'll be one of hope at the very least. Which is why the worshipers of a demon god of despair are trying to keep her from being born."

Lucy leaned back into Angie's comfy yellow couch and shook her head. "My life has gotten very strange since meeting all of you," she said, before taking a drink of her wine.

Little tendrils of her red hair had fallen out of her high bun and

41

framed her heart-shaped face. Lucy looked a little like a doll some-times. She was pretty and petite with thick red hair, pale skin, and brown eyes set against high cheekbones and a cutely pointed chin. She even had a high-pitched, sweet voice that added to the illusion.

She also had a bunch of blackbelts, trophies from martial arts competitions, owned her own dojo, and could kick the ass of men four times her size. In fact, that's how she and Cary had met years ago, when Cary had come across Lucy in a fight with a bunch of big guys. Cary had thought she'd needed to protect Lucy, but Lucy was easily tossing the men around. It had been an awesome thing to witness.

Lucy was also the only "mundane" human among Cary's three closest friends.

Angie was a witch, a psychic, and apparently had some demon hunting history in her past that none of them could get her to talk about. She was tall, thin, gorgeous enough to be a model, and when working in her business as a psychic, she wore a lot of flowing hippy clothes to play the part. When she wasn't working, she tended more toward casual chic clothes like the black pants and button-down blouse in emerald green she had on just then.

Her little moon earrings twinkled when she pushed her curly light brown hair from her face and shook her head. "I have lived through some pretty weird stuff in my life," she said, "but even I have to admit, this ranks up there with one of the weirder things."

"Yeah," Marianne said, "this definitely goes beyond even my strange life."

"Even the goblin king trying to kidnap you all the time?" Lucy asked, her eyes wide.

Marianne waved a hand. "That was just boring ordinary stuff." She pointed her own glass of wine toward Cary. "This is weird shit."

Cary snorted. "Gee. Thanks."

Marianne was a seamstress extraordinaire, and could do literal magic with needle, thread and cloth. Technically, she was called a weaver—like from the old stories where women could weave wheat into gold. Her two sisters were weavers as well. And for years, the goblin king had tried to coerce, con, and occasionally kidnap them to his kingdom so they would do some gold weaving for him.

Marianne and Cary had met before Cary became a Protector, but they'd gotten to be best friends after Cary had gone to Marianne for some help with her clothes, protected her from an attempted kidnapping by the goblin king's minion, and they'd both learned they were not, technically, mundane humans. That and the fact that they bonded over 80s music and no-pineapple-on-pizza had ensured a tight friendship.

Marianne was, as always, dressed in beautifully made clothing, this evening a wrap dress that showed off her curves in a deep purple color that complimented her dark brown skin. After years of keeping her hair short and tight to her head, she'd just recently gotten a new weave of long blond braids that she had pulled up into a high ponytail that night.

Cary had asked Marianne about the new hairstyle, but she'd given a vague explanation of needing a change. Cary had been trying not to worry about her friend, but there was tension in Marianne's relationship with her girlfriend, and Cary had an uneasy feeling there was more going on there than Marianne was telling any of them.

"So what happens now?" Angie asked.

"I wait until the other Protector finds the new surrogate." Cary shrugged. "Not much else to do. Although, this does mean I'm in Protector mode twenty-four seven now."

"Well that's good, given the whole wizard vendetta thing," Lucy said.

"Yeah," Cary said, "and likely the vampires too."

"Wait, what about the vampires?" Angie asked. She folded her legs up under her, cradling her stemless wineglass between her palms.

"Apparently, Gabriel knows who I am. I might have an issue with the vampires soon."

"Oh good," Angie said. "That'll help keep you alive for the rest of the year."

Cary made a face.

Marianne shook her head. "My friend, you have serious issues in your professional life."

"Tell me," Cary said with feeling. She gulped at her water. "I have to tell you, I'm not so sure about this being pregnant thing. My sister has not exaggerated the hell that is morning sickness."

"I will happily never know," Angie said with feeling. She was content to remain childfree for life. She had nieces and nephews from her brothers to fill any need for baby and kid time.

"Yeah, I always assumed Marianne would be the first of us to have kids," Lucy said. "Given she's been practically married for years now."

"I'm *not* having kids yet," Cary said firmly. "This is just part of a job, not a life choice."

"And I'm no longer practically married," Marianne said quietly.

"What?" Cary said leaning forward.

"Gina has moved out," Marianne said. "She's living in the club." Her girlfriend owned a nightclub in central Portland.

"What happened?" Lucy asked, setting her wineglass aside so she could wrap her arms around Marianne.

"And how long ago did she move out?" Angie asked.

"Why didn't you tell us?" Cary said. All thoughts of her own weird situation got shoved to the side.

"Remember how I was worried she was cheating on me?" Marianne said, her tone dull and sad.

"Oh no," Lucy sighed. She hugged Marianne closer.

For the next two hours, their entire world was comforting their friend. And some ice cream—with Baileys mixed in for everyone but Cary.

They had started into a post-ice cream discussion of Marianne's next steps when Angie suddenly stopped in mid-sentence and frowned in the direction of her front door.

"What?" Cary asked, following her gaze.

"Someone is knocking at my circle?" she said.

Angie had set up a circle of protection around her house when she'd moved in, a circle of buried salt and magic that she could activate whenever she needed her place to be safe from outside evils. Ever since she'd used it to keep Cary safe from a wizard attack, she'd activated it as soon as Cary arrived for their visits, opening it only long enough to let in food delivery people or expected guests. Because Angie was a powerful witch, her protection circle was strong enough to hold off most otherworldly beings.

"Can you tell who?" Cary asked.

"No," Angie said, still frowning, "but they're not trying to force their way in or disrupt it. They're just tapping it to get my attention. I'd be prepared to call it a respectful knock except I'm not expecting anyone else tonight. I don't like uninvited guests." She glanced at Cary meaningfully.

Cary agreed. "Shall we see who's there? Since I'm safe no matter what at the moment, I'll go first. Keep everyone shielded. Just in case."

"Marianne and Lucy, you want to stay inside?" Angie asked as she headed toward the front door with Cary.

"We've got your backs," Marianne said. She and Lucy didn't even hesitate to join them.

This was why Cary loved her friends.

At the door, Angie paused and closed her eyes. "Still there and not hitting at the circle. No signs of aggression at all. Pretty sure that's on purpose."

"Why?" Lucy asked.

Angie glanced at her. "To get us to come outside."

Cary opened the door and stepped out onto Angie's small wooden porch. The long front yard, with its neatly cut grass waiting for the spring thaw and its stone walkway down to the sidewalk, separated them from the stranger standing just outside the edge of Angie's invisible circle. When he tapped the shield, it briefly lit blue, but otherwise, no casual observer would notice it even existed.

The stranger looked up at them, his eyes glowing faintly under the streetlights. He smiled.

Cary raised her brows. Huh. A vampire.

Well, this couldn't be good.

6

The vampire dipped his head in greeting. "I assume you won't be dropping your shield, witch?" he said to Angie.

The "witch" part was said with casual respect, not distain. He wasn't throwing names, just acknowledging Angie for what she was.

"No," she confirmed. "We can talk like this."

He raised his hands, palms up, an elegant shrug of acceptance. "As you wish."

Cary narrowed her eyes. That was a line from one of their favorite movies, but she was pretty sure it was just coincidence the vampire had used it. The vamps couldn't possibly know *that* much about her.

"Ms. Redmond," he said, with another dip of his head in her direction. "As you might have guessed, I'm here to talk with you."

"Sure sure. Happens all the time, visits from vampires. What's up?" She raised her brows expectantly, showing no outward signs of fear.

Frankly, standing behind Angie's shields and knowing her own magic was working because she had to protect the baby god *and* her friends, left her feeling ever so slightly smug about her chances with a vampire. At this distance, without any sense of his powers, she had no idea how old he was or how strong. Nothing in his demeanor or appearance gave him away. He was wearing black slacks and a black turtleneck. The cliché of vampires liking black was a cliché for a reason. So so many of them enjoyed dressing in the color. He had blondish-brown hair, cut short and neat. His eyes were dark but with the jaundiced yellow glow of his nature just at the edges. He was pale, lean, tall, and contained. Not a lot of wasted movement or fidgety gestures.

Unlike Cary who frequently couldn't stand still.

"Would you care to step closer so we can talk in private?" the vampire asked.

His tone was gentle and sincere. No order or compulsion in it. She got the sense that if she refused and remained where she was, he wouldn't bat an eyelash. He was being extremely careful not to come across as aggressive or demanding. All politeness and gentlemanly behavior.

Interesting.

But probably not in a good way.

Cary stepped off the porch and walked along the path toward him. "You realize I'm just going to tell my friends everything you say, even if you can manage to speak to me without them hearing right now? I mean, you are aware I don't have vampire hearing, right? Just the ordinary human kind. They'll probably hear everything you have to say at this distance."

"You're not afraid of me," he said. Not asked. Said.

She shrugged. "Are you a threat?"

He smiled, lips closed so he wasn't showing his teeth. But the effort didn't look like it was difficult for him. A practiced smile. He was probably pretty old, if he'd mastered that trick. And likely powerful if he'd managed to survive so many years.

"I have a message," he said, instead of actually answering her question.

Well, she hadn't expected him to say he was a threat outright anyway. "From Gabriel, I take it."

He raised his brows. She flattered herself she'd surprised him, but with a vampire, you could never really read their expressions unless they wanted you to.

"Gabriel requests your presence to his court," the vampire said.

"What's your name?" she asked, mostly because she liked throwing vampires off their game with non sequiturs.

"James," he said without missing a beat.

Damn. He was good. "That's a nice name," she said. "Gabriel knows he can't order me around, right?"

"Of course. This is a request."

"And if I refuse because I have other things to do right now?"

"Like surviving your test year as a Protector?" James said.

Cary felt her breath stop. It was a weird sensation, forgetting how to breathe, even if it only lasted for a split second.

James smiled that closed lip smile again, his eyes glowing ever so slightly stronger. He knew he'd hit the mark. She had no way to hide her physical reaction. She just wasn't that controlled.

She held perfectly still for several long moments. "Who told?" she asked when she trusted her voice to come out steady. Her heartbeat was pounding hard, which James would hear, but she didn't have to let out a wobbly, weak sounding squeak. That would just be embarrassing.

"Gabriel is more than a thousand years old," James said. "The Protectors are not that old." The vampire shrugs. "You hear things."

She snorted, a kind of knee-jerk laugh that was more a reaction to her nerves and shock than to actual humor. "Request, huh?" she said quietly.

"Request," the vampire confirmed. "But a strongly encouraged request."

"Right." She'd stopped about ten feet from him. Which meant he could scent her, and easily hear her blood pulsing, but she was still far enough away to watch him carefully. At this distance, he'd also likely scent the baby god's presence. If Deacon could, the vampire probably could.

Except they hadn't met before. James would have no scent comparisons the way Deacon did. And Cary didn't have the first clue about gestation timing, especially with something like this that was magical, so she wasn't even sure if the little god fetus had a heartbeat yet. When did that happen? She narrowed her eyes. Deacon might be able to hear a heartbeat. She'd better ask him what vampires would know before she presented herself to Gabriel.

Argh, she was going to present herself to the Master of Portland. That was *such* a bad idea.

"Have the vampires started feeding on innocent kitty blood again?" she asked James, kind of stalling but also curious—because she'd be really angry if they had. "Has Gabriel changed any laws I should know about?" Like feeding from the willing only, she thought but didn't say aloud.

She had no idea how much James knew, about her, about her history with the Portland vampires. She didn't know him either, didn't recognize him from her one visit to the hive—although that didn't mean he hadn't been there. She'd been pretty overwhelmed by the sheer number of vampires. She wouldn't have remembered any one's face in particular unless they'd made themselves known to her by being an asshole.

A few had done that.

"The laws since Ariel was overthrown have been...adapting," James said with a slight, elegant shrug.

"You know, I've always appreciated how you guys shrug," Cary said. "All grace and elegance and all. How many years does that take to perfect?"

Another closed lipped smile. "If you're asking my age, it's old enough to recognize you're stalling."

"Ha! I want to get back to my girls' night. If all you're going to tell me is that Gabriel wants to see me, I guess we're done."

She turned to head back to the house.

"Wait."

The vampire's voice stopped her. She slowly turned to face him, giving him a politely neutral smile.

"When you're ready to come to the hive," he said, "send word. You will be escorted in and out. For your own safety."

She snorted, purposefully unladylike and rude. "Right. Who's my escort?"

"Me," James said, his smile widening enough to reveal teeth his time.

"Safety, huh?" She shook her head. "My boyfriend is probably gonna insist on coming with me, by the way. I wouldn't argue with him, if I were you."

"The leopard? No, we wouldn't. He's welcome as well."

"You guys gonna try to eat us? Cause that won't work?"

The threat went out of James's smile and he dropped his head back to bark out a laugh. It was the most natural reaction Cary had ever seen from a vampire—that didn't involve anger that is—and she watched in a moment of stupefied awe. Huh. She'd made a vampire laugh with actual humor. That was rare.

"Your fearlessness does you credit, Cary Redmond," James said, still chuckling. "This will be a very interesting meeting."

"Hey James," she called, as he started to turn away. "Are you a Master? I'm not close enough to you to tell."

It was *super* rare to have two Master vampires living in close proximity to each other. Too much potential for power struggles and fights that would lead to a lot of deaths. Hives were very regulated places—they pretty much had to be—and the Master of the hive never shared power.

"If you were close enough, could you tell?" he asked curiously.

"If you tried using a vampire trick on me, then yeah. Though, I might end up barfing on your shoes if you do, so just telling me whether you are or not would be simpler. And less messy."

"This will be a very interesting meeting between you and Gabriel," James said.

"You're avoiding the question, James."

"Yes. I am. Goodnight." He nodded to her and then to her friends all arrayed on the porch behind her.

Cary blinked and he was gone. Not even a wisp of wind in his wake.

She shook her head. She'd *almost* gotten used to how fast shifters could move. Almost. But vampires, especially old ones like James obviously was, the way they moved, the way they gave the illusion of instantaneous movement, that was impressive.

She was a little envious. It reminded her of teleportation again. Boy, she'd love that superpower. Not least because getting out of a vampire hive would be so much less deadly.

She set a hand on her now obviously thicker midsection and thought she'd better get this meeting with Gabriel done sooner rather than later. Too late, and she'd be a lot less likely to survive.

7

---

*W*hat did one wear to meet a Master vampire? Cary stared into her closet the next day. She wanted to get this part over with so it wasn't hovering over her head. She was acutely aware that Frank could show up with the Nags and the new surrogate at any minute. Which would be lovely for the baby god's sake. But it would also end Cary's indestructibleness, which would be not so lovely for her own survival when facing vampires.

She'd managed to talk Deacon into going to work this morning, but of course he'd insisted on going with her tonight. And he was still leaning toward taking more time off to guard her. His protectiveness was both sweet and annoying. But she'd been leaning more toward sweet the last couple of days. It felt really nice to know he had her back. She couldn't help but wonder if that was the pregnancy talking, or her own acceptance of their relationship.

She rubbed her stomach, the skin over it a little itchy from the sudden stretch of a pregnancy she hadn't built up to slowly. To her relief, the morning sickness seemed to have abated, but the weird taste in her mouth lingered. That wasn't fun. The hard candies helped, though, just like Frank had suggested. Thanks to her expanded waistline, though, she didn't have a lot of clothing choices. Vampires were pretty persnickety about clothing and appearance so sweatpants wouldn't go over well. But she really didn't want Gabriel to think she was trying to impress him by dressing up in the beautiful wrap dress Marianne had made for her, or her one fit and flare skirt that had an elastic waistband.

Sighing, she went to the bathroom for lotion for her itchy skin and considered calling Marianne. Spending money on maternity clothes would be a waste, but she needed to do something. Her jeans wouldn't button. If she had to protect the growing fetus for much longer, she'd need to invest in at least one pair of maternity pants.

Ah.

The whole suddenly-pregnant thing was messing with her mind a lot. Her hormones were jumping all around the place—she'd burst into tears not long after Deacon left for work and she still had no idea *why* —her body didn't feel quite right, she had aches that didn't have anything to do with a too-hard workout with Lucy, and all she wanted to do was hole up in her house and cuddle her dogs. Worse, she couldn't even discuss all this with her sister, who'd been through it before, because it wasn't something that would last. Valerie wouldn't understand that, or she'd misunderstand it. And while Valerie did know Cary was a Protector—unlike their parents—she didn't *really* know what that meant. She'd never seen Cary in action.

Cary didn't want to make her baby sister worry about her. That seemed like bad big sister behavior.

An hour later, she was still staring blankly into her closet when her front doorbell rang. Thanks to the glamour on her house that kept it a safe haven, impossible for people to find if Cary didn't want them to, the person ringing her doorbell had to be someone she'd want to see. She just hadn't been expecting anyone.

The long, extended ring that accompanied her short walk to the door confirmed the visitor's identity, though. Or should she say intruder.

"Jaxer," she said, throwing the door open. "Long time no see." She narrowed her eyes. "Why are you here? What's wrong?"

He grinned at her and stepped inside without being invited. Her former faery mentor was all blond haired, blue-green eyed handsomeness, angular face, perfect physique. Which he showed off in dark green slacks and a silk shirt, opened enough to real the perfect muscles of his chest. And because his greatest skill was magical glamour, the ability to make people see and feel whatever he wanted them to see and feel, she'd always suspected all that gorgeousness was a pale façade for his real appearance.

After six years of working with him, she'd never seen him without some sort of glamour in place, something to make him appear at least a little more like a normal human. She'd decided after the first couple of years she was grateful for that.

She noticed, with some surprise, that as he passed her, he didn't try to kiss her or hug her or any of the touchy feely things he normally did in greeting. She'd ask him to stop all that since she now knew those greetings were more than just casual friendship stuff. But she honestly hadn't thought he'd abide her wishes without more warnings and reminders.

"Pregnant, huh?" he said by way of greeting.

She made a face and closed the door. "Did the Nags tell you?"

"They asked me to check on you."

"I thought that was against the rules." She was supposed to survive this year without his help. Yet the Nags kept sending him to her for various reasons. "They don't think I can do this on my own, do they?" she asked as she headed toward the kitchen, knowing he'd follow. "They think I'm gonna get killed without your help."

"Actually, no," he said. "They won't say one way or the other, because they aren't supposed to, but I get the feeling they're rooting for your survival."

She snorted and tossed Jaxer a disbelieving look over her shoulder. "That's probably just because they don't want the last six and half years to have been a waste of time."

He shook his head but grinned.

"You're in a good mood," she commented as she pulled out a glass from the cabinet next to her fridge. She had given up caffeine, despite the headache the next day which, thanks to Protector healing, she'd gotten over in an hour. She did miss the ritual of coffee, though. Almost as much as the taste and caffeine. Water and juice just weren't a substitute.

"You're handling being unexpectedly pregnant very well," Jaxer returned.

"Not really. I keep crying at random moments. And my irritableness is epic right now." She lowered her brows to look at him. "You have been warned."

He laughed. "I love you."

"Shut up. Why are you here?" She worked hard to ignore his comment, but her chest still tightened at his words. She really wished he'd get over that. "If the Nags wanted to check on me and the baby god, they could have come themselves."

"The vampires have demanded you appear before the court," he said.

"And how the hell do you know that?"

"Angie told me."

Cary frowned. "Why?"

"Why else? She's worried about you."

"I'm indestructible now. No reason to worry."

"But you won't be indestructible forever, and the vampires have long memories," he said, more seriously now.

She sighed. "Are you here with a plan or just to raise my anxiety levels?"

"Wisat and Liruk want me to go with you."

That got her attention. She nearly dropped her glass. "They *do*?"

"They do." He leaned against the counter and crossed his arms over his chest.

"Is this because of the baby god, my being a bad Protector, or... what?" she asked. "Cause I'm certain this violates the Seventh Year rules."

"The vampires will know about the pregnancy," Jaxer said.

Confirming what Deacon had told her last night. Vampires would smell the hormones in her blood, even without having to hear a heartbeat. If James didn't already know, and report the news to Gabriel, then Gabriel himself would know the minute she stepped into the hive.

"Gabriel knows who you are," Jaxer said, "and likely what you are now."

"He knows," she said with a sigh. "Although I don't know how." Sure Gabriel was old enough to know Protectors existed, but she kept that information as quiet as possible to prevent enemies from knowing. Most people assumed she was a witch.

"The Master that fought with Holland," Jaxer said quietly. "Holland knew what you were, and so the Master likely knew."

Just before the start of her seventh year, she'd helped keep a demon and his army from invading a magical Naga city. The demon—Oliver Holland—had recruited all kinds of preternatural creatures, including an actual Master vampire.

"But a Master working for a demon in some other Master's territory wouldn't turn around and voluntarily present himself to the Master of the city," she pointed out. "That would be a death sentence."

"If he had information valuable enough, he could negotiate that sentence."

"How on earth would information about me be that valuable to Gabriel?" she asked. "Until the last few months when vampire attacks started going up, I wouldn't have even been on the Master's radar."

Jaxer shrugged. "I don't know for sure who's told him about you. I could be wrong. You do have a few enemies."

She rolled her eyes. That was true enough, but he didn't need to point it out. "He knows about my test year, too," she said. "At least the emissary he sent to 'invite' me to this meeting knew."

Jaxer frowned, a faint line appearing between is brows.

"That's not good, is it?"

"It's not optimal." He shook his head. "At any rate, however you came to Gabriel's notice, he knows enough that he wants you to appear before him now. And he's not likely to forget about you after this appearance."

"Oh good," she said, heavy on the sarcasm. "Which means if things don't go well this time, while I'm safely pregnant…"

"He's more likely to come after you again when you're not safely pregnant," Jaxer finished.

"Shit."

"Hey, things could go well. He could be taken by your charming personality."

She snorted. "Yeah, that's likely."

"It worked with Ariel."

"The former Master and I had a mutual concern." Because vampires shouldn't drink poor innocent kitten blood. "But I doubt her amusement with me would have been enough to prevent her from killing me at some future date if the mood had struck her."

"It worked for Holland," Jaxer pointed out.

"Sure. Right up to the point that he tried to kill me with an army of bad guys. The big and powerful are terribly amused by me and my little ways until I get in the way too often, and then they have no qualms about trying to crush me. That's one of the *lovely* side benefits to my job."

Her little pack of dogs chose that moment to walk in from the backyard, taking advantage of the doggie door to amble into the kitchen. Buck sat and stared at Jaxer while Fred charged Cary and bounced off her leg before racing back to throw himself on the floor next to Buck. Pickles flopped onto the cool tiles, resting her snout between her short front legs, her jowls spreading out around her mouth. She glanced between Buck and Jaxer, let out a deep "woof", then closed her eyes.

Pickles wasn't much bothered by Jaxer. He was just another one of the beings that popped in and out of Cary's world. Unless that being was an actually threat to Cary, Pickles saw no reason to get involved.

Lately though, Buck had started paying more attention to Jaxer whenever he appeared at her door, keeping an eye on the faery in a way he'd never bothered with before. Cary still wasn't sure why.

Jaxer stared down at the dog, holding his intent gaze without blinking.

"How is it outside?" she asked the dogs, half hoping to distract Buck. Since he'd gone full on demon dog last December, she hadn't been able to shake a low level of worry for him. And these recent staring contests with Jaxer weren't helping.

"Woof," Pickles said, only barely cracking open her eyes to respond.

"Nap time is it?" Cary asked the basset, smiling.

Fred hopped up and raced to her again, standing on his hind legs, leaning against her thigh with his front paws while she scratched behind his ears. "Did you see Scratchy?" she asked him. Scratchy was the stray cat who deigned to drop in for food sometimes, and to torture Fred by staying just out of the terrier's reach.

Fred yipped out a high-pitched bark and let his tongue loll out as he leaned into her hand.

"Still haven't caught him, huh?" she said. "Well, there's always tomorrow." Not that Fred would know what to do with the tomcat if he did catch him. He'd probably just stare, waiting for the cat to run away. Fred was all about the chase.

"Why are you and Buck staring at each other?" Cary asked Jaxer, watching the two through narrowed eyes. "This is going on longer than usual."

"Just assessing," Jaxer said quietly.

"Don't you hurt my dog," she said, very seriously. "Don't even think about it."

He glared at her, breaking eye contact with Buck. "I would never hurt any of them. Why would you say that?"

"I don't want any of you hurt and that means whatever this staring thing is has to end. Okay? In this house, I'm the big dog and that's the pecking order, and all other arrangements are unnecessary."

Jaxer shook his head. "We are not having a dominance stare off," he said with an amused snort.

"That's a relief." She glanced between him and Buck. "But one day, you're going to have to explain."

"In the meantime," he said, neatly avoiding the topic, "when did Gabriel request you appear?"

"He didn't give me a time. They said to send word and someone would show up to escort me—James, the vampire who brought the 'invitation.'" She made a face over the word. "I'm gonna just go tonight and get it over with."

"Without sending word?" Jaxer raised his brows.

"I know where the hive is. I figure showing up outside *is* sending word. James can come up and collect us."

"You don't think Gabriel has moved the hive since Ariel?"

"They don't usually. Why would he bother?"

Jaxer shrugged. "He might not have. He's pretty powerful so no doubt strong enough to protect the hive from enemies. But there was a Master working with a demon in his territory not long ago. Gabriel might have moved it to keep any demons from finding it."

She hadn't thought of that. In Cary's view, demons and vampires both fell safely into the bad guy category, but she'd never thought about whether they were a threat to each other or not.

"I'll still show up at the old hive. If it's moved, I'm sure James will be waiting for me to take me to the new location."

"What makes you say that?"

"James never told me *how* to send word I was ready for the meeting," she said with a shrug. "He'll be watching the old hive's entrance for me."

She headed with her glass of water—she missed coffee—back to the living room. Her feet hurt and she wanted to sit down. Her dog pack and Jaxer all followed.

"That's a leap," Jaxer said. "You can't know that's what he meant."

She settled onto the couch, finding the process of sitting stranger than it used to be. Her body wasn't balanced right anymore, and she had to bend and settle with the help of the couch's armrest. She pressed a hand to her stomach. She felt bigger today. Could that happen?

"How fast do baby gods grow?" she asked Jaxer as he lounged next to her.

She took note of the fact that he stayed on the opposite side of the couch, though, keeping more than the usual distance between them.

"It differs, depending on the god," Jaxer said. "The Nags wouldn't tell me anything about this one. I'm not even sure what she's supposed to be the god of."

"They told me they didn't know yet. But something to do with hope."

"Hope is always good."

"Yeah it is," she said with feeling. "But does this happen a lot? I mean, little baby gods having to be carried around by human surrogates?" She rubbed the skin along her arms, which had started to tingle.

"Depends on the baby god," he said.

"You keep giving me that same answer." She scowled at him. The tingling was moving across her stomach now, so she rubbed that area.

He lifted a shoulder in his irritatingly graceful shrug. "It does depend. Some of the gods have to be born via a human surrogate. Some are born from god parents. Some are born from magically protected sacred objects. Some are born from seashells. It depends. You've heard the stories about how gods came to be in Greek and Roman myths and legends? Things don't differ much across the spectrum of gods."

"My little human brain is going to explode with all this, you know?"

"You can take it." He grinned.

She sighed and rubbed her hands along her arms again. The tingling was running across her skin like a tickle of water, just enough to be noticed but not enough to irritate.

Jaxer frowned. "Are you okay?"

"Fine." She shrugged. "My skin is just tingling everywhere. Reminds me a little of the reaction I have after someone throws magic at me."

"You can feel magic hits while protecting?" His frown deepened.

"No, not while they're happening. I mean outside of when something gets through and I get hurt."

Her medical records for the last six years were appalling and often got her that *look* from doctors because they suspected she was an abused woman. She couldn't blame them, but it was tiring to have to make up so many excuses for her injuries. None of them were ever the kind of the thing that might kill her—a cracked bone or huge bruise mostly—and she healed fast now thankfully. But the occasional injury was unavoidable. Especially when she was jumping between a bad guy and a good guy at the last minute.

"But when I'm done protecting someone," she continued, "if I was keeping them safe from magic, my skin gets all tingly afterwards."

"Doesn't happen when you're protecting someone from, say a shifter attack?" he asked.

"Not usually." She studied him, the faint crease across his brow and tightness around his mouth. "What's wrong? It's happened from the beginning, even with the puppy-kicking demon. I just thought it was normal."

"Your skin tingled after saving Buck?"

"Yes. What's wrong? What don't I know? Why is this suddenly a big deal?"

"Not suddenly. You've never told me before."

"Because I thought it was normal. It's not?"

He glanced away from her. "Maybe it is for you," he said quietly, but he sounded like he was asking instead of telling.

Before she could grill him further, though, he stood. "I need to go. I'll be back tonight before you go to the vampires." He lowered his chin to meet her gaze. "Do not go without me. Even with Deacon. You need backup meeting Gabriel."

"Wait." She had to use the armrest to stand. Ugh, that was weird. "Where are you going? What the hell?"

"I just need to check on something," he said, trying for a casual smile.

Which wasn't convincing at all, and that made her really suspicious, because if he'd wanted to show her a convincing smile, he could have with his magic glamour powers. "What aren't you telling me? It has to do with the tingling stuff doesn't it?"

He cupped his hands on her cheeks, the first time he'd touched her since he'd arrived. The sensation made her blink, and to her utter shock, she felt a jump in her midsection that was not *her*. The baby god was moving now?

"I promise to tell you soon," he said. "But for now, it's nothing to worry about. I swear."

She stared at him for a long moment. Unfortunately, she believed that promise. "Fine, but if you leave me hanging in the dark too long, I will hunt you down and hurt you until you tell me the truth."

He laughed, one of his rare, true, honest laughs. "I won't say it again. But you know that's just exactly the kind of thing that makes me…"

She snarled. He grinned. And then he walked out her door without waiting for her to open it.

"Don't forget to wait for me tonight," he called as the door swung shut behind him.

8

Cary finally had to settle on one of her few pairs of dress pants —she mostly wore jeans because they were easier and she didn't have to think about them getting damage while she was protecting someone; Marianne made sure they fit without gapping open at the waist and that they had magic pockets—but she had to leave the top button unbutton to accommodate her larger stomach. It felt like she'd gotten bigger since just that morning. Very weird.

Her skin tingled on and off most of the day, too, only settling when she leaned back into a warm bath. The tingles had her a little worried now, thanks to Jaxer's reaction, but she wasn't sure what she was worried about. They'd been going on even before the baby god situation. It couldn't be baby god related right? And they didn't hurt or anything. It was more like static electricity dancing across her nerves. A little shiver of sensation. Nothing painful. Though occasionally it did feel like bugs crawling on her skin.

She stared at herself in the long mirror hanging on her closet door. The untucked blouse was a nice shade of sapphire blue that suited her, and it was long enough to hide the unbuttoned top of her pants. But the overall look wasn't particularly elegant.

Oh well. Gabriel was just going to have to deal with it.

Her doorbell rang as she was pulling out her handy dandy, Marianne-made leather coat with all the really good pockets. Both Jaxer and Deacon were waiting on her doorstep, glaring at each other.

She rolled her eyes and motioned them inside. "Not this again. Guys, really. Could we set the testosterone poisoning aside for just one night? You used to be friends. I'm sure you can find something to agree on long enough to *not* irritate me, right?"

"We agree we're going to guard your back tonight," Deacon said, though he sounded reluctant to admit it.

"So we'll keep our personal issues to the side. For now," Jaxer added.

She supposed that was the best she was going to get. To Jaxer, she asked, "Did you find anything out about the tingles that I should know before we present ourselves to the super scary Master vampire of Portland?"

"Tingles?" Deacon asked.

"Yeah, I get them after a protection where I've had to shield against magic. I thought it was normal." She gave Jaxer a look. "Apparently, I was wrong."

"If you'd have mentioned it before, I would have told you it wasn't normal," Jaxer said, sounding defensive. "This one is on you."

"But since I'm pregnant with a baby god and feeling grumpy, I'm going to blame you," she said without an ounce of remorse. "So what did you find?"

His lips twitched like he wanted to laugh. "Nothing yet. I'll let you know."

She huffed out a deep, irritated breath.

"That's what you're wearing?" Jaxer asked.

Which made her scowl deepen. "Unless you've got some maternity clothes tucked away somewhere that I don't want to know about, then yes. Deal with it."

He grinned. "I could glamour you up, make Gabriel see you however you want."

"No thanks. I'd rather he knew exactly what he was getting when we face each other. It might even help."

"If you say so," Jaxer said.

"I think you look lovely," Deacon said, pulling her close.

Her stomach actually got in the way. She frowned down at the bump. "You're just saying that because you're my mate and you have to, but I appreciate it anyway." She met his gaze. "This all feels really really weird. I haven't had four months to build up to it like a normal pregnancy. It's freaky."

"I agree," he said, with feeling.

She grinned at him, glad she wasn't the only one finding all this strange.

"All right, if you two are done making moon eyes at each other," Jaxer drawled.

She raised her brows at him over her shoulder. "Moon eyes?"

"It's a thing. You're doing it."

"Ha!" She stepped away from Deacon, a little reluctantly, and they headed out to Deacon's SUV.

Jaxer, as usual, waved them on and said he'd meet them at the hive entrance. He didn't get into human-made vehicles if he could help it because of his relatively-slight-compared-to-other-Fae allergy to iron. He had his own way of traveling around, and she'd only just learned recently how he did it. Well, not really *how*. He hadn't explained the mechanics. But she finally knew it had something to do with opening a door into Faery and crossing from one place to another that way.

She was still annoyed he'd hidden that from her for so long.

"You could have just done that part," Cary pointed out reasonably. "Met us at the hive directly rather than showing up here first to insult my outfit."

"But then I would have missed out on the chance to insult your outfit." He grinned at her snarl and disappeared into the dark.

She shook her head, but inside she was smiling. That was the Jaxer she'd known for six years, before he'd had to go and mess things up with *feelings*. She missed her friend. And it was nice to see him again, even if it was rare these days.

Despite it being home to all the resident city vampires, the hive entrance was actually located just a little outside of town, in the direction of Mount Hood. Cary hadn't had the guts to ask Ariel why they'd done that. For all she knew, it was traditional in Portland since the underground in the center of the city had had such an active history. She'd just assumed that the vampires didn't want to risk their hive being discovered by the crimps or the Chinese gangs that had built escape tunnels under Chinatown—not to mention bumping up against the Mor-gin, a bubble realm a group of Chinese wizards had established under the city—so had located their home well beyond the scope of the city port.

When she'd first been forced to meet with Ariel, she'd read up on the Portland vampires a bit. Apparently, Ariel had brought them here in the mid-1800s when the city was just coming into its own as a port town, at first extremely puritanical, later becoming a lot more dangerous and raucous. Just the sort of place a hungry vampire might find a meal without anyone noticing. The hive here had thrived in that period, under Ariel's strict rules. They'd remained safe from discovery while being able to stretch their natures. In fact, Gabriel's ousting of Ariel was the first major disruption to the order of things among the Portland vampires. Cary was both curious and afraid to find out what this had done to the hive.

The entrance into the hive, at least the one Cary knew about, was a simple, nondescript wooden farmhouse on a small plot of grass-covered land, carved out of the woods at the base of the foothills. There was a huge, red wooden barn with a peaked roof just behind the farmhouse—which she'd learned after her previous visit held vehicles of various types for the use of hive members—and beyond the barn, nothing but trees for several miles. The road leading up a steep slope to the front of the farmhouse was paved but roughly. Nothing about the area screamed vampire. Or even really drew attention to itself.

Until you walked *inside* the farmhouse. The interior was really just one big foyer, a formal entrance area where guests were screened and either allowed inside or ignored. Or killed. Depending on their intent.

The foyer was all gold and white and pale blue, the floor covered in white tiles marbled with lines of gold. The crown molding was shaped into an elegant pattern and gilded with gold paint. The few pieces of furniture were delicate and elaborately carved, white wood with gilt accents and pale blue silk upholstery, the sort of stuff that didn't look like it should be used by actual people or it might break. The lighting was muted and soft, coming from wall sconces. And while they were obviously electric, the bulbs gave the place an almost pinkish hue. There were mirrors in gilded frames over delicately carved side tables. And thick pale blue, ceiling to floor length velvet curtains covered the windows.

Once you stepped through the ordinary looking white wooden door, it felt like moving into another time and place. Like crossing into a Parisian palace. Only on a miniature scale. Even the ceiling seemed higher than the outside of the farmhouse would indicate.

The farmhouse door opened for them without them having to knock—a trick Cary knew was the result of security cameras over the door rather than some cool vampire magic. And just as she'd expected, James was waiting for them.

"Told you so," she murmured to Jaxer who was standing just behind her left shoulder.

He snorted an unintelligible sound that made her grin.

Deacon had taken up position just behind her right shoulder, the two men flanking her like bodyguards. She wanted to feel cool and powerful, but instead she just felt a slight sense of nausea and that tingling along her skin getting worse again. She rubbed her stomach, the bump making her feel oddly off balance, and sighed. Jaxer was probably projecting a gloriously beautiful and powerful image. Deacon had slipped into his super controlled Leader of the Leopards aura, all animal strength and contained deadly instinct.

And she was an ordinary human woman with her hair pulled back into a ponytail and the top button of her pants undone.

At least her hair was thicker and pretty glossy at the moment, one of the nice side effects of carrying this baby god. Because the rest of her was a pale match to the magnificence around her.

James was dressed in a charcoal gray suit, white shirt, and black tie with a subtle pattern stitched into it that she couldn't see from the safe distance she kept between her and the vampire. His blondish hair was combed neatly, his dark eyes not even showing the vampire glow. He looked perfectly elegant but harmless.

Which made the hair on her arms stand up in alarm.

"Welcome," he greeted, his gaze steady on hers. His smile grew when she stared back, not needing to drop her gaze.

"Gabriel free for a chat?" she asked. Her heart was hammering, and everyone except maybe Jaxer could probably hear it. She was certain both Deacon and James could smell her contained fear as well. But she pretended to be relaxed and comfortable for appearances sake. They might know she was nervous as hell but she didn't have to show it visibly.

"He conveys his pleasure that you've chosen to meet with him."

"Chosen? Right." She resisted rolling her eyes, but she couldn't help the sardonic twist to her mouth.

James nodded to Deacon and Jaxer. "Leopard, we expected you. Greetings." He tilted his head. "I am surprised you'd return, Faery. Given the general...tastes of vampires for your kind."

Cary felt her hackles rising, but Jaxer brushed off the not-so-subtle threat.

"Oh, I wouldn't miss this meeting for the world," he said, sounding very amused. And a lot more Irish. "I can't wait to see Gabriel's reaction to our Cary. Doubt he knows what he's gotten himself into."

"He knows more than you might assume," James said. Though his smile turned a little tighter around the edges.

That surprised Cary, that she could see the change in reaction. Vampires as old as James appeared to be didn't show their emotions unless they wanted to.

Jaxer laughed, completely unconcerned. Cary couldn't help feeling jealous. She'd love to be so relaxed right now. Her stomach did a little flip that didn't feel entirely like her own jumping nerves. She rubbed the bump unconsciously.

"Nothing could have possibly prepared the old man for our Cary," Jaxer said.

James lifted his brows and glanced at her, meeting her gaze. She stared back, pretending at casualness. James lifted one side of his mouth in a look that could have been a smile or a snarl, depending on one's perspective. Cary decided it was safer to assume amusement and smiled back.

"Perhaps," he said faintly. Then more loudly. "This way."

When he turned toward the rear of the open foyer, Cary murmured to Jaxer, "'Our Cary'? Your Irish is showing."

Jaxer's accent changed depending on who he was talking to. He had ties to both the English and Irish Fae courts, though exactly how he'd never told her. Sometimes he sounded quite English—especially when talking to Thomas the leprechaun, his nemesis. Other times, the accent swung Irish. With Cary, he mostly kept to a soft Irish lilt she barely noticed after all these years. But he'd kicked that accent up several notches with James.

"James is English," Jaxer said quietly. "And he didn't support home rule for the Irish."

"You two have met?" Cary asked, surprised. She glanced at Jaxer.

He smiled at James's back but didn't answer her question.

Oh good. This was a positive turn of events. She did roll her eyes this time and faced James again.

Just what she needed. Her vampire escort and her faery bodyguard nursing a political grudge while she had to face off against a super scary monster in just a few minutes.

This was going to be fun.

9

*C*ary was always just a little surprised that the door at the rear of the farmhouse lead into an elevator. She had no idea why this surprised her. Why wouldn't vampires use elevators to take them into their subterranean living spaces? Hell, she'd even seen it in a vampire movie before. But still, she expected the door to lead to a long and winding staircase every time—well the two times she'd been here. And when it opened onto a comfortably large elevator, she was always startled.

To be fair, the elevator was at least luxuriously decorated and not just a steal box. It had an armless bench with red upholstered cushions against the rear wall, a soft Turkish rug underfoot, and dark stained wood paneling covering the walls. The controls were an old fashioned crank handle and the levels ticked down on a circular, wrought iron dial over the door. None of the levels were actually marked with a number, just a pointed hash mark, but still, she could track the elevator moving. Which was reassuring because otherwise she couldn't actually sense the movement. She had a feeling that beneath all the old fashioned trappings, this elevator was a high tech marvel.

The fact that the décor had such a different look from the foyer was also a bit of a shock, like a visual non sequitur. She had a feeling that was done on purpose as well. Most everything the vampires did in their lair was done for a reason, even if she had no idea what that reason might be.

Keeping the prey off balance probably.

Jaxer shifted from one foot to the other behind her. It was a subtle move, but she was so hyper aware of everything going on around her while they were trapped inside an elevator with a strange vampire, she noticed the gesture.

She glanced a question at him, not wanting to say anything aloud that might alert James to a possible problem.

Jaxer shook his head very slightly, and then let his eyes wonder around the enclosed space.

She winced. How the hell had she forgotten that? Jaxer and his very slight but still there allergy to iron. No matter what kind of alloy was used to make the elevator, chances of it having some bits of iron in it were pretty damned good. Even the wrought iron dial—which looked real and not a like a plastic facsimile—would have enough actual iron in it to irritate the faery slightly.

She mouthed, *Sorry.*

He shrugged and offered a faint smile, but she could still see the tightness around his eyes and mouth.

She'd forgotten how uncomfortable this descent had been for him during the last visit. Mostly because she'd been so worried about confronting a Master vampire. She'd only been a Protector for a little over two years when she'd faced Ariel. Her own fear had overwhelmed her sense of awareness for Jaxer's discomfort, and she'd only realized how bad it had been for him afterward when he'd told her.

She felt pretty crappy now, having forgotten all over again.

He leaned in closer, so she could feel him pressing against the back of her shoulder, and whispered in her ear, "I'll survive."

Deacon growled very low, a sound almost impossible for her human ears.

But James heard it. He glanced back at them.

Jaxer had already moved away from her. And Deacon was no longer making any noise. She gave James an innocent, wide-eyed look that asked silently what he wanted. The vampire glanced between the two men behind her then faced the elevator door again, his hand still on the lever that operated the thing.

She gave Deacon an "Are you crazy? Stop that!" look—at least that's what she tried to convey with her urgently raised brows and the tight line of her mouth. She mouthed a brief thanks to Jaxer for his reassurance. Then she faced forward again, rolling her head on her neck until bones cracked.

Dealing with Deacon and Jaxer's issues while she was about to face a super scary monster was really distracting.

Her stomach moved again, the muscles across it seemed to contract a little, a weird but not uncomfortable spasm. That was strange. She settled her palm on the side of her stomach. Geez had she gotten bigger in just the last few hours? It was hard to tell because the whole baby bump was such a bizarre sensation. Not anything like the soft squishy bump she got after too many weeks of eating too much pizza.

She swallowed hard when James moved the elevator handle to lock the giant box into place. He smiled, closed lipped, over his shoulder at her. Then opened the elevator doors.

The smell hit her almost immediate. She hadn't noticed it so strong the first time, though now she did remember thinking the way this place smelled was odd and disconcerting.

This time around it smacked her across the face like a bloody rag. So much blood and earth. With some strange underscent like sweat or body odor but with a reptilian punch to it rather than that mammalian musk. And just under the surface of all that, the very faint, sweet scent of decay. That was a part of this she hadn't picked up the last time around. She narrowed her nostrils, trying not to pull in the smell, but it coated the back of her tongue and throat, making it impossible to escape.

The weirdest part was that it wasn't a super unpleasant smell. It should have made her gag. It should have repelled her, like the smell of fish did. But no, this sweetish, metallic, earthy smell was almost magnetic. It drew her into the undergrown cavern rather than scared her away.

Vampires. So many vampires in one place.

Actually, she was pretty sure there were only about forty or so living in the hive. But given their speed and ability to hide themselves in plain sight, it was impossible for her to really tell how many surrounded them as they left the relative safety of the elevator behind. The cavernous entryway was, as one might expect, dark with only a single recessed light high overhead and halfway into the cavern to give the barest amount of light needed for eyes to work—well vampire and probably shifter eyes. Cary was still blinking in the darkness, trying to get her bearings. Because her Protector magic was working, she'd be able to see in a moment. Under normal circumstances, she probably wouldn't have been able to see hardly at all.

The scent clung to her as she stepped into that darkness, shadows moving all around the open space. The floor was stone tiled and covered with thick rugs which took out some of the chill in the air, but not enough for her to want to take her jacket off. They cut down on echoes too, although she was the only one making any noise when she walked.

Unlike the last time she'd been here, when the walls were covered in black silk and there were scatterings of elegant French couches and chairs around the area, now the walls were bare and there was no furniture. The walls were reinforced, heavy concrete blocks, with no adornment, curving along the arched ceiling and disappearing into the darkness. She suspected those same walls had been underneath Ariel's black silk, but Ariel had been about drama and style. The bareness now was strange. It reminded her a little of the Washington DC subway stations, except without the weird uplighting in the subway.

At the far end of the huge room was another door, steel-reinforced oak. It was, like everything else here, large, austere, and surprisingly plain, right down to the rounded steel knobs. There was a lock plate under the knob, so obviously this door could be cut off from the rest of the hive. She supposed that was a necessary security precaution. And suddenly she started wondering if there were any other ways out of here. The being trapped underground, locked into a room with vampires thing started a little drop of panic in her gut which was going to grow into hyperventilating, full-on terror if she wasn't careful.

Her stomach contracted again, the muscles across her abdomen pulling tight and releasing in a wave-like motion. She pressed her palm against the bump and thought, *We're good, baby god. Don't worry. I've got you.*

Both the panic she was feeling and the tightening of her stomach muscles eased. Yay for a calm baby god. The tingling along her skin was a constant hum in the background now, covering her entire body in a blanket of tickled nerve endings. It was so pervasive she was getting used to it, and only just realized in the moment they stepped up to the huge oak door that it had gotten stronger as the baby god moved and was easing a little as the baby god settled.

That was really weird.

James paused outside the door and glanced back at them. "Are you ready?"

"Sure," Cary said, not entirely sure at all. She knew she was safe, thanks to having a baby god in her womb to protect. She knew that thanks to the threat the vampires posed to Deacon and Jaxer she could keep them safe, too.

As those oak doors opened, though, she worried about how *long* she might have to protect everyone. Because if the vampires locked them in, she had no idea how to get back out again. At least not how to do that and still be alive.

Why hadn't she worried about this with Ariel?

Anger was apparently great at giving her a lot of false confidence. She pulled in a deep breath and let it out slowly through her nose as they stepped into the dim area beyond the door.

They were greeted by another austere setting, directly in opposition to Ariel's elaborate décor. Where Ariel had had the cavernous room decked out in white and gold and crystals like a French palace, empha-sizing the courtly aspect of the room, Gabriel had it stripped back to simple smoothed tiled floors and bare wood paneled walls. It was a bit warmer than the concrete area outside, but still bare and echoing in its emptiness. There was no furniture, no decorative lighting, no elegant paintings or wall hangings. Just a few very large pillow-like mats stacked against one wall and a line of recessed ceiling lights which barely provided enough illumination for Cary to see, even with the super vision her Protector magic gave her.

In fact, for the first few seconds they were inside the room, Cary thought it was empty. Then a shadow at the far end materialized into a man sitting on one of the pillow mats. His eyes glowed yellow in the darkness.

"Welcome, Cary Redmond," he said, his voice deep and melodious. Hypnotic. "It's about time we met."

10

*C*ary thought she could have gone on significantly longer without meeting this particular vampire, though she kept that thought to herself.

As her eyes adjusted to the dim light, she took advantage of her apparently shifter-level ability to smell to assess her surroundings. A weird woodsy, earthy scent seemed to float in the air over the musky, sweet metallic scent of vampire. The scent reminded her a little of the incenses Angie occasionally burned in various ceremonies, and sometimes as a prop for her customers who wanted to make sure they were getting their psychic readings from a real witch—if they only knew!

It took some moments before Cary recognized the smell, as she'd never come across it mixed with vampire and blood before, but she was pretty sure it was that very hippy of incenses, patchouli. Neither her nor Angie's favorite.

She wrinkled her nose. Sight might be a better friend in here because nothing that she was smelling was particularly appealing. In fact, she'd kind of preferred straight up vampire to this mix with the growing-stronger-by-the-minute patchouli stuff.

"Nice place you have here," Cary commented, gesturing to the empty space.

Neither she nor her erstwhile bodyguards had moved more than a few feet into the room. Standing twenty yards away from a vampire still wasn't enough space to be safe, not given how fast vampires moved, but it gave her the illusion she'd be able to turn and run if she needed to.

Not that she would. She had that freeze-in-the-headlights reaction to danger, which as it turned out was a very useful instinct for a Protector.

"I'm pleased you approve," Gabriel said.

"Very Zen," she said. "The only thing you're missing is a meditation bell."

Even from this far away, she saw the flash of his very white teeth in the dark. A slight sound, the faintest ring of a melodious note echoed through the room.

"Huh. Bell," she said with a slight tilt of her head in acknowledgement. She hadn't seen him tap the hanging gong, but its swinging caught the faint light on its brass surface so she could see where it was now. "Guess you've got all the cool stuff."

"I was told you were amusing," Gabriel said, not sounding either amused or annoyed.

"I try. So why are we here? I'm pretty sure it's not for tea and a philosophical discussion of various meditation techniques."

"No. I would like to know why you keep interfering with my vampires feeding."

"They're breaking the law set down by Ariel and that you claimed you would uphold. I've only stopped vampires attempting to feed from the unwilling."

"And you were sure those…humans were unwilling?"

"Yes."

"How?" His voice took on an ever so slight sibilance, like there might be Ss in that question that she'd never noticed before.

"Because I was able to stop the vampire," she said. Her skin tingled across her abdomen and arms. She wanted to rub her hands along her skin to calm the sensation but was afraid Gabriel would misinterpret the move as nervousness.

She was pretty sure he was reading more than enough of her nervous energy as it was.

"Say that again?" Gabriel said, his voice low enough it was difficult for her to hear.

"Not a shifter," she said. "You'll have to speak up."

"You're a witch?"

She smiled. "I get that a lot." But she didn't confirm or deny his guess. According to James, he already knew she was a Protector, so she didn't feel the need to elaborate.

Unless, of course, James had lied about Gabriel's knowledge.

Silence followed, that kind of silence that rang in her ears and made the space around her feel like it was closing in.

Cary tightened the muscles in her thighs to keep her knees from shaking. Even this far away, she could feel Gabriel's power emanating toward them out of the shadows. It was the middle of the night in a place where no light reached them except for the faint glow of artificial lights from overhead. This was his place, his seat of power. And he was powerful. His age and strength were like a living thing in the room, a thing that crawled toward her and wrapped around her ankles, twisting up her body. The sense of that twisting, creeping, searching power made her want to tremble. Why the hell wasn't her Protector power keeping it at bay?

The sensation reached to just above her knees before it stopped, and with a suddenness that almost made her wobble, it vanished, retreating so fast she was tempted to think she'd imagined the whole thing.

Only with a Master vampire, she knew better.

Her stomach muscles did that roll and settle, almost like the baby god was turning over. She did set her hand to her stomach this time, silently calming the active little entity.

Gabriel's glowing eyes narrowed. It was too dark in the cavernous room for her to get a good look at him. All she saw were teeth and glowing eyes in a dark shadow. She was sure that was deliberate, but the impression was still disconcerting.

"I have someone here who'd like to speak with you," he said.

Cary raised her eyebrows. A list of possible people raced through her head. The first and most likely suspect was the Master vampire who'd worked with Oliver Holland. She kind of assumed if that Master survived it was because he'd left Gabriel's territory. But you couldn't trust vampires.

The person who stepped out of the shadows, however, was quite literally the last person on her list.

"You!"

She'd only glimpsed the older wizard once, when he'd tried to kill her for the second time. The parking lot outside the diner had been poorly lit, and she'd been scared and trying not to move so she hadn't picked up much detail. Just the gray hair, blue eyes, and pale, leathery skin. In the underground darkness of the vampires' lair, the wizard managed to look exactly like he did in her memory. Right down to the black turtleneck and pants. The clothes made his face look like it was floating, bodiless, in the dark.

Cary snarled. "Why the hell have you been trying to kill me?"

The wizard snarl back. "Why won't you die?"

"Because I don't feel like it," she snapped. "I know who you are. And that little shit Sheldon deserved what happened."

Sheldon had tried to steal Deacon's body. She had no sympathy for the little shit, even if she had been conflicted about his supposed death. She wasn't sure how she felt about his survival either. But she wasn't about to discuss that with his murderous mentor.

"You think I'll let you steal my apprentice's powers without retribution?" the older wizard growled, taking a step toward her.

"What the every loving fuck are you talking about?" Cary said.

"Thief," he said, his voice low. The blue glow of an energy ball filled his palm.

Under any other circumstance, this might have been a scary sight. The wizard *knew* how to kill her. No one else here was under threat from him. Just her. So he would be able to get around her powers.

Ah, but not today, wizard, she thought. Not today.

Even without needing to protect Jaxer and Deacon from the

vampires, thanks to the baby god she needed to keep safe, no one else's petty grudges were getting through her shields.

She smiled at the wizard's threat. "Try it, buddy. I dare you."

His eyes narrowed. Deacon's low growl made the hairs on her neck stand up. He knew better than to try getting around her to attack the wizard at this point, but she recognized that he really wanted to. She could hear it in his tone.

The wizard glanced at Deacon briefly. "Your mate would like to rip my throat out," he said.

"Yeah, well. Can you blame him? You're threatening his mate, and you let your apprentice try to steal his body. You brought his anger on yourself."

"Yet he doesn't attack me when I threaten you," the wizard said, almost thoughtfully. "Why?"

"You already know." She glanced at Gabriel and snarled. "And you told the damned vampires, didn't you?" That's how Gabriel knew what she was. The stupid, grudge-holding wizard told him. "You bastard," she said to the wizard.

"Gabriel promised me you'd be alone," the wizard said. Not quite a rebuke of the Master vampire, but close enough that Gabriel glanced at the man. The wizard either didn't notice the look or ignored it. "You are never alone!"

"I'm a popular girl," she said.

The wizard brought out her snarky side. And all the fear she'd been swallowing since getting into the elevator got subsumed under her anger. She really hated people trying to kill her for stupid reasons. And getting revenge for Sheldon was a stupid reason as far as she was concerned.

"You're a thief," the wizard said. "And you need to die so I can get the lost power back."

"What the hell do you mean I'm a thief?" Cary said, her tone sharp. "You keep saying that, but I have no clue what you're talking about."

The ball of sizzling blue energy in the wizard's hand expanded, making it the size of a soccer ball. The glow reflected on his face, distorting the shadows in the hollows of his cheeks and the sharp edges of his jaw and chin. It gave him that demented evil look people got when they shined a flashlight up under their chin. Highlighting his inner personality, Cary thought irritably.

"You stole my apprentice's powers, bitch. That will not stand."

"I don't know what you're talking about," she said. Again. "Sheldon killed himself, or whatever happened to him, he did it to himself."

The tingling along her skin spiked, almost painful now, but she was too angry to pay much attention. The sensation fed her irritation instead of distracting from it.

Behind her, Jaxer murmured her name quietly. She ignored that, too.

Deacon placed a hand on her shoulder, but it felt like a shock of electricity against her jumping nerves and she flinched away.

"I'm fine," she said over her shoulder to him. "Just pissed off." She glared at Gabriel. "And I don't like being set up."

"Really?" Gabriel said. "Because I'm finding this meeting fascinating."

"Fuck you," she said. She was all snarls and hissing anger and her skin was jumping and she wanted them all to stop being assholes and leave her alone.

"Language," Gabriel said.

She snorted. "Seriously? You're going to check my language? That's rich."

"Don't like vampires much, I see?" Gabriel said.

Cary was busy glaring at the wizard's energy bolt, so she couldn't gage Gabriel's tone. He sounded mild. She suspected he was offended. She really didn't care.

Her nerves were so sensitive at this stage, she wanted to scream with it. Strangely, it still didn't hurt. The sensation was just overwhelming. She couldn't channel it away because she didn't know what the hell was causing it. Probably the stupid Master vampire. She would have glared at him, but she didn't want to risk looking away from the wizard.

"Are you going to use that damned energy bolt or not?" she finally snapped. "Either throw it or put it away."

"You want me to kill you?" the wizard snarled.

"You can't, and you know it. That's why you're posturing. But it makes you look like an amateur. Like the petulant child your apprentice was. Is. Whatever. Is that little shit still alive or not?"

"You stole what was rightfully his," the wizard snarled. "What should have been mine to control."

She raised her brows. "Did Sheldon know you wanted to control his powers yourself? Cause he might not have been too happy about that."

"It hardly matters now. You left him weakened."

"Still alive then," she said. "Good to know. By the way, still don't have the first clue how *I* left him weakened."

The wizard snarled and raised his hand as if he meant to throw the energy bolt at her.

She smiled, with a lot of teeth, and waited for him to try it. With luck it would rebound around the room, killing vampires, and then both the vampires and the wizard would end up too busy fighting each other to worry about her anymore.

From the corner of her eyes, she saw Gabriel raise a hand. Really, he just raised a finger, but the gesture was enough to make the wizard lower his arm. The energy bolt in his palm winked out, and Cary had to blink against the spots dancing in her eyes after the extra light vanished.

"You don't understand what he means, do you?" Gabriel said quietly, staring at her.

"You know what I know," Cary said. "That setting someone up like this is rude. We're here to talk about how vampires need to mind the rules. And if you've changed the rules, you're gonna be dealing with me a lot, so maybe don't change the rules. Also, this wizard and his apprentice are assholes, so the fact that he's here makes me think less of you."

There was a part of her that recognized taunting a Master vampire was a really bad idea. Especially since she wasn't going to be technically indestructible forever. But there was another part of her that was too edgy and angry to care. She wasn't even entirely sure where the anger was coming from. It was, she thought, justified. But the level of rage building seemed dangerous given the situation.

She didn't mind pissing off bad guys. She did it all the time, and sometimes even on purpose because they talked more when they were angry—which had the dual effect of them not killing her immediately *and* giving away their future plans. Sometimes anyway. Sometimes, it was just a stalling tactic.

This felt different, though. Even the fear that she'd walked into this room with wasn't there anymore. She wasn't even a little afraid of these monsters.

She should have been. Logically, she really really should have been.

Logic started to remind her of this when a ripple of movement fluttered through the room.

Vampires she hadn't realized where there moved and shifted, shadows in her peripheral vision. She felt Jaxer and Deacon both moving behind her, too, putting their backs to her back, forming up into a defensive wall.

The wizard's snarl turned into something that looked like anticipation. His blue eyes narrowed, and a spark of electricity danced along the fingers of his right hand.

And then Gabriel smiled.

Wide enough to show the points of his canines.

Oh boy.

11

*C*ary swallowed hard against the jump in her pulse. She braced herself. It helped a little knowing her Protector magic was already working, that none of the vampires flowing around her in shadows could get near her or her charges.

But there was a lizard-brained instinct that kicked in, no matter how much experience she had keeping people safe from bad guys, that always whispered doubts and fears into her ear.

What if the magic doesn't work this time? What if someone gets killed and she doesn't stop it?

Unfortunately, she'd faced that failure before. Someone *had* died. She really didn't want to face that again.

She took her gaze off Gabriel long enough to scan the cavernous room. The vampires in the shadows were a moving mass of darkness now, but they weren't getting closer to her little group. The near silent swish of clothing and a very faint breeze created by their movements filled the large space with a kind of irritating hum. She caught the glow of yellow eyes in the darkness, and some sibilant whispers too quiet for her to decipher, although she suspected Deacon knew what they were saying.

"Can you hear them?" she murmured to him.

"You don't want to know," he said back. The growl of his leopard near the surface was clear in his voice.

She shivered a little—inappropriately, because she liked the sound, not because she was scared.

She shook her head. This mate business had the *worst* timing. But on the other hand, the reaction did something strange. It settled her nerves. She met Gabriel's gaze.

And smiled back.

"Well, this has been interesting for a first meeting, hasn't it?" she said. "You threaten me and make sure I meet an enemy face-to-face for the first time—thanks for that, by the way. Always good to get to know the person trying to kill you even if you don't know why they're trying to kill you."

"You haven't been listening to him, then," Gabriel said.

"Yeah, yeah, I'm a horrible person who did something terrible to his awful and evil apprentice."

Gabriel made a slight sound, like a snort of amusement but too subtle to be called more than maybe an exhale of air. Since he didn't need to breathe much, the sound was quite a gesture.

Outside of the flash of white canines and the glowing yellow eyes, she still hadn't gotten a good look at the Master. Even when the wizard's energy bolt added more light to the room. Unlike Ariel, who'd sat on a throne and demanded admiration of her glorious grandeur— and she had been an unearthly being of awesome beauty—Gabriel continued to hide his features in the shadows, his gestures like moving bits of darkness and nothing more, as patchouli smoke circled his head. She was sure that was a vampire trick now. Her eyes were adjusted to the dark. She should be able to see him.

"I see why Ariel was so amused by you," he said.

"I have that effect on people."

"You stole his apprentice's magic." Gabriel glanced at the wizard who was still glowering at her. "At least some of it. Enough to have angered the master who wanted that magic for his own."

"I still don't have any idea what you're talking about. I can't steal anyone's magic. That's not how mine works."

She didn't need to go into detail about how her magic did work. Since Gabriel and the wizard—what the hell was his name?—had been talking, Gabriel knew at least as much as the wizard did about Protectors. Since that was enough to get Cary killed, it was more than enough as far as she was concerned.

"You're pregnant," Gabriel said, changing the subject.

She went with it because bad guys did that a lot. To be fair, so did she because it was a great technique for throwing people off balance. "Yup." Again, he didn't need to know more.

Gabriel glanced at the two men behind her. "But neither of theirs."

"Your point?" She smiled as if she wasn't bothered by the implication, designed to anger her mate no doubt. Since Deacon was edgy about this whole thing, she just hoped he kept his leopard under control.

"The mate doesn't mind?" Gabriel asked, confirming her suspicions.

"I'm a very understanding man," Deacon said, his voice very deep.

She glanced over her shoulder. He wasn't looking at her or Gabriel. His attention was firmly on the other vampires in the room. Which was good. He might not like this subject but he wasn't letting it distract him.

"You'd have to be," Gabriel said dryly. "The wizard tells me I can't kill you right now."

"You can't," the wizard said. "But that won't last forever."

"What the hell is your name?" Cary asked the wizard. It was starting to bother her that no one had introduced him. "Or do I just call you Sheldon's guy?"

The wizard snarled. She grinned and blinked innocently.

"You don't get my real name, witch," he said.

"Now, you know better than that," she said as condescendingly as possible, referring to his calling her a witch. They both knew that part wasn't true. "And if you don't want to give me something to call you other than 'wizard,' fine. You can be Sheldon's guy. No skin off my nose. Sheldon's guy."

"I'm going to kill you slowly," Sheldon's guy snarled.

"But not yet," she said with a grin. Then she faced Gabriel. "This stopped being fun almost as soon as James showed up at my friend's house to invite me here. So I think we should call it a night. You ambushed me. I was a smart ass to you. You know you can't kill me. And my feet are hurting from standing this long." She rubbed her stomach. "Pregnancy, you know."

"We haven't settled anything," Gabriel pointed out.

"You haven't brought up anything we can negotiate a settlement to," she reminded him. "You've avoided the topic of any new laws I need to know about regarding vampire feedings, and instead, decided to show me your hand, revealing that you now know what I am. I have taken note."

"The laws haven't changed," Gabriel said. "At least, not yet. Does that make you happy?"

"Yes. But I'm pretty sure that's not why you haven't changed the laws."

"True."

She narrowed her eyes. "Why haven't you changed things? And more importantly, why are so many vampires drinking from the unwilling if it's still law that they aren't allowed to?"

Gabriel's slight smile returned, a faint slash of white teeth in the shadows of his face. "How else could I get your attention?"

She gave him a look. "Right. All this was for my benefit? I seriously doubt that. Who the hell am I to you?"

"You're the Protector in my territory," Gabriel said quietly, for the first time naming aloud her job.

Somehow, hearing him say it out loud was a lot lot worse than just knowing he knew. Why the hell did so many powerful and dangerous people have to figure out what she was? Her life was a lot less complicated when people thought she was a witch.

"And having a Protector in my territory could be very useful," Gabriel finished. "I wanted to take your measure."

"Gee, I'm flattered?" She pressed her lips together. "For the record, I don't protect anyone I don't want to protect."

Technically, not true, but mostly she could manage to avoid

protecting bad guys from other bad guys. She really hated when she had to protect bad guys. It rubbed her the wrong way.

"I find it interesting that you still don't care to know what the wizard means about you stealing his apprentice's powers," Gabriel said in another non sequitur.

But two could play that game. "He wouldn't tell you his name either, huh? I find that pretty paranoid, really. Don't you?" She glanced at the wizard before meeting Gabriel's gaze again. "He's okay with Sheldon's guy apparently. You can use that."

The wizard snarled. She ignored him.

"Attack her if she's making you angry," Gabriel said. "Why not try to get through her defenses, since you know how?"

The fucking Master vampire of Portland knew how to kill her. She really hated this. Her Seventh Year survival odds had dropped significantly.

Her stomach did another roll, and her side flexed and relaxed. Poor baby god must be getting upset at all the anxiety that kept storming through Cary's system. She tried to calm the movements with a hand to her side.

The wizard actually rolled his eyes at Gabriel. That was ballsy.

"While she's pregnant, as she is not so subtly pointing out, I can't kill her. Even though I don't care about killing the infant, killing this bitch will kill it, and that triggers her powers."

"You are such an asshole," Cary said to the wizard as he outlined for *all* the vampires in the room to hear exactly how her powers worked.

It was one thing for the Master to know. That was bad enough. But now his entire hive knew. She'd pissed a number of that horde off over the years, especially in the last month. Even if Gabriel wasn't interested in killing her right away, that didn't mean the others wouldn't try for revenge.

Deacon reached back and took her free hand, squeezing briefly before letting go. She took the gesture for the reassurance it was meant to be, then looked Gabriel right in the eyes.

"Are we done here?" she asked. "I think there's been enough 'revelations' tonight. Without any real reason for me to have shown up."

"It's been some time, several centuries actually, since someone met my gaze so easily," Gabriel commented quietly. "I'm not sure I like it."

"Tough." She sighed. "This is a lot of not getting anywhere. Will your vampires keep attacking unwilling food?"

"No."

He said it with such certainty, she blinked. Another shiver of movement went through the shadows.

Huh. If Cary wasn't misinterpreting the whispers, his people didn't much like that pronouncement.

Gabriel didn't look at the other vampires, but the whispers died down until even the restless movements were stilled. She raised her brows at him. She was so tempted to question him, to ask if he was sure his people would follow that rule. But doubting his hold over the hive while the hive was watching, and while he couldn't kill her, seemed like tempting fate. Because before long, he'd be able to kill her, and they both knew it.

"Then we're good," Cary said instead. "So we'll be going now. Thanks for the…" She narrowed her eyes at the wizard. "I suppose calling it an interesting meeting would be accurate." She started back toward the heavy oak and steel door.

Gabriel's voice stopped her. "You absorb magic, Ms. Redmond. That's what the wizard meant. In a way, he's right about you being a thief."

She frowned and faced Gabriel. "The wizard is wrong."

"Then why is your skin glowing?" he asked.

She glanced down. Blinked a few times. Raised her hands to stare at them.

Whoa.

"That is so weird," she murmured. Her skin *was* glowing with a faint, pale light. Along the back of her hand, where her nerves were still tingling, little sparks danced. "Are you guys seeing this?" she asked Deacon and Jaxer.

"You've been glowing since the wizard appeared," Jaxer said quietly.

She dragged her gaze from her hand to stare at him. "I have?" She looked at Deacon.

He nodded. "There's a scent with it too," he said quietly. "Very faint, but there. Like…cocoa."

"I smell like chocolate?" That sounded nice.

"The unsweetened powder."

She scowled a little. "I lack sweetness, huh?"

Deacon's serious expression broke for a slight smile. "It's enhanced by your own natural sweetness."

She snorted a laugh. "Right."

Looking down at her hands again, she shook her head. It had to be the baby god. Nothing to do with her. She knew full well she was ordinary. Even the Nags—particularly Liruk—reminded her of her very human frailty without her Protector magic. She'd have to ask Frank about this because it was too weird.

She glanced back at Gabriel, then at the wizard. Would it be better if they thought she could do something she couldn't? Thought she had skills and magic she actually didn't? Maybe. Although, if they ever called her bluff, she was toast. But with these guys, she was probably already toast.

"This is pretty interesting," she said, "but nothing to do with Sheldon and his magic and whatever Sheldon's guy here thinks I did." There. Sort of giving them truth without actually admitting anything. "You've been misinformed," she said to Gabriel.

She watched the wizard from her peripheral vision as she said this, trying to gage his reaction. He was trying to kill her because he thought she could so something she couldn't. Maybe if he realized she couldn't, he'd stop trying to kill her? She doubted it. But a woman could hope.

Unfortunately, he didn't look any less angry and annoyed with her. And in fact, her comment made him wince, glance at Gabriel, and then scowl harder at her. Was he worried about being in trouble with

Gabriel? If he was busy dealing with vampires, he'd have less time to come after her so that could only be a good thing.

Gabriel didn't glance at the wizard, not even a little. He continued to stare at her. And nothing changed in the shadows around his face. But the glow in his yellow eyes brightened briefly.

Sowing the seeds of mistrust between two people she didn't like or trust. Yay, her.

"We're finished now, right?" Cary asked Gabriel. "All satisfied with 'taking my measure' and seeing how I'd react to the wizard?" She glanced at the wizard. "I assume we're done for a while now too? Since, you know, can't kill me yet and all?"

The wizard's lip lifted in a faint sneer, but he didn't answer. Okay, maybe they weren't done. She supposed since he knew he couldn't kill her while she was pregnant that at least he'd leave her alone for another few months. Hey, maybe if she could stall him long enough, she'd get through her Seventh Year trial before he came after her again. Or better yet, he'd get tired of waiting and move on.

She had very little hope of that last option, based on the rage in his eyes.

When no one answered her, she shrugged and turned back toward the door. One of the dark and whispering shadows finally detached and flowed forward to block her way.

She was a beautifully stunning vampire. Her dark hair hung in thick waves to her ankles. Her skin was a light brown shade that Cary thought might have even been a few shades darker in life. Her eyes were nearly black, not glowing yellow like Gabriel's. She was dressed in a form-fitting black dress with cut-outs here and there to show off her fantastically curved figure. The woman had the kind of curves that usually only showed up in drawings because real life women couldn't manage that without surgery.

"You smell yummy," the vampire hummed. "Two for the price of one. A dinner for a queen."

"Gee, thanks?" Cary commented.

"Gabriel says I'm not allowed to eat you."

"That's good to hear." She supposed.

The woman flowed even closer, close enough Cary worried a little and was tempted to step back. She wasn't entirely sure how the vampire could get so near without her shields reacting.

"Once he says I can," the woman said, her voice dropping to an almost inaudible whisper, "I'll drink slowly and savor every last drop. Wouldn't want to waste any." She dragged in a breath through her nose, close enough now that Cary could smell her too—the faint scent of blood and dead meat.

"You know that's not happening, right?" Cary said, leaning a little closer too, despite the smell. Her stomach rolled and the morning sickness she thought she was done with came back in a less intense wave of nausea.

The woman reached for her, her fingers tipped with long, pointed nails painted a deep, wine red. Her hands hovered around Cary's cheeks, like she wanted to cup her face. "So pretty. I will enjoy eating you."

Well. Cary felt an unaccountable blush at the innuendo, whether the vampire meant it or not.

After a moment, the woman jerked her hands away and shook them like they stung. She hissed, going from seductive to pissed in a blink. And then vanished back into the shadows like she'd never been there. The darkness shifted and moved a bit around them, the hum of faint noise growing and dropping.

Cary's heart was pounding, but she didn't dare wait to see what might happen next. She headed out the door without looking back at Gabriel, the wizard, or the other vampires.

James was waiting for them just outside. He closed the heavy door and led them back to the elevator without a word.

They were outside in the cold night air before James spoke. By that point, Cary was shaking a little, an internal quake she hoped wasn't showing on the surface, like her inner muscles were trembling, but she hadn't started shivering in a visible way yet. Her knees were weak, though, and she desperately needed to get into the car before she embarrassed herself by falling down.

"He'll try to make you a pet," James said quietly. "However he can.

He'll enthrall you, blackmail you, threaten you, seduce you." He flicked a brief look at the men still flanking her. "He'll threaten the people you love. He wants to control you."

"Is this a warning, James? Or just an fyi?"

His serious expression didn't change. "He'll let Petra turn you. She's especially good at making other vampires, even without being a Master herself. Something in her blood is powerful despite her youth."

"Petra? That vampire who was talking about eating me?" She felt her cheeks heating again, but ignored the blush. "Thanks for the update. I'll bear it in mind. But I'm not becoming a vampire. I have a job already."

"And all the vampires know what it is now," he said, his voice even quieter. "You're no longer safe in this city."

She snorted. "That's not news. I haven't been safe in years." Except at home. And maybe, just maybe for the next few days while she carried a baby god around with her.

He stared into her eyes. "You'd become a Master. That's both threat and temptation to Gabriel. Guard your back."

"Got that handled," she said, gesturing to her mate and her mentor and pretended at a casualness she didn't feel.

In fact, the longer James went without cracking his serious expression, the more worried she got. Having the vampires after her—knowing how to get to her—was scary as all hell. She had no idea how to get out of that. She'd hoped appearing here tonight and being indestructible would help.

Obviously, it hadn't. A temporary fix at best.

"Question, though," she said. "Why would Gabriel want another Master in his territory? Why are *you* in his territory?" She wasn't sure James was technically a Master, but she got the feeling he was close.

"A Master strong enough to control other Masters is…powerful," James said. He leaned in to her, getting as close to her as Petra had but without the accompanying reaction against her shields, and dropped his voice to a whisper she almost couldn't hear. "Whatever you do, don't become his pet. You'll regret it. We all will."

For several seconds after he'd gone, vanishing instantly like he'd never been there, she continued to blink at the spot where he'd been standing.

"Well." She leaned toward Deacon. "This was all weird and scary."

Deacon pulled her close, wrapping his arms around her expanded waist. "Let's get home."

"Yeah. Yeah, I think we'd better."

She couldn't be sure, but she thought she heard whispering, and she'd swear she could see faint points of yellow in the trees behind the pretend farmhouse. It could have been the breeze moving through the branches and her imagination, but she didn't want to stick around long enough to find out.

"I'll meet you there," Jaxer said, his tone serious. "We need to talk."

When Deacon didn't object or even growl with his usual annoyance, Cary realized just how seriously they all saw this turn of events. Her heart started to hammer hard.

She'd come tonight hoping to settle things and then go back to flying under the Master of Portland's radar. She'd ended up in an even worse situation.

Now what?

*D*eacon pulled Jaxer aside while Cary disappeared into her bathroom. The dogs followed her, waiting just outside the door as if they knew she needed guarding.

"What was that glow?" Deacon asked the faery who'd been his friend at one time. He wasn't sure what they were now. Not friends. But maybe allies. At least when it came to keeping Cary safe. "It was the baby god?"

"I'm not sure," Jaxer said. "Honestly."

Deacon glanced at the bathroom and lowered his voice even more. "You once told me she wasn't supposed to get hurt while protecting, but she does." Cary had ended up hurt the first time they'd met, when she'd been protecting him from Sheldon. He still hadn't entirely gotten over that. "You didn't know why. The wizard is convinced she's stolen Sheldon's magic somehow."

"She can't," Jaxer said. "How could she?"

He didn't sound as sure of that as Deacon would have liked. "Could the glow, the wizard's reason for his vendetta, her injuries, the tingling that she thought was normal but isn't, could it all be related?"

"That's a leap, Deacon. The baby god could explain the glow. We don't know what kind of god it is and there's no reason to think her skin glowing had anything to do with anything else."

"But the wizard is trying to kill her because of what happened between her and Sheldon. Even if he's wrong, he thinks Cary can steal magic. We need to find out why. And we need to find Sheldon."

"None of my spies have seen Sheldon in months, not since one of them spotted him at his old apartment while you and Cary were in Eugene."

"Then we look harder. I'll put the leopards in town onto it."

Jaxer nodded. "I'll talk to Liruk and Wisat. About the glow and what the wizard said. Maybe they'll have a better idea." He frowned a little. "I haven't found anything about the tingling either, but Renee might know something. I'll check with her next."

"Renee?"

"The current proprietor of the Bookstore," Jaxer said. "Knows a lot about everything."

"What about a bookstore?" Cary said, coming back into the living room.

Deacon tried not to pull in a surprised breath, or breathe too deeply. Cary smelled amazing. He always loved her scent, but right now, while she was carrying around that baby god, she smelled so delicious he wanted to bury his face against her and just stay there.

And he was having serious issues with that reaction.

Not because he wouldn't happily indulge himself in his mate's scent for hours, but because this added element was due to the baby she was carrying—which wasn't his. And while on a logical level he understood this situation, his instincts and his leopard were mightily confused. His animal side being confused was not a safe thing.

"I just need to drop into the Bookstore," Jaxer said to Cary.

The way he smiled at her made Deacon want to snarl. He pressed his lips together.

"Oh," Cary said. "I'm jealous. Tell Renee I said hi. And that Pickles is doing well."

Deacon frowned a question at her.

"The Bookstore was Pickles's home before I adopted her. Or rather, she adopted me." Cary grinned down at the basset hound. Pickles woofed in answer. "What do you need at the Bookstore?" she asked Jaxer.

"Research."

"On…?"

"Stuff," Jaxer said.

She stared at him, glanced at Deacon, then back to Jaxer. "Baby gods or what the wizard said about me stealing Sheldon's magic? Or the fact that my skin tingles when it shouldn't?"

Jaxer's attempted innocent expression dissolved into a grin. Deacon looked away so he didn't "accidentally" punch Jaxer in the face. Even after all these months, he couldn't quite rein in his reaction to the fact that his former friend was in love with his mate. He was trying, for Cary's sake. And for the sake of his previous friendship with Jaxer. None of this was anyone's fault, just bad luck and bad timing. And frankly, he didn't blame Jaxer for his feelings. How could he? Cary was amazing and Deacon felt lucky to have her as a mate. But his leopard was less logical about all this. About everything.

"All of it," Jaxer said to her perceptive questions.

"You know I can't steal magic," she said, rubbing her lower back absently. "How could I possibly do that? Can anyone do that?"

"Certain magic wielders can," Jaxer said. "But it takes spells or rituals or power stones or…"

"Oh, like the two gems Justin Klein made that we used in the fight with the demon god," she said, her face brightening. "That's right. I'd forgotten about that. Kind of a scary idea, actually. But obviously, I don't have a magic amulet that lets me absorb someone else's powers. And I've never been a magic wielder. And I haven't done any magic stealing rituals or spells—which even if I had wouldn't work because of the whole not being a magic wielder thing."

"The wizard obviously has a misconception," Jaxer said. "But it'd be helpful to find out what that is exactly."

Deacon narrowed his eyes and glanced at Jaxer. The faery wasn't exactly lying, but he wasn't being honest with Cary either. She didn't know she wasn't supposed to get hurt while protecting people. No one had told her that though. Even Deacon, who'd learned the truth from Jaxer, hadn't told her yet. He'd threatened to. But since no one understood *why* things sometimes got through her powers, he was afraid he'd scare her if he told her.

And he'd rather she blamed Jaxer for withholding the information, so he wanted the faery to tell her.

Guilt poked at his conscience. He shouldn't be keeping things from his mate. He'd made that mistake already, not wanting to scare her, and he'd almost lost her because of it. Maybe he should tell her. Given she'd just learned she was experiencing something else she wasn't supposed to while doing her job, it was probably time everyone came clean. Before Cary got seriously hurt.

"It would also help to know why the baby god is making my skin glow," Cary said. "That was weird. Pretty, but weird. My skin is still tingling, but not nearly as strong as it was while we were in the hive."

"It got more intense?" Jaxer asked. "Even though no one was throwing any spells or magic or anything at you?"

"Yup. It had to be baby god's doing. I suspect these tingles are probably different to the ones I get after shielding against magic. Just feels similar. It'd be good to know what the little god is up to."

Jaxer frowned, his gaze turning inward.

Deacon pulled Cary close and took over rubbing her back. "Any side effects from all that?" he asked quietly.

"Not that I can tell. I feel great actually." She leaned in close and whispered in his ear. "You smell really really good right now."

His gut tightened at the brush of her breath against his skin. "So do you," he murmured back. "Too good."

She pressed into his touch, her lids heavy, her mouth curved in a faint smile. And it was all he could do not to drag her back to bed.

He glanced down at her stomach, and the bump that had gotten bigger over the course of one day. He blinked. At this point, could they even have sex anymore? He hadn't expected things to move along quite so quickly. They'd been fine last night, and the night before. But she looked...farther along now. More than four months at any rate.

He frowned. "Why is the pregnancy moving this fast?" he asked

Jaxer, nodding to Cary's stomach. "She looks more than four months pregnant, since this morning."

Cary winced. "Does it look bad?"

"No. Beautiful actually," he assured. "Just…faster than I was anticipating."

"Yeah, me too." They both looked at Jaxer.

Jaxer raised his brows. "I haven't a clue. I've never had a protégée who's had to be a surrogate for a god before. And Wisat and Liruk haven't filled me in on the whole process."

"All the damned secrecy is starting to really piss me off," Cary said.

Jaxer flashed a grin. "Nothing new there."

"Don't smile. I'm mad at you, too."

He put a hand to his chest. "Me? What did I do?"

Deacon had to work not to smile. His leopard settled a lot when Cary was angry with Jaxer.

"Nothing," she admitted reluctantly. "I'm just mad in general I guess."

"Then be mad at Deacon," Jaxer said.

"Why?"

"I don't know. Because. Same reason you're mad at me for no good reason."

She made a face, but there was amusement in her expression. "Right. Sorry. I'm being irrational. The night, and the pregnancy hormones, are messing with me."

"Definitely grumpier than normal." Jaxer shook his head and glanced at Deacon. "Good luck."

Deacon didn't comment, primarily because he didn't want to incur his mate's annoyance.

"I'll see you both tomorrow," Jaxer said. To Deacon, "You going in to work?"

"Not now."

"Deacon…" Cary's tone was exasperated. "I'm fine. You can go to work."

"One day off won't hurt things."

He was always reluctant to be away from her. He had to be, more often than he liked. Life didn't allow him to stick to her side twenty-four seven, which would have left her feeling stifled anyway. She needed time for herself and time with her friends, and he needed to respect that—even if his leopard didn't want to. He could manage their time apart better now than he could a few months ago, too. But it was still a strain. He was almost grateful for the excuse to not have to leave her tomorrow. If her life wasn't in jeopardy, he'd be downright delighted about the prospect of keeping his mate in bed all day.

"I'll call in after lunch, then," Jaxer said.

All morning anyway, Deacon corrected.

When Jaxer was gone, he pulled Cary around to face him. "So that vampire, Petra…"

"What about her?" Cary leaned into him.

"She wants more than your blood."

Cary's eyes widened. "I thought there was some sexual innuendo there but I wasn't sure. It's hard to tell with vampires sometimes, given how they feel about drinking blood."

"It was there. She wants you. My leopard wasn't happy about it."

"Your leopard gets jealous at the drop of dime." She huffed, exasperated but not mad.

He had absolutely no control over his jealousy. It was bone deep instinct and chemical reactions. She'd gotten a little taste of that herself a few months ago, so she'd stopped trying to talk him out of it. Frankly, he found it annoying too. Mainly because it was so damned dangerous. They'd been surrounded by vampires. If he'd followed through with his leopard's suggestion to rip Petra's head off, they could have all been killed.

There were times, since meeting Cary, when he really missed his former control. He wouldn't trade her for it, he wouldn't give her up, but he missed being able to trust himself.

She rubbed a hand over her back again, near the base.

"How are you feeling?" he asked, taking over the job of massaging muscles along her spine. "You've been rubbing your stomach and back a lot."

"I seem to be collecting a lot of aches and weird twinges. And the baby god is rolling and moving. I'm almost certain it's too soon for that. Either something is wrong, or baby gods gestate faster than human babies. Or the Nags and the other Protector lied about how far along the previous surrogate was before she was killed."

Which reminded Deacon, "Outside of vampires and wizards, you still have the people who killed her to worry about."

She waved that away. "They don't have any way of finding me. I doubt we'll hear anything from them. For all we know, Frank could show up tomorrow with the second surrogate and this whole pregnancy thing will be over."

"And then we'll *just* have the vampires and wizards to worry about."

"Sure. Simplifies things a lot." She shook her head. "Anyway, we know for sure Sheldon is alive and it wasn't just his master running around looking like him. That's something at least. And we know why the stupid wizard is trying to kill me. So I suppose the night wasn't a waste."

He nuzzled her neck, her scent too delicious to resist any longer. "I can think of other ways to end the night so it's not a waste," he said against her skin, before nipping a sensitive spot between her throat and shoulder. He wasn't sure how they'd manage because he'd never made love with a pregnant woman before, but he was more than happy to figure it out.

She shivered and he reveled in it, in the way her desire rose in her scent, adding spice to the vanilla and cinnamon that made up her ordinary flavors and the cocoa powder undertone which was so new. His hands tightened around her back, pulling her close. The bump between them was awkward, but not unpleasant he realized. A deep well of protectiveness filled him, more than usual. She laughed when he picked her up, carrying her easily back to the bedroom. He loved that sound. He loved her.

A vision of what their future could be like spread out before him, a future he hoped they could have.

They both just had to survive long enough to see it.

*C*ary pushed into the seamstress shop with a sigh of pleasure. Marianne's place was always so clean and bright, filled with sunlight—when there was sunlight—and splashed with color from all the bolts of material against a simple background décor of light wood and white walls.

"I need maternity pants," she whined to Marianne when her friend came out from the back room and greeted her with a hug.

Marianne winked at Deacon, who stood behind her like the bodyguard he was currently playing. "Good to see you, big guy."

"Nice to see you again, too, Marianne."

His voice was all deep and sexy and Cary wanted to roll her eyes. He wasn't doing that on purpose. It was just how he sounded. But she knew Marianne approved by her little shiver.

She met Cary's gaze and mouthed, *Damn.*

I know, right? Cary mouthed back.

None of them had ever quite gotten over Deacon's...well, Deaconness.

"Don't worry about pants, I will sort you out," Marianne said.

"You are the best of all people. And I love you," Cary said.

"Come to the back so we can get some new measurements." Marianne grinned at Deacon. "You keep standing there looking all handsome. People walking by will spot you and come in, and I'll end up with more clients."

Deacon chuckled, crossed his arms over his chest, and leaned against the cash register counter.

Looking deliciously, ridiculously handsome, Cary noted. Marianne might be on to something. He really could attract more people into the shop—Cary would have walked through the door to get a closer look.

The back room was a huge space filled to the rafters with bolts of cloth, drawers full of needles, threads, buttons, zippers, and all the other things Marianne needed that Cary couldn't identify, several sewing machines, a couple of places to press and iron clothes, some racks for hanging things, and very bright overhead lights. The scents of material and starch gave the place a clean, fresh smell. To one side was a section draped off from the main room where clients could change clothes when they were here for alterations. Floor to ceiling mirrors covered one full wall, while the rest were a clean white behind the stacks of colorful cloth.

The space was neat, colorful, bright, and felt like Marianne in a way Cary couldn't have put to words. This was definitely Marianne's domain.

Marianne motioned her to a small area set up with a raised platform so she could take measurements.

"It's just my waistline that's changed," Cary said. "And way too fast."

Marianne looked her over. "You do look like you've progressed a month in two days. Is that normal?"

"How should I know? No one else seems to know either. Although I haven't had a chance to talk with the Protector who got me into all this."

"Your bosses?"

"Not a word from them. I suspect they're looking for the second surrogate, too."

"I'm sure it'll all be fine." She pulled out her handy measuring tape from a desk. "I'll make you something with an expanding panel over the stomach, like regular maternity pants. How many pairs do you want?"

"Oh geez. Only one. I think. I hope." She made a face. "I really hope I don't need more than one pair."

Marianne glanced up at her. "I'll make you a skirt you can wear, too. Elastic waist and able to sit under the bump, loose and comfortable. You can wear it after, too, so you don't have to worry about wasting money."

Cary sighed. "Thanks." She didn't wear skirts or dresses that often because of her job. But maybe she wouldn't have to dive in front of people much for the next couple of days. "I really hope this only last a couple more days."

"Why?"

Cary looked at her. "What do you mean, why?"

"Why? You're safer this way, no one can kill you. Deacon's obviously handling things well. Why rush it?"

"Because..." Cary raised her hands. "Because it's really weird since it's not mine. Since I didn't think this through and volunteer for it all—surrogate, baby, none of it."

"Do you want kids?" Marianne asked reasonably. "Is that why it's bothering you? Because you never intended to get pregnant."

"No. I actually would like kids someday." She met Marianne's gaze. "If I survive. And if I can find a way to have that life while still being a Protector."

Marianne nodded, her mouth pursed in consideration. "Fair enough. What kind of material do you want for the pants?"

Cary grinned. "What else? Denim please."

Marianne shook her head. "So predictable."

As Marianne puttered around, writing down Cary's new waist measurements on the card she kept with all Cary's measurements, Cary sat on one of the comfy waiting couches next to the raised dais.

"How are you doing?" she asked.

Marianne's shrugged, her back to Cary. "Managing."

"You want to come over tonight and talk? I'll send Deacon home, and we can just hang out all night eating ice cream and watching old

80s movies." They'd originally bonded over all things 80s and that love had never died.

"No need," Marianne said, turning to smile at her. "Though I do really appreciate you'd pick nursing my broken heart over a night in bed with your beautiful man."

"Obviously," Cary said.

"I'm okay. Really. Plus, I have an old friend coming in from New York this week for a visit. We'll be so busy catching up and gossiping, I won't have time to worry about my heart."

"Good. But if you need me, I'm a phone call away."

By the time they finished picking material and a style of maternity jeans Cary thought wouldn't make her head explode, the conversation had moved on to more pleasant topics, and Marianne was laughing as they walked back out into the main room.

Deacon, true to his word, had remained leaning against the counter looking shockingly sexy. And there were three women in the store stealing looks at him and pretending to be there for actual business.

Marianne leaned in close to Cary and whispered, "I'm gonna make you bring him here once a week for the foreseeable future."

Cary snorted and elbowed Marianne in the ribs. She settled the bill —Marianne sometimes tried to wave her off, but Cary insisted on paying her because Marianne did excellent work, and always included magic pockets, and she was a business woman who deserved to be paid. Plus, for all the ups and downs of her job, the Nags ensured Cary made a good living from being a Protector. Hazzard pay was good pay.

Now that the three women were inside her shop, and Marianne had their attention, it looked like at least one of them would end up commissioning some clothes. All three stayed behind after Deacon left, which was a good sign.

On the street, Cary said, "You know you're welcome back now any time you like. Just to stand there and draw in customers."

He chuckled. "If it'll help Marianne, I'm happy to oblige."

"Of course you are."

"I overheard your conversation earlier. What's happened? Why is her heart broken?"

"Ah. She and Gina broke up. Gina was cheating."

"Damn. I'm sorry to hear that." He put a hand to Cary's lower back and guided her around a corner to where they'd parked his car on the street. "Is there anything you need me to do?"

"She'll be okay. But I might have to send you packing a few nights so I can hang with her."

"One of the very few reasons I will be only too happy to be away from you." He kissed the top of her head.

She leaned into him, sighing. Loving that he understood how important her friends were to her. She was just starting to get distracted by his smell, by the heat of him so close, when the man and woman walking toward them on the sidewalk screamed and charged at them.

With very large knives raised high over their heads.

14

_C_ary took a step forward, putting herself between the attackers and Deacon. Thanks to more than six years of doing that as a Protector, it was an instinctive move she didn't even think about.

Which was fortunate, because all of her self-defense training with Lucy—who'd been focusing on teaching her how to deal with things exactly like this with knives and all—went out the window. She just stood there, watching those two pointed blades in the hands of screaming humans plunge down toward her head and shoulder.

Lucy would be disappointed.

But to be fair, four months of real effort at self-defense training paled in comparison to six years of training to stand still and watching bad guys try to reach her.

The razor point of steel stopped several inches away from Cary, hovering in the air as the attackers tried to force the blades closer, going so far as to grip the hilts with two hands. When the knives didn't budge, both people jumped backward, snarling at her.

"That was rude," Cary said, putting her hands on her hips. "You could have hurt Deacon. What the hell are you doing?"

"You must die," the woman hissed, throwing herself at Cary again, swinging her knife in a slashing motion aimed at Cary's chest.

"Why is that?" Cary asked, trying to remain reasonable in the face of all that crazy.

The man lowered his head and dove at her, as if he was attempting a tackle. She raised her brows as he bounced off her shields and fell backward onto his ass.

"You both need to stop that or you're going to hurt yourselves," she said. Wow, she sounded just like her own mother. That was...

Horrifying.

She glanced back at Deacon. "You okay?"

She wasn't referring to injuries. He sometimes had trouble *not* reacting to people trying to kill her. Which was really sweet but since she was the Protector and could keep him safe, she didn't want him doing anything silly like trying to attack her two attackers.

"I'd be better if they'd stop trying to plunge knives into you," he growled. His eyes were starting to glow.

"Okay, big guy, you need to calm down. The poor humans won't know what to do with themselves if you get too mad." She really really couldn't help it. She faced the two attackers and said, "You wouldn't like him when he's angry."

Neither of them reacted. Humph. A waste of a perfectly good superhero joke.

Deacon leaned close and whispered, "I thought it was funny."

She grinned at him over her shoulder before facing the attackers again. "Want to explain all this?" she asked. "In words," she clarified as the woman screamed and charged her again. "Words, not screeches. I don't speak screeches."

"The baby cannot be born," the man said, slowly getting back to his feet, almost stumbling to one side like he was drunk. "The baby must die."

Cary frowned at his drunken wobble. "You're those people, huh?" she asked. "What the hell do you call yourselves again?" Frank had told her the name of the group, hadn't he? She couldn't seem to remember.

But to be fair, that night had been a blur.

"How did they find you?" Deacon murmured against her ear so only she would hear.

"Damned if I know."

She watched the man wobble some more and the woman, her blue eyes wide and wild, thrashing her knife toward Cary's neck in long swinging chops, holding the hilt with two hands. The point plunged into Cary's shield, stuck, and then bounced away. It was like watching someone try to stab a bounce castle with the toughest skin ever.

"How did you guys find me?" she asked when there was a pause in the woman's attack.

"She tells us," the man said. "She tells us and we obey."

"That doesn't sound good," Cary said. "Who's 'she?' For the record."

"The One Who Will Rule," the woman said. Then tried to stab Cary from the side.

Cary shook her head. "Name doesn't exactly roll off the tongue, does it?"

"The demon?" Deacon asked.

"It better not be," Cary said. "I've had more than enough of demon gods for one lifetime thank you very much. I will not be a happy woman if I have to deal with yet another one." But since Frank said these people worshipped a demon, chances were unfortunately good that she would have to.

"She's no demon," the woman screamed. "She's the One! She will rule and turn our world into a place of perfection."

"Uh huh," Cary murmured, distracted by the woman's stumble. Geez, it was like they were both drunk. Drugged maybe? Or spelled?

Oh shit, what if they weren't doing this of their own will? What if someone was making them do this? That meant she'd have to figure out a way to protect her own attackers from the bigger bad guy.

Argh, she hated when that happened.

"Okay." She raised her hands in a calming gesture. "Why don't you guys tell me a little more about this One Who Will Rule, and what she's promising you. Maybe she and I could meet, have a coffee, talk this all out…?"

"She would singe you're very brain if you tried to talk to her," the man said. He lunged at her, a clumsy jab of the knife that even she could have deflected. "She is a god. She is the One!" He dropped to his knees but was still swinging his knife at Cary.

"You okay?" she asked.

"Cary…" Deacon said.

She waved him off. "Yeah, I know he's trying to kill me and the baby and all, but look at him. Does he seem…healthy to you?"

"Mentally? No," Deacon said, his tone hard. After a pause, though, he added, "But I see what you mean."

The woman threw herself at Cary again with another ear-splitting scream, and then she also collapsed to her knees and foam started to bubble up out of her mouth.

"Oh, that's not good," Cary said. She pulled out her cellphone and dialed for an ambulance.

The two were still sort of swinging their knives at her, but without any strength or power. The man fell onto his side and started to convulse. Cary frantically gave the emergency operator her location as Deacon kicked away the man's knife and knelt beside him to keep him from smacking his head off the sidewalk as he spasmed. Cary stayed on her toes, prepared to move between the man and Deacon if this was all a ruse, but she was pretty sure it wasn't.

The woman started to jerk and shake, her jaw tight. Shit. They had been drugged. As she continued talking to the emergency operator— who was very calmly working to keep Cary calm—Cary knelt beside the woman and removed the knife still tightly clenched in her hand. It took a few tugs for her to budge the weapon, and she suspected if it wasn't for her Protector magic, she wouldn't have been able to remove it without hurting the woman.

The next fifteen minutes felt interminable. She remained by the woman's side as she jerked and convulsed, getting first aid advice from the emergency operator, passing that advice on to Deacon who was gently keeping the man's head in his palm, keeping him turned on his side as foam and liquid choked out from between the man's clenched teeth.

Cary had faced many horrors in the last six and a half years—including failing to protect someone who had ended up dead, murdered by a demon because Cary wasn't fast enough. The helplessness she'd felt in that moment, the failure, rose back to gut her. She couldn't do anything but wait and watch and try to keep her attackers from getting hurt any further, and it was maddening this helplessness.

When the ambulance finally arrived, other people arrived with it. A few passersby stopped to help, another few started taking videos on their phones. Cary kept her head ducked, hoping her face didn't get caught on film. As the paramedics took over, she and Deacon stepped closer to a building, staying out of the way. She'd palmed the woman attacker's knife and slipped it into her jacket pocket—it was a pocket made by Marianne so it was magic and would keep the knife safe and hidden. Deacon had scooped up the other knife while no one was looking, and he passed it to her subtly so she could hide it in her jacket too.

"What the hell?" she murmured to him.

"Got me. But I'm betting drugs gone bad."

"So is there really a One? Or is this just some weird human thing with a human bad guy drugging people to get them to attack?"

"Guess we'd better find out," Deacon said. He glanced down at her. "You're glowing, just a little," he whispered.

She blinked and looked at her hands. "Shit. That's not good. What if someone notices?" What was the baby god doing? This was a really really bad time to glow—in the middle of the day, surrounded by emergency personnel, human bystanders, and cellphone cameras.

Fortunately, everyone seemed to be focused on the two people on the ground and not Cary.

"They're all talking about the people," Deacon murmured near her ear. "They assume their druggies, overdosed..." He trailed off, listening with his super shifter hearing. "No one has commented on us yet. If we leave now, we can avoid any more attention. But we'd better go quickly."

"The emergency services people have my cellphone number now," Cary said as Deacon put a hand to her back and edged her away from the scene, toward his car parked farther down the street.

"They aren't going to contact you unless the police need information. And there's no reason the police will need to question you over this since no one knows they attacked us. The scene looks like two drug addicts in overdose. You'll be okay."

She hoped so. She worked hard to stay below the radar of the human authorities. Sometimes she had to cross paths with them, but she tried really hard not to. The last thing she needed were human police pestering her while she was trying to protect people. Way way too complicated.

"I'll get Trevor to check on things later," Deacon said. "But in exchange, he'll insist we finally come over to dinner with him and his family."

Cary winced. She'd been making excuses not to have dinner with Deacon's cop friend for months now. She probably was going to have to give in eventually. But, "Not while I'm like this." She gestured to her midsection and the really obvious baby bump. "They will have way too many questions we won't be able to answer. But after this job is done."

Deacon gave her a look, raising his brows.

"Yes, yes, I will finally go and stop stalling. Are you happy now?"

His lips lifted in a little grin. "Trevor and Sue Ann will be delighted."

Oh boy.

"*I* need to talk to the Nags," Cary said to Jaxer when he arrived late that afternoon. "It sucks that they can just drop in any time and I can't ever contact them when I need them."

"You've been complaining about that for six years," he said, as he sauntered toward her kitchen.

"It's been true for six years." She frowned at his back. "Where are you going?"

He paused. "Don't you need...?" He blinked. "Huh. You don't have a coffee mug in your hand, so I figured you'd need some coffee to discuss all this. You've given it up while carrying the baby god, though, haven't you?"

"I have. Even though it's a myth that caffeine is an issue."

His mouth quirked up at one side. "Habits, though, right?"

"Habits." She smiled, then sighed.

"Where's Deacon?"

"In the yard with the dogs."

"Not guarding you from my nefarious plot to win you from him?"

"We've had an interesting morning. I'm not in the mood for anyone else's nefarious plots, and he knows it."

"What happened?" Jaxer changed directions and settled on the couch, lounging in that way only Jaxer could, taking up half of her comfortably cushy blue couch.

She sat in one of the two chairs bracketing her wooden coffee table, the one farthest away from him, not so much to keep distance between them but because it was easier to see him this way. And she was finding it easier to stand up from the chair than the couch. She could still manage, but why make her life *more* awkward than it already was?

"So some of those people who want the baby god dead attacked us this morning," she started. "Not far from Marianne's shop."

Jaxer leaned forward. "You're obviously okay, but how did they find you?"

"Good question. Even better question, why did they collapse into seizures, foaming at the mouth when they couldn't manage to kill me?"

"What?"

She told him everything. Right down to the ambulance's arrival and all the cellphone video of the event.

He waved that away. "I'll take care of that."

She raised her brows. "You can do that?"

"Who do you think *has* been doing that for six and a half years?"

She blinked. "Oh. I didn't realize it needed doing all that often."

"To be fair, for you it hasn't. You've managed to stay under the radar pretty well." He grinned like he was proud, which she found weirdly pleasing. "But between my glamour and Chris's skills with technology, we've concealed any of your shenanigans that did make it into the public domain."

She scowled at the "shenanigans." But also that was cool to know. Chris was Cary's computer guru, the one who'd set up Cary's secret computer in her attic and gotten Cary connected to the parts of the internet that had all the good information on supernatural and preternatural matters—a place most ordinary people couldn't get to. She supposed for Chris, messing up video footage that showed up online would be easy enough. Especially with Jaxer's glamour magic help.

She narrowed her eyes at him. "Doesn't that violate the Seventh Year rules, though? Isn't that helping me?"

"This isn't something I do just for you. Chris and I do it for all the Protectors. So no violation."

"Wow. Why didn't I know about this before now?"

"You never asked."

She gave him a look. "And if I had asked?"

"You didn't." He shrugged.

"I hate all the things I don't know that I should have known by now, you know that right?"

"That's a lot of 'know's in one sentence."

"Shut up. Can you get the Nags here or not?"

"I can. I can tell you, though, Frank hasn't found the second surrogate yet."

That wasn't exactly good news. While Cary didn't mind the being indestructible part, she was getting nervous about the growth of the baby god, and the effect all this was having on her. Not the least of which was the glowing skin.

"My skin glowed again during the attack," she told Jaxer.

"And the tingles?"

"Yeah, still there. Did you talk to Renee?"

"She sends her greetings and asked you to give Pickles a hug from her."

Cary grinned. "Will do. What did she say?"

"She suggested a few books," he said.

Cary narrowed her eyes. His tone was casual, his body language was casual. There was nothing about him or what he'd said to suggest tension and evasion. And yet, he was tense and he was evading the topic. He was keeping something from her.

"What?" she asked, her tone very serious.

"I still need to do more research," he said, feigning innocence.

"What?" she repeated.

He sighed. "How can you read me when no one else can?"

"Practice." And likely some part of him wanted her to or she doubted she'd be able to. "What's up, Jaxer?"

"I don't want to say anything until I know more. It could be a wrong direction and that won't help you. She did say the baby god is likely responsible for the glow. Gods have a habit of sparkling and glowing and doing all kinds of things before being born."

"Does Renee know a lot about gods?"

"Renee knows a lot about everything," Jaxer said.

Cary supposed if you owned a bookstore that was magical and not really tethered to this world, or this time for that matter, and held books on every topic under the sun, it just made sense you'd be well read on all that stuff. Also Cary got the impression Renee might just be multiple centuries old even though she looked like she was in her mid-thirties. If she'd been human.

"Is Renee a god?" Cary asked. Renee had stars in her black eyes and green blood. Cary had never really come out and asked Renee *what* she was, at least not after that one time when they'd had to save the Bookstore from a person who also had green blood.

"Technically? She could be considered one," Jaxer said. "But she wouldn't call herself a god."

Cary's eyes widened. That was…cool.

She'd have to find time to visit the Bookstore soon. She hadn't been in a while and she missed the peaceful ease of the place. And maybe she could get the information she needed about herself directly from Renee, instead of waiting on Jaxer to give her answers.

In fact, though she hated to admit it, that *was* supposed to be what this year was about—doing things on her own without his help. Some-how, they were getting away with him helping her a lot more than he probably should, because the things he was helping with were at the Nags' orders. But maybe uncovering the truth behind the wizard's misconceptions and the effects of the baby god on her should all fall to her…

That felt like a very grown up plan. Huh.

She blinked and refocused on Jaxer. "Thanks for your help. I appreciate it."

"Of course." He frowned a little. "Are you okay?"

She made a face. "Yes. I can say thank you. I have before. Now, when can I talk to the Nags?"

"Let me go ask," he said, flowing to his feet with a grace that was even more irritating now that she required the arm of the chair to lift up.

He reached out a hand to give her a boost and his gaze dropped to her stomach. "Things really do seem to be…progressing faster than they should be, don't they?"

"Yes," she said with feeling. "And it's making me nervous. I've only been in charge of this baby god for a few days, but the pregnancy seems to have advanced a month or more. That's not a good thing."

"I'll go get the Nags," he said. "Hold tight. We'll get this fixed."

She was still staring at the front door when Deacon came in from the backyard with the dogs in tow. "What did Jaxer say?"

She gave him a look. "You heard everything."

"I was trying to be polite."

"I appreciate the pretense. He's worried about the pace of the pregnancy, too. And I think I'm going to visit the Bookstore myself. He's hiding something from me and maybe I need to do my own research." It wasn't the kind of information she had up in her secret attic—which she still hadn't told Deacon about. She only went up there when no one was around.

That was two things she hadn't told him about yet, and as she looked at him, she realized that was one secret too many for her mate.

"I have something to show you," she said. "Not even the girls know about this. Just Jaxer, the Nags, and my computer guru Chris." She glanced at the dogs. "And my dogs, of course."

He frowned a little but didn't say anything.

"It's not a huge deal. It's just were I do my research." She winced. "I can't leave all the weird books laying around for my mother to find when she visits."

That earned her a slight smile.

She went to the laundry room to get the pole that helped her press and open the hidden panel in her ceiling. The pole was about four feet long and topped by a flat metal plate with an old kitchen towel wrapped around it to pad it. She studiously ignored the piles of laundry that had built up in the last week as she headed back to the living room.

After six years, she found the section she needed to press without having to hunt around for it. The panel clicked and then released, drop-ping down a few inches. She used the pole to hook the edge of the panel and dragged it down far enough for her to reach the folding ladder. Once she had the ladder extended, she set the pole against the wall and faced Deacon.

"Welcome to my secret lair," she said.

He continued to frown just slightly as she proceeded him up the ladder.

"Are you sure you should be climbing that?" he asked, keeping a hand on her hip to steady her.

"Yeah, this is more awkward at the moment than it usually is. I'll be fine." She was grateful for his presence behind her, though. Just in case.

She boosted herself into a seated position once she'd cleared the attic floor, leaving her legs dangling as Deacon climbed the rest of the way into the room. He helped her to her feet while looking around her bright, tidy office.

"You've had this up here the whole time?" he asked.

"Since about a month after becoming a Protector." She gestured to the shelves and the handful of books stacked on her wide, solid desk at the center of the open, airy space. "Up here to keep my parents from finding it, or trying to access the regular internet on my computer." A nod to said computer, also on her desk. "It's set up to go to places that normal internet users can't access."

He nodded. "I've been there."

Of course he knew all about the supernatural dark web. She resisted making a face.

"Why have you kept this place secret from me? From your friends?" He pulled a book off her desk and looked at the spine. His eyebrows rose. "I see why you hide it from your parents."

She smiled at that, wondering which book he'd picked up. Probably one of the vampire ones since most of her recent reading had been on that. She glanced around the room, at the light creamy colored walls, and polished wood floor with bright area rugs. Light—when there was sunlight—came flooding in through a skylight and a few small circular windows in the walls where the roof peaked. When there wasn't enough sunlight, the overhead lighting was both bright and soothing. No irritating florescent bulbs for her office. She kept the room comfortably heated, having it connected to the central air like any other room in her home, and in the summer, the circular windows opened to let the breeze flow through. The place smelled of books and she loved it.

She wrinkled her nose. Could use a dusting soon, though.

"I've kept it a secret from everyone so I didn't accidentally reveal it to anyone," she said. When he looked at her, she shrugged. "If I didn't make an effort to keep it a secret, it would be very easy for me to get too comfortable about this room, coming up here even when there were people around. Before I knew it, my mom would be up here wondering why I had books on vampires and demons and demanding my father find me a good psychiatrist."

His lips quirked. "I can't wait to meet your mother."

"Yeah, you can. So..." She gestured at the space. "What do you think?"

"Thank you for showing me," he said, setting the book he'd picked up back on her desk. "It looks like you."

"It does?" She looked around. She was extremely comfortable up here, but then, she was comfortable in her whole house, so she didn't see the difference.

"Given it's a secret superhero lair, I figured it would be all dark and foreboding," he said.

She snorted. "Right. Because I'm all dark and foreboding."

While she did like him calling her a superhero, since she liked to pretend she was one, she really was an oddball out in her current occupation. Not particularly stunning, seductive, and powerful like all the vampires. Not strong and fast like the shifters. No magic to speak of except what the Nags gave her. And even that she just channeled. She didn't control it. She was human, unlike the Fae and various beings she'd come across over the years. She didn't even have the willpower to be a demon hunter—but really, giving in to pizza and chocolate just made good health sense, didn't it? The only thing she had going for her was a seemingly innate ability to freeze in the face of danger and hold that position indefinitely so she could protect good guys.

She was shockingly ordinary in her very unordinary world.

The little baby god choose that moment to adjust her position, and the muscles of Cary's stomach contracted and relaxed with the shift. She patted her tummy and said mentally to the baby god, *Thanks for the support.*

To Deacon, she said, "Are you mad at me for keeping this place a secret?"

"No. You had your reasons. The fact that Angie, Marianne, and Lucy don't know about it, but I do now, is actually pretty humbling. Thank you for trusting me."

"You're welcome." She smiled, relieved and please.

And now she just had one last secret from him that she still didn't know if she should admit. But that was for another day.

Right now, "I need to do a little internet search. You want to hang out up here with me, do some reading? Or do you want to go hang with the dogs and watch TV?"

16

In the end, he chose to stay with her and read, though they did check with the dogs, all arrayed around the ladder, to make sure they didn't mind. Fred barked and threw himself on the floor, his tail wagging. Buck settled onto his side, his tongue hanging out in contented panting. Pickles let out a deep woof, then spread out on the floor, feet stretched out in front and in back so she looked like a basset hound pancake. Even her jowls spread around her head. She closed her eyes, settling in for a nap.

Cary spent a good hour hunting around the internet, doing various word searches, trying to find more about baby gods. Unfortunately, everything she read just frustrated her as much as discussing all this with Jaxer had. He wasn't being purposefully difficult with his evasive answers to her questions. There really weren't any definitive answers. It all "depended."

She was getting super sick of the term "depended."

She switched gears to searching for the group that was trying to kill the baby god. There had to be something about them in here, right? Except, she couldn't for the life of her remember their name.

"Did I ever tell you the name of the people trying to kill the baby god?" she asked Deacon, most of her attention still on her computer screen.

He glanced up from the book on demonology he was reading. "No, why?"

"I can't remember it. It's weird. I don't have a super memory or anything." Which was a pity because in her work a really great memory would have been helpful. She had so much to learn that it was irritating when she had to go look something up again even though she'd read about it already. "But the name Frank told me, I just can't call it up again. I think it started with an R? Or maybe it was a P..."

"Wish I could help," he said.

She glanced at him. He was sitting in one of the oversized cushioned chairs she had set up near the wall of bookshelves—shelves that were only four-foot tall because they had to accommodate the roof arching overhead, but still, it was a whole wall of those four-foot shelves and they were full of books. Deacon had one leg hooked over the armrest and was lazing to one side, the book resting in his lap now as he talked to her. He looked incredibly sexy, and cat like, and much much too distracting. Her blood started to hum a little. Maybe she didn't need to do research right now?

She blinked. Except she did. She shook her head a little and said. "I'll ask the Nags if they ever show up. It's just frustrating that I can't remember. And random searches for 'the mean people who want to kill baby gods because hope' aren't really working."

He smiled, that slow sexy look of his. Was he doing that on purpose? She focused on her computer again so she didn't go crawl onto his lap. Damn but she was randy this afternoon.

After another few minutes of fruitless searching for fanatical groups devoted to demons who wanted to destroy hope—there were too many to choose from and no way for her to pick; even looking at the names of the various groups didn't trigger her memory—she finally gave up that line of research. She'd have to deal with that when someone reminded her of the group's name. She glanced at Deacon again. This was nice, and very convenient, having him here, knowing about her secret attic. It meant she could actually do research while he was around, because he was around a lot and she didn't have the willpower to send him away most of the time.

He glanced up and caught her smiling at him. "What?" he asked, little wrinkles forming between his brows. His beautiful golden eyes narrowing.

She grinned. "Nothing. Just admiring how you look in my secret superhero attic."

He chuckled and raised the book he was reading. "This is fascinating. Until meeting you, I hadn't had to deal with a lot of demons. Just enough to know how they smell, but not anything like what we've faced."

She winced.

"I never bothered to learn much about them. There's a lot."

"Yeah there is," she said with feeling.

"Did you know there's a whole group of demons dedicated to just…irritating humans? Their whole aim is to raise as much irritation as possible."

She nodded. "And they're very good at it. Probably a good thing I've never gotten one attached to me, huh?"

"Why?"

"You really want me to be more irritable than I already am?"

He tossed his head back and laughed. She loved that sound. Full throated and deep.

"I think you're perfect as you are," he said, "but yeah, it's good you haven't encountered that particular demon." He glanced down at the book. "It doesn't say how the little irritants get out of their realm, though. They can't just pass into this one without being called, right? And who would call something that's whole aim was to poke at you until you were annoyed?"

"That's in another book. I don't know why all the details aren't compiled in one big tome—probably because it would be too huge. They tag along with other demons when they get called from their particular realm, and the irritant demons aren't contained by any of the precautions the human caller might take. In fact, the assholes are incredibly difficult to contain once they slip through."

"Have you had to deal with any of them before?"

"Only once, thankfully. And the little bastard did *not* want to go back to its realm."

"You got it to go back, though. Right?"

"Not…quite." She shook her head. "You don't want to know."

He chuckled. "Probably not. How many get here? They can't have that many opportunities to slip through."

"More than you'd think—humans are stupid about calling on demons and do it a lot more frequently than is healthy, at least according to all my readings. Angie says it's true but won't tell me how she knows. Anyway, the irritant demons dodge into this realm at every possible opportunity, which is not rare, and then go about gleefully spreading annoyance."

He frowned at the book. "That's scary."

She chuckled. "Could be worse. There's a species of demons dedicated to creating chaos in small ways, not giant havoc, but just little things that eventually snowball into absolute mayhem. Fortunately, there aren't very many of them, and they don't get through into our realm easily. Or have you gotten to the part about the demons who drink sweat and turn it into acid glop that they spit at victims where it becomes a cocoon for the demon's eggs?"

He raised his brows. "Do I want to get to that part?"

"It's pretty fascinating biology, if you're interested."

"Maybe later." He set the book aside, glancing at her bookshelves. "Have you read all of these?"

"I'm working on it. They seem to double on me every time I come up here. I still haven't had the nerve to tackle a few of the magic books."

He raised his brows. "Magic books?"

"Yeah, they require special methods just to open them so you don't accidentally blow anything up or release any super dangerous spells. I got one the first time I went to the Bookstore and it's still wrapped in the protective paper Renee put it in because I'm too afraid to open it."

"That sounds…sensible." He gave the shelves a sideways look. "I'm impressed, though."

"With what? My book buying addiction?"

"With the fact that you've been studying all this stuff all these years."

She shrugged. "It's my job. And the studying part isn't as impressive as it could be. I try, but there's just so damned *much*, I never feel like I've got a handle on all of it."

"Beyond not being able to find the group after the baby god, how's your research going?" he asked, changing subjects.

Which was good because she was getting a little sad about how much she still had to learn. He probably smelled her changing mood. Smart man.

"Not great," she said, glancing back at her computer screen. "There's too much 'it depends' in all this. 'It depends on the new god's origins, their history, their purpose...' Which by the way, you won't even know until well after they're born because up to the being-born point they aren't actually little gods yet, just possibilities and hope. They're all 'hope,' which makes pinpointing specifics impossible. The glow is not unheard of, just like Jaxer said. But my tingling skin doesn't seem to be a common feature of gestating a potential god."

"Maybe the two things aren't connected?"

She hummed under her breath. "That's kind of what I'm worried about."

"Why?"

"If this sensation isn't specific to the baby god, it really is tied to me and how I react to magic. But..." She bit her lip. She wasn't entirely sure how to put this into words. Finally, she settled on, "I'm worried about what that might mean."

"It's obviously nothing horrible or you'd have had answers by now," he said.

But she heard something off in his tone, something that made her narrow her eyes at him. "What do you know that I don't?" she asked.

After a few moments, during which he held her gaze, he finally said, "The Nags and Jaxer have kept something from you. I told Jaxer if he didn't tell you, I would."

"What?" She turned in her seat to face him more fully.

He held her gaze for a beat longer. Then, "You're not supposed to be getting hurt when you protect someone. Nothing is supposed to get through. All those injuries you've been racking up over the years? They're not normal. And neither Jaxer nor the Nags know exactly why they happen."

17

*C*ary blinked, staring at Deacon for a long moment as her brain worked to catch up to what he'd just told her.

She wasn't supposed to get injured.

Nothing was supposed to get through her bosses' magic.

She wasn't supposed to get hurt.

The Protector shields should keep everything out.

She wasn't supposed to get hurt.

"What the fucking hell?" she exploded, launching out of her desk chair.

Deacon remained sitting, but his gaze was steady on her, watching.

She started pacing the room, absently rubbing her stomach as the tingling on her skin intensified. "They've been letting me get hurt for more than six years, they let me enter my test year with this thing still happening... And. It's. Not. Supposed. To. Be. Happening!" She faced Deacon. "How long have you known?"

"I learned right after we met."

She narrowed her eyes. "Why did you wait to tell me?"

"Jaxer said he would, but he was worried if you knew, you'd hesitate or flinch or...not be able to do your job. He thought if you knew, you might get hurt more, or worse, because you'd stop trusting the Protector magic."

"Damned straight he should have worried about that," she growled. "How can I trust it? It's not working right for me."

"It does still work," Deacon said carefully. "You get hurt but not killed."

"Well, that's a nice consolation," she said, heavy on the sarcasm. "Why are you telling me now?"

"Jaxer said he would tell you. He hasn't. You need to know. But…"

"But?" Was that her voice? It sounded very deep and very angry. Which made since, because she was so angry the phrase "seeing red" made sense to her now.

"I was hesitating, worrying you'd get hurt more if you knew. I'm still worried about that."

"Yeah, well…" Frankly, she was worried now too. She plopped back down into her desk chair and stared at him. "What am I going to do? What if I do…flinch and someone gets killed now?"

"I'm most worried about you getting killed," he said quietly.

She wanted to wave that away, but she could get killed if she flinched.

"I asked Jaxer if the sensation you feel after getting hit with magic might have something to do with it. What the wizard said… Maybe it's all tied together."

"What did Jaxer say to that?"

"He thought it was a stretch."

"But said he'd look into it?" she asked.

Deacon's mouth quirked. "Yeah."

She let out a long breath and stared at nothing, absorbing all this. Her getting hurt because her Protector magic didn't work exactly right, the tingles she felt after getting hit with magic, the wizard's accusation that she'd stolen Sheldon's magic… The more she let the various anomalies bounce off each other in her mind, the more she wondered if Deacon wasn't right. Maybe they were all tied together?

She faced the computer again and typed in "ways to steal someone else's magical powers" in her secret search engine. The list of results was surprisingly small. There weren't many ways to steal someone else's magic. Most of the articles seemed to be about the thing that Justin Klein could do—putting a spell on some object and that object would suck up powers. It was a rare magical skill, apparently, and people who had it were usually targeted and killed if anyone found out about them. It didn't seem to be associated with strong magical talent in other areas, necessarily, but the ability to turn an object into something that would absorb magic was always associated with someone who could actually *do* magic.

Cary was pretty sure she hadn't accidentally created a magic amulet to steal Sheldon's powers. She never even wore the same piece of jewelry every time she was on a job—at least until recently.

She had been wearing the same necklace for the last few months, a present given to her by a girl she'd saved in January. The little gold Fatima Hand charm on the necklace was a stylized hand with three finger-like loops pointing upward and two "thumbs" curving off to the sides. And it had just a touch of good luck magic in it, though Cary wasn't sure Jasmine knew that. Since Cary hadn't died at the hands of Deacon's ex-girlfriend while she'd been wearing the necklace, she was inclined to think that good luck had helped. So she slipped the necklace on all the time now.

But good luck didn't steal other people's magic. And she'd been gifted the necklace *after* the incident with Sheldon.

She wore her Marianne-magicked leather jacket all the time. But she'd been a Protector for six months, and getting hurt occasionally already, by the time Marianne made that for her. She'd double check, but her friend would have mentioned putting a spell to absorb magic into the jacket.

None of the articles mentioned someone with a magic absorbing amulet actually feeling anything afterward, like tingles in their own skin.

There were a couple of articles on how someone's magic could be cursed to not work. That was a different thing all together, though. The magic wasn't taken from the user. They just couldn't access it anymore because of the curse. If they got the curse lifted, their magic came back. No permanent loss—unless of course they couldn't get the curse lifted. From what Cary could tell, those curses were ancient and triggered by accessing something the magical person wasn't supposed to. No one in several millennia had been able to create that kind of curse.

Cary would *definitely* remember creating a curse of that magnitude —because she couldn't—or triggering an ancient curse—which would have been aimed at her anyway and since she didn't have any magic to curse, it wouldn't have been an issue. That was definitely a deadend as far as her situation was concerned.

Although now she was worried about the fact that there were ancient curses floating around the world that could do that kind of damage. She did have friends with magic who could be affected.

She skimmed the articles again, tried a few different keyword combinations, and still didn't see anything that might apply to her.

Maybe Jaxer was right, and Deacon was stretching to think her getting hurt, her tingles, and what the wizard had said were in any way connected. There was no reason for them to be. In fact, it was entirely possible the wizard had just been lying. Or confused. Or maybe Sheldon had lied to his own master about his magic…?

She rubbed her temples. There weren't enough keyword searches for her to figure this out.

And since even the Nags and Jaxer didn't know why she was getting hurt, thinking she could do a few internet searches and miraculously find the answers was pretty silly.

She leaned back in her chair and absently rubbed her stomach. Then faced Deacon. He'd sat quietly during her search, no longer reading, but watching her carefully.

"Nothing," she admitted. "Everything that has to do with stealing someone's magic requires magic to begin with. I don't have magic, so that's not me."

"Are you sure?" he asked.

"Sure that I don't have magic? Uh, yeah. I would have known something like that, Deacon. And even if I didn't know for certain, there would have been hints in my past. Strange things happening around me…that kind of thing. But I had a very very ordinary life up to meeting Jaxer and the puppy-kicking demon."

"Yet you stood up to a demon and, according to Jaxer, you're an outstanding Protector who can channel the magic better than anyone he's trained before."

"He said that?" She blinked. "Huh. He never told me." She made a face. "If I can channel the Protector magic better than anyone else, then how am I *also* not channeling it well enough to prevent getting hurt? None of this makes any sense."

"Maybe because you do have some kind of magic," he suggested, his brows raised.

"No. Deacon, if I had magic, I would have known. Also, Angie would have mentioned it at some point in the last few years. Jaxer would have known. The *Nags* would have known. It's like…what they do. Make Protectors, see potential futures, detect magical happenings. Someone in my life over the last six and a half years would have noticed I had magic of some kind. It would have come up."

He let out a frustrated breath and shrugged. "I don't know."

"Yeah, me neither and it's irritating as all hell."

"It is. Especially because you're getting hurt when you shouldn't."

"Yeah, Wisat and Liruk are going to hear about that the next time I see them."

"Did you tell Jaxer you wanted to talk to them?" Deacon looked around for a clock, which she didn't have up here, then pulled his cell-phone out to check the time. "It's almost seven."

Cary blinked. She glanced out her overhead skylight and realized the sky had faded to a darker gray shadowed dimness that meant sunset was approaching. "Damn, I didn't realize so much time had passed." She rubbed her hands over her face. "We should get some food. The baby god will start to complain and make me nauseous again if I don't eat."

Deacon went down the ladder first, and kept his hands up to catch her if she fell while she came down after him. She shook her head. His protectiveness was sweet, even if unnecessary.

She'd just cleared the ladder and was leaning over to push it back up when a familiar sweep of sensation rolled down her spine. She narrowed her eyes and straightened.

"It's about time you guys showed up," she said, turning to face her bosses.

"*I* shouldn't be getting hurt," Cary said, her tone accusing. "And you haven't bothered to tell me that little detail. What the hell?"

Both Liruk and Wisat stood on the opposite side of her couch, near the small fireplace, next to her TV, looking as stunningly Fae as always. Even used to them, she still occasionally blinked at just how beautifully strange they were. Right now, however, she was not impressed.

They exchanged a look, then Wisat said, "Who told you?"

"You should have," she said, settling her hands on her hips.

While she didn't want to tell them Deacon had been the one to spill the beans—and she suspected that was obvious given the way he'd taken up position at her back during this confrontation—she was super tempted to throw Jaxer under the bus for this. But her ire was focused on her bosses just then. She'd deal with Jaxer later.

"You would have quit before you fully realized your potential," Liruk said.

"Ha! This from you, Liruk? Who kept pushing me, kept criticizing me, kept at me like I wasn't ever going to be any good at this job? So what if I had quit?"

"You are an outstanding Protector," Wisat said. "One of the best we've ever worked with. We did not want you to quit."

She opened her mouth, but the words caught in her throat. They didn't often compliment her. In fact, Liruk was almost always critical of Cary's efforts. Except when she'd taken on the baby god. And now, Wisat was giving her a huge compliment.

Something was definitely not right about all this.

"Okay," she finally said, "what's wrong? Why are you being so nice? There's more, isn't there? Something worse than the fact that I shouldn't get hurt."

Another look exchanged. Finally, Wisat said, "We have been unable to save the second surrogate, Cary."

She felt her breath pause in a way that didn't seem good. She waited for it to start again before squeaking out, "What?"

"The second surrogate, for the baby god, she was killed by the Polrom," Wisat said. "Some of their members reached her before Frank could."

Cary pressed her lips together—mainly to keep from screaming—and nodded a few times. Several moments went by during which her brain did not want to work. She patiently waited for it to start functioning again before opening her mouth.

The first thing her brain managed to latch on to when it did start working again was, "So that's the name of the group. Thanks for the reminder. I'd forgotten." Another scream bubbled up her throat, so she stopped talking.

Deacon moved closer to her back and she leaned into him, his hands coming up to her upper arms, squeezing gently.

"What does this mean?" he asked, his voice dangerously deep and cold.

That was his iceman voice. He fell into that tone when he needed to maintain control at all costs so he basically cut off emotion. The fact that he was having to exert that kind of control now meant she wasn't the only one about to scream and lose their minds.

"We are now in a very difficult situation," Wisat said, his tone quiet and gentle. "There is only one other person who might take over for Cary to gestate the fetus until term. And Frank is balking."

"Frank is?" Cary asked, finding her voice. "Why? Who is it?"

"His wife."

Well shit.

Cary leaned into Deacon and closed her eyes. Now what? Could she ask another Protector to risk his love, his own family, because she wasn't ready and didn't want to take this particular protection job to the full term —pun intended. She wasn't remotely ready for this. And what happened to the baby god after it was born? Shit, she hadn't even thought of that.

"What happens when the baby is born?" She opened her eyes and looked at Wisat. "Who was going to raise the baby?"

"The surrogates were also going to function as parent," Liruk said. Her tone was as quiet and gentle as Wisat.

Which was extremely disconcerting. "Why are they 'surrogates' then? How was the baby god...conceived?"

Her head was starting to hurt. And the tingling in her skin had increased. There was a hint of heat in the tingles now, too. Not just a run of energy along her nerves, but a warmth was spreading through her limbs, like the sensation of settling down into a warm bath. Was that a good thing or something she should worry about?

"This particular god was conceived of two other gods," Wisat said. "Minor deities in a pantheon no human worships."

"From this realm? Or some other place?" she asked. "Like Faery or a demon realm or...something?" There were realms, worlds, dimensions innumerable apparently—or so the theorists in othernatural phenomenon claimed.

"Something," Liruk said. "Not of this realm."

"Is that why the demon the Polrom worship is after this particular baby god? Because maybe it's from a similar realm or an enemy realm?"

Wisat and Liruk exchanged another look.

"As far as we know," Liruk said, "the two realms have nothing to do with each other."

"Then why this god? Just because…hope?"

"We don't know," Wisat admitted. "None of our usual methods of seeing…things are working in this situation."

"So you have no idea what's really going on?" Cary said slowly. "And you don't know if you'll be able to find another person to carry this baby god to term? And raise it." She frowned. "It has to be raised here? Or it can go back to its parents? Why couldn't it be born and raised in this other realm?" She pressed a finger to her temple. "This is all really confusing and weird and you haven't helped with the explanations so far so I'm going to need more."

"Everything," Deacon said, still in that cold tone.

Wisat sighed, a rare gesture. "The gestation and birth of gods doesn't fall into the same simple process as humans or other biological entities in this realm. The deities from this particular pantheon require…hosts."

"Like parasites?" Cary asked.

"Biologically speaking," Wisat said with a shrug, "that's not a bad analogy."

"Oh good," Cary said, heavy on the sarcasm.

"And anything as vulnerable as a baby," Liruk said, "even a baby god, cannot survive in the realm this one's parents call home. The… environment, for lack of a better term, is too hostile. A certain level of magic and power is required to navigate those environmental dangers. The baby will be born with some, but not enough."

"They why bother to go through all this trouble for offspring they can't even meet?" Cary asked.

"The same reason any creature wishes to reproduce," Wisat said. "Many are driven to, even if their biology prevents interaction with the offspring. Even on this planet, in this realm, many animals don't have anything to do with their offspring, and yet are still driven to reproduce."

Well that was true enough. Cary hadn't really thought about it in those terms. The idea that something called a god or a deity might operate on the same basic level of biology as a fish or a turtle just never occurred to her. And the idea of it now wasn't helping her headache.

"All right, putting aside the question of *why* this is necessary," she said, "the fact is that this baby god has to be gestated in a host?"

Liruk nodded.

"A human host?"

"Those have proven quite effective over the recent millennia," Wisat said.

Which brought up a whole plethora of other questions, but she wanted to stick to her current point. "And she has to be raised outside her parental realm until she reaches a certain level of power?"

They both nodded.

"And until that point, she's vulnerable?"

More nods.

"And for some reason no one can quite pinpoint, there's a group of humans who worship a demon that they call a god who shouldn't have any interest in this baby in particular, but the humans are still trying to kill her."

"Yes," Wisat said.

"Did Jaxer tell you about my run-in with two humans from Polrom?"

Liruk blinked very slowly. "We have looked into that."

"And..." Cary gestured for more information.

"They were drugged," Wisat said.

"Like a real drug? Like a human thing. Or something magical?"

The two Fae exchanged a look that had Cary narrowing her eyes.

"What?" she snapped at them.

"A human drug," Liruk said. "A hallucinogen in such a high dose it killed them."

"They died?" Cary felt like she'd taken a punch to the solar plexus. A mix of emotions she couldn't quite sort out flowed over her, a mix of guilt and sadness and confusion and frustration and more things she just couldn't name in that moment. "So they took the drug or where given it?"

"We don't know," Liruk said.

"And we don't know why a drug was necessary," Wisat added.

"Maybe they weren't the type of people to kill a baby and had to be drugged to do it?" Cary guessed. With the two people dead, there was no way to know for sure. "Did the people who attacked and killed the first surrogate… Were they drugged?"

"Frank didn't notice at the time," Liruk said.

"And he had to evacuate the dying surrogate to a safe location quickly, so he didn't see what happened to those attackers after," Wisat added.

"You still haven't said what will happen with Cary now," Deacon said.

"Uh, yeah, because I didn't sign on to this with the idea of giving birth and raising a baby. In fact, you both specifically promised that wouldn't be the case. I'd very much like for this little god to survive." She rubbed her stomach. It was impossible not to *feel* things for the baby at this stage. The influx of hormones alone would have guaranteed her compassion for the growing little god. But this wasn't *her* baby and she hadn't agreed to all this and she wasn't ready for it and she wasn't supposed to be the baby god's parent. She was the baby god's Protector. "But I didn't agree to be more than her temporary bodyguard. So to speak."

Wisat nodded. "We never intended to put you into this position, Cary. We will ensure an alternative is found."

Cary didn't miss the side look Liruk gave Wisat.

"What kind of alternative?" Cary asked. Then, before they could answer and potentially tell her something she didn't want to hear, she said, "Can I speak to Frank and his wife? How does his wife feel about all this? I'm assuming she's volunteered or she wouldn't be an option, right?" She narrowed her eyes. "Right?"

"She did volunteer," Liruk said. "It is Frank who doesn't wish her to get involved."

"Because he doesn't want to raise a baby god or because he doesn't want his wife to take the risk?"

"He worries for his wife's life," Wisat said.

"I understand his concern," Deacon said, some of the cold control in his tone slipping into a little more heat. His anger was getting out. That couldn't be good.

Wisat nodded in acknowledgement.

Cary paused, waiting for more, then said, "Isn't this up to his wife, though? I mean, he can protect her—that's his job—and she's the one who would have to carry and give birth to a supernatural baby who will eventually have enough power to leave this realm and return to her parents' realm. That's a big ask. If she's volunteering for that—besides being a spectacularly wonderful person—she must have a damned strong reason."

"She is a very good person," Liruk confirmed. "And she would make a wonderful surrogate for the god."

"I'd like to talk to her. And Frank," Cary said. "Can that be arranged?"

Another look passed between the two Fae. Then Wisat nodded. "Will you allow them to come here?" he asked.

Cary really really appreciated that Wisat didn't go into detail about why he was asking the question that way, or why her home would be a good meeting place, since Deacon didn't know that one last secret yet. She needed to give permission for Frank and his wife to find her home, thanks to the Nags' glamour. That glamour also made this a very safe place to have a meeting without the Polrom being able to find them.

She assumed Frank's home had the same type of glamour on it. That would ensure his family was safe so long as they were at home.

But no one could stay home all the time.

"They can come here," she said aloud. "That would be fine." And in her head, she gave the other Protector and his wife permission to find her home. Then, "When?"

"We'll go discuss the meeting with them now," Wisat said.

"Does Frank have your permission to port into your backyard?" Liruk asked. "It will be easier and less visible."

"Sure." She glanced down at her dogs who were arrayed around her. "Don't bark or go after the two people who arrive through a black doorway into our backyard, okay?" She gave Fred a particularly stern look. Not that Fred would be able to do much, but he was loud and excitable and loved a good chase.

"How long?" Deacon asked, while Cary was still starting down Fred.

"Perhaps tonight?" Wisat said.

"No sooner," Liruk said.

"But not much later," Wisat said.

Cary glanced at them. "I may still have vampire issues."

"You have more vampire issues?" Liruk asked, her smooth brows creasing. "Why didn't you take care of that last night when you met with Gabriel?"

Ah, that was the frown and disapproval Cary was used to. She'd been starting to worry about Liruk.

"Jaxer told you Gabriel knows what I am? That the stupid wizard trying to kill me told him everything?"

Liruk's mouth flattened into a line that Cary could interpret in a number of ways, all of them uncomplimentary. So she ignored the expression.

"Well, Gabriel might want to bribe me to working for him." She waved that away. "The usual. No big deal." At Liruk's look, Cary said, "I already have a job. I know. I'm not going to work for a bad guy." She let Deacon take more of her weight because her feet were starting to hurt. "But the night does come with its own set of issues at the moment, so just warn Frank."

They'd be safe here. But that didn't mean she might not have to leave to take care of vampires at some point tonight.

"Ensure it's not much later than tonight, though," Deacon said. "The baby god is growing faster than she should. There isn't a lot of time to fix this situation."

Wisat narrowed his electric green eyes at Cary's midsection. "The fetus is growing fast?" he murmured, almost to himself.

The fact that Wisat looked confused and Liruk's frown had

changed to one of concern made Cary's pulse kick. "That's not good, is it?" she asked. "Didn't Jaxer tell you?"

"There wasn't time after…" Wisat trailed off, speaking so quietly, she barely heard him. He pulled in a deep breath and smiled, though the expression looked forced. "We will ensure all is well in the end," he said, trying to sound reassuring and confident.

Boy, did he fail miserably.

---

19

*A*fter eating a weird meal of cold pizza and toast with strawberry jelly, which was apparently what the baby god wanted, Cary decided they needed to go to the Bookstore. Since her internet search had turned up no help, and Jaxer was being cagey about what Renee had told him, Cary wanted to go directly to the source. She needed more information. So much was happening at the same time, and she needed some answers.

It was fully dark by the time they reached the Bookstore. She stared at a flickering streetlight while Deacon locked up his SUV. The vampires would be coming out soon. If not out already.

A part of her wondered if she'd see James appear from behind a lamp post to pass her a message from Gabriel.

Deacon put a hand to her lower back and glanced around the industrial neighborhood. The sounds of the freeway only a few blocks away competed with some local traffic. The cool spring day had been sunny and left a sort of damp heat smell in the air that wasn't unpleasant, but it was tinged with the smell of cars and that didn't help. The few struggling sidewalk trees made thin little shadows under the overhead street lights. Across the street, a sign for a construction equipment rental warehouse hung over closed metal doors.

The Bookstore's entrance had moved several times since Cary had first been introduced to the store. It remained in this section of the city, but the block it was located on occasionally shifted. Not that that had much to do with the actual physical movement of the store. It wasn't actually anchored to a particular time or place. And you had to know about it to actually find it. From the outside, it always looked closed. At least the store front Cary saw.

"You're sure this place is open?" Deacon asked as they approached the door.

The windows to either side were dark with a few empty boxes stacked in them, the glass in need of a good cleaning. "The Bookstore" was etched in white in a plain script on the front door's glass. But beyond that label, the place looked locked up and unoccupied. There was even a cardboard sign in the window to the left of the door that said, "Moving sale."

Cary grinned. "It's open. I'm surprised you didn't know about this place. I thought it was an open secret in the paranormal community."

"I've never heard of it," Deacon said.

Huh. That made her wonder how many people did know about it. It was always full of customers when she came. But to be fair, those customers arrived from all different locations around the world—and possibly other planets; she'd never been entirely sure about that part—and different times as well, so the fact that there was room to move in the store probably did indicate only a select few knew it existed.

Well now she felt special.

She pushed open the glass door, which swung inward easily for her, and a little bell over the inside of the door let out a delightfully happy tinkling sound. The scent of books and wood polish greeted them as they stepped inside.

Once over the threshold, the full glory of the Bookstore opened out in front of them. Tables piled with stacks of books, walls lined with shelves, some standalone shelves making a labyrinth of the floor space. All filled with volumes of glorious books—paperbacks, hardbacks, some bindings Cary didn't care to think about too closely in the sorcery section. Each shelf had a hand labeled sign indicated the subjects. Demonology. Practical Magic. Magical Systems. Theoretical Sorcery. Biology and Evolution. Several shelves on Shifter species. A shelf specifically for Secret Societies—she'd have to look there in a bit and see if they had anything on the Polrom. Whole sections on History, Mythology, and Cosmology. Cary tended to avoid the shelf on blood-letting techniques.

On first glance, the space seemed cluttered and too crowded, especially with all the beings wandering the stacks, but somehow she always managed to maneuver through the store without knocking things down. And the back of the room extended out much farther than the physical space of the store indicated from the outside.

In the center of the main room, a wooden u-shaped desk served as the checkout counter and customer information booth. The store's owner/proprietor stood behind the desk, ringing up a woman of diminutive stature wearing a sexy, smart white business suit and stiletto heels that still only managed to get her tall enough for her eyes to clear the countertop. For some reason, the customer reminded Cary of her acquaintance—she wasn't sure if she could call him a friend since he sometimes worked for bad guys—Thomas. Thomas was a leprechaun with a glorious Irish accented and an outstanding sense of style.

Once the small woman who may or may not be a leprechaun walked away with her purchases, Cary walked up to the desk. "Hey, Renee!"

"Cary!" Renee came out from behind the counter to give her a hug. "I haven't seen you in a while. How's the test year going?"

Renee knew what Cary was, even though she never actually said it out loud, and Cary always had the impression the store's owner knew more about the Protector world than Cary did. Which, to be honest, probably wasn't hard to do since sometimes Cary got the feeling she didn't know anything about her own world at all.

Renee was about Cary's height, though her gloriously full afro gave her an extra couple of inches. Today she was wearing bellbottom jeans and a fitted button up flower print shirt in bright orange tones that complimented her dark skin and really made her look like she was living in the seventies. The era of Renee's clothing changed all the time, and sometimes Cary didn't quite recognize the styles. She'd often wondered if Renee's outward look was as detached from time and space as the Bookstore's location. For the most part, Renee looked like an ordinary thirty-something year old human woman with nothing in particular to make her stand out in a crowd. But when you looked into the woman's dark eyes...

A field of black strewn with points of light like stars.

"Things are interesting," Cary said in answer to Renee's question.

Renee glanced down at Cary's expanded midsection and nodded. "Jaxer mentioned. You doing okay?"

"Could be better." She glanced around at the milling crowd and said, "Long story." She couldn't really explain in front of so many people because she wasn't sure who might be listening. And some of these creatures had hearing as good if not better than Deacon.

Renee glanced past her then as if just noticing Deacon for the first time. "Hello," she said pleasantly. "You must be Deacon Jones." She stretched out a hand in greeting. "It's a pleasure to meet you."

"You too," Deacon said and asked at the same time.

She smiled. "Jaxer's mentioned you once or twice."

"I'm sure." Deacon didn't even try to hide his feelings about the faery.

Renee raised her brows at the tone but didn't comment. Instead, she said to Cary, "I think I have just the book you need."

"You know what I'm here for already?" Cary asked.

"Given what Jaxer came looking for recently, I have a pretty good idea. Deacon, why don't you peruse the store." At his narrowed eyes, Renee gave him a gentle smile. "She'll be fine." Then to Cary, "Follow me."

Deacon hesitated, but Cary gave his hand a pat. "Don't worry. The place is neutral and safe." At least, it was usually safe. Except for that time when the guy with the green blood had tried to hostile takeover the Bookstore. But that was a story for another time.

She kissed Deacon's cheek, which made her blood hum. That never cease to surprise her. How could simply being close to him do that to her? And it always seemed to happen at the oddest, most unexpected moments. She watched him walk away toward a shelf on shifters, admiring the view. Then she followed Renee toward the back of the store.

They wove through the stacks, Cary having to take extra care because she felt more awkward in her own body at the moment. When she squeezed past a man with a thick leather coat and a huge hat covering his face, she realized she couldn't just suck in her gut to make room. That was a startling realization.

Did other pregnant women feel like this, or did they just get used to the bump as it grew so they didn't have these strange moments? She really should talk to her sister if she could figure out a way to do that without it getting Valerie excited that Cary was considering having kids. Valerie was good about not pressing her older sister with questions about settling down and having a family—unlike their mother— but Cary still got the impression her sister wanted familial company in the kid-raising journey.

At the rear of the store, Renee lifted a small key from her jean's pocket and unlocked a door Cary hadn't ever noticed before. She raised her brows.

Renee shrugged. "Some books are safer locked up."

Given what Cary had *bought* out in the open in this store, she was more than a little nervous about the kinds of books Renee thought needed a safe room.

According to Renee, the Bookstore's magic, or whatever it was, kept all those unruly books in line while they were here and they only had the potential for trouble once they were sold, if they were handled wrong. There was a lot of magic and strangeness in the store. And not just because of the books. This was a place for beings from almost every realm—there were a few demon realms not allowed in anymore —and Renee used her own magic, whatever it was, to keep the store balanced and safe. The fact that she felt some books were better behind lock and key, and that Cary needed to see one of those books, made Cary's pulse pound.

The pervasive tingles tickling her skin increased just a little, and the baby god adjusted positions with a slight, very gentle kick to Cary's ribs.

She set a hand against that side of her stomach and followed Renee into the new room.

A strong smell of parchment and electricity greeted her. Was that a good combination? Seemed like maybe a fire hazard, right? The room's lighting was dim but not too dark to see. The air was clean and cool, almost cold. The space was cylindrical, with the curved walls all lined with bookshelves going up two stories. The books on the shelves were all faced out, though, and there were a lot fewer in here than out in the main store. The ceiling overhead was domed almost like a church, with stone arches and gargoyle carvings at the joints between ceiling and wall. The stone floor was covered with a simple dark blue circular rug. In the center of the room was a large standing bookstand, made of intricately cut and inlaid wood, which was currently empty.

While the room was tall, it wasn't otherwise very large, although size in the Bookstore was relative, so the bookstand actually took up a lot of the walking room. Cary could see why Renee didn't want Deacon here now. They'd have been cramped if all three of them had tried to fit. Moving around without knocking into something would have been tricky.

Faint colorful flashes popped in and out of Cary's peripheral vision, but when she turned to see what was causing the light, the flashes vanished. Her skin fairly crawled with tingles now, like the electricity she could smell was racing over her skin and lighting up her nerve endings. That was strange since she was pretty sure nothing was attacking her...

Although, really something could be and she wouldn't know. Without the visual aid of *seeing* something coming at her, she had no way of judging. She couldn't feel the Protector shields coming up, and she couldn't sense magic, at least not in the traditional way, like Angie could. She did have a sort of Protector-sense that let her know when someone needed her particular brand of help. But at the moment, with her magic working full time, she hadn't been getting those feelings either.

"Are we getting hit by any of the magic that's obviously permeating this room?" Cary asked, warily eyeing the shelves.

"You shouldn't be," Renee said. "But the ambient magic might be revving up your powers to keep the little one safe."

Cary nodded, still leery.

"The book you want isn't here because it's dangerous per se," Renee said, turning back to the shelves. "Ah, here it is."

She pulled a small, slim, unobtrusive little book down. It looked like an ordinary modern-day hardback only without the cover jacket. The bare cover was a dark blue material, and the title was printed on the spine in gold leaf.

Renee held up the book. "It's here because it's just safer that as few people as possible know about the information in it."

She handed the book to Cary, who hesitated to take it. "Is this what you gave Jaxer?" she asked.

"I let him read it." She motioned to the bookstand. "It doesn't leave this room so I couldn't give it to him. Well, sell it. I am a business woman after all."

Cary chuckled. "He said he still had some reading to do." She narrowed her eyes. "He's not telling me something."

"Maybe he thinks this isn't information that will help you," Renee said reasonably. "But I'm inclined to think this is your answer."

Cary carefully took the book from Renee. "Why?"

"Because I've been a little suspicious of this since we first met and you helped me defend the Bookstore."

That got Cary's attention. She dragged her gaze from the book to meet Renee's star-filled eyes. "What do you mean?"

"You told me your skin was itching, tingling after fending off the magical mayhem. That isn't a typical side effect for a Protector. In fact, as far as I know, you shouldn't feel anything after you've channeled the Protector shields, no matter what you've been defending against. But that sense of tingling, that is a very distinct symptom of..." She nodded to the book. "And Protectors don't tend to be ordinary humans. They always have something else."

"But I don't. Even the Nags...my bosses don't think I have any other powers." She gestured to her stomach. "That's why I got roped into this. Because there was no other magic to possibly complicate and mix with the baby god's powers and development."

Renee narrowed her eyes just a little as she glanced at Cary's stomach. "I hadn't considered that but... Read the book. Then we'll talk. Do you need a chair?"

"You can fit one in here?" Cary's lower back did tend to ache a little if she stood for too long, but the bookstand was sturdy enough to lean on so she'd be okay if a chair was too much.

"I can make it work." Renee stepped outside and came back in with a small, padded chair that hadn't been just outside the door when they'd come in. "I'll be back in a bit. Take your time."

She left Cary to the strange room and her little mysterious book, closing the door behind her as she left. For a brief moment, Cary worried the door wouldn't open again when she was ready to leave, but when she tested the knob it turned easily. She didn't try to open it yet, but knowing she could get out was a relief. She eyed her surroundings, waiting a beat to make sure none of the books *did* anything in Renee's absence, then she settled onto the chair and carefully placed the little hardback on her lap. The baby god changed positions again.

Later—Cary wasn't sure how much time passed while she read— Cary closed the book and blinked at the shelf across from her without actually seeing it.

This couldn't be her. She'd have known. She'd have *felt* it.

Wouldn't she?

She opened the book again, flipping through the pages. "Extremely rare," it said. "Usually end up dead," it said. She let out a long breath.

If she believed this, if she bought that this was true and this was her, it meant admitting that maybe the crazy wizard trying to kill her was right.

Oh, she'd hate having to do that.

20

When Renee came back into the room, Cary was still staring at the shelf, trying to process what she'd read.

"What do you think?" Renee asked.

"I think I know why Jaxer didn't want to tell me this yet," Cary said, finally blinking and looking at something beside the inside of her own mind. "He knew I'd freak out and not believe him." She held up the little book. "How would this be possible? Shouldn't I be dead?"

Renee shrugged. "If you didn't come into contact with magic before becoming a Protector, why would you? Someone with this biology hasn't existed for a long long time."

Given how relative time was inside the Bookstore, Renee's comment struck Cary as significant.

The little book outlined a very rare trait of seemingly normal humans who could literally absorbed magic. Into their cells. Like a sponge. Soaking it up when it was tossed at them. They didn't just randomly absorb magic from their surroundings, which Cary had to admit was something of a relief, but try to hit one of these people with magic and their cells just took it all in. And kept it.

Exactly the thing the damned wizard had accused her of doing.

Dammit.

According to the book, though, these rare and seemingly ordinary humans got killed the first time they came into contact with enough magic for anyone to notice their ability to steal it. Their cells absorbed the power, just like good little sponges, but that didn't protect them from the effects of whatever spell had hit them. Their first contact with big magic didn't usually end well enough for them to realize that magic had changed hands, so to speak. It didn't, for example, prevent an energy ball from a wizard from frying them. It's just that the magic that went into the energy ball got absorbed by the human's cells before they died, and so the wizard tossing the energy ball lost that amount of his power when killing one of these humans.

And most of the time, neither the dead human nor the now-less-powerful wizard had any idea what had happened.

There was a three page chapter in the already spare book about what happened if someone like this was hit by non-lethal magic—apparently that didn't happen as often as being hit by lethal magic?—and it was that part that really had Cary's head spinning.

"The tingles," she said to Renee. "The fact that my skin feels buzzy every time I have to protect against magic… That's my cells soaking up some of it."

"That's my suspicion, yes," Renee said. "But because of the Protector shields you're not taking in as much as you might otherwise. Just little bits that get through the barrier."

"Since the shields keep me from actually taking the magical hit directly and deflect it around me?"

"I would assume so. Jaxer says you occasionally get hurt. That things get through your shields?"

She made a face. "And he failed to tell me that wasn't normal." Her voice sounded like she was growling. She cleared her throat.

"The fact that you absorb magic probably leaves space for things to get through the shield. And it's likely the shield keeps you from absorbing too much magic at any given point. I'd say that's why no one's noticed before. The effects, for both you and the person losing magic, would be a lot harder to detect since you wouldn't be absconding with that much."

"Either that or they ended up dead after my shields deflected their magic back on them," Cary said. "Hard to notice your power is drained after that."

Although, she'd been hit by some pretty strong magic over the last six years and a lot of those people had survived. For some reason, she thought of the three witches who'd been working for the demon Oliver Holland, and the power they'd thrown at her. They'd walked away just fine, or so Cary had thought. But she hadn't seen them among Holland's army outside the Naga city.

The idea of going to look for them to find out if she'd accidentally stolen some of their magic seemed like a really bad idea, though. Given how Sheldon's master was reacting.

"Plenty of people have walked away from an encounter with my shields and not complained about losing their magic," Cary said aloud. "Or tried to kill me because I stole their magic."

"Most people wouldn't have a clue the possibility exists," Renee said reasonably. "If you don't know something is even possible, you're not likely to make the connection."

Even the Nags hadn't made the connection. Or Jaxer. So, yeah, Cary supposed it wasn't an obvious leap.

"How did the wizard guess this?" she asked, not really expecting an answer.

"Either he absorbs magic too," Renee offered, "or he's seen this book or had experience with someone like you. Though, to be honest, I haven't heard even a hint of someone like you existing for, oh, centuries."

"You've been alive for centuries?" Cary asked, her eyes widening.

Renee waved that way. "The Bookstore drops into all times and spaces."

That didn't exactly answer Cary's question. But she let it go. "So he might have read this book? Would you know him if you saw him again?"

"Of course. I know everyone who comes into my store. I can tell you, though, I don't let very many people back here. The list of possibilities is short."

"Because the books are dangerous?"

"Because I can't sell any of them," Renee said.

"Fair enough. The wizard that's after me is a white man, older, gray-white hair, blue eyes, about six foot tall. Likes wearing black." She winced. "Pretty generic description. There wasn't much about him that stood out physically. I mean, he seems physically fit and he moves easy and lightly for someone who looks pretty old. But he's a wizard so maybe that comes with the territory?" She'd noticed both witches and wizards tended not to look their age, but ordinarily they looked young for their ages, not older than their age. "He might have come in some time in the last six months—relative to Portland time—since I apparently stole his apprentice's powers in October. Halloween actually." There was something both spooky and appropriate about that timing.

Renee's gaze unfocused as she thought, though the stars in her eyes remained in place. Cary kept waiting for them to whirl and spin like she was checking time and space itself.

"There was a wizard here in what was November your time," Renee said. "He didn't look like your wizard, though. He was very young, thin, tall, pale, and had a few pimples, greasy dark hair. He wore glasses he didn't need and was dressed in sweat pants and a leather coat that hung awkwardly on him."

"That sounds like the apprentice I supposedly stole powers from," Cary said, sitting up straighter. "Sheldon. We all assumed he was dead at the time. We only found out later that he was still alive. How did you know he didn't need the glasses?"

"There was no prescription in them, just clear plastic."

"You could see that just looking at him?"

"Yes," Renee said as if everyone would notice that kind of detail. "He asked some questions after going through the shelves in the magical section and a more frantic scan of the mythical beings shelf. He seemed frantic in general. I felt sorry for him. When he asked about people who could steal magic, without amulets, I brought him in here and showed him the book because he seemed harmless enough. A little desperate, but he didn't have any real magic to speak of. I assumed he was the one who was worried he'd stolen someone else's powers."

"But if he had, wouldn't he have still had that magic in him?"

"You haven't read the last chapter of the book, have you?" Renee asked.

Cary shook her head. "When I hit the part about non-lethal magic, I got caught on the realization that this could be me."

"The last chapter discusses the stuff that's most theoretical. Because, again, the rarity of the condition and the frequency that someone like this ends up dead means they can't be studied."

Cary winced at the mention of both death and being "studied." "Can you give me the highlights?" she asked, not sure she could take reading any more.

"In short? The magic that gets absorbed can't just remain indefinitely in the person. It has to eventually release. The theory goes that the lower the amount of magic absorbed, the longer it can remain. But it builds and accumulates. Eventually, it has to get out again."

"Or what?" Cary asked, her eyes widening with each word.

Renee shrugged. "No one knows for sure. Either the magic just comes out in one big whoosh of pure power, likely to mow over everyone in the vicinity. Or..." She frowned and glanced at Cary's stomach. "Or the power builds to a degree in the cells that the cells start to explode."

"Explode?"

"Pop? I'm not sure there's a good word in any of the human languages to describe it more accurately. The cells go poof under the pressure of too much absorbed magic."

"How many of them?"

"All of them."

"Which means...?" Cary was starting to feel ill.

"The person dies."

"And the magic?"

"Again this is just theory, but it's thought the magic is released with the death of the human. Either violently, like a real explosion, or like smoke that dissipates back into the environment."

"Oh, this is not good." Cary stared at a wall of books.

"It's theory, remember," Renee said, her voice gentling. "No one is really sure what happens. There haven't been enough humans like this for proper research, and even the anecdotal evidence is sparse. It's possible the power just…leaks back out again, or the cells adapt so it's their normal state, no matter how much power is soaked up."

"I flattened an army of supernatural beings," Cary said, her tone sounding flat and emotionless to her own ears. "I was standing between the army and a Naga city, buying time for the Nagas, and the army threw everything they had at me. Magic, shifter strength, powers of all kinds. A demon had recruited a bunch of beings…" She swallowed. "I thought I'd die. My shields were contracting under the pressure of so much power. I could actually feel the shield getting smaller, moving in closer. I don't remember what happened clearly. I know I was looking for space, just a few inches of space to breathe so I could hold out a little longer, give the Nagas the time they needed to save their city." She stared up at Renee. "I…pushed out something, I thought it was my Protector shield, and it just whooshed out over the army. I think I killed some, definitely disabled some."

"And what happened to you after?" Renee asked quietly.

"I was exhausted, drained. I made it through the next couple of hours, then the next thing I knew I was waking up from a three-day healing sleep. I've had healing sleeps before, periods where I've had to rest for twenty-four hours and sleep a lot to heal. But I'd never been knocked out for days like that before."

"What did Jaxer say about it?"

She shrugged. "He didn't know what I'd done either. We all figured because I'm so ordinary, I somehow managed to use the Protector magic offensively and it took a toll on me, channeling that much of the defensive magic. But…"

"But maybe it was something else?" Renee filled in. Again she glanced at Cary's stomach and the obvious baby bump. Creases formed between her thin eyebrows.

Cary set a hand to her stomach and the baby god kicked. "I'm absorbing her magic," she said, her voice so quiet she wasn't sure she'd spoken aloud.

"This is all still guess work," Renee said. "There's a reason Jaxer didn't want to worry you with this just yet. Even if it's true, it's nothing to panic over. Your Protector magic, when it's working, keeps you from absorbing much, right? And your shields are up constantly with the little one, to keep her safe. I'm sure, even if it's true that you can absorb magic, you aren't pulling in very much from the baby."

But Renee didn't sound like she believed her own words. At least not entirely. And Renee was one of the smartest people Cary knew.

"For the sake of argument," Cary said. She choked a little and had to clear her throat before continuing. "For the sake of argument, say I *am* one of these rare unicorns that can soak up other people's magic..."

Renee smiled a little at the mention of unicorns, which almost distracted Cary because now she wanted to ask about unicorns and if there were any on this planet any more.

She shook off the distraction. "I can steal people's magic—unintentionally—and because I also channel Protector magic, I don't get killed when I do it. In fact, the shields keep most of the magic from me so only a little gets through at any given point, which means..." She squinted, trying to work her way through her own thoughts. "Which means even if I have been up against really powerful beings, I've likely only absorbed a very little bit of what they've thrown at me. So no one has noticed this yet. And the people I've picked up more power from either ended up dead—" she thought of the supernatural army, "—or didn't make the connection that they lost power to me."

Renee nodded. "That would make sense. If all this was true."

That much getting through her shields would probably only happen in those moments when she had to jump in last minute, those moments when she tended to get hurt, because physics was a real thing even in the supernatural world, and there was only so much space available for things to move or stop in any given period of time. Although, even last minute, she was apparently not supposed to be getting hurt.

When she'd supposedly stolen Sheldon's powers, she'd had to jump between him and Deacon at the last second. She'd taken the teenage wizard's energy bolt to the ribs—ending up with a few broken ones for her troubles—and been tossed away by the collision of power with her shield. Sheldon took the brunt of that recoil and, they thought, ended up dead.

Apparently, everything they thought was wrong.

"Okay," Cary said. "So the magic gets through, sometimes in large chunks, because my own abilities are somehow affecting the Protector magic, but for the most part I channel the Protector magic well enough to stay safe and alive. And because the magic has been absorbed in mostly small quantities, nothing really bad has happened."

Renee nodded. "Again, if all this is true."

"If it's true."

Cary was having a really hard time dismissing it, though. Maybe if she hadn't had that encounter with Holland's army, she could write this all off as impossible. Maybe. She pressed her fingers to her temples.

"If it's true… I have a baby *god* growing inside me. A god that's been making my skin glow at odd times, and I've been tingling practically from the beginning. My shields are up to protect her from the outside world, not to protect me from her magic. I've never been in a situation like this before. And we are pretty sure, if this is all true, the Protector magic is disrupted by my absorbing magic. The injuries, the tingles, all this is tied together and a result of me being not quite as ordinary as I thought."

She met Renee's star-filled eyes, her heart thumping hard enough in her chest to hurt. "If I'm absorbing baby god magic," she said quietly, "what is that doing to my shields and my ability to protect her? And what's it doing to me?"

21

*D*eacon stalked the bookstore, making a few attempts at scanning the shelves but his attention kept drifting to the back of the store. When Renee had come out the first time, leaving Cary behind, she'd assured him Cary was just reading. Deacon had stalked to the closed door and listened. He could hear pages flipping slowly, even through the thick wood. He'd forced himself to remain calm.

But something about all this was raising his hackles and his leopard was prowling around inside his head, ready to leap at whatever threat he sensed.

Maybe an hour passed—it was hard to tell—before Renee returned to the back room and Cary. Deacon hovered at a book-stacked table a few yards away, waiting. At this distance, he couldn't really hear what was being said beyond the door. He wanted to give Cary her privacy. She'd tell him what she could when she came back out. All he could pick out was the faint faint murmur of voices. Even their tone was hard to discern.

Around him, customers quietly perused shelves, some sat in the large chairs scattered in nooks throughout the store, others held quiet conversations, but it was almost like a library with most people not doing much talking. It had taken him several minutes to realize there wasn't even any music playing like there often was in ordinary human bookstores.

A sharp bark of laughter from a huge man who looked human but from his scent was a bear shifter—a bear shifter from a different century if his clothes were any indication—disrupted the quiet. The sudden, loud noise attracted some attention, but less than Deacon would have guessed. And not nearly as many scowls. Only a vampire sitting nearby gave the bear shifter a disapproving look. Everyone else either ignored the noise or glanced up, then went back to what they were doing.

The entire place had a sense of peace and serenity to it. Surprising given the sheer number of *different* creatures here. The scents of all those different beings should have been overwhelming, too, because his leopard was on edge, which meant filtering his senses got harder. To his surprise, he wasn't having to exert a great deal of effort to block out the various smells. He could pick out individual scents when he focused—like the vampire's faintly metallic damp earth smell and the bear shifter's obvious bear musk—but otherwise, he wasn't being assaulted by the sensory input.

The front door opened a few times while he waited, and it was obvious from the snow on one customer's shoulders and the board shorts and sweat soaked t-shirt on another that the entrance to the Bookstore wasn't set in the same location any more than it was set in a single time. Strange magic at work here, but he could see why the place was busy.

He tried keeping himself distracted with the store, the curiosity of it: how it knew to let everyone back out into their own time and place; could it be used to pass through to different places; how it managed to stay so peaceful here; how creatures that didn't like each other managed to pass and even stand close to one another without starting a fight… He'd been sure something bad would happen when the gazelle shifter stopped to study a shelf right next to a lion shifter. He'd been on his toes, prepared to step in. But nothing. The gazelle even smiled at the lion when the lion walked away. All of it was fascinating. The people watching alone should have been enough to keep him occupied.

Yet he kept glancing toward the back door where Cary and Renee were still talking. Peaceful and safe or not, his leopard was worried, and no amount of distraction would settle his animal until his mate was back at his side.

When the door finally opened, he sped to it—he didn't have to pretend he could only move at human speeds here. Renee stepped through first and held the door for Cary. Cary walked through, her expression shocky, looking like she'd been run over by a truck.

He scowled at them both and instinctively pulled Cary close. "What happened?"

"She needs to talk with Jaxer and her bosses," Renee said quietly.

"Are you in trouble? Hurt?" he asked, pulling her around to look at him.

"Not hurt. Maybe in trouble." She set a hand to her stomach. "Maybe we're both in trouble. Or maybe none of it is true and I'm worried for nothing."

She sounded like she was trying to convince herself of that last part.

"Tell me," he said quietly.

"Let's get home. I'll tell you on the way." She turned to Renee. "Thank you very much for helping me. I'll be even more grateful once it's all settled in."

Renee smiled faintly. "I understand the shock. Don't worry. Come back and talk to me more once you've talked with Jaxer. You should still read that last chapter for yourself."

Cary's eyes widened a bit. "Right. I will. Thanks again."

As they wove through the stacks of books, Deacon glanced back. Renee was still watching them with her unique, star-speckled eyes, frowning just a little. Then a customer edge cautiously up to her, her expression changed to pleasant helpfulness, and she went back to managing her store.

At the door, he asked Cary, "How does the Bookstore know to let us out at home?"

She smiled, some of the color coming back to her cheeks. "Apparently, the doorway takes an imprint of your DNA and matches it to your time and place, so you can only return to your original location."

"Ah, so the store can't be used as a passage into other realms."

"Nope. Renee was very clear on that."

Deacon glanced at the demon in human guise hovering near the alchemy shelves. "That's probably a very good thing."

On the drive home, Cary told him what she'd learned. He stayed quiet, letting her "it's just a theory, but…" her way through the telling, letting the information sink in. If all this was true, it explained a lot. But given the dangers, he understood why Cary was reluctant to accept. He wasn't sure he wanted any of this to be true either, even if it did give them the best explanation for…everything.

"And the baby god?" he asked. "How would all this affect the two of you?"

"Good question. And one Renee couldn't answer. Neither could the book—which was pretty lean on detail anyway." She frowned as he turned down the street to her house. "If it was Sheldon who read the book, he probably got to the last chapter, the one I didn't finish. Which means he knows that the magic has to come back out eventually, so the theory goes, and that no one knows what happens to it when it does." She glanced at Deacon. "Why risk killing me if the magic will still be lost?"

"Anger. Revenge. Bitterness." He shrugged. "They obviously don't care if you're dead, so they're willing to take the chance in the hopes Sheldon—or his master—will be able to reclaim the magic."

"Gee, isn't that scientific of them," she said.

Her sarcasm made him smile despite the situation.

"But if Sheldon really was in those woods with Holland's army, wouldn't he know the outcome of that stand off? The fact that I likely unleased all that built up magic, including his, onto the army?"

"If he stuck around that long," Deacon said, parking in front of her house. He came around to open her door, helping her down from the SUV. "He might have gotten away while he could and not even seen that part of the battle."

The sidewalk lights cast a soft glow on the night in her quiet neighborhood. From the house across the street, Deacon could hear a man and woman laughing loudly over the sounds of dishes clinking. It was always quieter here during the day. At night, he picked up more from the surrounding houses, people going about their lives, a kind of oblivious peace he found he enjoyed. A contrast to his own life—and even more so, his mate's life.

She sighed. "You're right. And even if he had stuck around and seen what happened, that wouldn't necessarily make his master any less eager to kill me." She pushed into her house and her little dog pack immediately surrounded her.

Deacon watched the dogs vie for her attention, gratified when Fred broke off from the group long enough to bounce off his thigh in greeting. "Good to see you too, Fred."

Fred barked and charged back into the fray. It was a routine that seemed to happen more when Cary was in trouble. The dogs were always in a hurry to greet her, and there was a lot of noise and petting and checking in, but he'd noticed when something was a little off in her world, their welcomes got more enthusiastic. Since Buck was a demon dog and apparently Pickles was a foo lion, he suspected they sensed the paranormal trouble brewing. Fred was a mundane mutt and just liked to be in the middle of things.

Once she and the dogs were finished, Cary headed toward the kitchen, a sort of knee-jerk habit after she'd taken off her jacket, hung it in the front closet, and dropped her keys into the bowl on a small table in the entry. He smiled at her back. Even in the middle of mayhem, she always followed this routine. He wondered if she even realized it.

In the kitchen, she stared at the coffee machine and sighed. "It's too late for coffee anyway, I know," she said. "I need to sleep. But…" She sighed again.

He pulled her into his arms, holding her close, mostly because it was one of his favorite things to do. "You've had a long day, long couple of days. And no matter what's happening with the baby god, you do need sleep."

"You suppose the reason I seem to be farther along in the pregnancy than the first surrogate is because I'm…absorbing some of baby god's powers? You think maybe she's rushing the process so I don't drain her?"

"I doubt a fetus has that much forethought, love. Even instinctively. And even though she's a potential future god." He rubbed a hand down Cary's back, frowning at the quietly humming fridge without seeing it. "But it's possible the faster growth does have something to do with all this. If it's true."

He wasn't as reluctant to believe it as Cary—the facts all seemed to line up—but the impact of it was immense, and he wasn't *accepting* it any faster than her. His mate having this kind of trait could cause her a lot of danger. And he wasn't happy about that part at all.

"Can you use the magic?" he murmured. "Did the book say if you could actually use any of what you absorb?"

"Technically, you could say I did when I flattened Holland's army," she said quietly. "Although, that might have just been the magic rushing back out, not anything I had control over. According to what I read, though, no one knows. Rare trait, too few case studies, too many end up dead."

Her voice got very quiet on that last.

"You're not going to end up dead," he said, a growl he couldn't help in his tone.

She snorted. "Me ending up dead over the course of this year was always a possibility. This is just one more layer of complicated crap." She shook her head. "I still can't quite accept it. Despite the evidence. I'm… I've always been just an ordinary person."

"Cary Redmond," Deacon said, tilting her face up to meet her gaze, "I have known you for six months now, and I can say with absolute certainty, you have never been just an 'ordinary' person."

Her mouth quirked in a slight smile. "Compliment or insult?"

"Always a compliment." He smiled back. They'd had this exchange before.

He started to lean in for a much-needed kiss, but her eyes widened and her faint smile turned into an irritated huff.

He sighed. "The Nags?" he asked, although he already knew. Her expression always changed when they showed up.

"The Nags," she said.

As they turned back to the living room, Deacon noticed the dogs had arrayed themselves in a little semi-circle near the kitchen door, a kind of barrier between Cary and the newcomers. That was new. They usually ignored Cary's bosses or watched from a spot near the big living room window overlooking the backyard, the spot they all slept in.

This time, however, they kept their little semi-circle position between Cary and the newcomers even as they all walked into the living room...

And Deacon realized the dogs weren't reacting to Liruk and Wisat.

Two strangers stood in Cary's living room. And one of them smelled of magic.

22

*D*eacon had encountered Cary's bosses often enough now that their strangely compelling appearance didn't throw him off anymore, but they were still as beautifully odd as anything he'd ever seen. Even stranger, though, was their scents.

Neither of the Fae revealed themselves through their scents. The only thing he ever picked up was rich soil and the heady thickness of dense forest. They smelled like the woods all the time, right down to hints of animal musk and the faintly sweet smell of rotting detritus. Nothing that he could parse out as emotion or anything he might associate with other beings. Their expressions and tones of voice revealed feelings—from Liruk mostly annoyance; from Wisat mostly extreme patience—but for a shifter, not being able to read their scents was irritating. It left him feeling edgy and uncomfortable.

Next to Cary's bosses stood two perfectly ordinary looking humans. A man and a woman. The man was about six-foot tall, physically fit looking but nothing that would stand out in a crowd, brown hair, brown eyes with dark purple circles underneath, and a little paler than Deacon thought looked healthy. But overall pretty average.

Deacon didn't need an introduction. He'd caught faint hints of the man's scent on Cary when she'd returned newly pregnant with a god. The man was the Protector who'd gotten her into this mess.

Which meant the woman was probably his wife. She was a pretty woman with hair a few shades browner than her husband's, dark eyes ringed by long lashes, and pale brown skin. She was the one who smelled of magic. It was one of those scents Deacon had never been able to explain fully to Cary. Her friend Angie had it. And Marianne, too. There was something about magic…a kind of electrical smell, but not quite, maybe more like heated ozone, that tended to infuse the scent signatures of magical humans. There was variation—he could tell Angie and Marianne didn't share the same *kind* of magic—but that underlying scent of heat and electricity was always there.

He realized even as he analyzed the scents of the newcomers that he never picked up that scent of magic in Cary—at least not when she wasn't freshly covered with someone else's magic after a protection job. And that always faded away so that she just smelled like herself again. She had a unique additional flavor to her scent now, but it wasn't exactly like the smell of human magic because the baby god wasn't a human.

If Cary was absorbing magic, wouldn't he smell it?

Maybe he had been this whole time and just didn't realize it, though. Maybe it was so much a part of her, he'd never noticed it was real magic mixed in with her essence? He had thought she was a witch the first time they met—although not because of her scent. Or maybe her body changed the magic she absorbed, giving it a unique scent that didn't translate to magic in his olfactory lexicon?

More to parse out when they were alone.

"Thank you for coming, Frank," Cary said, confirming what Deacon had already assumed about the man.

"It's my responsibility that you're in this situation," he said. To Deacon, his voice sounded strained. "This isn't the solution, but we do need to find one."

"Frank Schmidt, this is a great solution," the woman beside him said. "Hi, my name is Elizabeth Adams."

"Nice to meet you, Elizabeth. I'm Cary Redmond. This is…Deacon Jones."

Deacon glanced at the top of Cary's head. She still occasionally stumbled over introducing him as her mate or boyfriend or partner or anything similar—unless she was goading one of her enemies. Was it the words she found awkward or the relationship?

"Nice to meet you," Deacon said to Elizabeth. He gave Frank a noncommittal grunt of greeting. He was still reserving judgement on the other Protector. While he completely understood the man's reluctance to put his wife in danger, Frank had put Deacon's mate in danger instead. And he wasn't ever going to be happy about that.

"This is not a great solution," Frank muttered, giving his wife a look that obviously meant something to them both. She rolled her eyes at him and shook her head. The exchange looked like it had happened more than once already.

Deacon analyzed their scents again. Franks had that sharp, bitter flavor of fear he was trying to hide. Elizabeth's carried notes of annoyance, love, and determination. The determination was strong at the moment, like solid packed, rock heavy earth. Her mind was made up.

Elizabeth put her hand on her husband's cheek. "I love kids and being pregnant, and I will be happy to raise this baby god until she can move back to her own realm. If she moves back. Because maybe she loves us so much she stays and brings hope to our world forever."

"Liz," Frank said in a low voice, his tone warning. "She won't be like our kids."

"Of course not! But then our kids aren't like each other. Frank, this is a great solution. I'll have you around twenty-four seven with your Protector powers, and I have a few handy spells to keep us safe when you're not home. Why are you fighting this? It'll be fun."

He scowled. The brief flash of anger that spiked in his scent also put a little color into his cheeks. Deacon studied Elizabeth closer. Had she done that on purpose?

"None of this is fun," Frank said.

"Oh, sure it is. It's a *baby*." She faced Cary. "I love babies. I love being pregnant."

"No morning sickness, then, I take it," Cary said. "Cause that wasn't even a little fun."

Elizabeth shrugged. "Mine wasn't ever very bad, just a little weird taste in my mouth."

"Lucky," Cary said.

"Agree," Elizabeth answered with a light laugh. "My cousin, Yolanda, had horrible morning sickness. So bad, she had to be taken to the hospital. And I have a friend from a mommy-and-me group who threw up during the entire nine months. She's sticking to just her one baby."

Cary nodded. "I can't blame her."

"I feel very lucky I don't have much of that issue," Elizabeth said. "Though, I'd probably deal with it just to have more babies."

"How many kids do you have now?" Cary asked.

Deacon didn't miss the hint of panic in her tone.

"Only three." Elizabeth laughed. "I wanted ten, Frank wanted two, so we've compromised with four."

"You're intending to have another baby anyway?" Cary asked. "Then..."

"Then this is excellent timing," Elizabeth said.

"No," Frank said. "It's not. Liz, this is a magical baby with growing god powers. You have magic that will have unforeseen inter-actions with the baby's magic. You. Can. Not. Carry. Her."

Elizabeth waved that away. "You don't think witches have figured out how to have kids who also have magic without it damaging them both? That's very sexist of you, love."

"Damn it," Frank said, "this isn't just an ordinary magical fetus, this isn't another witch. This is a *god*. And we don't know, no one *can* know, how that will affect you. That's why gods always use ordinary human surrogates. That's why no other Protector could be tapped for this job."

Cary's shoulders tightened, the move almost imperceptible, but Deacon was aware of everything about her at all times even when he didn't realize he was, and he noticed the flinch. He settled his hands on her upper arms and squeezed gently. They hadn't discussed if she was

168

going to talk about what she'd discovered tonight with anyone but her bosses and Jaxer, who already knew. Deacon wanted to blurt it out, to warn them that Cary wasn't a good surrogate either. But this was her information. And Frank and Elizabeth were strangers.

He noticed Liruk watching Cary. The Fae's expression was impossible to read, but if he had to guess, he'd say Liruk looked concerned. Wisat was focused on the arguing Protector and his wife. Not being able to pick up anything from them worried him *a lot*. Had Jaxer told them about this magical absorption possibility yet? He'd read the same book Cary had. Did her bosses know she shouldn't keep protecting the baby god this way for much longer?

Cary's dogs were still arrayed in front of her in a half-circle, though Pickles had flopped onto the ground in a basset spread that made her look almost flat, and Buck had also laid down in a more comfortable lounging position. Fred, of course, was still sitting up and vibrating with energy, but his tongue was hanging out to one side. If the dogs had relaxed, Deacon supposed he could. He wasn't going to. But at least the demon dog and foo lion weren't on full alert anymore.

"I should probably mention something," Cary said into a heavy silence that fell between husband and wife as they stared at each other, both stubborn and not backing down. "It will affect our decisions."

Her cellphone chose that moment to ring. She grunted a curse under her breath and looked at the screen, then cursed again. "I have to take this." She answered and Deacon heard Angie's voice on the other end.

"You asleep?" Angie asked. Her tone was serious and no-nonsense.

"No. What's wrong?"

"So I've got about fifteen vampires trapped between my house and my protection circle—they were threatening my neighbors."

"I'll be there in twenty minutes," Cary said, "faster if I catch the traffic lights and there aren't any cops."

"Don't crash," Angie said. "I'm safe in my house. No invitations from me, thank you very much. And they can't get out of the protection circle to hurt anyone at the moment. But they're threatening to camp out on my lawn—which would really disturb my poor mundane neighbors—until I call you. They want to *talk*."

"Right. Talk," Cary said. "Stay safe. I'll be there soon."

As Angie disconnected, Deacon heard her shouting, "Hey, you break that window, you're paying for it." Then the line went dead.

"You heard?" Cary said him.

"I'll drive," he said.

"We'll have to talk later," Cary said to the others, already heading for the front door. "Friend in need. Vampires."

"I'll go with you," Frank said.

"I help, too," Elizabeth said.

"No." Frank turned to her and took her face in his hands. "Remember our deal. Only one of us in danger at any one time. No orphaning the kids if we can help it."

Elizabeth let out a loud, annoyed breath, but nodded. "I can handle vampires, you know?"

"I know. But one of us needs to stay out of it. And I'm the walking shield."

Elizabeth snorted in response but kissed Frank soundly on the mouth. "Watch your back."

Cary opened the front door but Frank stopped her, his cellphone in hand. "Give me your friend's address. I can teleport us there, but I need a visual." He showed the satellite map on his phone. "Technology is a wonder," he said with a brief smile.

"Yeah it is," Cary said and gave him Angie's address.

"Got it." Frank studied the image, showed the phone to Cary. "Which house is hers exactly?"

Cary pointed. "The one with the little porch. She's got a protective circle activated around the place, though, so we probably can't come in too close."

"No problem. I'll bring us in a few houses away." He studied the image another few seconds, then stuck his phone into the pocket of his jeans. To Liruk and Wisat, he said, "Can you get Elizabeth home, please?" To his wife, "I'll meet you there later." To Cary and Deacon, he said, "Hold onto my shoulders and don't let go. It'll be like stepping through a doorway, but you won't be able to see for a few seconds. The exit will feel a little disorienting. And you might get nauseated."

He made a motion with his hand, opening a black rectangle the size of an actual door in the middle of the room.

Deacon had never teleported before. His leopard objected on principle, loudly in his head. Pulling Cary close, he held her to his side as they both gripped Frank's shoulders and followed him into the blackness.

23

Cary blinked as they emerged onto Angie's street under a dim streetlight. Frank had been right. The very quick journey left her both disoriented and a little nauseous. She pressed a hand against her stomach and swallowed hard. The baby god kicked Cary in the ribs, as if she'd also noticed the disorienting move through space-time and wasn't very happy about it.

To be fair, the baby god had done it before, at least once, so Cary wasn't sure what she had to complain about.

They had arrived two houses away from Angie's but close enough to see the small throng of people on her long front lawn. There were easily ten to fifteen of them, pacing around, hissing taunts up at the second floor of Angie's house. Cary looked up to see Angie watching the vampires from her bedroom window, the lights on behind her throwing her form into silhouette.

Cary took a deep breath. Her friend seemed fine, hands on hips, shaking her head at the crowd on her lawn. Having a best friend who understood the preternatural world and its rules—like no inviting vampires into your home—was a very handy thing. She waved at Angie as they approached her house, and Angie pushed open the window.

"You okay?" Cary called up even though she knew Angie was.

"Sure. Fine. I'm billing Gabriel for the window they broke in the back, though."

Cary glared at the vampires that had started to flow—there was no other word for it; they moved like they were made of water—toward the sidewalk. All of them stopped just inside Angie's circle, while Cary, Deacon, and Frank were stuck on the outside. The vampires hissed and murmured, specific things Cary chose not to hear, but there was an awful lot of low level noise. The sounds rubbed wrong against her nerves, making her even more irritable than normal.

"What the hell?" she said to the group in general. "There was no reason to break a window, you assholes." She hunted for a familiar face in the crowd and spotted one she really hadn't wanted to see.

Petra, the vampire who'd threaten to eat Cary, swayed to the front of the crowd. "Cary," she hissed, drawing out the "r" sound. "We've been waiting for you."

She ran her finger down the invisible barrier that circled Angie's house. A trail of blue light followed her movement, smoke rising from her skin, her flesh blackening. The injury healed as soon as she pulled her finger back from the circle's barrier, but Cary was relieved it worked so well on vampires.

"Why are you here?" Cary snapped. "Angie isn't part of this, and it's extremely rude to drag her into it."

"We couldn't find you," the vampire sang. "We looked. We followed. We couldn't find you…"

Cary hadn't realized they'd tried to follow her. That was bad Protector-ing. Damn. She glanced at Frank. He'd know why the vampires couldn't find her house. He kept his gaze on the threat, not acknowledging the information from the female vampire in any way. Like a good and proper Protector. Cary sighed. He probably wouldn't have missed them trying to follow him home.

She shook her head and looked at Petra again. "That's no reason to threaten my friend or break her window. You want to talk to me, send a message. Like through James who knows better than to break windows." She glanced around. "Where is James, anyway? He's more fun to talk to."

Petra pouted, an expression that was horribly sexy and alluring. Cary glared. Evil people really shouldn't be this beautiful. Okay, she didn't *know* if Petra was evil or not, but it was prudent to err on that side with vampires.

"You don't want to see me?" Petra said.

"Well last time you did threaten to drain me dry," Cary said, "so I'm gonna say no."

"You would enjoy it before you died," Petra whispered. "I promise I'd make it good for you."

"No, thank you." Cary shook her head. She'd lay money that line usually worked on poor humans. How could it not coming from a being so ethereal and gorgeous? There was no doubt some mesmerism in the woman's tone, too. Thankfully, it didn't affect Cary right now. "Why have you bothered my friend just to get my attention? I *just* met with Gabriel last night, and we settled things." Sort of. "I'm not his lap dog. Ariel's rules stay in place. You cannot drink from the unwilling. All's good in Portland."

"Not settled," Petra sang. "Not even a little bit."

Cary sighed. Yeah, she'd been afraid of that. "Where's that asshole wizard?"

"He got away." She pouted again. "Gabriel said he could be my pet. I need a new pet. My last one died."

Cary tried not to shudder. Geez, this chick was creepy. Cary wasn't a big fan of the wizard trying to kill her, but still, she wouldn't want anyone subjected to unwilling "pet" status for Petra.

Petra held Cary's gaze as she rubbed her hand along the circle barrier again, the smell of burning flesh rising between them. Gross.

"Come in a play, Cary Redmond," she whispered. "We want to play."

Cary rolled her eyes and glanced up at Angie. "This isn't going anywhere. Can you let us in without letting them out?"

She'd feel better if she could get between the vampires and Angie so she'd know for sure Angie was safe. Yes, Angie was a powerful witch who could take care of herself. But her powers involved casting spells that took time to recite and manifest. Unless Angie kept some anti-vampire spells prepared and stored nearby, she didn't have any way to fend them off beyond just staying in her house. And Angie couldn't stay inside forever.

Angie shrugged. "Not really. I'll have to drop the barrier for you to get past it. But since they're here for you, they aren't likely to run away. You sure you want me to, though." She nodded down at Petra. "She seems a little preoccupied with eating you."

Cary shrugged. "She's just being scary." Cary looked Petra in the eyes, holding her gaze. "You gonna try to eat me if I come through this barrier?"

"Yesss," she hissed.

Cary sighed. "Why, when you'll just get hurt? Just…don't."

Petra smiled slowly, a sexy look that nevertheless showed her teeth. "Come in and play with me, Cary. We'll have such fun."

"You are so creepy," Cary muttered. She looked around the crowd. "Anyone else want to explain what this is all about before I come in there? Reasons for hunting me down? Threatening my friend?"

"Breaking windows," Angie shouted, sounding very annoyed.

"Breaking windows," Cary repeated. "Anyone?"

The vampires were like one big shadow of menace, moving behind Petra in a flow of shifting faces, blurring and reappearing in new spots, the hisses and whispers like nails on a chalkboard. None of them stopped moving long enough for Cary to really get a good look at them.

It finally occurred to her that they were doing that on purpose, another kind of mesmerism. A group effort to seduce and confuse and lure into a trap. As Cary watched the flow, she could see how this would work, and probably on stronger beings than her. It was entrancing and hard to look away. Disorienting, scary, and fascinating at once. The sounds, the flow of shadow, the flash of light from their glowing eyes and white white teeth. There was even a new smell filling the air, not the heady vampire musk so prevalent in their lair, but something that called to a primitive part of her, urging her to lean in and take a deep breath.

"This affecting you?" she asked Deacon over her shoulder.

"Not much," he said. "But probably because you're between me and them."

Fair point. "Would it affect you if I wasn't here?"

"Might," he admitted. "But not long enough for them to eat me. It's a predator trick. I'm not prey."

She smiled at the growl in his voice. No, he most definitely was not. But still... The fact that this show might get to Deacon, even for a moment, was terrifying. An ordinary human wouldn't stand a chance.

"How you doing, Frank?" she asked.

"Glad I'm a not the one she's looking to play with," he said.

Cary snorted.

"Their mesmerism isn't getting to me," he said quietly. "Not much anyway. The defenses are working."

Cary was relieved to hear his Protector powers were functioning. He wasn't currently indestructible because of a baby god. Although...

She maybe should have warned him that the Portland vampires knew she was a Protector. And knew what Protectors were and could do. And how to kill them. Oops.

"What's the plan?" Frank asked.

"I'd like an explanation," Cary said, putting her hands on her hips. "I can't be running over here every night just because these assholes want to pester me. And I don't like that they're endangering my friend."

"I'll be better prepared for it next time," Angie called. "There are... things I can do."

Cary grinned at that. She was sure there *were* things Angie could set up.

"Come in a play, Cary Redmond," Petra sang again. "We just want to play."

"No. You want to feed. Does Gabriel even know you're here?"

"No," a new voice said.

Cary jumped and instinctively put Deacon behind her as she faced the newcomer. She let out an annoyed breath when she recognized him. "James, what the hell?"

"Petra is a little…taken with you," he said, his gaze moving from the group of vampires to her. "Gabriel doesn't know she's stalking you."

"Will he be upset?" Cary asked, hopefully.

"No," Petra said. "He needs me. He loves me. He wants me to be happy. You will make me happy, Cary. I need a pet."

"No," Cary said to Petra without looking away from James. "Your Master owes my friend a new window," she said to him.

"He'll pay. But this won't end. Gabriel didn't order it. But he doesn't care, either."

The noise from the vampires behind Petra rose, a song like torture and release. Cary's heart pounded for reasons she couldn't entirely pinpoint. Fear? Panic? Or just an involuntary reaction to the threat? She wasn't sure.

"Why are you here?" she asked James. "And not inside with the others."

"I'm here to keep the peace. No fighting."

"They started it."

"Drop this barrier and we can play," Petra said.

She pressed her hand into the invisible shield again and blue light flared brightly around her, so bright Cary had to look away. Spots danced in her eyes.

From the house, Angie gasped loudly and cursed.

"What?" Cary called. "You okay?"

"No. Damn it. I made an amateur mistake." She cursed again. "This circle's good at keeping things out and letting me feel what's going on outside it without the shots actually hurting me. Didn't build it to protect from stuff happening *inside* the damned thing. Stupid. I've been retired too long and got careless."

Retired from what? Cary wondered, knowing she wouldn't get an answer in front of a bunch of strange vampires, so she didn't ask aloud. There was this one thing in Angie's past—which seemed like it might be a pretty big thing from the hints—that Angie never talked about.

One day, Cary really hoped her friend would tell her exactly what she'd been doing before they met.

"So that means…?" Cary said.

Petra pressed against the barrier again, ignoring her hand as it caught fire, glowing blue and red. Angie grunted.

"It means she's feeling me push at her circle," Petra said with a grin, and a lot less sing-songy creepiness in her voice. Now she sounded deadly serious, sly, and smart. Not the slightly insane scary thing she'd been a moment ago. This was a woman who knew exactly what she was doing. "And it hurtssss." She pressed harder against the barrier, leaning into it, the flare of blue light turning her black eyes a sickly green.

Angie screamed.

"Drop the circle," Cary shouted. "Drop it!"

The blazing blue light standing between Cary and Petra vanished. And the vampires swarmed.

ary automatically put her back to Deacon's as he turned to face the threat. She had him safe inside her Protector powers, but it was nice to know he had her back as much as she had his. Frank formed up with them, facing the horde.

The vampires swarmed around them like a whirlwind of dust and shadow and glowing yellow flashes from their eyes. Their hisses and whispers grew into a cacophony of noise that hurt Cary's ears. Long skeletal arms and fingers reached through the swirl toward them, hit against the shields of two Protectors and caught fire briefly before being sucked back into the vortex.

It all happened so fast, so chaotically, the arms and fingers looked detached from their owners, like they were limbs without bodies. Faces appeared in the swirl, mouths opened wide, jaws unhinging in a way human jaws couldn't, sharp teeth clacking together before the face vanished back into the shadow void.

The wind of their attack whipped at Cary's hair, pulling strands loose from her ever present ponytail to slash across her eyes. She pushed the strands behind her ears with an irritated swipe. Then jumped involuntarily as another face pushed through the shadows right at her, stopping only inches away. The stench of rotted meat and blood from the vampire's breath made her stomach role. Its canine's glistened in the dim light from the streetlamps, dripping a liquid Cary didn't want to think about too closely.

The baby god kicked her in the ribs. "Yeah, I understand," Cary said to the protesting little god, pressing a hand against her belly. "But there's not much I can do right now."

The tingling over her skin intensified. She rubbed her arms to help tamp down the feeling. Her nerves were already on edge, what with a vampire tornado swirling around them and all. She didn't need the added tingles.

Over the noise, she heard Angie calling her name. "Stay inside that house," Cary shouted at her. "We're fine. They'll wear themselves out eventually."

Between Cary and Frank's shields, the vampires couldn't touch them, but that didn't make being inside the stinking, terrifying eye of this storm any easier. The ground shook with it. Cary's ears rang from the noise. And Angie's fear that this would disturb her neighbors seemed a moot point now because if they weren't hiding under their beds after hearing all this, they had a death wish.

The storm of rushing vampires tightened around Cary, Deacon and Frank, leaving only the space created by the Protector shields. This got the reaching fingers and screaming faces much too close for comfort as far as Cary was concerned. Still, none of the vampire got through to so much as touch them. Which was good.

Cary braced as the winds buffeted her, pushing her against Deacon. He reached back a hand to steady her, wrapping his arm loosely around her waist. The gesture had the duel effect of also putting the baby god under his hand, and Cary's softer side got a little emotional at the protective gesture. She rolled her eyes. Pregnancy hormones had really sucky timing.

The storm of shadows and terror started to slow, the winds calming as the group stopped racing around them and came to a stop. No one was breathing hard—since vampires really didn't breathe all that often anyway—and no one showed any signs that all that exertion had been any kind of a strain.

That was irritating. If they were going to terrorize her, they should at least be exhausted by the effort.

"Are we finished?" she asked as Petra stilled in front of her.

The vampire's head swayed on her neck, giving her even more of a reptilian aura than her sibilant hissing. She flicked out her tongue as if she was tasting the air, lapping up a spot in front of Cary's face. Cary raised her lip in a snarl. That wasn't even a little pleasant to watch.

"You're mine, you know?" Petra said, getting her face as close to Cary's as she could with the Protector shield in the way.

"Actually, she's mine," Deacon said from behind her.

Cary nodded. "He's right. I'm his. He's mine. We've got this whole commitment thing going."

Petra's smile was sharp as glass. "Time. Time. Time," she sang. "I have time. Lots of it. You don't. Don't don't."

"Back to creepy, I see," Cary muttered.

"I will have you. I will eat you. I will turn you. You will thank me."

"I'm not sure how many more ways I can say no to that."

Petra reached toward her, stroking the air near Cary's cheek. "So pretty. Gabriel wants you too. Not like me. But he wants you. You'll be ours. I can share."

Cary sighed and pretended to be annoyed. Inside, she started to tremble. Petra was right. Vampires had all the time in the world. And they could just keep coming at her until they caught her in a vulnerable moment. The thought of being a vampire's pet, of being their food, made her pulse pound hard in her throat.

Petra's gaze dropped to that frantic beating vein and she smiled, showing her teeth.

Deacon's hand flexed against her waist, his arm tightening, pulling her closer to him and away from the vampire.

"We'll kill him," Petra said in a low tone. "He's not invited to the party, even though he's a yummy shifter. A king. He'll feed us for weeks. And then we'll kill him so you can be mine."

"No," Cary said, the threat to Deacon spiking something besides fear in her blood. Anger was good. Anger was strengthening. Anger beat back her fear. "You touch him, and I will end you." She leaned in toward Petra, putting her face only inches from her. "I *know* how to kill vampires."

"We know how to kill you now, too," Petra said.

"And I am gonna fry you all right this minute if you don't leave," Angie called from her porch.

All eyes turned to her. Cary frantically motioned her to get back inside. Angie raised a vial, the purple glass bottle looked like a mini version of a djinn's lamp.

"You don't leave," Angie said, "this little spell will dissolve you in about five seconds. Just long enough for you to feel yourself dissolving. Little something I picked up from the vampire hunters in Europe. You know, the ones who are really really good at slaughtering your kind?" She shook the vial and the liquid inside sloshed enough for even Cary to see the movement. "You ready to die now?" Angie asked Petra.

Petra snarled. "You're bluffing, witch."

Cary used the distraction Angie had created to shift positions and put herself between Angie's house and the vampires. She tugged Deacon with her, so she could keep him safe—especially after Petra's threat—and motioned Frank around. To her surprise, he opened a portal, walked through it, and reappeared at a spot on Angie's lawn closer to the porch, putting him and his Protector shield between Angie and the vampires.

Whoa. Cool trick.

Now that the vampires weren't surrounding her anymore, Cary was able to relax a little. She shook her shoulders to release some of the tension that had tightened her muscles.

To Petra, she said, "You're not going to get what you want here. Go away."

"Why can't I find you?" Petra said, sounding pained and hurt. "Why do you hide from me?"

The switch in mood was so lightning quick, it made Cary's head spin. "Cause you're a scary bitch, and I don't want you to find me," she said. "Petra, call it a night. Go home. Don't come back. Angie will kill you. And I'll let her because you threatened my mate *and* my best friend."

"And I will kill you," Angie said, "because you're a threat to *my* best friend. Back off my lawn. Now. This is your last warning." Angie raised the vial again and pointed it at Petra.

All the vampires backed away, snarling and hissing and cursing. Petra was the last to move. She held her place for a long moment, holding Cary's gaze, not speaking. Her black eyes flared to an incandescent yellow glow for a beat.

Then she vanished, gone at speeds too fast for Cary's human eyes to perceive.

"I hate when vampires do that," she murmured.

When the metaphorical smoke cleared, only James remained, standing several yards away on the sidewalk, just watching.

"Got something to say, James?" she asked.

His smile was faint, closed lipped, and Cary might have imagined it. "I'll send Gabriel your regards."

He vanished as well.

Cary rolled her eyes at his theatrics. Then she faced Angie. "What's in that vial? And since when have you had vampire-killing juice in your house?"

"It's just water," Angie said with a shrug, pocketing the vial. She was wearing loose flannel pajama pants, a t-shirt, slippers, and had wrapped up in a long wool coat in deference to the cold spring night. "But they didn't know that."

Cary laughed. "They obviously thought it was a real threat. What did you *imply* it was?"

"The European vampire hunters have developed some really wicked killing water in the last century, combing chemistry and magic. Huge progress since they discovered the secret to alchemy was nuclear physics. Good stuff. And it's a nice coincidence that it ties neatly into the holy water myth."

"Cool," Cary said.

"I have a friend in New York who can probably get us some. Might not be a bad idea to have a few vials on hand, just in case."

"That would be fantastic."

"Hey Deacon," Angie greeted.

"Hello, Angie," he said.

"Your skin is glowing," Angie said to Cary with a nod.

Cary looked down. "Ah hell." Her skin was glowing again.

"You find out why yet?" Angie asked, coming down from her porch to stand with Cary on the stone path between her door and the sidewalk.

"Maybe. We need to talk."

"I'm always here for you." She faced Frank. "We haven't been introduced."

"Sorry," Cary said. "Frank Schmidt, this is my friend Angela Jordan. She's a witch, if you didn't realize. Frank is a Protector." At Frank's frown, Cary said, "She works with Jaxer sometimes. She knows what we are."

He nodded, but his slight frown didn't go away. "The vampires know what you are, don't they?"

Cary winced. "You noticed that, huh?"

"That's not good."

"No, it's not. I figured that part out already."

He had the grace to look embarrassed at his comment. "I mean, them even knowing about Protectors is bad for all of us."

"Not my fault," she said. "It was this asshole wizard who's been trying to kill me. He told Gabriel."

"The Master of Portland? He knows you're a Protector."

"Yeah." She sighed. "Very inconvenient."

"You think?" Frank said.

"Hey, don't you start with me. This wasn't my fault."

"Why is a wizard trying to kill you?"

"That's a really long story." She glanced at Angie. "And that's some of what we need to talk about. It's more your specialty than mine."

Angie's brows creased with a faint frown but she nodded. "I've got a reading at noon. Then I can come over to talk."

"Why is your skin glowing?" Frank asked.

"The baby god," Cary said.

Although, she still wasn't entirely sure what about the baby god was making her skin glow—if it was the little fetus herself just being all god-like, or if it was this possibility that Cary was absorbing some of her powers. Either way, it was something to do with the baby god, so she'd given him an honest answer. She hadn't committed to telling Frank about her suspicions yet. She probably had to because it affected her ability to keep protecting the little god by actually carrying her inside her womb. But she still hadn't absorbed the impact of this knowledge yet, and she hadn't had a minute to really let it sink in.

"The other surrogate didn't glow," Frank said.

"Maybe the baby god wasn't old enough for that yet," Cary said.

"You're farther along than you should be," he said. "I didn't realize before, because I've been worried about Liz taking this on, but you look six months pregnant, not four. You should only be four."

"Are you telling me I look fat?" Cary said.

"I'm telling you something is wrong. You know it's wrong. That's why you wanted to meet with Liz and me."

Cary sighed, knowing the jig was up. "Yes. And it's too long a story to tell on someone's lawn in the middle of the night. We'll need the Nags in on this too. It's important." Guess she'd made up her mind and she was going to admit all. Probably for the best.

Frank's lips twitched when she called their bosses the Nags. "We'll come back to your house tomorrow morning, then. If that's okay?"

She glanced at Angie. "Might as well do all this at once. Say about two?" she said to Frank.

"We'll be there." He opened a portal door and before Cary could speak, stepped through and disappeared, the door closing behind him.

She blinked at the empty air. "Frank, you were our ride," she said with a huff.

Angie chuckled. "I'll get my keys and drive you home." She started back to the house when a black rectangular portal door opened again.

"Sorry," Frank said, stepping back through. "Forgot I'd ported us here." His sheepish expression went a long way toward earning Cary's forgiveness.

She hugged Angie. "Call again if the bastards come back. Sorry about the fuss for your neighbors. Is that going to be a problem tomorrow?"

Angie shrugged. "I'll sort it out. Thanks for coming."

"I always have your back. Especially when it's my fault you're in danger."

"Don't dare blame yourself for other people's actions," Angie said, holding her gaze. "We've discussed this before."

"Fine." She hugged Angie again. "See you tomorrow."

Deacon held her hand as they followed Frank into the portal. She glanced down to where their fingers intertwined. Her skin was still glowing.

2 5

---

*C*ary slept late the next day because she needed it. But she didn't sleep well. Between the worry and the fact that she couldn't sleep on her stomach anymore, the night was restless. Even Deacon's calming warmth next to her only helped a little. By the time she dragged herself out of bed at nearly noon, her eyes were gritty and she felt like she could sleep for a month.

She might have to when all this was over.

Deacon had gotten up sometime before her and already had the coffee going—decaf because she way buying into the myth, but still, it satisfied her morning ritual. She wasn't sure what to do with herself without hot coffee in the morning. It didn't feel natural.

She wandered out to the back porch, wrapped in a thick, padded flannel shirt against the chill. The day was surprisingly sunny and she could feel the stirring warmth of approaching spring. Deacon sat on the porch, throwing a ball to Fred as the mutt zipped around the yard.

Fred got distracted from the game by the appearance of the stray tomcat Cary had dubbed Scratchy. The cat sat on the brick fence encircling the small backyard, licking his front paw and making a show of ignoring Fred's barking. Pickles was laid out flat on her stomach next to Deacon on the wooden porch. Her front legs were stretched in front of her, back legs stretched out behind, and her ears flopped out to the sides, making her look almost like a basset hound rug. Buck was sniffing the perimeter fence, and when Fred barreled into him, jumping around a little, Buck joined into Fred's game.

Cary grinned at that. It was nice to see Buck having ordinary dog fun. He hadn't done as much playing these last few months, after his demon dog episode. He was usually pretty mellow anyway, and didn't bounce around like Fred, but he had still played before, and it did Cary's heart good to see him playing again.

She sat next to Deacon on the top step leading down to the grassy yard, cradling her coffee mug. "Thanks for the coffee. Decaf isn't the same, but it's better than nothing."

He bumped her shoulder and smiled at her. "You're welcome. Didn't sleep well, huh."

He wasn't asking. She sighed. "Sorry. Did I keep you awake?"

"Worry or the baby god kicking you?" he asked, avoiding her question.

She made a face at him. "Both. Mostly worry though. Lots and lots of worries."

He wrapped an arm around her shoulders. "I was talking to Trevor this morning, before you got up."

His cop friend. That could only be about one thing. "The two over-dosed fanatics?"

"They can't identify the drug used yet. Some sort of hallucinogen, but not a standard."

"Kind of quick turn around for a drug panel anyway," Cary said with a shrug. "It'd help if we knew what killed them I suppose, but that's the police's job to handle. Hey, do you suppose they'll find the main bad guy behind the people coming after the little god and save us a lot of trouble?"

Deacon gave her a look. "Do you want them to? What if it is a demon?"

"Ugh. Right. No. If I have to protect actual cops from a demon, they're gonna know there's something strange about me."

He chuckled. "But in a good way."

"Does Trevor suspect there's something strange about me, since he knows about you?"

"He's a good investigator. And observant. But he hasn't said anything, so if he does suspect you're unique, he's keeping it to himself." Deacon met her gaze. "He did remind me that the dinner invitation he keeps extending to us has continued to go unanswered, and his wife is getting suspicious that you're not good for me."

"Ha! I'm probably not. How many times have you had to fight demons and vampires and weird shit since meeting me?"

"I'm a shifter. Weird shit has always been a part of my life."

"Yeah, yeah, but still. Maybe I'm not good for you." She was joking, too tired and punch drunk to think about what she was saying.

"You're the best thing that's ever happened to me," he said, very seriously.

She met his gaze. "Yeah? Well, I'm not prepared to let you go yet either, even if Trevor's wife doesn't like me."

"She'll like you." He paused. "Why did you say 'yet?'"

"Life is a strange and complicated thing," she said, also very serious now. "And my life is hanging in an awkward balance this year. Letting go of each other might not be a choice. But," she said, touching a hand to his cheek, "it won't be voluntary on my part."

"I love you," he murmured. "And if I have a choice, maybe even if I don't, I won't let you go either."

She smiled, letting the moment and his words settled into a warm spot in the middle of her chest.

Her life was chaotic. And dangerous. And had been flipped upside down yesterday with what she'd learned at the Bookstore. She wasn't even sure who she was anymore. She hadn't had time to process the news. She was worried about the baby god and what all this meant to them both. And she was certain the vampires were going to be a big problem for her over the next...well, maybe forever since they lived so damned long.

But for this one instant, sitting on her back porch, wrapped in

Deacon's embrace, her dogs content and healthy, she had a little peace. And she was grateful for it.

The words she hadn't said yet bubbled up, on the tip of her tongue to say out loud finally. She felt them. But she was afraid to let them out into the real world.

Afraid the real world might take them as a challenge to destroy this peace.

Her front doorbell sounded at just that moment. Someone leaned onto the button, turning the little ding dong into an irritating drone. She closed her eyes. Words or no, there went her peace.

"That's Jaxer," she said, opening her eyes. "You want to get it to establish your dominance in my territory?"

He snorted at that. "You just don't want to stand up yet."

She grinned. "It is getting harder to get up and down. My center of balance is really weird right now."

He kissed her, hard and quick. "Stay there. I'll let him in. It'll be fun to watch him scowl."

"You two need to get over this and make up," she called after him as he disappeared into the house.

He grunted something rude.

Smiling into the heat of her mug, she waited for the two men to do their irritating little dance around each other. That was a sight she was happy to miss out on.

"You went to the Bookstore?" Jaxer asked from behind her a few minutes later.

"You should have told me," she said without turning to look at him. "At least warned me what might be happening."

She heard his sigh. "I didn't want to scare you. It's not a certainty."

"Renee seems to think it's likely. And she's super smart. She lives in a bookstore." And might well be a god in her own right.

"No one, not even Renee, can be certain, Cary. This...ability is really really rare."

She finally faced him. "I flattened an army, Jaxer. How the hell did I do that?"

His mouth turned down, but he held her gaze. "I wanted to talk with an acquaintance before I said anything to you," he said. "Someone very old, older than either Wisat or Liruk, who might have actually come across a person who could do this."

"And?"

He settled on the step next to her, the spot Deacon had left just moments ago. He didn't touch her, which she appreciated, but Deacon still growled a little, and Buck stopped playing with Fred to sit at the bottom of the steps, looking up at Jaxer. Fred charged across the yard and hopped to a sitting position next to Buck, his tongue lolling out as he also stared at Jaxer.

"Your pack is getting a lot more attentive to me," Jaxer said with a frown at Buck.

"Pickle's is indifferent," Cary said, nodding to the basset still sprawled on her stomach like a rug, her eyes closed.

Jaxer's mouth quirked up at one corner. "Someone on my side at least."

"What did this old friend of yours say?" Cary asked, getting Jaxer back to the subject at hand.

"If you hadn't done something impossible with Holland's army," Jaxer said slowly, "she wouldn't have been able to say for sure. The wizards could just be making excuses. There are other reasons Sheldon could have lost his powers when he tried to kill you and Deacon. Especially because he was…is—" Jaxer made a face, "—so young. He might have had unstable powers to begin with. Sheldon's master might have been draining him the entire time through a spelled object and that object just got broken during Sheldon's confrontation with you. There are lots of things that could have happened there."

"But the tingling, the injuries I take even through the Protector magic…"

"All could be explained away as something else." He shrugged. "Okay, something we couldn't explain it, but it didn't have to be this."

"Leveling Holland's army was the deciding factor?"

He nodded. "There's nothing about you, or the Protector magic that you were channeling, that should have made that possible. Protector magic doesn't work that way. Even for someone who can channel it as well as you do. I thought, maybe... But Wisat, Liruk, and I have looked into it, gone over the histories of Protectors back to the beginning."

"Did they find anything at all?" she asked.

"Nothing. The rare human who can absorb magic has never become a Protector. And there's never been a hint of anyone using Protector magic offensively, the way you seemed to with Holland's army."

"The damning evidence is stack up," she murmured, looking down at Buck and Fred. "Not sure this is a good thing, guys."

Fred let out a cheerful, "Arf!" that didn't really do much to answer her unspoken question, but it did make her smile.

Pickles rose from her sprawl and sat next to Cary's hip, putting her chin on Cary's knee. She looked up with her big brown eyes, all sympathy and love, and Cary's chest tightened. "Thanks," she said, and set a hand on the back of Pickles's head.

"So..." She faced Jaxer. "What does all this mean? Besides the asshole wizard was right, which I have to say, is the worst part of all this. I really really hate that he's probably right."

Jaxer's mouth quirked at one corner. "I won't tell him if you won't."

"Thank you. What now?"

"Now..." He paused. "We talk to Frank and Liruk and Wisat. We settle the issue of the baby god. Because if you can absorb magic, you can't remain the surrogate. That's magic your human cells won't survive."

She blinked. Hearing that reality put into words was enough to start her pulse pounding with just a hint of panic. As her adrenaline surged, the tingling on her skin intensified and the baby god moved.

Oh boy. Yeah, they needed to take care of all this.

She patted Pickles's head and gestured for her to ease back a bit, then reached toward Deacon for a helping hand up so she could stand

—between the pregnancy and the mug in her hand, she wasn't getting to her feet gracefully without help.

She'd felt the Nags arrive. They were waiting inside the house for her, likely with Frank and Elizabeth. Time to confront this reality.

Like it or not.

*H*er living room wasn't big enough for all these people.

Cary sat on the couch next to Deacon with Jaxer leaning casually against the wall to her left, next to the large window that looked out over the backyard. Elizabeth sat on the couch with her and Deacon, though it was a tight fit, and Frank sat in the chair closest to them. The Nags stood, as usual, and kept themselves closer to the fireplace across from the couch. The dogs had decided to stay in the backyard—Cary couldn't blame them.

And in the second seat next to her couch, opposite Frank, sat a stranger who'd been introduced as Mrs. Benson. Mrs. Benson—no first name given—was one of the people whose age could have been anywhere from her mid-thirties to her mid-fifties. She was attractive in an unadorned kind of way. Neatly dressed in a conservative knee-length skirt and button up blouse, all in a dark blue color that sat neutrally against her tan skin, her shoes low-healed and beige. She wore clean, neutral makeup that highlighted her features without seeming to draw attention to anything in particular, no jewelry but for a ring on her third left finger—a simple gold band with a single diamond in the center—and her nails were neatly shaped and painted a soft pink color.

Her black hair was pulled up into a large bun that sat on the back of her skull, a position that made Cary wince. When she wore her hair that way she got headaches. Also she didn't have enough hair to make such a thick, attractive bun anyway. But still, the position made her scalp ache in sympathy.

Everything about Mrs. Benson said class and grace, and Cary felt her own awkwardness in her bones as she watched the woman. How did someone go about displaying so much class with so little apparent effort? She had to practice, right? No one was that casually elegant without practice? Right?

No one had mentioned *why* Mrs. Benson was at this meeting yet. But it was clear from the way Frank had deferred to her seating choice, and Elizabeth asked after her comfort, that she was someone they considered worthy of consideration.

Which was all well and good, but Cary really really wanted to know who she was and why she was here because they had some serious things to discuss and she wasn't prepared to talk about those things in front of a stranger.

Yet no one seemed in a hurry to start the conversation.

Cary sighed. To Frank, she said, "Thanks again for last night."

He waved that away. "Part of the job." He smiled a little and she smiled back.

There was something kind of refreshing about talking to another Protector, someone who actually understood her job from the inside. And not a mentor who wasn't the one who kept diving in between bad guys and good guys, but the actual person who did the job. When all this was done, she wondered if she'd be allowed to talk with Frank about the job and the process. She had a feeling she wasn't allowed under the test year rules, but maybe they'd give her a break given what she'd been through the last week.

She glanced at the Nags. Maybe not.

She couldn't read either of their expressions, not even Wisat, and she couldn't tell if there was sympathy there, or if they were annoyed. Or if they were just remaining neutral until everything got laid out on the table.

"So," Cary said on a slow breath, "where do we start?"

"Shall we finally discuss the fact that the Master of Portland knows you're a Protector," Liruk said.

And now Cary heard the disapproval. "You know that wasn't my fault. Blame the wizard trying to kill me. And before you say anything, that wasn't my fault either. I was protecting Deacon from his protégé. And before you say anything, I know I wasn't there on one of your jobs, but you can blame Jaxer for that."

"I'll take the blame for that," Jaxer said.

She smiled at him. He hadn't used to take the blame for stuff he did to her that got her into trouble with her bosses, but since her Seventh Year started, he'd been better about not throwing her under the bus. That, at least, was a nice change.

"This isn't going to make the rest of your year easy," Wisat said.

As usual, he tried to sound calm and reassuring, but Cary heard the strain. "I've figured that out already, Wisat. Not much I can do about it now. Unless you know a way to wipe his mind so he doesn't remember me?"

Wisat didn't react, but Cary caught movement from Liruk from the corner of her eye. She focused more fully on her. Liruk looked her usual disapproving self. No hint of movement or any change in facial expression. Huh. Maybe she'd imagined the slight gesture.

"Anyway, while the vampire thing is a pain in my neck—ha!—it's not the biggest issue we have at the moment, right? The baby god, me moving through this pregnancy too fast..." She glanced over at Jaxer. "The reason why the wizard might want to kill me." She faced her bosses again. "Has Jaxer told you what he found?"

Wisat nodded. "It is...not likely. You realize that."

"It's rare. Not impossible," she said. "I've been trying to talk myself out of the idea since learning about it. I'm not having much luck. If you've got information to make disbelief easier, I'm willing to hear it."

Wisat and Liruk exchanged a look.

"What are we talking about?" Frank asked.

"The likely reason I can't keep carrying the baby god," Cary said. "It's entirely possible I'm not as ordinary as we all thought."

"In what way?" Elizabeth asked. "You have magic of some kind you haven't known about?"

"Not…per se," Cary hedged.

She really wasn't sure she wanted to say this out loud. The more people who knew about this, the more likely she was to get killed. It was even worse than people knowing she was a Protector in some ways. At least then, they usually only wanted to kill her because she'd saved someone's life and it pissed off the person wanting to do the killing. She didn't really mind pissing people like that off. In fact, sometimes, it was one of the rewards of the job, getting to irritate bad guys. Like sticking your tongue out at a bully.

But this other thing, people might try to kill her just for being her, for something she couldn't control. It was just the kind of thing some human beings were very good at—killing because they didn't like or feared someone else for something that other person couldn't control. Those particular human beings sucked. And they were dangerous as all hell.

She stared at Deacon, silently asking what he thought. This was one of those times she was sorry she wasn't a shapeshifter. If she was, she could scent some of what he was thinking and maybe even get an answer to her unspoken question.

Elizabeth stepped into the silence. "I'm still okay with taking over the pregnancy. Eager even. And seeing as how *something* isn't quite right with you continuing to harbor the baby, whatever the actual reason, it's enough to confirm you can't any longer." She stared at her husband. "Right, Frank."

His mouth flattened into a line, a gesture that didn't hide his unhappiness with the state of things. For Cary's part, she wasn't particularly happy either. This was, technically, his job. And he'd gotten her into this. And Elizabeth was glad to take over.

Despite all that, though, Cary understood why he still hesitated. It seemed to be a required trait for Protectors. Get in the way of things and then just stand there.

"I can't keep carrying the baby," Cary said quietly to him. "This other thing, it's affecting us both. If the little god is going to make it through to actually being born, she can't travel in me anymore."

He faced Mrs. Benson, the first time since they'd started talking that anyone had acknowledged the extremely elegant woman. "What do they say?" Frank asked her.

They?

Mrs. Benson closed her eyes and pulled in a deep breath. Her lids flickered, as if she were dreaming, her hands rested on her knees and gripped tight. A shudder travelled visibly through her frame, ending in her shoulders as she gave a hard shake. Then she opened her eyes.

The blackness was absolute. No light, no star-specks like Renee, no hint of white around the edges. Black. And solid. With no sense that there was someone looking out through the darkness. In fact, her eyes didn't look like eyes anymore. They looked more like obsidian rock, solid and faintly luminous but with nothing underneath, no visible inner workings.

When Mrs. Benson opened her mouth, the sound that emerged was so far removed from the soft elegance of her voice when she'd been introduced, Cary actually jumped and moved closer to Deacon.

"You have called," the voice said. Deep, gravely, and echoing as if from a great distance. In fact, even after the sentence finished, there seemed to remain sound moving in the background, a noise like echoes of words and maybe thunder, even though Mrs. Benson's mouth was no longer moving.

From the corner of her eyes, Cary saw Liruk and Wisat straighten slightly, and Jaxer no longer leaned casually against the wall. Deacon's arm tightened on her shoulders.

"Thank you for coming," Frank said, deferentially. "A decision must be made."

"The offspring is alive?"

"Yes. Her surrogate can no longer carry her, though. We must move her."

Mrs. Benson's rock eyes moved in her head as if refocusing. But without a pupil or any inner light, it just looked like a smooth marble rolling in the socket. It was so disconcerting, Cary didn't realize the woman's focus had moved to her until the voice emerged from her again.

"You are not the original surrogate."

Cary jerked as the sound sent an involuntary shudder through her bones. A weird sort of vibration that happened at the level of molecules. She shook herself a bit and said, "I'm not. There was a problem. I took over. But I can't continue to carry the baby."

"I will take over," Elizabeth said, not waiting for her husband to comment.

He gave her a look, but she ignored it.

The rock eyes moved a little. "You are the Protector's mate. You have carried new life before."

None of the words sounded like questions. Elizabeth nodded anyway.

"You are volunteering for this task," the voice said, again not a question.

"I am," Elizabeth said.

"Your...husband is not happy."

"Frank will adapt."

"And he will protect our child," the voice said.

Cary blinked as the reality of what was happening really hit her. Holy shit. They were talking to a god. Mrs. Benson was channeling a god from a different realm. Holy shit!

"We both will," Elizabeth confirmed. "Cary was obligated by circumstances to take over. It's not her duty to continue."

"It is not yours either," the god—or gods?—speaking through Mrs. Benson pointed out.

"I'm happy to take it."

"She will be hope," the voice said.

Cary got the impression that was a reference to the baby and not Elizabeth, although as far as Cary was concerned, Elizabeth was *her* hope of getting out of this without anyone getting hurt.

"Why will you no longer carry her?" the voice asked.

Cary assumed the god, or gods, was talking to her but without eye contact it was impossible to be certain. Still, "There are complications. And I'm not sure it's good for the baby to continue with me."

"You have not produced new life before," the god said.

"A valid point," Cary said.

Silence for a moment, but another echo of thunder emerged from Mrs. Benson's closed mouth.

Oops. Had Cary offended the god? Wasn't thunder and lightning a sign of a god's annoyance? It was Thor and Zeus's go to when mad.

"We thank you for taking over," the god said.

Cary frowned slightly. Were they talking to her or Elizabeth?

"I will talk with the offspring," the god said, and Mrs. Benson shifted forward in her seat, her hands stretched out.

Cary gave Frank a panicked look. "What am I supposed to do?"

"She needs to touch your stomach," he said quietly. "With your permission, of course."

The god hadn't exactly made it clear her permission for the physical contact was required or solicited. But it was nice to know she was being given a choice in the matter. She patted Deacon's leg and he reluctantly loosened his hold on her. But when she stood, he moved to the edge of his seat, ready to leap up if needed.

Cary nudged her coffee table aside so she could stand in front of Mrs. Benson easier. Mrs. Benson's rock eyes stared straight ahead—or at least that's what Cary assumed was happening—and her perfectly manicured hands reached out to gentle settle on the sides of Cary's baby bump. As soft as a leaf, Mrs. Benson set her forehead against Cary's stomach.

The tingling in her skin increased, like champagne bubbles moving over her in a warm bath. It was both pleasant and strange. Not like the usual tingles. These were more intense and almost overwhelming. She was reminded of the moment outside the Naga city, with Holland's army throwing everything they had at her, and she could barely breathe through all the magic. But this time, her breathlessness didn't come from the sense of being pummeled with stones. This felt like a blanket of warm comfort weighing her down into a deep, soft bed.

Her knees wobbled, and Deacon's hand was there at her elbow, keeping her upright.

"You okay?" he murmured.

She nodded, unable to speak around the sensations flooding her. She wasn't entirely sure she was okay, but she wasn't in pain and she was pretty sure she wasn't under attack here, so that was a good thing, and maybe as close as she was going to get to okay while an actual god and the baby god in her womb were talking.

Even the idea of that was so mind-bending, she couldn't think around it.

A sensation like static electricity danced over her fingertips. She flexed her fists and glanced down. Her skin was glowing again. And to her astonishment, little sparks of blue electricity were dancing across her hands, around her fingers. She opened and closed her fists again. The sparks crackled. The baby god moved, a gentle change of position that made Cary's stomach flex. She glanced at where Mrs. Benson still had her head pressed to her stomach.

What the hell were they talking about?

She gave Deacon a look and waved her hand very gently. He nodded, his eyes on the sparks around her fingers, his expression serious. She glanced at Jaxer. He was also watching her hands, frowning. The Nags moved a few inches closer to her, and Wisat actually looked upset. Cary couldn't tell what Liruk was thinking from her expression. From behind her, she heard Elizabeth gasp and Frank murmured something under his breath.

She wanted to say *told you so* to the group at large, but she couldn't actually speak at the moment. Her body felt odd. She was in it, in control of it, but it also felt like someone else was using it at the same time, like at any moment someone else might also move her hands or head.

She only realized she was trembling when Deacon's grip on her arm tightened and he stood to take more of her weight.

A gasp from around her stomach area drew her attention. Mrs. Benson was leaning back now, looking up at her with normal eyes, not the obsidian rocks of the god's eyes. Her expression was a horrified, wide-eyed, open-mouthed one of shock.

"You're sharing her powers," Mrs. Benson murmured, her voice harsh and choked, like her throat had been scrapped raw. "How?"

Cary sighed. Guess the cat was out of the bag on this one. She didn't want to lie because this wasn't just about her. But boy, she did not want to admit this in front of so many people.

So she stalled. "What did the god say to the baby god? Do you know?"

"I don't know what the gods say through me unless they want me to," Mrs. Benson said. "This one didn't deign to reveal the conversation with you or with the offspring. Only that you are…sharing the baby's budding powers. Once she's born, the powers will go into a kind of hibernation for years so that she may grow more easily and without complications. She will come back into her powers when she's ready. But now, those powers are building in her, developing along with her external body. And they are being…shared between the surrogate and the god."

"Why do you keep hesitating over the word sharing?" Frank asked.

So, Cary wasn't the only one who'd heard that part.

"The god revealed this truth as a sense of the thing rather than through words so it's more difficult to interpret. I got the impression of sharing, but there was some sense of…taking. That the baby god was both willing but not in control of the sharing of powers." Mrs. Benson blinked. "And it's the sharing that is bringing her development along faster than typical."

"Is she in trouble?" Cary said, panic setting in. She glanced at the Nags. "We need to move her. Now."

"She is not in trouble," Mrs. Benson assured, sitting back in her chair. Her eyelids drooped low, and her breathing grew deep and slow. "She is…content…eager?" Mrs. Benson blinked and focused on Cary again. "The god accepts that she should be moved one last time, though."

"Because of the sharing?" Cary asked.

Mrs. Benson nodded. "It isn't good for you." Her voice trailed off, her eyes closed, and her head listed to the side. Mrs. Benson was out cold.

"It takes a lot out of her," Frank said, as he went to the woman and ensured she was comfortable in the chair where she'd passed out.

Cary let herself drop back to the couch—an easier process than getting up from the couch—and stared at the fireplace, not looking at any of the others in the room. After a moment, she felt a hand on her knee.

"It will be okay," Elizabeth said. "I'll take over." She narrowed her eyes at Frank, whose mouth compressed in a line, but he didn't comment. "We talked more last night. And now the parents of the baby have spoken. Frank agreed that if they wanted the baby moved, we should go ahead." She squeezed Cary's leg. "I promise, I want this. I'm delighted to do it, and I will be ecstatic to have a new baby in our home. I'm not making any sacrifices here." She glanced at the unconscious Mrs. Benson. "And it sounds like it's better for you if we do this."

Cary nodded, but she was too busy thinking to say much. The tingling, the glowing, the sparks along her hands—the baby god, but it was the baby god sharing her powers with Cary. Not voluntarily, though. Cary was drawing magic from the little fetus, which meant she was storing god magic in her cells.

She set a hand to her stomach. The baby's parents thought continuing would be dangerous for Cary, not the baby.

Any doubts and worries that Cary was neglecting her duty by passing the guarding of this baby to someone else went out the window. She wouldn't be any good to anyone, including the baby god, if she died in an explosion of god magic.

Holy hell. *God magic.*

She glanced at her bosses. "This needs to be done," she said.

Liruk answered. "It does, Protector. We thank you for your part in saving her life."

"What about the people after her? The ones that attacked me and Deacon? The ones that died of a drug overdose."

"The Polrom are fanatics," Frank said. "They likely took the drugs themselves to martyr themselves once the killing was done."

Cary didn't like "likely" as an answer. But as soon as the baby god moved to her new home in Elizabeth's womb, it was no longer Cary's job to worry about it.

She just had to worry about no longer being invulnerable to the vampires who now knew how to kill her, and the wizard who wanted revenge for something, as it turned out, she probably did do.

Sure, no problem. That was the easy part.

Oh boy.

he process of moving the baby god went more smoothly than the first time because there was no panic and no dying surrogate—much to Cary's relief. They were even a lot more comfortable, with Cary stretched out on her couch, Deacon behind her cradling her, and Elizabeth standing next to the couch, holding Frank's hand.

Cary didn't miss their knuckles going white from the tightness of their grip on each other.

Mrs. Benson was still unconscious on the chair, but Frank assured Cary she'd sleep for a few hours after channeling the god, so they left her resting while they got on with things.

The light Liruk lifted from Cary was larger than it had been when Cary had taken over as surrogate. And it didn't flicker this time. It pulsed with health and color. Cary grinned at that, glad she'd done well by her charge. Tiny sparks of blue light flickered around the glow, reminding Cary of the light and sparks that had danced around her hands as the baby god was communing with her parent gods.

The idea of that was still a bit mind-blowing. More than a bit.

As Liruk gently guided the ball of glowing light toward Elizabeth, Elizabeth began to murmur something under her breath. After so many years of being friends with Angie, Cary recognized it as a spell. Elizabeth mouthed the words more than whispered them, very few of them emerging as sound, but from what Cary could hear, they were as much prayer as spell. She'd have to ask Elizabeth about that afterward.

The ball of light waffled in the cool air, rocking as if on a swing, moving closer to Elizabeth but occasionally swinging back toward Cary. Liruk's smooth brow creased as she changed the position of her hands slightly to ease the god toward her new surrogate. A collective gasp went up as the little ball of light suddenly bounced in a long arch that brought it right to Cary's face. Cary blinked. What the...?

A tendril of energy from the ball flicked out and brushed Cary's cheek, filling her with the buzz of static shock, and then the light was back in the open cups of Liruk's hands, as if it had never bounced away. Liruk pulled in a deep breath and eased the light toward Elizabeth's womb. This time, the light moved willingly and easily, almost in a hurry as it flowed into Elizabeth. A tinkling sound like tiny bells tickled Cary's ears, but she wasn't sure if she was imagining the sound because no one else seemed to react to it.

For a few moments, Elizabeth's stomach glowed with a soft white light, casting shadows onto her face as she smiled down. Then the glow faded. And Elizabeth's stomach was noticeably larger. Maybe even a little larger than Cary's stomach had been.

"Is the baby god still..." Cary murmured. "Is she okay? Is she still at the six month gestation point?"

Elizabeth patted her stomach lightly. "She just moved so she seems to be okay." She glanced up a Liruk. "Can you tell how far along she is, technically?"

"Based on the feel of her energy, she has about twelve weeks of gestation remaining," Liruk said. "She should not leap forward with you the way she did with Cary. But watch for that reaction, just in case the little one is in a hurry. With gods, it is always hard to predict."

Cary and Elizabeth both chuckled at that. Frank looked less pleased.

"How do you feel?" he asked his wife.

Her smile positively glowed. "Wonderful. I love this feeling. Maybe we could have one more after this?"

At the slight panic in his expression, Elizabeth took pity and patted his cheek. "Okay, we'll put that discussion to the side until after we get through the birth of this baby."

"Yes, please," he said, still looking like he might pass out from worry.

Cary tucked in her lips to keep from laughing. The feel of Deacon's hand covering her own stomach startled her and she glanced down. The baby bump was gone as if it had never been there. Her stomach was back to its usual shape, a lot smaller, but with a little extra space for pizza. The stretchy fabric addition of her maternity pants fell loosely across her abdomen. She put her hand over Deacon's.

"How do you feel?" he murmured in her ear.

"Weird," she said. "Like myself. Like my body belongs to me again and is mine. But also…weird. It's hard to explain."

"Bad?"

"No. Not bad. Which I suppose is a little surprising. I feel like I might cry for no reason, but that doesn't feel any different to PMS."

"Your hormones will need some time to return to normal," Elizabeth said. "So you probably will be more emotional than normal."

Cary chuckled and glanced up at Deacon. "You're in for a fun ride this week."

He smiled and his hand on her stomach flexed. "I think I can handle it."

"Do you feel any lingering emotional trauma?" Liruk asked.

The question startled Cary. "Should I?"

"It was always a risk," she said softly. "Carrying offspring can be emotional, even if you do not keep them."

Cary leaned into Deacon to consider that. She'd never thought of the baby god as hers, so maybe that was why there weren't any emotional hits. She felt a little sad to see the baby god go. But in the same way she felt when she said goodbye to a charge she'd been protecting for longer than a few minutes. She supposed this would all feel different if she'd been in a place to want kids or been trying to have kids. Since she was not in that place, she really just felt…like herself again.

"I think I'm okay," she said, trying to be honest with Liruk because Liruk was so rarely compassionate it seemed important to respect her concern. "This all feels right."

And once Elizabeth and Frank left, she'd discuss why she was also a little relieved to have the baby god residing in a more appropriate surrogate—no matter what the god parents said, sharing god powers couldn't have been good for either the baby god *or* Cary.

She got up from the couch, startled when she realized she could move normally again and didn't have to do any strange contortions to accommodate her stomach. She blinked down at the couch. Well that was weird. Almost as if nothing had happened or changed in the last week. But some of the adjustments she'd had to make while protecting the baby god, not having to do them anymore was going to take a little time to settle in.

She folded the stretchy material at the waist of her pants over a few times to keep the extra bulk in place and out of the way. She'd have to go change soon, back to her normal jeans. And she was going to need an appointment with her gynecologist to replace her IUD. She wondered how she was going to explain that.

But hey! Caffeinated coffee again. That was a really good thing.

The dogs came inside from the backyard and Buck bumped his head against her hand. She smiled and gave him a scratch behind the ears. Fred sat with a great deal of enthusiasm, his tail wagging. And Pickles let out a soft woof before sitting next to her.

As Cary leaned over to give Pickles a scratch under the chin, Buck turned toward the still unconscious Mrs. Benson. He vibrated as he stared at the woman, and Cary gave him a little nudge, trying to redirect his attention. At least he wasn't staring at Jaxer, but she wasn't sure she liked that he'd taken such an interest in Mrs. Benson either. He didn't move close to the woman, but he did lift his nose and sniff the air. His quiet growl made the hair on Cary's arms lift.

"Buck," she murmured under her breath. A warning and a question. "Sit."

After hesitating a moment, he sat, giving the impression of being a normal dog, which was good given they had company.

When she was sure none of her dogs—including Fred who looked like he really wanted to jump on someone for attention—were going to cause any issues, she faced her guests.

"You're sure you're okay with all this?" Cary asked Elizabeth. It was an unnecessary question. Elizabeth was glowing. Cary had definitely not felt that way while tossing up her cookies right after the baby god had been moved into her.

"Of course," Elizabeth said. "She's very active. I won't have the fun of being pregnant for long this time it seems, but we'll enjoy it while we can. Right, little one?" This last she directed to her stomach.

Cary shook her head. She'd never meet anyone who actually enjoyed being pregnant this much. Not that Cary considered herself an expert on the subject, but still…

To Frank, she said, "As far as the Polrom are concerned, do you want my help with them? Is there anything I can do?" She dipped her head to Elizabeth, who was looking at her stomach and cooing at the baby, not looking at her husband or Cary. "Need an extra Protector hand?"

"You cannot leave your territory," Wisat said quietly. "Not this year."

"I've done it once already," she said. "I think we can safely say my test year isn't going to be a normal test year."

Wisat and Liruk exchanged a look.

Cary ignored them.

Frank said, "We should be fine. The house is safe for her and the kids. I'll be with them all the time when they leave."

"Kids in school?" Cary asked. She'd had to protect a kid while he was still in school and that had been…interesting.

"We homeschool them," Frank said. "We tried the public schools but…things happened. This is safer. They have some group classes and friends for socializing. We'll just cut back on a few things for the next couple of months."

Cary hadn't thought much about it since the night she'd first met Frank—she'd had a few other things on her mind since then—but she again wondered how he managed to have kids and do his job. How he kept his enemies from using his kids to get to him. She supposed his comment answered some of those questions.

"He keeps forgetting I can keep the kids safe even when he's not around," Elizabeth said. "Homeschooling is convenient and flexible for us, which is important. But I could have arranged their safety in a public school."

Cary wanted to frown. It was as if Elizabeth had been reading her mind.

"Not every Protector is lucky enough to have a witch for a partner," Frank murmured, and kissed her cheek. Elizabeth smiled and patted his cheek in return.

It was all very comfortable and loving and partnership-y, and it made Cary smile. But her gut started to worry at something, something that had nothing to do with their current bad guy issues or the impending birth of a new little god. Something she'd have to think about later when there were less people in her house and her hormones had settled down again.

"Thank you for everything," Frank said, shaking Cary's hand.

The gesture felt strangely formal. "Thank you for helping fend off the vampires from my friend's house."

He shrugged. "It's what we do."

She let out a snort. "One day you and I will talk more about this job. I want to know if it's just me, or do all Protector's end up with bad guy enemies building up all around them, wanting to kill them. Like Master vampires and crazed wizards and stuff."

"Yeah." Frank narrowed his gaze. "I think we probably should talk."

Liruk made a throat clearing sound. Cary and Frank both ignored her.

"Anyway, if you need my help, I'll be there," Cary said. "I don't know where there is." She grinned. "But just send one of those handy teleportation doors for me, and I'll be there to lend an extra Protector hand. Or, you know, you could call."

"You got a piece of paper?"

She dug up a couple of sticky notes from her bill paying desk and they jotted down cellphone numbers.

Handing his to her, he smiled. "Thanks. Again."

He tucked Cary's number into his pants pocket, then set his hand to Elizabeth's lower back as he led her a few feet away from everyone else. He opened the black rectangular door in a space just in front of Cary's house door, which made it look like he was just leaving the house and it had gotten dark outside. He returned to lift the still unconscious Mrs. Benson into his arms before rejoining his wife at the black door. Buck stiffened under Cary's hand but didn't growl this time. She gave him a little head rub in thanks.

They remained silent as Frank, carrying Mrs. Benson, and Elizabeth stepped through the teleportation portal. Elizabeth turned to wave goodbye, and Cary noticed her stomach was glowing, just a little. Then the black rectangle collapsed into a pinpoint and winked out of existence.

"That is the coolest power," Cary said into the silence. "I always wanted teleportation as my superpower."

"Instead, you got an excess of bravery and compassion," Deacon said.

"Ha! I think I might use different words. Maybe idiocy and stubbornness?"

Jaxer chuckled from his place near the window. Cary flashed him a sour look, and he grinned in response.

Deacon pulled her into his arms, a welcome distraction, and held her gaze for a moment. "We have some things to talk about later, don't we? Personal, future-related things," he murmured.

"Yeah, I think we do. But it might be too early for that conversation."

"Maybe. Maybe not." He brushed his fingers over her cheek. "In the meantime…" He glanced back at the Nags. "I think there's more to discuss right now."

"Like how did you guys *not* know I could absorb magic," Cary said, also facing her bosses. "Aren't you as old as the continents? Shouldn't you have figured this out?"

Before Liruk or Wisat could answer, Cary's doorbell rang. She frowned, then remembered Angie was coming over. She glanced at the clock on her fireplace mantel as she headed toward the door. Angie was more than an hour late.

"Why are you late? Was there any trouble?" Cary asked as she opened the door.

"You're not pregnant anymore, I see," Angie greeted.

"Long story," Cary said. "Why are you late?"

"Client didn't want to finish and paid for an extra hour." She stepped inside. "I like the money, but she really should just go to a therapist. Anyway, I'd rather discuss your long story." She noted all the visitors, and then looked at Cary again. "I have a feeling this conversation might take a while."

Cary closed the door with a sigh. "You might as well have a seat." She gestured to the place where Mrs. Benson had so recently been unconscious. "Do I have some stuff to tell you."

Angie chuckled and sat. Almost as soon as she touched the fabric, though, she launched up and spun around, frowning down at the chair.

"What the hell?" She looked at Cary, her eyes wide. "Why did you have a demon here?"

"Demon?" Cary shook her head. "No. That was where Mrs. Benson sat and she channeled the baby god's parents so we could talk to them." Cary widened her eyes. "I was talking to a god," she said in a hushed voice. "That was really weird."

To be fair, she had talked to a demon god before, but talking to a non-demon god had felt very different. Mostly because this god wasn't trying to kill her.

"Your Mrs. Benson must be channeling more than just gods," Angie said. She was staring at the chair as if it might bite. "I got a definite flash of demon laughter and the scent of sulfur."

Cary edged Angie away from the chair, holding her arm as she dropped onto the couch. "You're sure you're not just picking up the god and getting it mixed up with a demon?"

Angie was psychic, as well as being a witch, and picked up many of her visions from touch. She could touch someone or something and see, sometimes feel and smell, events from the past. Her clients came to her for future predictions, and she was good at that too—good enough that she'd just finished paying the mortgage off on her house last month from the money she earned from her private psychic readings business; they'd had a party to celebrate—but when she touched things, she often *knew*, in an instant, events that had already happened.

Fortunately, Angie had learned a long time ago how to control that particular gift, or she'd never be able to touch anything. She only occasionally got visions she didn't anticipate now, the skill flaring up unexpectedly. But according to Angie, those accidental readings were rare.

"I'm sure that wasn't a god I just picked up," Angie said. "Because I got a sense of the gods, too. But the sense of the demon, the laughter. That was stronger. More recent."

"No." Cary shook her head. "Literally, the god, or gods—I was never really certain—was talking to the baby. Mrs. Benson passed out from channeling the gods. And we moved baby god to her new surrogate. There was no time in there for Mrs. Benson to channel a demon."

"Unless it entered while she was unconscious," Angie said.

"That can happen?" She faced the Nags. "Could that happen? Would you know?" She looked at Deacon. "Did you smell anything? You can smell demons in human form, did you pick up anything?"

He shook his head. "I could smell the god when it was here. Kind of. It's hard to describe, like smelling energy more than a scent. But I was distracted by your scent and the baby god being moved once Mrs. Benson was unconscious." He sighed. "All my senses were focused on you during that period. I didn't notice anything else."

Cary's heartbeat hammered. What the hell? She glanced down at her dog pack. And suddenly Buck's reaction to Mrs. Benson while she was unconscious made more sense.

She turned to Jaxer, growing frantic. He had pushed away from the wall, looking as worried as Cary felt. "Are Frank and Elizabeth in trouble?"

Liruk and Wisat both winked out of her living room without a word. Cary cursed. She assumed they were going to check on Frank and his family, but without telling her, she was left to guess. Sonofabitch. She didn't even know where to find Frank right now.

"Can you get to them?" she asked Jaxer.

He shook his head. "I wasn't Frank's mentor. I know he lives in Austin, but I have no idea where. I'm not invited to his home."

"What?" Angie asked.

"What does that mean?" Deacon said at the same time.

Another pulse of adrenaline raced into Cary's bloodstream. She glared at Jaxer who had the grace to look annoyed with himself.

Cary waved away his comment. "We'll worry about that later." She dug into a pocket for her cellphone, realized she'd left it in her bedroom, and hurried to get it. She might not know where he lived, but she did have Frank's phone number now.

By the time she got back to the living room, Wisat had returned. "They are not at Frank's home. His mother is looking after their kids and said he and Elizabeth are out on a date." Wisat's worry was palpable.

"Not home? Shit. Where are they?"

"Liruk is attempting to obtain a location now," Wisat said.

"You have something of Frank's here?" Angie said. "I could try scrying. It won't work if they're too far away. Or not in this realm. But I could try."

Cary looked around the room. Frank hadn't left anything behind that she could see. She hunted on the couch, but there was nothing from Elizabeth either. She pulled the sticky note that Frank had written his cell number on and after entering the number in her phone handed the note to Angie.

"This wasn't his, but he held it and wrote the number on it. Maybe that will help?"

Angie frowned but took the note. "Give me a few minutes. I have what I need in the trunk of my car."

Cary rang Frank's number while Angie was gone but wasn't hopeful. It went to voicemail. She looked at Deacon. "This feels really really bad."

He rubbed her shoulder but didn't comment. The first hint of a golden glow lit his eyes though, his animal side rising to the surface to face a threat.

Her every instinct screamed at her to hurry to Frank and Elizabeth and the baby god, to protect them, but without knowing where they were she couldn't do anything. She hated waiting. She wasn't good at it.

"I will go help Liruk," Wisat said. "If we uncover their location, we will let you know immediately, Protector. And if you discover them before we do, don't wait on us."

Cary nodded as Wisat vanished. She turned to Jaxer. "Any ideas? His cellphone is going to voicemail. And Angie is good, but a note Frank touched isn't going to be as useful for scrying as something he actually possessed."

Jaxer frowned. "If a demon snuck in after the god, if a demon has been using Mrs. Benson while she's unconscious, that could be the demon directing Polrom to kill the baby. It could be how they've known where to find the surrogates, how to find you. Frank would have talked with the god through Mrs. Benson. Maybe explained moving the baby to you."

"But Mrs. Benson said she doesn't hear or know what's said in those conversations unless the god wants her to. How would the demon overhear? Can she channel more than one entity at once? And if so, wouldn't a *god* have known a demon out to kill their baby was sharing the same human conduit?"

"If the demon comes in after Mrs. Benson is unconscious, it's possible Frank has let things slip aloud, thinking no one else was listening."

"Shit." Cary pressed a hand to her stomach, an unconscious gesture she'd been doing a lot since taking on the role of surrogate. When her hand came down on her normal stomach and not the baby bump, her sense of dread climbed. "Do you think Mrs. Benson knows any of this? Would she be…in on the demon's plot?"

"Impossible to know," Jaxer said. "We'll have to ask her."

He didn't say the "if we find them" part of that sentence, but Cary heard it anyway. The tension tightening her gut ratcheted up another level.

Angie came in and shook her head. "Nothing," she said. "Either this isn't enough to link to Frank, they're not in this realm, or they're just too far away. He teleports. They could be anywhere on the planet."

Cary started cursing again.

"It's a demon whose likely responsible," Angie said. "Let me make a few calls. I might turn up something."

"Aiden?" Aiden was a demon hunter, a legendary one who pretty much lived up to the legend part, who'd helped Cary fight the demon god a few months back. Angie had introduced them.

"She's in France right now," Angie said. "But I know a few other hunters. Let me see what I can find out."

"One day, I'd love to hear about this demon past of yours," Cary said.

"I doubt that very much," she said with a sigh and moved away to make her calls.

With adrenaline surging through her blood and no plan of attack to help her use it, Cary started pacing, nibbling at a fingernail. She was really not good at waiting. She'd been horrible at hide-and-seek as a kid. She used to get too tense and just come running out shouting, "Here I am!" after about five minutes of trying to hide.

To her relief, neither Deacon nor Jaxer tried to get her to calm down or sit down. She might have taken their heads off if they'd tried.

Jaxer seemed to be deep in his own thoughts, a frown creasing his normally smooth brow. Deacon stood to one side of the couch, gently rubbing Buck's head. The Labrador had tucked up next to Deacon's leg and pressed in for a scratch.

A new worry hit her. "How does he feel?" she asked Deacon. "Is he warm? Like he got when the demon god was giving us trouble?" It had been the first time in Buck's life that his demon dog nature really came out. He was about that age, but it had, nevertheless scared the hell out of her. Not for herself but for Buck. She didn't want him to go through that again until he was ready.

"He feels normal," Deacon said. He squatted down to put his face near Buck's. "Any problems, boy?"

Buck nudged his nose against Deacon's cheek in answer.

Cary let out a long breath. "Oh good."

Buck had been face-to-face with a demon prior to the demon god incident—when they'd encountered the demon god's son Oliver

Holland, in a park of all places. That confrontation hadn't brought out Buck's alter ego. Only the god had.

Which meant whatever demon had been here wasn't an actual demon god.

"Oh, that's really good," she said. When Deacon looked a question at her, she said, "This is likely just an ordinary demon causing trouble, not a god of some kind. Buck only reacted when the god came to town."

"One less thing to worry about then," Deacon said. "Sort of."

She snorted. "Yeah."

Even an ordinary demon was a disaster of epic proportions. And since Frank, Elizabeth, and baby god's lives were in danger, the level of the demon responsible was only a side detail.

"Any news?" Cary mouthed to Angie when she turned to face the living room.

Angie shook her head.

"Where the hell are the Nags?" Cary asked Jaxer.

He blinked to refocus on his surroundings. "They work in premonitions. It's not any more consistent than Angie's scrying."

"But don't they have some way of tracking us Protectors? They always seem to find me, no matter where I am." And drop in at some really irritating moments, too. Almost like they'd timed those moments to annoy her the most.

"They do. Because they can follow the powers they've given you to channel. Frank's powers will be in full shield mode at the moment. It's a matter of time before they find them. The demon will only be able to hide them from Liruk and Wisat for so long."

Cary looked back at the clock on her mantel. It had only been about a half hour or so since Angie had declared a demon had been here. Not much time at all really. Cary's anxiety swore at least four hours had passed, though.

Remembering Frank was a Protector, and that he'd be keeping Elizabeth and the baby god safe right now, helped Cary's panic a little. No matter where they were in this realm, he'd be channeling the Nags' powers. And even a demon couldn't get through that with Elizabeth and the baby god under threat.

So, they hadn't been killed yet. And probably taking them into another realm would be tricky with a baby god in tow. Right? Maybe. It was something to hope for anyway.

They had time. She had time to find them and reach them and help. They were still alive and she would reach them in time.

She kept repeating that mantra as she paced and bit at her now non-existent nail.

After the fourth time the maternity pants slipped and turned, she cursed and went to her bedroom to change. It felt weird buttoning up her old jeans, being able to button them easily. Baby god wasn't safely tucked into her womb anymore.

And the people protecting her were missing.

She returned to pacing in the living room, her gaze darting to the clock as time ticked by with no word.

When her cellphone rang, she nearly jumped out of her skin. Fumbling for it, she checked the number. Damn. Not Frank.

"Marianne," she answered. "What's up? We have a little crisis here, so…"

"Got a little one here too," Marianne said. "Sort of. I have a vampire just outside my shop and he's refusing to leave until I call you."

"Not these guys right now." Cary snarled. "They have to stop pestering my friends or Gabriel and I are gonna have serious words. Did the vampire give you a name?"

"James. And he's dressed slick enough that he's not an insult to my shop. But still, he's hovering and it makes some of my customers nervous. It's also distracting a few of them in other ways that might be dangerous to them."

"I bet. He's not trying to come inside, is he?"

"He's been disinvited, so he can't."

"You're so smart."

"Yes, I am. What do you want to do about him? You have a crisis of your own?"

"Fellow Protector and the baby god are missing. Likely a demon involved. Waiting to find out where they are so I can ride in and rescue everyone." Not that she knew how she'd do that. Plans weren't her strong suit. But she fully intended to do…something.

"Yup, a crisis," Marianne said. "Not carrying the baby anymore, huh?"

"I'll explain when we can sit down and talk. You want me to come shoo the vampire away?"

"He's listening to me right now. I'm standing in my doorway. I can tell you what he wants if he's willing to speak more now."

Marianne sounded annoyed, which didn't bode well for James.

Cary couldn't hear James's response without vampire or shifter hearing—which kind of sucked in her job, being at that disadvantage.

Then Marianne said, "He says Gabriel has something to show you, and if you don't come to—" a pause, "—the barn? The barn, whatever the hell that means, at eight o'clock tonight, your friends will die." Marianne hissed. "If he's talking about Angie or Lucy, I'm gonna stab him through the heart with a needle before meeting you at this barn, wherever the hell that is."

Cary grinned. "I'm looking at Angie. She's safe. You're safe?"

Marianne snorted. "I've been fending off worse things than vampires for years."

"Yeah you have," Cary said, thinking of Marianne's run-ins with the goblin king. "Ask him if he's talking about Lucy. Although if he is, he might lie cause you just threatened to stab him with a needle."

"He says it's not about Lucy, and he's not afraid of a needle."

"He doesn't know about your needles, does he? Probably for the best. So Lucy's safe. I would have heard if it was one of the leopards. Who the hell is he talking about?"

There was another pause. Then Marianne said, "He says it's your baby."

"What?" Cary gasped. Deacon took a step closer. "He said to go to the barn, right?"

"He's gone," Marianne said with a curse. "Walked away after

saying that last part. Even in full daylight, those damned vampires move weirdly fast."

"Thanks for passing on the message," Cary said as the panic already rushing through her blood threatened to choke her. "Stay safe."

"You need my help."

"I'll call if I do. Thanks." She hung up. For Angie's sake since she hadn't heard the conversation the way Deacon had—and probably Jaxer, although Cary had never been sure if he had super hearing or not because he never admitted to it—she said, "Gabriel wants to see me at eight tonight or he claims a friend will die. His messenger says it's to do with the baby god. I don't know if they're lying to get me to their lair."

"I'm coming with you," Angie said.

"No, this isn't your fight. And there's a demon somewhere in all this. I might not know the backstory, but I know you avoid anything to do with demons."

She shrugged. "Can't run forever. And if I have to get dragged back, it might as well be for a friend and a baby god."

"No," Cary said. "You've done what you can. If this was witch work, there's no one I'd trust more. But I don't want you getting involved in something you don't want to be in. You can wait here and tell the Nags where we went if they don't show up before we leave. This is my job, not yours."

"I love you, too," Angie said. "And I'm coming with you."

Cary opened her mouth to protest more, then realized she didn't have time. She glanced at the clock. They had a few hours until the rendezvous, but she wanted to be there before sunset, not after when the vampires reached full strength.

She faced Deacon. "Can you drive? I might crash a car right now."

"I'll meet you there," Jaxer said.

"Thanks."

"He gets a thanks and I get protests?" Angie said.

"I love you more," Cary said.

Jaxer made a face before walking out the door.

"I need to swing home and pick up a few things," Angie said. "Where are we going?"

"Vampire hive," Cary said.

"Same place it's been since Ariel?"

"Same place."

"I'll meet you there." Angie waved on her way out.

Cary looked down at her dogs. "You guys good while we go save the day?" She was most concerned with Buck after having inadvertently exposed him to a demon.

But he just laid down under the window and rested his head on his forepaws, looking up at her with content brown eyes. Pickles flopped down next to him. Fred barked before charging around in a tight circle until he was satisfied with his spot, then he also laid down and closed his eyes.

At least someone was safe.

Panic and worry churning in her gut as she climbed into Deacon's SUV.

If this was a trick, if the vampires were luring her away from Frank, Elizabeth, and the baby god, she was gonna be really pissed.

29

They reached the vampires' lair as the sun dipped behind the trees. There was still plenty of light, but Cary could feel the night closing in, the progression of time in the cooling air and deepening shadows. The sense of approaching darkness settled in her bones, an awareness that the vampires would be rising sooner rather than later.

The farmhouse looked as ordinary as always. No signs of either the vampires or Frank, Elizabeth, and the baby god. No James to greet them.

Behind the farmhouse, the old red barn with its peeked roof and huge sliding doors also seemed deserted.

James's message specified the barn. Not the farmhouse.

She waited at Deacon's car until Angie pulled up fifteen minutes later, slipping her Marianne-made courier bag over her head as she joined Cary and Deacon.

Then Cary started across the rough, rocky dirt path that led back to the barn. A breeze carried through the trees, heavy with new growth, pine, and the damp scent of earth. Cary pulled the lapels of her leather jacket closed, zipping it up to keep out the breeze. Her fingers brushed against her necklace.

Jasmine had told her to wear the Fatima Hand with the fingers pointing up for good luck. But she could also turn the fingers to point downward to ward off the evil eye. As Cary looked up at the huge sliding oak doors of the barn, she debated which she needed more right now—good luck or defense against evil eyes.

Given her situation, she decided she needed all the good luck she could get.

Jaxer came out of the woods as they reached the barn, joining her, Angie, and Deacon.

"No one's loitering in the trees," he said, glancing at the barn door. "Are we supposed to go in?"

"Yeah, that doesn't seem like a wise idea, does it?" Cary said, thinking of being trapped inside with vampires. She supposed it couldn't be worse than being trapped with vampires deep underground with no back door out. "But we have to find out if Gabriel was bluffing or not. Any word from the Nags before you got here?"

"Not yet. They say the traces they're getting are contradictory."

"Meaning?"

"They'll pick up the link to Frank's Protector magic, and then lose it, and then it will seem he's in a different place, and then that's blocked."

"Is he teleporting?"

"They can't tell."

"So this might all be a ruse, with the vampires." She looked up at the barn again. "If Gabriel lied to get me here, we aren't going to have a very friendly relationship going forward."

"Liruk and Wisat are still looking," Jaxer said, moving to stand just behind her left shoulder. "If this is a trick, we have time to deal with it and get out."

She nodded. "Okay. Everyone stay behind me. I might not have baby god invincibility now, but there's no way we walked into a vampire lair without them being a threat to any of you, so we should be good." She glanced back at Angie. "You still sure you want to do this?"

"I've got your back, hon. This isn't my first rodeo, you know. I've been playing in this world longer than you."

"Doesn't mean I want you hurt helping me," Cary said.

Angie had come to her rescue more than once. In fact, Angie was a lot better suited to arriving in and saving the day than Cary, being a powerful witch who had actual offensive magic to fight bad guys with and all. Cary was just the shield here. Everyone else had skills for fighting and destroying vampires—strength and speed and magic and…all the stuff Cary didn't actually possess.

But Cary felt responsible for them all. They were here because of her. Because of Gabriel's interest in her thanks to the stupid wizard who was trying to kill her. She needed at least one of them here for her powers to even work. But she wasn't happy about it. If any of them got hurt, Cary would never forgive herself.

"Is that why you rarely call me or Marianne in for backup?" Angie asked idly as a figure moved from the woods.

Jaxer cursed. "He wasn't there a minute ago."

James sauntered toward them, taking his time instead of moving at rapid vampire speeds and just appearing before them. Cary had to wonder about that. She could do without the show and the tension, but you couldn't get away from drama with vampires.

"Yes," Cary answered Angie's question while they watched James. "Marianne doesn't want to fight these battles. She just wants to run her shop. And I do call you when it's magic, but I don't want to keep dragging you into things that aren't your job."

James stopped in front of Cary and smiled. "I wasn't sure you'd take the bait."

"Of course you were. That's why you waited until I was on the phone before dropping the baby comment." She leaned her face in close to James. A move that caused the vampire to raise a brow. "But if you lied to me, James, I will kill you. Despite the damage to that pretty suit."

She'd never killed a vampire on purpose before. Accidentally… It happened. On purpose, not so much. But James didn't know that—at least, he didn't know that the previous times had been on accident. For all he knew, she was good at killing vampires, she was just very restrained.

The idea of that almost made her snort in amusement.

"You've met Mrs. Benson?" James said and he stepped aside.

Mrs. Benson. No longer unconscious, standing in her elegant suit with her elegant posture, her elegant hands folded together in front of her. She was smiling, her muted lipstick in place.

Cary straightened, swallowing her gasp. How had none of them noticed her there? Or maybe Deacon had with his super shifter smelling. But James's and Mrs. Benson's trick had worked on Cary. Her heartbeat thudded hard in her chest, and a panic of adrenaline raced into her blood.

"Mrs. Benson," she greeted. "Or should I call you by the name of the demon currently moving around in Mrs. Benson's body?"

The smile on Mrs. Benson's face stretched. The voice that emerged was deep and echo-y, like the god's had been, but closer and rockier. Like literal rocks rolling over rocks. "How did you know?" it asked.

Cary shrugged. "I have talented friends. Why and what do you want?" No point in prevaricating. "And where's Frank and Elizabeth?"

"Safe for now."

At least the stupid demon answered the most pressing question first.

"What I want..." The demon chuckled, the sound really strange coming from Mrs. Benson's mouth. It *almost* fit. *Almost* seemed like the kind of chuckle you might hear from that face. Just with more echo involved.

That was really really weird.

"Does Mrs. Benson call you in on purpose or does she even know about you?" Cary asked. A distraction from her original "why and what" questions, but she wanted to know if she should be mad at Mrs. Benson or trying to save her.

"Humans in the woods," Deacon murmured close to her ear. "Behind the barn. And vampires are in the barn now."

"Thanks," she whispered back. It was good to have a boyfriend with super senses.

"This body is a very good channel," the voice coming from Mrs. Benson said. "Once I can fully take over, I will enjoy staying here."

Well, that wasn't good.

She had no idea if the demon was even able to stay with Mrs. Benson permanently. Cary didn't know much about mediums who could channel gods and demons. Up to this point, she'd only ever read about mediums who channeled ghosts, and since ghosts terrified her, she'd avoided mediums and the subject of them as much as possible.

Over her shoulder, she whispered to Angie, "Can it do that?"

While she might not know much about mediums, she did know that a demon possessing a human host was a lot more difficult than people thought. Even if they managed it—and that took time and prepping the human host through magic and sacrifices—the human couldn't survive having a demon occupy their body for long. The more powerful the demon, the faster the host died. And once the host died, the demon was tossed back into its own realm.

Most demons just tried to outwit the humans who summoned them in order to escape into this realm. It cost them some of their power to do it that way—possessing a human host didn't have that drawback— but it gave them a lot more time in this realm.

All that was with an ordinary human host, though. Would a medium who channeled them from their realm be the same?

"Depends," Angie said.

"On?"

"The bargain it's made with her. How much power it has to start. How well prepared the human host is—and since she's a medium who can channel things as strong as gods, she's likely to survive this longer than an ordinary human. How long it's prepared her for the full possession." She paused before saying, "And the power of the final sacrifice it makes."

"Shit." A baby god would make a hell of a powerful sacrifice.

"It might even be able to remain here after the host dies if the sacrifice is strong enough," Angie said quietly.

Cary glanced at the various humans starting to stumble out of the trees. They were all walking a little funny. Focused on her and her group, but tripping and uncertain on their feet. Drugged like the ones who'd attacked her and Deacon? Or something else?

Shit again. She had a lot of people to protect now, and she still didn't know where some of them were.

The sun was setting, the shadows growing longer. Cary, even with her human senses, could hear the vampires inside the barn now. Gabriel probably wouldn't make an appearance while the sun was up —couldn't be seen in a weakened state; even if weakened for a Master wasn't what anyone generally thought of as "weak"—but that wouldn't stop the others from peeking their heads out and causing trouble.

She needed to find Frank and Elizabeth. Soon.

"I am told you are a Protector like Frank," the demon in Mrs. Benson's body said.

"Were you?" Cary said, studying the approaching humans. They were lining up behind Mrs. Benson, and their eyes glittered. Not supernaturally. Their eyes were rounded and wide, their pupils dilated, and tears filled them, creating a shimmer.

Yeah, probably drugs.

"I am also told you can be killed," the demon said.

"Really?" she said. "That's very interesting."

James had moved away from the demon, to the barn doors. She still wasn't sure what to make of him—ally or enemy—but she was inclined to put him into the enemy category just to be safe. Warning her that Gabriel wanted to use her as a pet wasn't the same thing as being an ally. He'd shown up when Petra had come after her and just stood there watching. So yeah, probably not a friend.

"Gonna answer my earlier question?" she asked the demon, mostly to keep it talking. She didn't expect it to tell her where Frank and Elizabeth were just yet.

She'd edged out ahead of her group so she could keep them safe, but she could hear Angie murmuring something behind her, a spell of some kind in one of the languages Cary didn't know because she sucked at languages. Not Latin. That much at least she was sure of.

Mrs. Benson lifted a finger and one of the human women standing next to her raised a hand and threw a knife at Angie, the move so fast

Cary didn't realize the woman had thrown a knife until she saw it hovering in the air to her left and about a foot in front of her. After hovering for a second, the knife dropped with a dull thud to the rocky earth, settling into the sparse grass.

"You have a powerful shield, witch," the demon said to Angie.

"Yup," Angie said, without missing a beat. She went back to murmuring.

Cary raised her brows. Did the demon *not* know that had been Cary's Protector shield? The demon said it knew what Protectors were. It couldn't have really understood, though, or it wouldn't have just tried to have Angie killed.

But also, yay for the fact that it had tried to kill Angie. Because that meant Cary's powers were working, these guys were a threat to her friends, and even if everyone here knew how to kill her, they couldn't because they'd likely also try to kill the people she was protecting.

Protector magic was tricky that way. Thankfully.

Also, whatever it was Angie was doing was enough to distract the demon—enough it tried to kill her. That had to be a good thing, too, right?

"You're not a god, are you?" Cary asked the demon. The line from *Ghostbusters* ran through her head, about if you got asked if you were a god, you should always say yes, but she was pretty sure demons from other realms didn't watch human movies. Even if they got channeled through a human medium.

"What do you know of gods, human?" the demon said.

"Just that I've already sent a demon god packing so, you know, an ordinary demon isn't all that impressive to me."

Oh boy. That might have been a step too far. Especially since it wasn't *precisely* true.

She knew she really shouldn't irritate the demon. That was like poking a dragon and expecting not to get burned. But it was her only real skill—distraction and irritation so the bad guy did something stupid that she and her friends could take advantage of to send it away.

She was kind of counting on Angie's ability to deal with the demon while she kept the demon from killing anybody. Deacon's skills laying in fighting and right now they weren't fighting, although with the vampires waiting around just inside the barn, a fight was probably inevitable.

Jaxer... Well, he could make people see what he wanted, so there was no telling what he was doing to the humans right now. She noticed a few of the ones not standing right next to the demon had started staring at something in the air, little smiles overtaking their mouths as they batted playfully at the unseen something.

Cary wanted to laugh at that. But she kept her expression serious. No point in giving away the glamour. So to speak. Mostly because once you knew there was a glamour spell at work, it was easier to see through. Maybe not Jaxer's glamour, but most Fae glamour came with that weakness.

The demon stepped closer to Cary, coming within a foot before her shield stopped further progress. It studied the air just in front of it.

And for the first time, Cary noticed the red glow in the depths of Mrs. Benson's dark eyes. Not the same as when the god had been there. But definitely not Mrs. Benson's eyes now either. The glow sort of reminded Cary of what happened to long time demon hunters. All that exposure to demons meant they ended up with the red glow, too.

The demon lifted Mrs. Benson's hand, running it over Cary's shield. Her skin sizzled, and Cary wince.

"Strong," the demon murmured. It met Cary's eyes. "Yours. Not the witch's."

Cary met the demon's gaze without answering.

"Not impossible to breech," the demon said.

"If you say so. Frank and Elizabeth?"

"Will be here soon."

"You can teleport, too," Cary guessed, taking a swing in the dark.

She wasn't even sure how all this was working with the demon. It wasn't confined by a circle, the way most called demons were. It wasn't technically a free demon, as it was looking for permanent control of Mrs. Benson's body through a sacrifice. It might not even be *in* this realm right now, any more than baby god's parents had been. That didn't make it any less dangerous.

How did they kick the demon out of Mrs. Benson without hurting Mrs. Benson? What were the rules here?

She really shouldn't have skimmed over the stuff about mediums all these years.

"I'm drawn to others who can teleport," the demon said. "Like attracts like. It's rare in humans. But a handy skill, don't you think?"

"Definitely," Cary said in all seriousness. "I'm jealous. I always wanted to be able to teleport."

And that explained why her bosses couldn't locate Frank and Elizabeth. The demon had been moving them around.

Probably why Jaxer hadn't come across all these humans in the woods either. And why Mrs. Benson could show up behind James without any of them knowing she was there. All a lovely bit of magic trickery.

Cary might have applauded. But the sun dipped below the horizon in that moment, plunging the surroundings into darkness.

The barn doors opened, releasing the vampires.

30

A whirl of hissing, whistling movement surrounded Cary and her group, like a creature made storm dropping onto them. Not the same tight hurricane of the attack in front of Angie's house, but a storm of menace and hunger nonetheless.

Mrs. Benson was left inside the circle of vampires with Cary. Her demon's red glow gaze never left Cary's face.

Which was probably for the best. Cary needed to focus on something or she'd get dizzy trying to watch all the vampires. They were moving too fast to see and the blurs of color were disorienting.

A snap. And everything fell still and silent so suddenly Cary rocked back on her heels.

She finally looked away from the demon.

They were surrounded by vampires, at least thirty, maybe more. More than the night outside Angie's house anyway. Cary didn't turn to see the ones behind them. Deacon, Jaxer and Angie had all moved back to back with her so everyone had their own group to watch.

The ones Cary could see looked like glowing moons in the deepening darkness, their skin illuminated from within in a way she'd never seen above ground. She'd seen them do that deep in their lair, but not up here where they'd give themselves away too easily to uninitiated humans.

Obviously, the drugged up demon worshiping group didn't count?

The vampires' eyes glowed yellow, their pupils stretched into lines like cats. There wasn't any attempt to disguise their nature, nothing to tamp down the pure…vampireness of them. They were beautifully, dangerously grotesque. Some so skeletal she had to blink a few times to see their skin. Most of them had dropped the lure of a pretty face to reveal their true natures beneath. There was still beauty and attraction there, but it was a striking snake's beauty, an attacking shark's beauty.

Deadly and horrifying when those sharp sharp teeth snapped near your face.

And damn but there were a lot of them right now.

Vampires. Demon. Demon worshiping humans. A missing baby god, fellow Protector, and witch. And just Cary, Angie, Deacon, and Jaxer to do something about all this.

Oh boy.

The only thing they were missing was the wizard.

Cary did search the crowd for him. Or even Sheldon. But there was no sign of them. When Gabriel stepped from behind the circle of vampires just to the right of Mrs. Benson, it was the first thing Cary asked him.

"Where's your pet wizard with the big mouth?"

Gabriel's own mouth twitched. She couldn't tell if it was amusement or irritation, but there were some really pointy canines involved peeking out from between his lips.

To be fair, he'd put on an impressive show with the vampires storming out to surround them. And his entrance into the little standoff was probably supposed to be dramatic and impressive, too. She'd sort of robbed him of that by not being impressed.

"Not all of my pets were invited to this meeting," Gabriel said.

He'd put that lure into his tone, that seductive little come-hither sound that drew unwitting humans. He was very very good at it.

A little shiver danced down Cary's spine in acknowledgment of his skill. The sound, that deep resonant note of danger and sex, he hadn't bothered with that tone in the hive at their first meeting. He was working hard at the drama and magnetism tonight.

Shame it was wasted on her.

She did have to admire his effort, though. Especially since this was her first close look at him. He'd kept to the shadows in the hive, giving her only glimpses. She hadn't even really been able to tell what he was wearing during that meeting.

But out here, he glowed with otherworldly beauty.

Still austere and sleek, though, like his choice of decoration in the hive. Nothing like the flamboyance of the previous Master. His dark blond hair was pulled into a sleek low tail, which displayed the sharp cut of his high cheekbones and angular jaw. His black pants and button-down black shirt added to the brightness of his illuminated pale skin. His eyes glowed more gold than the usual jaundiced sort of yellow of the other vampires. And his pupils were round, almost human. The rubies glinting at his wrists cut through all the black, like drops of winking blood.

While a vampire dressed in black with some red accents was verging on cliché—James was sporting a black on black suit tonight with a red tie—all the vampires surrounding Gabriel were dress in extravagant costumes in white and red. Flowing material, baroque coats from different centuries, hoop skirts, and wigs in hairstyles that looked better suited to an eighteenth century French court. Their flamboyance set Gabriel off even more, allowing him to stand out among all that glitter behind him, a darkly stunning contrast to their grotesque beauty.

He left no question who was the Master here.

Mrs. Benson—or rather the demon in Mrs. Benson—glanced at Gabriel as he stepped up beside her. Gabriel didn't bother looking at the demon. All of the demon's human servants had been pushed back behind the vampires, as well. The demon stood alone inside the circle of menace without its own acolytes, not even the few who'd been standing right next to it.

Beyond the crush of vampires, Cary glimpsed the Polrom humans.

They were exchanging looks and shifting around as if they didn't quite know what to do now.

What was the balance between demon and Master vampire she wondered? Which was more powerful?

She'd seen a Master go to work for a demon once, but she didn't get that sort of relationship here. So...

Why were they working together? What was the plan here?

Angie was still murmuring quietly, almost beneath what Cary could hear. But the vampires would hear it.

Which meant Cary needed to do her irritating thing to keep everyone distracted.

"So, this is all pretty and impressive and everything, but what's the point? I mean, yes yes, all you lovely vampires look quite good in your costumes." She pointed at one impressively dressed male vampire and gave him a thumbs up. "Nice coat," she said. "But really, it's kind of wasted effort. And Gabriel, you know you look good. There's no objectively arguing with that. But since it's not having any of the effect on me or my group you might want it to, why bother?"

She flicked a glance at the demon. "And lowering yourself to work with a demon?" She tsked. "I mean, that's what Antonio did, getting mixed up with Oliver Holland. But I expected more from you, Gabriel."

Some of the vampires behind him growled and hissed. She could hear the rise in anger all around them. She smiled at Gabriel. There was a facial twitch around his lip that might have been a snarl if he weren't so controlled.

"I'm surprised at you, Cary," Gabriel said, his tone still pitched to lure and seduce. "Taunting us, when I know how to kill you now."

Already on first names. That was never good with these old creatures.

"I'm an enigma," she said. "Also, I know you'd rather have me as a pet. For the record, I would make a horrible pet. I will rip up your favorite shoes, and if push comes to shove, I will not hesitate to pee in your closet."

Jaxer laughed.

She glanced around. "Speaking of pets, where's Petra?"

"You're eager for me, Protector," Petra said in her hissing murmur, flowing out from behind Gabriel.

She draped herself over his shoulder, but her gaze remained on Cary. She'd also kept up the outer stunning countenance. Her face glowed softly but there was no skeletal grimace or too tight skin. She almost...almost looked human except with that kind of gorgeousness that rarely appeared in humans. Her dark hair hung in thick waves around her and her black eyes glowed without any hints of yellow. Her lips were full and red. Her outfit a concoction of white veils wrapped around her lush body in a way that looked like they might fall off at any minute.

The woman had gone out of her way to be as sexy and seductive as a woman could be. The effect of her and Gabriel standing together in one spot was a little overwhelming. Even for Cary.

She defaulted to smartass to cover her surprise. "Not particularly," she said. "Deacon's starting to get jealous."

Deacon grunted.

Petra smiled. "Shifter blood is electric. If I drain him dry, he won't be jealous anymore."

"Yeah, I think we'll pass. So... Where's my friends?"

"You are very concerned with the other Protector," the demon said, its first comment since Gabriel had arrived.

"Yup."

"Why?" the demon asked.

"Empathy and caring and all that. If you don't get it, I can't explain."

"You want to save the god?"

"Well, yeah. That's kind of my job."

"Why?"

"Why do I have a job? Puts food on the table. Keeps my dogs in treats."

"And you in coffee and pizza," Jaxer said sounding reasonable.

"True. True. Wouldn't like giving up coffee and pizza. A woman's gotta earn."

"Why do you want to save the god?" the demon said. There was a growl of impatience in its tone now. That tone suited Mrs. Benson's face. It was really weird how *well* the demon's voice fit in Mrs. Benson's mouth. "She will be a god. A god who will destroy you."

Cary narrowed her eyes. "You use that line with your acolytes, don't you? I'm not buying it. Why would I worry about baby god destroying me?"

"She is a god."

"Well, technically, not yet. Right now, she's just potential god. She's still gotta get born." Cary felt this point needed to be made.

"And once she is? She will destroy this world. It is what gods do."

"Is that what demon gods do?" Cary asked.

She was watching the vampires from the corner of her eyes. This conversation was a great distraction—and Angie was still murmuring away with no one paying her any attention thankfully—so Cary was trying to stretch it out. But she could see the vampires' subtle movements, almost like they were waving in the wind. Impatient seaweed, restlessly shifting in the breeze, and ready to feed.

Petra had eased forward, dropping her hold on Gabriel and standing so close that Cary's shield was making the vampire's skin glow red like it might catch fire at any moment. Petra ran her hands over the barrier, no doubt hunting for a way through. Her tongue flickered out, a snake tasting the air.

There was debate in the literature over whether vampires could actually do that, if they had a reptilian nature or a mammalian nature. After years of mostly trying to avoid them but still having to deal with them occasionally, Cary was inclined to think it depended entirely on the vampire.

Petra definitely had that reptilian thing going. Cary liked snakes in general. She liked all animals. But Petra's particular brand was pretty creepy.

"Gods always destroy," the demon answered Cary's question. "It is their role."

"Their role. They destroy." The demon's human acolytes, still stuck just outside the ring of vampires, started murmuring the chant. "They destroy. No hope. She will destroy us. Must kill her."

The sound was like nails on a chalkboard to Cary. She winced. "Anything you can do about them?" she murmured to Jaxer.

"The drugs are interfering," he said. "Whatever high they're on, it's more compelling than even my illusions."

"Poor dumb bastards," Cary said.

She needed to find a way to get the humans safe, but while they were drugged, they were kind of the enemy because they'd attack if she tried to protect them. She hated being in this position.

The vampires were ignoring the humans at least, which kind of surprised Cary. They were easy prey. Was that out of deference to the demon who controlled them or...?

Cary looked at Gabriel. "You're upholding the 'no feeding from unwilling victims' rule right now, aren't you?"

He tilted his head. "My laws are always obeyed."

"Huh." She nodded. "Well then. One less thing, right?"

He frowned a little. She loved confusing the bad guys.

"This feels a little like a Mexican standoff," Cary said. "Although, wait no, I think I'm using that wrong. I'd have to look it up. Maybe not since the vampires aren't trying to eat the demon people? Maybe just an ordinary standoff? I don't know. Anyway, where are my friends?"

The demon blinked Mrs. Benson's eyes. "The time of sacrifice is not arrived."

"Yeah, I'm not gonna let you sacrifice anyone, so we can set that aside. I'm here for my friends. Once I've collected them, we'll be on our way. Easy peasy. So... Bring them out." She nearly added please just to really annoy and confuse them all. But she thought that might be a little too far.

"You're very good at this," Jaxer murmured to her. "The irritating part."

She grinned. "Thanks! I've been practicing a lot over the last six years."

"Good job, protégé. I'm a very proud mentor right now."

She chuckled.

This exchange pulled a growl from the demon. And Gabriel's eyes flared more yellow.

Wow, she really was good at annoying bad guys.

Her heartbeat thumped a little harder as a jolt of fear she tried to ignore moved through her. It was always a risk, taking this much attention, making them even angrier than they already were. Angry was unpredictable. But it was also talkative and less cautious. Angry bad guys revealed things.

And the longer they talked, the better chance Cary had of getting out of these kinds of messes.

She was desperate to know what Angie was doing but didn't dare ask. And she really really wanted to see Frank and Elizabeth to know for sure they were okay. She had to keep reminding herself he was a Protector and she was witch. They would be safe-ish, even if they were being teleported around relentlessly.

Cary winced when Petra's hands caught on fire as she continued running them over Cary's barrier. "You know you really shouldn't do that," Cary pointed out the obvious.

"Pain is delicious, sweet one," Petra murmured. "Didn't you know that?"

"I'm not one to judge other people's kinks, Petra, but pain is not one of mine."

The flames had fully engulfed the vampire's hands now. Why the hell was she still doing that? Ouch.

"Your shields are very strong," Petra murmured.

"But not impenetrable," Gabriel said.

"Thanks for reminding everyone," Cary said, heavy on the sarcasm. "Listen, you really have to stop doing that," she said to Petra as the flames licked higher around her hands. "There's dry grass around here. You're going to start a fire."

Probably not, but still it was worth trying. She couldn't actually feel the vampires attempts at getting through her shield—which kind of surprised her; she usually got nauseas when a vampire that strong pushed at her shields this long—but the sight of flames crawling over Petra's now blackened skin was creeping her out.

Angie leaned in and whispered, "The area's enclosed. We can work now without the demon getting out. Demons and vampires in. Most of the humans outside the containment circle."

"Cool." And probably best for keeping the drugged humans safe. "Does that leave Frank and Elizabeth out?"

"Yup. It can't sacrifice them if it can't get to them."

"Ah! Good point. Okay." She looked at Mrs. Benson who was snarling at Angie. "Now what?"

"We need to send the demon back," Angie said.

"You know how?"

"I don't have the will for it," she said. "I have…complicated feelings that interfere."

Cary would really love to know what Angie kept hidden about her links to demons and demon hunters, but right now wasn't the time.

Most of the process for banishing demons—the candles and chants and offerings and such—that was all outer trappings that were only vaguely useful. Sending a demon back to its realm really required only one thing. Will. A will stronger than the demons.

Which, unfortunately, was a rare trait among humans. Otherwise, the world would be full of demon hunters, and no one would ever have to worry about demons.

Her one exposure to using her will against a demon—who'd been a god and really was probably just playing with her at that point—had taught Cary a valuable lesson.

She wasn't cut out to be a demon hunter.

So, now, they had a demon they had to banish with no demon hunters conveniently around. A demon who'd gotten into this realm, or was accessing it, in a way that Cary had never learned about. A Master vampire and his entire hive ready to break in and eat them. A bunch of drugged out humans ready to do the demon's bidding. And no sign of the good guys they were here to save because they were busy jumping around the world via the demon's teleportation powers.

On her side, she had a shapeshifter whose magic didn't work on any of these particular creatures, a faery whose greatest magic wasn't doing much through the drugs the humans had taken, and a pretty powerful witch whose unknown history with demons made her ability to help with the demon a little shaky.

They were all safely trapped inside a containment circle—except the humans—so that meant none of the seriously dangerous bad guys could get out—yay!—but also that Cary and her friends couldn't leave without breaking the circle.

And she had no idea how to rescue the good guys and get out of this mess without everyone getting killed.

Right. So.

Just another day at work.

he breeze shifted, rushing the stench of Petra's burning flesh into Cary's face. She tried not to gag, but wow, she wished Petra would stop testing the Protector shields. Beyond the vampire circle, the human acolytes continued chanting about gods destroying things. A sliver of moon rose above the barn's peaked roof, its faint glow paling next to all the vampires.

"How are you teleporting Frank and Elizabeth without actually being with them?" Cary asked the demon occupying Mrs. Benson. Out of curiosity but also so she could stall and hope some miracle answer to the standoff occurred to her.

She really was curious, though. She and Deacon had had to hold on to Frank to go through his teleporting doorway. And he'd been holding Mrs. Benson in his arms while Elizabeth had kept a hand on his shoulder when they'd left Cary's house. But there were different ways to teleport. Maybe the demon used something besides big black doorways.

"The other Protector's skills are quite rudimentary compared to mine," the demon said.

Which didn't answer her question.

"So, how do your powers work?" Cary asked with what she hoped sounded like patience.

She also wanted to know if the demon could still teleport while trapped inside a containment circle. But one thing at a time. If it couldn't, did that leave Frank and Elizabeth trapped in some sort of in between space? That would be bad. But then maybe Frank could take over and get them somewhere safe?

So many unknowns!

"This isn't a university, Cary," Gabriel said.

"I didn't ask you, did I?" She sighed. "Fine. Don't tell me how everything works. I'll look it up when I get home."

"I do not have to be present to enable teleportation," the demon said, smiling slightly.

"Was that a warning? Cause, you can't teleport me right now, you know."

The demon narrowed Mrs. Benson's eyes. There was a long pause.

And Cary realized it was trying to.

"I told you, that won't work right now," she said.

"I can teleport the other Protector, even as he protects his wife and new child." The demon sounded a little confused. "Why not you?"

Cary shrugged. "The containment circle maybe?"

Cary was more inclined to think it was because teleporting her would endanger her charges. Although, why the demon couldn't just send them all away...?

She frowned. "Hey, I just realized, you all got me here on purpose for some reason. Right? I mean, you didn't drag me here only to teleport me away while you ate my friends because you didn't know who'd be with me. You could have sacrificed the baby god without me being anywhere around. You didn't need the vampires." She straightened a little. "What are we doing here?"

"I'm here to recover your body once the demon is done with you," Gabriel said. "I intend to keep you."

"No," she said, pointing at him without looking away from the demon.

"The vampire knows how to kill you," the demon said. "You are a test."

"Ah," Cary said. Now she got it.

If the demon could kill her, or at least find a way through her shields, it would know how to kill Frank in order to get at Elizabeth and the baby god. Couldn't sacrifice the baby god if you couldn't get at them, and Frank's Protector magic would have started working the minute the baby god moved to his wife.

"How did you learn about the vampires?" she asked.

"Frank tells his wife everything. Sometimes, he tells her things after speaking to the new god's progenitors. When the medium is unconscious, I am here. I can listen. I have learned so so much."

Cary shook her head. "Well, that all kind of sucks, but at least I understand now. We're here to push at my shields until you find a weakness." She glanced at Petra and her burning hands. "That's not gonna work. I've fended off entire armies of bad guys, and no one's gotten through yet."

Well, okay, just that one army. But still. She'd survived and a lot of them hadn't. So there.

The demon lifted Mrs. Benson's lips in a snarl. How did that look right on the elegant face? That face shouldn't snarl. At least, the snarl should look awkward. It didn't.

"I will get through, and I will eat your bones," the demon said. "There will be nothing left for the vampires to drink."

"Demons say that kind of thing a lot," she said.

She glanced at Gabriel. He didn't react to the comment outwardly. Maybe he didn't care if she ended up demon food before he could turn her into one of his pets. Either way, he'd be rid of her interfering with his vampires.

She faced the demon again. "What's up with eating bones? Don't you get them stuck in your throats? Aren't you worried about choking? You never did tell me why you think the baby god will destroy our world."

The demon blinked. So did Gabriel. Cary raised her brows in innocent inquiry.

She was good at non sequiturs. She was hunting for information that might help, some way of finding Frank and Elizabeth, really any kind of answers or inspiration for getting out of this mess. The containment circle kept the bad guys in. Her shields kept them from hurting her or her friends. But none of that solved the fundamental issue of getting rid of a demon and rescuing her fellow Protector and his family.

Overhead, fireworks starting to go off. Cary heard some oohs and aahs from the crowd of humans. And even a few vampires glanced up at the display.

"That you, Jaxer?" she asked.

He chuckled. "Just having a bit of fun. You go back to irritating the bad guys."

"Fair enough." She focused on Mrs. Benson. "So, baby god, world destroyer, where's that idea come from? How does it make you feel?"

Lay down on my couch and tell me about your mother.

She wondered if Gabriel picked up on her tone and the humor in it. Probably not. He looked entirely too serious.

Petra's lower arms were black now, the fire crawling unnoticed over her skin. She hadn't pushed through Cary's shield, but she was leaning on it. The flames starting to dance around her hair. Her white veil dress had blackened too, some of the material flittering to the ground, still dangerously alight. Cary watched a small flame start in the grass, but Petra, whether consciously or not, stepped on the new flame with her bare foot, putting it out.

Cary winced. "Would you tell her to stop," she said to Gabriel, nodding at the burning vampire. "She's gonna kill herself. That has to hurt."

"It hurts deliciously, pet," Petra said through the flames.

"You need to seek some professional help. This isn't healthy." To Gabriel, Cary said, "You're going to let her kill herself? That's pretty rude."

He flicked a glance at Petra, shrugged. "She'll live or die at her own hand. She's disobeyed me by coming for you when the time was inappropriate. She'll get no leniency from me. Perhaps she wants to die to appease me."

Cary closed her eyes. "You're both using her to test my shields and find the weakness. If she dies, she dies. But since she wants me more than the others, you think she can get through."

When she opened her eyes, Gabriel was smiling at her as if she were a child who'd just learned a new word.

There wasn't a lot Cary could do about internal vampire politics, or even the way Gabriel punished his hive for disobedience. But she didn't appreciate being used as the method of punishment.

In fact, it made her feel like Gabriel was already using her as a pet, despite her best efforts.

"Petra," she snapped, "seriously, stop. The smell... Just... I can't with watching you burn yourself. It's gross."

The vampire smiled, the skin on her face starting to blister and peel. Her pointed canines stood out in a skeletal grimace. No longer the beauty she'd been at Gabriel's side, but neither did she share the grotesque beauty of the other vampires. She was like a nightmare, worse than a demon in its natural form.

Terrifying as she spoke through lips that were melting away.

"I will eat you. I will have you." She sang the words over and over, even as more of her skin blackened and burned.

Cary had never had someone purposefully kill themselves on her shields before. She'd had people *accidentally* kill themselves on her shield. But she'd never watched someone purposefully embrace the damage her shields caused them.

And it went against everything in Cary, letting the vampire do that. Especially since it was also a punishment from the Master.

Petra was a threat, or the shield wouldn't be burning her, but Cary's every instinct wanted to stop the vampire from doing this to herself. Even though she was dangerous and was chanting about eating Cary. Even though this was Gabriel and the demon's fault, not Cary's. Even though...

Sometimes her protective instincts were really screwed up.

She pointed at Gabriel. "I am not okay with being used as a way for you to punish your vampires. And you..." She faced the demon. "You can't get through my shield. Or Frank's. You need to return to your realm. Now. Because I'm not letting you kill the baby god."

To Cary's surprise, the demon took a step backward. It frowned and moved forward again, getting closer to Cary's shield than it had been. The flames dripping off Petra continued dropping onto the grass, and a small fire lit up next to the demon. Gabriel stepped away from the burn, but the demon stepped into it.

Nothing happened to Mrs. Benson's body. She didn't catch on fire, her clothing didn't start to burn. The flames roared up around her, as if she'd been oxygen to them, engulfing her and making the red glow in her eyes stronger. She was like living flame now. And yet the woman herself under all the fire wasn't harmed.

An illusion or just the demon's nature?

"You are not strong enough to send me back," the demon said, its voice deeper and more resonant than before.

Loud enough to shiver through Cary's bones.

She didn't take a step back from it, but only because she was still standing back to back with her friends and Deacon took her weight when she leaned away from the demon.

But the demon's comment made her frown. "Aren't I?" she asked absently.

Had she managed to will the demon backward that step?

No. That wasn't likely. Despite suggestions by the legendary demon hunter to the contrary, Cary *knew* she didn't have the willpower to just...send a demon back to its realm. Especially since she didn't understand the connection between the medium and the demon in this case.

The demon was in control, and seemed able to control what happened to Mrs. Benson's body. But it wasn't exactly *here* in this realm either.

What would happen if she snapped Mrs. Benson out of her trance or whatever it was that happened to her when she was channeling something from another realm? Could that even be done? Would it harm Mrs. Benson?

She still didn't even know if Mrs. Benson was in on all this or not.

Meanwhile, there was way too much fire inside this containment circle. The vampires, except for Petra, had all moved to the very edge of the circle. There was a lot of low level hissing and raised hands to block the light from the fire engulfing the demon. Even Gabriel was well away from all the fire now. But they were all stuck inside Angie's circle.

Well. This made things interesting.

"You ready to die too?" Cary asked Gabriel. "Lots of fire going on here. Me and my friends are safe. But your hive...? Not so much. Vampires burn like matchsticks."

Gabriel didn't snarl or hiss at her, but most of his vampires did. One even charged her, so fast Cary only realized it had happened when the vampire hit her shield and was thrown backward. Not on fire, she noticed. Must be one of the younger, weaker ones.

The Master raised his hand and the hissing silenced. "We aren't the ones in danger here."

"Sure. Sure. Except you're trapped with a burning demon. And I'm comfortably safe inside my shield. And you guys just keep reinforcing my shield with all this. So..." She shrugged. "Hey, not my place to tell you what to do. Burn, don't burn. Up to you."

She looked into the demon's eyes. The flames around it had taken a kind of shape, like a larger body superimposed over Mrs. Benson, but less solid. Its eyes were no longer coming through Mrs. Benson's face, but seemed to be two glowing orbs inside a roughly inverted triangular shape that hovered over her head—the demon's head maybe?

Cary found herself meeting those glowing orbs as if they were the demon's eyes. She wasn't entirely surprised to see a mouth form at the bottom point of the triangle.

"I will not be denied entry to your realm, human. I will not be denied."

To Angie, Cary said, "Can it get here without the sacrifice? Is this killing Mrs. Benson? Can it do that to get into our realm?"

"It's being channeled. It's not really here," Angie said. "Not all of it anyway. It's...it's in two places at once. And doing that is draining.

This could kill its host, but that will just send it back to its realm and it'll have to start over. This is one of the harder ways for an ordinary demon to enter this realm."

"So," Cary said to the demon's flaming head now more than a foot over Mrs. Benson's. "You hear that? Don't want to risk killing Mrs. Benson. You'll wreck all your planning."

The demon reached out to Cary at the same time as Mrs. Benson reached toward her. It was weird, like two different beings taking up the same space and doing the same things, but superimposed one over the other. It was making her brain hurt, trying to sort it out.

A large boom sounded through the darkness as the demon's flaming hand hit Cary's shield. She sound made her wince. Some of the vampires moaned, others screamed. Beside her, Deacon sucked in a breath that she felt more than heard over all the noise.

"You okay?" she asked him.

"I don't think my ears are bleeding," he said. "But they're definitely ringing now."

Cary leaned into him and he wrapped one arm around her waist, reaching backward to do it. She took strength from that touch. The little charm on her necklace seemed to warm against her skin. But maybe that was just the fire.

Smoke blackened the sky overhead. They were going to start a forest fire soon. She glanced at Petra. Her charred, skeleton of a face didn't look even vaguely human anymore. Narrow, sharp bones, a wide-open mouth with sharp, black teeth. Her hair was gone. Her clothing burned away. She was still leaning heavily into Cary's shield. She shouldn't even still be alive, but somehow she was.

And she was laughing, her voice ruined, the sound bubbly and choking.

The flame shapes encompassing Mrs. Benson grew, leaning over Cary now, looking down at her.

"You will die," the demon said. Its voice was still coming from Mrs. Benson, so the sound of its words came from the area of the flaming shape's stomach. Which was really disorienting. Cary didn't know where to look.

"Getting kind of smoky in here," Angie commented. Sounding calmer than Cary felt.

Cary was pretty sure they were safe from the fire. She'd kept people protected from fire before, but still… She couldn't stand under thick ropes of black smoke without it being just a tiny bit terrifying to her most basic survival instincts. Sweat trickled down her cheek as the area around them heated.

"Everyone doing okay?" she asked her friends.

"Brilliant," Jaxer said. He didn't sound concerned. That was reassuring.

"Breathing just fine, which is nice," Angie said.

"Are you okay?" Deacon murmured.

"Sure. Sure. Just waiting for the bad guys to give up and go away."

Deacon snorted. "How often does that happen?"

"Not very," she admitted.

Angie was chanting quietly under her breath again. Cary kept her attention on the demon.

A hand the size of a small car but made out of flames hovered above her, and the vague upside down triangle that was the demon's head grew more defined, the pointed ends of the triangle resembling horns at the top and an elongated chin at the bottom.

How very demon, she thought as the hovering hand descended and slammed into her shield like a meteor.

Another loud boom shook the area, nearly throwing Cary to her knees. Some of the vampires—including Petra—fell down. Some covered their ears and screamed. The wind from the kickback churned up dust and swirled the smoke around.

Cary squinted to where the demon's human acolytes were. Some had pressed forward, trying to reach the demon through Angie's circle. Some had fallen down and were curled up with their hands over their ears. Others were on their knees, hands out to the side and faces turned up to the demon as if in prayer.

That last was pretty disturbing.

The demon slammed its hand down on Cary's shield again. Another ear-splitting crack tore through her. She clapped her hands over her own ears against the ringing noise. She couldn't feel the attack. The heat, the sounds, the ground shaking, yes. But not the reverberation in her shield.

Deacon still had his arm wrapped backward around her, holding her close. His balance remained solid despite the trembling earth—it was good to be a cat—so she relied on him to keep her upright.

On the other side of her, she couldn't hear Angie anymore, but she wrapped her arm around her friend to help keep her upright. All four of them were leaning back into each other, using each other for balance.

As the demon slammed her shield yet again, and the sound robbed Cary of hearing, she tried to look past it, hunting for Gabriel. She couldn't see him through the demon's glow, but the vampires she could see all looked in pain, all screaming, though she couldn't really hear them over the noise, just saw a lot of open mouths and writhing bodies.

Petra had collapsed into a heap of blackened bones and ragged, pealing remnants of skin. Cary couldn't tell if she was even alive. But at least she wasn't still burning and spreading fire around.

The demon had taken over that effort.

The stench of sulfur, burnt flesh and bones, burning grass, smoke, clogged Cary's throat and nose, choking her and coating her tongue. The heat was almost unbearable now, sweat soaking her t-shirt under her leather jacket, making her jeans stick to her skin. She wanted to shout at the demon to stop, but when she opened her mouth, the stink made her gag.

The demon struck again. A sound like a plane crash, ripping metal and tortured engines, broke over them.

From the blackness, Gabriel stepped forward, standing closer to the demon's flaming shadow body than Cary would have expected.

He smiled at her.

"Shall I tell it to stop?" he said, his voice somehow discernible, despite the ringing in Cary's ears.

She shrugged. "I'm cool. Well, actually, it's gotten a little hot in here. But I'll be fine." She nodded at his hive. "Not sure your vampires will survive all this."

He waved a hand. "They'll recover. It's what we do."

"Even Petra?" Cary didn't look at the husk that remained of the vampire.

"Even me, Protector," a voice came from the direction of the crumpled form. It didn't sound healthy. "I will drink. And I will heal. And I will feed on you."

Cary shook her head. She was starting to think Petra was a little too focused on that last point for her own good.

She made a concerted effort not to look at the fallen vampire. She was going to have nightmares about that burnt husk still housing a living being as it was. Seeing her speak through the burnt face seemed like it might be too much for her psyche.

Pointing to the space around her and her friends. "This is what I do. I'm pretty good at it. All this banging and such is pointless. You know that. And you know why."

The demon slammed her shield again. She winced.

"If I save you, will you serve me?" Gabriel asked.

"No. Plus, I don't need saving."

"If I love you, will you serve me?"

"Ha! If that doesn't work for a goblin king, it's not going to work for you."

Gabriel frowned.

"You don't watch movies, do you?" she asked him

"Love that movie," Angie murmured.

Labyrinth was one of their favorites—thanks to Angie introducing them all to it. Unfortunately, in real life, the goblin king who'd occasionally tried to kidnap Marianne so she would weave gold for him was nowhere near sexy like David Bowie's portrayal.

"She already has a mate," Deacon said, his voice deep with the growl of his leopard.

"Also that," Cary confirmed. "Dibs on my love has already been called."

His hand flexed possessively against her stomach and she patted his arm. She hated that he was in danger here, but boy, she loved that he had her back. At the moment, quite literally.

The demon growled. "I will not be denied," it said, still speaking, incongruously, through Mrs. Benson's mouth. "I will have my sacrifice."

Cary wasn't sure whether to look at the fire face with horns above her or the human woman channeling the demon. She chose the fire face. "Nope," she said. "See, you can't get through my shield. You won't be able to get through Frank's no matter how much you teleport him around. You lost before you got started. Best to leave. Maybe try the old-fashioned way of getting here, trick some poor greedy bugger into calling you and then have them forfeit on the deal. I understand that occasionally works. If the demon hunters don't get to you before you get out, of course."

She probably shouldn't be giving the demon advice on how to break free into her realm, but honestly, she just wanted it gone.

The demon lifted both hands to slam down onto her shield, but stopped. She frowned up at it. Then looked down. Gabriel had reached through the flames of its shadow body to touch Mrs. Benson's shoulder. The flame head looked down at the Master.

Gabriel stared at Cary as he pulled his arm out of the fire. His skin on his hand had blackened but was healing fast. To her surprise, his shirt hadn't burnt away. What sort of material was that? She'd have to ask Marianne later.

"I believe," he said, pulling her back to the moment, "it's time to call the sacrifice."

She narrowed her eyes. What was he playing at? They'd just proven Frank's shields would hold.

"She can't be in two places at once," Gabriel said, nodding at Cary without taking his gaze off her. "She can't protect them while protecting her lovers."

Cary would have made a face at that description of her group, but Gabriel didn't give her time.

"If you sacrifice Frank and leave the witch and baby alone," Gabriel said, "you will succeed."

"No." Cary shook her head. "That won't work. Elizabeth and the baby will still be in danger. From you. From the humans. It won't work."

Her pulse raced. He was telling the demon how to get around Protector powers. It wouldn't work for her group. There were too many threats to them. But could it work against Frank? If Elizabeth and the god weren't in danger, if he didn't have to protect them, he'd be vulnerable.

But they'd be in danger here. There was no way around that. There was no way for them to be safe from the demon or the vampires. Not here.

Mrs. Benson looked at the Master even as the demon head above turned more fully toward him.

"If you content yourself with releasing the witch and god," Gabriel said, "you can sacrifice a Protector of great power. Enough to allow you to stay here." Gabriel's eyes narrowed. He hadn't looked away from Cary the entire time he spoke. "And she won't be able to stop you."

"No..." Cary breathed.

No. That wouldn't work. It couldn't work. Protector magic was tricky that way. Frank would be safe because his wife and the baby god were in danger. He had to be.

Right?

"I'd be willing to bet," Gabriel said, his voice even quieter in the now dead silence, "if you allowed the pregnant witch to join Cary, the other Protector will allow himself to be sacrificed."

"No!"

*C*ary lurched forward without thought, her instincts to stop disaster without a plan behind the movement. Deacon's arm around her waist kept her back. But for an unthinking moment, she struggled against his hold.

It took several moments for her brain to catch up to her instincts.

What did she think she was doing? She couldn't attack a demon, or a Master vampire. She trembled in fear for Frank, but she forced herself to pause. To think.

"It won't work," she said, mostly to herself. "It can't. Frank is too smart for that. He'll know he's safe if he keeps Elizabeth with him. He won't let them out of his protection. It won't work."

She was trying to convince herself. She didn't know Frank well enough to know what he would do. But she did know her own instincts to keep people safe sometimes made her do stupid things. It was the entire reason she'd ended up in this job—she'd done something stupid to save a puppy and ended up...here.

But Frank had to know he didn't have to give himself up to protect Elizabeth, right? He had to know the only way to end this was to *keep* protecting her and the baby god.

A breeze moved through the area, turning to a wind that cooled the sweat on Cary's temples. She shivered and watched as the smoke overhead dissipated. A light rain started, putting out the small fires that had started inside the containment circle. The flaming body of the demon smoked and smoldered, but a little rain wasn't enough to extinguish it.

The demon looked across the clearing, back toward the woods. Mrs. Benson also turned to look in that direction, her movements and the demon's perfectly synchronized.

It won't work, it won't work, it can't work, it won't work.

Cary chanted the reassurances over and over, her stomach tight with tension, her muscles trembling against the need to do something to stop a disaster.

Mrs. Benson's body turned back to face Cary. The fire demon's larger form collapsed back downward, sucking back into Mrs. Benson's body in a whirl of air currents and dust. Without the flaming shape engulfing her, Mrs. Benson looked ordinary again, but for the red in her eyes.

Through the medium, the demon smiled. And then Mrs. Benson collapsed to the ground.

It happened so fast, Cary blinked, not moving in time to catch the woman as she fell. "What the...?"

The vampires who'd been pressed against the edge of Angie's containment circle started to ease away from it, creeping slowly toward the fallen woman. Gabriel continued to stare at Cary, not even giving the collapsed form beside him a glance.

As the other vampire's crept closer, Cary's instincts wavered. Was the demon pulling a trick? Was it still there? It couldn't have left... right? So what was it playing at? Mrs. Benson looked vulnerable laying there on the scrubby, charred grass. Her elegant suit now bunched up and wrinkling, blackened soot smeared across the attractive blue color. Her face looked pale, but it was hard to tell in the dark, with only vampires' glowing skin and the last few flickers of fire inside the circle to see by. Her hair had pulled out of the tight bun and loosened around her face.

The medium looked like an innocent, vulnerable woman lying

there. And the vampires were creeping closer, sniffing or tasting the air with their tongues, a few hissing, a few laughing.

None of it felt good.

"What happened?" Cary said aloud.

She wanted to nudge Mrs. Benson's body with her toe, but years of scary movies kept her in her place, leery of a trick. The thought of Mrs. Benson suddenly sitting up and grabbing her foot, her eyes glowing red in triumph, sent a shiver through Cary.

Sounds from beyond the circle penetrated her confusion. The humans were no longer milling about uncertainly. They'd collapsed to their knees, facing the woods, their arms lifted in supplication.

It took her a moment to decipher their chants, the sound blending together in a white noise of murmurs.

"The god comes, the god comes, the god comes, the god comes..."

She frowned. Wait, were they talking about the baby god? Why were they chanting for the baby god since they worshipped the demon and thought that gods destroyed worlds?

"What's happening?" Cary murmured again.

Deacon's arm tightened around her. She glanced at him. He was staring into the woods.

"What do you smell? Hear?" she asked.

"Can't smell anything. Too much vampire and burnt...stuff. Can't pick anything out," he murmured. "Sounds like something is moving in the trees but..." His frown deepened. "Hard to tell over the chanting and hissing. I could just be hearing the breeze."

"Is the demon here?" She glanced down at Mrs. Benson's prone body.

It was so hard not to go to her, make sure she was still breathing. She was so still and looked so...crumpled.

This was exactly how bad guys got you in the movies, though. And then you ended up being that heroine Too Stupid To Live, running across the grass in your high heels and tripping and falling and screaming like an idiot until an ax dropped onto you.

Angie leaned around Cary to look at Mrs. Benson. "From inside the containment circle, the only place it could have gone is back to its own realm. But I can't tell unless I touch her. And I'm not getting close enough to touch her, just in case."

"I was just thinking I didn't want to be that dumb heroine."

"This is why we're best friends," Angie said, very seriously.

The trees rustled and even the vampires turned toward the woods now, ignoring Mrs. Benson—which was thankfully one less thing Cary had to worry about.

Although whatever was coming through the trees was probably not anything she would be grateful for.

"The god is coming. The god is coming."

"Are they talking about the baby god do you think?" she asked her little group.

No one answered.

Even Gabriel faced the woods now, so Cary couldn't see if he was smirking at her.

She moved restlessly from one foot to the other, anxiety crawling in her gut. She glanced at Mrs. Benson again as the chanting from the acolytes got louder and faster.

"It comes. It comes. It comes."

Baby god or…something else? Where the hell was the demon? What the hell was going on?

Her muscles tightened with so much tension she felt like she might snap.

And then movement, just inside the trees.

The acolytes started moaning and bowing over and over, prostrating themselves before whatever was coming out of the trees.

First, Elizabeth stumbled out, tripping over something in the uneven ground. Frank next, taking her arm to balance her.

Cary let out a sharp breath, seeing them both alive and looking uninjured as far as she could tell. They stopped before they got too near the acolytes.

"Frank," Cary called. "You guys okay?"

"So far," he shouted back. "He hasn't been able to get through me, but he's been bouncing us around the world."

"He? He who?"

Behind Frank, from the darkness under the trees, another human immerged.

It was all very dramatic. The man was tall, at least six and half, maybe closer to seven feet. Slim, but wide shouldered. He was wearing a tuxedo with tales and a top hat. His skin was dark and shadowed under the hat, his black hair long and straight.

If Cary didn't know better, with all that drama, she'd have thought the man a vampire. But as he got too near to Frank, he didn't light up from Frank's shields. He just got forced back a step.

Could still be a vampire, though, just a young one.

From her place a few hundred yards away, Cary couldn't see his eyes or any of his features in any detail. The impression of him, though, was one of strength and intensity. Like he was coiled, just waiting for something to happen.

He looked over the heads of the acolytes toward Cary, catching her eye. And smiled.

That was never a good thing.

"I've been waiting to meet you, Cary Redmond," he said, his voice a beautiful base that she might have admired if he wasn't one of the bad guys. "Too bad we don't have any time to talk."

"Huh?" Good come back, she thought rolling her eyes at herself. But it was all she could manage as she watched the man step around Frank and Elizabeth, forced to keep his distance by Frank's Protector magic.

The man raised his arms over his head, again all very dramatic, and the acolytes started to chant again, waving their own arms in the air.

"It comes, it comes, it comes…"

"Who?" Cary asked. "Are they still talking about the baby god?"

She only realized she'd said all that out loud, and it was audible to the people around her, when Deacon said, "They aren't looking at Elizabeth. They're all focused on the man."

"But then who's coming? They said the god was coming earlier. But baby god is officially here."

"They don't worship the baby god, remember," Deacon said, his voice low. "They worship the demon."

She looked at him, as a sudden horror swept through her. Then she faced Angie. "If the demon went back to its realm, it could get into another human conduit? Like it did with Mrs. Benson?"

"Only if it went to another medium who could channel demons and gods and had..." Angie started then she straightened and her skin paled. "Fuck me," she muttered.

Cary's head snapped back around to face the man in the top hat.

Above and around him, a figure made of fire rose, a shadow of flames with an inverted triangular head and glowing red eyes.

33

The glowing orbs of burning heat locked onto Cary from across the field, and the demon laughed.

"You wanted to confine me, witch," the demon said, its voice even deeper now, coming from the tall form of the man now channeling it. "I cannot be contained so easily." It turned its head, even as the human man turned his head, toward Frank and Elizabeth. "The time of sacrifice is upon us."

"You have a choice to make, Protector," Gabriel called to Frank.

"What choice?" Frank shouted, keeping his gaze on the demon bending over him and Elizabeth. The points at the top part of the triangle had grown into horns again, larger and thicker, curving backward like a rams.

"I will let your wife and the god go," the demon said.

"If?" Frank didn't sound convinced.

"You offer yourself up as sacrifice."

"No!" Elizabeth screamed. "Don't even think about it." She pulled at Frank's arm. "He can't get to me or the baby god. Don't listen to him."

"Don't listen, Frank," Cary yelled. "It's a trick. They're playing you." Something flung through the air and bounced off Cary's shields. She scowled at Gabriel. "Tossing rocks? That was rude."

"This is not your conversation, Cary," Gabriel said. "Don't interrupt."

"Oh right, I'm going to listen to advice on manners from a vampire." To Frank, she shouted. "They tried to break through my shields and couldn't. They were testing the demon's strength on me."

"They know," Frank said. "You admitted. They know how."

"It doesn't matter what they know, they can't get through you to Elizabeth. She's still in danger here, no matter what they say. Do you hear me? They can *not* get through you."

Frank was still staring at the demon.

Damn it. Cary couldn't tell if he was hearing her or not. Elizabeth was holding his arm, talking to him in a quieter tone so Cary could no longer hear what she was saying. Hopefully, she was continuing to talk sense to him.

"You have to let me out of the circle," Cary murmured to Angie, not taking her eyes off Frank.

"Once I break it, everyone will get out—vampires and all," she warned.

"Can you reform it?"

"Not in time to keep everyone contained." She paused. "I can keep Mrs. Benson inside a protection circle, though. At least that'll keep the demon from jumping between the man and her."

"But..." Cary faced Angie. "What if Mrs. Benson was in on this? You'll be in danger if you're inside the circle with her."

"I won't be." Angie shrugged. "And the little circle will be easier to build." She looked at the vampires. Everyone was watching the demon now, even Gabriel. "You're not going to have a lot of time once the circle drops. They're pushing at it. They'll fall out as soon as it's down."

"That'll probably help us," Cary said quietly. "No way Elizabeth will be safe with all those vampires roaring toward her. Frank will recognize that and stay next to her." She watched the demon leaned down toward Frank, the man channeling the demon leaning closer to

Frank's shield. "I just need enough time to reach them. I can keep everyone safe if I get there in time."

"I'll get you there," Deacon said.

"And I'll create some chaos to keep everyone distracted," Jaxer said. To Angie, he said, "Once Mrs. Benson's contained, you wanna play?" He wagged his eyebrows.

She snorted. "I haven't played those games in years." She narrowed her eyes. "But these vampires did break my window..." A smile that wasn't friendly spread over her wide mouth.

Cary hadn't ever seen Angie look quite so...eager before. The vampires were going to regret attacking her house.

"You're sure you'll be okay?" she asked Angie. "Without me here to protect you?"

Angie chuckled. "How many times do I have to tell you I can handle this? I've been doing this longer than you have."

"Yeah, but a demon is here. And you have demon issues. Which you haven't told me about. Yet."

Angie rolled her eyes. "Go save the day. I'll keep Mrs. Benson contained then help Jaxer cause some chaos. It'll be fun. I haven't really cut loose magically speaking in years."

Cary let out a long breath. Time to trust the people she loved to take care of themselves.

She stretched her neck, first one side, then the other, getting in a couple of very satisfying cracks. Then she jumped up into Deacon's arms, not surprised when he caught her without comment.

"Okay," she said to Angie. "Drop the circle."

Gabriel turned in that moment, his eyes narrowing. "Don't...," he started.

But Angie made a slashing gesture with her arm, and Cary actually felt the *pop* of the containment circle breaking open.

The vampires poured out, flashes of white and red streaming toward the vulnerable acolytes. Gabriel roared. And then the world blurred as Deacon raced Cary across the yards of open ground.

They stopped so suddenly, Cary gasped. Deacon had covered the space in a second.

"Like short range teleporting," she murmured as she slid to her feet, a little wobbly.

He'd stopped in front of Frank and Elizabeth, neatly inserting her between the rest of them and the demon.

Cary grinned up at the man channeling the demon—so far up! Holy hell, he was tall—and then farther up at the demon's head.

"Nope," she said simply. "Not letting you get at them." She wagged her eyebrows. "And whether Frank gives in or not, I'm protecting him now. Tricky, tricky powers."

The released vampires stormed around them, encircling the acolytes, demon, and all now. Cary didn't try to look for Gabriel in the mix. She'd just get dizzy. But she did wonder if he'd charged forward too.

She was also a little curious where Petra was since she'd somehow managed to survive near immolation on Cary's shield.

The demon growled. "You are not indestructible, woman. The vampire has told me you can be destroyed. I will take pleasure in breaking you."

"What happened to eating my bones?" she asked. "Your threats are weakening." Over her shoulder to Elizabeth, she said, "Don't you dare let him try to be a hero."

"You hear that, Frank," she said. "No heroics. I am safe."

"But it'll just keep coming. This is what I was worried about. This is why I didn't want you to do this."

"He's right," the demon rumbled. "I want free. I will not stop. And if I cannot sacrifice the god, I will take whoever I can get."

"Nope," Cary said again.

Then turned to look at Frank and Elizabeth. She felt a vague breeze overhead, looked up to see the demon dropping its giant shadow hand toward them. It bonged off her shield, the noise making the vampires and acolytes yowl in pain.

She winced and shook her head. "Slow learner." To Frank, she said, "We'll figure out how to banish this thing and you guys will be safe. But no sacrificing yourself. It's not necessary. That was a vampire trick, convincing the demon you would. Don't play into it."

"It'll just keep coming," Frank murmured.

"And you think Elizabeth and your kids will be safe if it gets free into this realm? Enough," she ordered in her firmest voice, channeling her own mother and sister's mommy voices.

Frank blinked and finally looked at her.

Ha! The stern mommy voice strikes again. "They are manipulating you because they can't get through our magic. We're safe."

Just then a series of fireworks went off overhead again. Cary chuckled. "Jaxer is playing," she said to a frowning Elizabeth and Frank.

The acolytes started oohing and aahing up at the pretty lights. The vampires stilled in their frantic circle racing. Then a series of rainbows—rainbows at night?—started running through the air, forming arcs overhead, disappearing, and forming again in a new place. Sparkles glittered down over the area, like a winking rain, only to vanish as they neared reaching hands. What looked like butterflies, only the size of bats, fluttered in circles, diving in and around the humans and vampires, landing on heads. The moment someone reached for them, the butterflies flapped away. A breeze, heavy with the scent of rain, blew past, gaining strength enough to blow off a few vampire wigs.

Cary pressed her lips together, wanting to laugh and watch longer, but she couldn't afford to be distracted by Angie and Jaxer's show.

"We will kill you eventually," Gabriel said.

Cary spun to see him standing next to the demon.

Petra, looking like a gross, melty burnt marshmallow, stood next to him. How the hell was she standing? Her face had healed just enough that there was some fresh skin visible around all the charred ruins. But she was naked now and still hairless, and the gleam of her black eyes glowing in the skeletal depths of all that burnt damage was like a nightmare. When she smiled at Cary, crackling stuff fell off.

Cary tried not to think about that too closely.

"No," Cary said to Gabriel.

"I will kill you," the demon said. "Perhaps, I should sacrifice you." He leaned a little closer and sniffed. The human man did the same motion at the same time. "You smell..." It straightened. "Like the god."

"Residual from being the surrogate," Cary said. But she leaned into Deacon and raised her brows at him.

He tapped his nose. "Getting too much input. I'm smelling the god on you, but...it could easily be left over from earlier today. You haven't actually stopped smelling of the baby since she was moved."

"I haven't? Weird." She shrugged. "I'm not a god," she told the demon. Probably should have said she was one, but since it was looking to sacrifice a god, this was one of those rare circumstances where it might be better not to be one. "Not a good sacrifice. Neither is Frank."

"He is sufficient," the demon said, but it sounded less certain.

She narrowed her eyes up at it, then at the man channeling it, then at Gabriel.

"A vampire might work, though," Cary suggested. At Gabriel's glare she shrugged. "Just saying."

"I am no one's sacrifice," Gabriel growled.

"But you'd sacrifice one of your people to an experiment?" She nodded at Petra. "You're a crappy hive Master."

Actually, Cary got the impression that Masters used and discarded hive members without much care, and all the vampires knew this was the risk of living in a hive, but what the hell. It was a crappy arrangement.

The ground bounced underfoot once, twice.

Cary scowled down at the earth. The little rocks were jumping around in the soil. She looked around as another low-level boom proceeded the ground bouncing. Angie was weaving her hands in a complicated pattern and every time she opened her palms and made a gesture like she was flinging something into the air, the ground would shake. Cool.

Gabriel raised a hand and the vampires stopped racing around in frantic circles, chasing glitter and butterflies and flyaway wigs. "We are no threat to any of you," Gabriel said, smiling enough to show teeth.

No threat. Right.

But...

"We are just here to witness the emergence of a fellow being of power." He gestured up to the demon. "We are no threat to anyone. We will not drink from the unwilling because I have decreed it. The acolytes are safe. I have no interest in killing you anymore, Cary."

Cary snorted at that. "Says the man who *just* said he'd kill me eventually. Don't think this will work."

"Intention is everything, though, isn't it?" Gabriel said. "I'm in control of the vampires. I will not allow them to hurt...anyone here. Not the witch, not the shifter, not the faery, not the humans." He motioned and the vampires fell back toward the barn like good little minions. "We're here to bear witness. That's all."

He moved away, taking a swaying Petra with him. She gave Cary a longing look, but didn't object to her Master's command. From the jerky, halting way she moved, it didn't look like she could have objected even if she'd tried.

Cary narrowed her eyes at Gabriel. "Still won't work. Big, giant demon here is a threat to us all." She motioned to its acolytes. "They're not exactly safe for us either. Nope. Not getting around me that easily."

She looked up at the demon. "You can't stay without a sacrifice. That makes you a threat."

"But what if the only sacrifice I want is you?" the demon said.

"We've been through this. You'll still be a danger to the others here, especially if you get out. It's your nature. If this plan won't work for Frank, it's sure as hell not going to work for me."

"I'll attack if you try to hurt her," Deacon said to the demon. He motioned to the tall man. "Your conduit will die before you can blink."

The man flung his hand out in a swirling circular gesture. Frank and Elizabeth drew in sharp breaths and moved closer together.

Cary frowned. Waited for something to happen. When nothing did, she raised her brows at the demon.

"What?" she asked.

It made the gesture again. And again.

To Elizabeth and Frank, she asked, "What's it doing?"

"Trying to teleport us," Frank said. "Why isn't it working?"

"It tried that before when it was in Mrs. Benson," Cary said. "Didn't work then either."

"But Mr. Benson can teleport too," Frank said.

Cary's mouth dropped open. "That's *Mr*. Benson? What the hell? And he can teleport?"

"Long story," Frank said, sounding more like himself and less like he was going to sacrifice himself to the demon now. "But yes. He's capable of teleporting. He's the one who attracted the demon in the first place apparently. And agreed to channel it so it could get into this realm."

"Wait, is he like his wife? Can he channel gods and demons?"

"Not as powerfully. His real skill is teleporting. But he can manage enough to let the demon in. He's been channeling the thing for years now. They've been hunting for a suitable sacrifice to bring the demon in permanently. Mr. Benson is the one who made the demon's bargain."

Shit. "Does Mrs. Benson know?"

"Not according to her husband," Elizabeth said quietly.

"How did you guys learn all this? When?"

"When Mr. Benson—Bartholomew—when he was teleporting us around the world, I got him to admit to a few things," Frank said.

"Ha. Bad guy monologuing strikes again. Did you irritate him into giving you answers? That's what I always do?"

"Actually, I did," Frank said, giving her a small smile.

"Irritating them and getting them mad really works, huh?" She faced the man who was Mr. Benson. Bartholomew Benson. What a name. "Is he there while he's channeling the demon? Or is it like Mrs. B and he doesn't know what's happening?"

"The demon lets him know," Frank said. "He's a party to this."

"They could have come for you before," Cary said. "You're not enough. They need the god."

"But two Protectors will suffice," Gabriel called from farther away.

"Shut up," Cary shouted at him. "You're not helping."

"I'm not here to help. I'm here to bear witness."

Cary snorted. "Right. So, Mr. B here can teleport, and he was able to teleport you despite you being in full blown Protector mode. And the demon can teleport." She huffed. "Everyone can teleport except me. That's not fair. But obviously, it can't just teleport into this realm because of all the rules about that sort of thing. It needs a pretty significant sacrifice to stay. No simple human sacrifice will do or they would have arranged that already."

Something in that was nagging at her. Something wasn't adding up...

More light bursts went off overhead. The acolytes were moving away now, opposite the vampires, following what looked like fireflies this time, only these fireflies were the size of huge birds. Flickers of light popped in and out around the gathered vampires, too.

Cary noticed a lot of them growling and swatting at the lights. Irritating vampires... Good idea or bad? Well, it was a distraction. Jaxer and Angie were good.

She focused on the only threat she had to worry about now. A demon that needed the baby god to stay. "Why something like a god?" she wondered out loud. "Most demons kill the person who calls them to get free."

"The bargain made dictates everything," Frank said. "The demon has to follow the rules of the agreement."

"The demon god killed the person who called him," Cary whispered to Deacon. "Guess gods don't have to abide by the rules."

The demon growled and both man and fire being leaned closer, close enough for Cary to feel the shadow fire's heat.

"Gods destroy worlds. I will destroy the gods."

"Which gods?"

"All gods," it said, stretching out the "all" like a breath—a promise and a curse at once.

Cary blinked up at it.

All gods? Oh boy.

34

"Wait, wait, wait..." Cary pressed her fingers into her temples, trying to work her way through this as a bunch of the stuff that didn't make sense started to coalesce. She grasped at the idea, tugging it into view.

"You haven't been looking for just any old sacrifice," she said. "Or you could have picked any powerful being. A human with magic. A shifter. A vampire."

She bared her teeth at Gabriel when she said this. He snarled back.

"But..." she continued, "you want something more. Something like a god. Why?" She tapped a finger against the charm hanging in the hollow of her throat. The gold was warm from all the heat and fire surrounding her. "You want to destroy gods. Not just demon gods. All gods. But you're not one, so you're not strong enough."

She snapped her fingers. "But you think you can absorb the powers of a god if you sacrifice one. Become a god yourself. And then go get revenge or whatever, right? I knew there was more to all this." She flicked her fingers at Gabriel. "See Frank is no good to them. Stupid suggestion."

"If Frank had moved away from Elizabeth," Gabriel said, "and allowed himself to be teleported away for sacrifice, who would have protected her from us?"

"Me," Cary said sharply. "Now stop taunting. You know none of that would have worked. You're just muddying the waters."

She had no idea why, either. What the hell was Gabriel playing at? Testing her powers, sure, but all that had gotten him was a crispy fried vampire. So what was his end game?

She hated dealing with vampires. Their thinking was all twisty and convoluted. Probably because they'd been alive for too long.

"Listen," she said to the demon. "I don't know what Gabriel told you about killing a Protector, but you're not getting through us to the little baby god, and I know you need baby god now, not just any old sacrifice. Frank knows it, too." She raised her brows at her fellow Protector. He nodded faintly. "So he's not walking away from his wife to be your sacrifice."

The demon and Mr. Benson waved their arm in that circular motion again. "Why can't I teleport you?" the demon demanded, sounding really annoyed.

"Because I'm stubborn that way, and I don't want to be teleported," she said.

That was a big fat whopper of a lie. She had no idea why the thing couldn't budge her, even though Mr. Benson on his own had been able to jump Frank and Elizabeth all around the world. But she didn't have to tell the demon she didn't know.

"You aren't just a Protector," the demon said, lowering its head closer, the flames hissing as they came into contact with her shield. "You have more powers than you admit."

"Nope. Just an ordinary woman with an extraordinary capacity to stand belligerently in the way of bad guys."

Deacon snorted out a muffled sound she suspected was a laugh.

The light show Angie and Jaxer were putting on all around them colored the demon's fire body, decorating it with sparkly rainbow colors. It should have looked funny, all those colors flowing across its fire like oil on water. Instead, the thing just looked like a psychedelic terror that would suck her into a vortex if she stared at it too long.

"You could try killing her friends," Gabriel suggested, casually. "She'll abandon the baby god to save the witch and faery."

Oh, she was going to hurt that vampire now. She didn't know how. But she was going to hurt him good for suggesting that to the demon.

"Won't work," she said to the demon. "Frank can still protect Elizabeth." To Gabriel she snarled, "Enough meddling. You can leave now."

She desperately wanted to motion Angie and Jaxer close, to get them into the circle of her protection, but she didn't dare reveal to the demon that Gabriel's suggestion might actually work. She didn't even want to glance at her friends, just in case that gave her fear away.

"You doing okay over there?" Jaxer called, which was perfectly timed for Cary to know he was still safe.

"Good. Good," she said. "Trying to talk our guest into leaving. You know. The usual."

"Fair enough," Jaxer said. "The acolytes are busy chasing illusions, so shouldn't be any trouble now. The vampires are attempting to remain harmless. They'll be good little minions. So Angie and I will take our leave."

She did look then, her eyes wide. Jaxer winked, opened what looked like a hole in the ground, wrapped an arm around Angie, who waved goodbye before closing her eyes tight, and then Jaxer stepped into the hole.

It sealed over him like it had never been there.

"Did he just take Angie into Faery?" Cary asked.

"Looks like," Deacon said. "But they can't be used as pawns now."

"He better keep her safe there," Cary muttered. Jaxer had told her Faery was no place for a human. That it could drive them insane.

"They won't stay in there long," Deacon murmured near her ear.

"So," Cary said to Gabriel. "Running out of useless ideas, aren't you?"

"One can never stop testing," Gabriel said, his voice carrying to her even though he didn't raise it. "And I will test you until I find your weakness."

Cary refused to let him know he'd found her weakness already.

Her friends, the people she loved... Threats to them. That was her Achilles' heel. Well, that and having no one around to protect. But he already knew about that part thanks to the stupid wizard. She didn't have to confirm any more of her weaknesses for him.

She faced the demon. "Your acolytes have fled. The vampire isn't any use to you because he keeps feeding you suggestions that don't work. You can't budge me from protecting the baby god. And you can't get the powers you want without her. So... Yeah, you've lost. Time to go back to your realm and rethink your plans. Like, maybe you just, I don't know, move to another demon realm with nicer demon gods? You can teleport, right?"

The demon growled, the sound actually making the ground tremble. The growl got deeper and louder, shaking Cary's bones.

The earth bucked. A rain of fire exploded from overhead, showering down over them, swarming over Cary's shield, leaving her, Deacon, Frank and Elizabeth in a bubble of safety surrounded by heat and death.

"Well, this isn't good," she said.

Then another sound so deep it wasn't really sound anymore vibrated in the air and shook the earth. She rocked on her feet, had to grab onto Deacon to stay upright.

Elizabeth gasped. "Something's wrong," she shouted above the noise. "The baby... Something's wrong."

Cary turned to see her covering her stomach, her skin blanched white. Blood spotted the front of her skirt near the apex of her legs.

"Oh no," Cary breathed. "What's happening? The demon can't be killing her? She's protected." She looked at Frank, but he was holding Elizabeth, his full attention on his wife.

Elizabeth gasped again, her head thrown back.

Cary didn't know what to do. The baby couldn't be hurt from whatever the demon was doing, but... Maybe something had gone wrong with the pregnancy during all the teleporting, or...?

She had no idea. She gave Deacon a frantic look.

He shook his head, his brows lowered, looking as confused and worried as Cary felt.

The flames around them roared. The sounds from the demon moving to a level Cary couldn't even hear anymore. The ground continued to roll and buck.

Elizabeth dropped to her knees, Frank falling beside her, not releasing his hold on her.

Cary swore she heard Gabriel laughing. Anger and fear, spiked with adrenaline and uncertainty, bubbled in her blood like the worst kind of drug. She wanted to burst apart from it.

She dropped to her knees next to Elizabeth. She'd trained—a long time ago!—with small animals, dogs and cats. And even then only as a technician, not a vet. She didn't have any human first aid skills, though she'd been to emergency rooms enough she should know more really.

But she certainly didn't know anything about maternity care or pregnancy emergencies. She'd been here, on the opposite side of the country from her sister, when Valerie was pregnant, only going to visit after the babies were born, so she didn't even have that experience to draw on.

"What can I do?" she asked Elizabeth, who had at least been through a few pregnancies before this. "What do you need?"

Above them the demon continued to roar in that subsonic way that shook the ground and vibrated in her bones. Fire rained on them, enclosing them in a dome of blistering brightness. Beyond the low-level, painful demon roar was the sound of vampires. Laughter, hissing, taunting noises. Cary couldn't discern the words, just the tone. But the tone was enough.

Elizabeth moaned and clenched at her stomach, her jaw tight. "Not sure what's happening?" she said between her teeth. "Something's wrong."

Cary glanced down at Elizabeth's stomach and realized the area was glowing, a white glow like the one that had infused Cary while she harbored the growing god. No other part of Elizabeth glowed, her skin wasn't lit from within like Cary's had been. And there were no sparkles.

"Your stomach," Cary said.

Elizabeth gasped again. Then she threw her head back and screamed.

35

_C_ary panicked. She leaned in and grabbed Elizabeth's shoulder, then placed her own hand over the baby bump because she didn't know what else to do and wanted to offer…something. Comfort or support.

Energy, like a shock of electricity, hit her the moment she touched Elizabeth's stomach.

She would have jerked her hand away, but she couldn't. She was stuck, fused in place, the pain of the connection running up her arm.

She gasped and leaned back, jerking her right hand away from Elizabeth's shoulder, but she couldn't remove her left hand from Elizabeth's stomach and the bright white glow.

The flow of energy turned warm and rushed, moving into her like water overflowing a glass. Her vision blurred.

Dimly, she heard Deacon call her name, heard the panic in his voice. She couldn't open her mouth to answer. The energy raced through her now, overwhelming her until she couldn't breathe.

Heat and ice danced on her nerves. There was pain, and the soothing warmth, and the overwhelm, and all she wanted was for it to stop. A sensation like bubbles in her blood turned to a raging white-water river of foam.

Too much. Too much.

She couldn't contain it. Couldn't hold it.

She needed space. Space. Room to breathe. She'd be able to take whatever was happening, if she could...

Just...

Breathe...

Gasping, groping for air, she tried to push the sensations racing through her out, away. She needed an inch, just an inch of space.

The rushing power moved and shifted. She took a breath, short but enough. The energy raced to her free arm, coalescing and flowing in faster and faster waves.

Pain dampened and tightened at once. A focused single line of electricity. No longer overwhelming her entire being. Now only burning the palm of her hand and her right arm.

She leaned away from Elizabeth. The hand she had on the other woman's stomach remained. But she was able to move her free hand, the right hand where all the burn was gathering. Moved it safely away from the others.

Holding that source of concentrated power out from her body, she looked up at the dome of her shield. The flames had lowered. The bubble of safety contracted around them.

No!

She had to concentrate. She had to keep them safe. She focused on pushing out her shield. She never had control of her magic, but she tried anyway. Without really thinking, she held her hand up to the barrier, a physical gesture to reinforce her need for that shield to push back, to protect the others.

An explosion of light, bright white, sharp as a laser beam, burst from her palm, carving through the flames, cutting apart the sounds beyond.

Cary screamed and swept her arm down.

The flames vanished in time for her to see the beam of energy shooting from her palm slice through the center of Mr. Benson's body, cutting him in half.

The demon screamed and the flaming shadow body collapsed with

Mr. Benson, smoking and writhing before winking out. Leaving a stench of burnt flesh and sulfur and spilled intestines behind.

The power still flowed from Cary. She couldn't stop it. Her body moved almost of its own accord, her arm tracking over the field, toward the barn. She wanted to shout a warning but she couldn't speak. Her vision darkened. The light flared like a sun exploding in front of her face.

And then everything went black and silent. So suddenly, so completely, it was like all of existence had ended.

Am I dead?

She sucked in a sharp, gaspy breath. Did you breathe once you were dead? Supposedly not.

Spots danced in her vision now, sparks of light and dark circles that made it impossible to see her surroundings. Her body trembled and shook but she realized she had control of it now. She lowered her arm and collapsed backward, only just then realizing she'd come up onto her knees during the previous few minutes. The rough ground was uncomfortable. A rock poked into her ass.

Yeah, probably not dead.

Another breath confirmed that assessment. She blinked at the spots and tried to find Deacon.

His hands came to her face. "Are you okay?" His voice sounded like it was coming from very far away.

She blinked a few more times and nodded. Her mouth tasted like electricity, or burnt creosote. Her throat was dry. Her nerves buzzed. But she was alive. And they were no longer engulfed in flames. That had to be good.

Right?

She let out another breath, grateful for each one, and tried to clear her vision. A frantic thought had her turning toward Elizabeth even though all she could see were shadows against a darker background.

"Elizabeth?" she forced out the single word, hoping all the questions she couldn't voice yet were understood.

Frank answered. "She's okay. She passed out, but she's breathing. The bleeding has stopped." He paused.

Cary squeezed her eyes tightly then opened them, hoping that would help her see.

"Her stomach is...bigger now," Frank said. "Like she's closer to eight months than six months pregnant."

"She'll be disappointed with that, won't she?" Cary murmured. Her voice was breathy and deep, like her throat had been roughed up.

Frank's chuckle sounded strained. "Probably. Are you okay?"

"I have no idea. What the hell happened?" Her vision was starting to return now, at least a little. She could make out Elizabeth's form, cradled in Frank's lap, her stomach definitely looking bigger now. Cary faced Deacon, relieved he looked uninjured. "You're good?"

He nodded, but when he tried to pull her into his arms, she stopped him. "My nerves are beyond sensitive right now," she said. "Like I might break with the barest contact. Just...give me a few minutes."

"Tell me when I can touch you," he said. "Because I need to make sure you're okay."

She smiled, as much as she was able. "I'm good. I think." She glanced around. Her gaze skipped over the fallen body of Mr. Benson. She didn't want to see the pieces. As she turned toward the vampires, she realized the barn was...gone.

She leaned forward, blinking, sure she was seeing that wrong.

Nope. Where the barn had been, all that remained were some splintered chunks of wood and part of a burnt frame. She hunted the darkness for the vampires. Several bodies littered the ground, a few with chunks of wood sticking out of them. Oops. She winced. Gabriel was going to be pissed that she'd accidentally killed some of his people.

She hunted the area for the Master, gasping when her gaze fell on a body dressed in black. There was no head attached to the body. The head had rolled several feet away, the face pointing at an angle to Cary so she couldn't see it clearly in the dark. Just a few ragged sweeps of dark blond hair still pulled back into a low tail, and skin starting to sluff off the skull. The sharp canines stood out white in the skull's death grimace.

"Is that...?" she asked, afraid to say the words aloud.

"Gabriel?" Deacon said. "Yes. That power you were channeling went right for him, slicing his head off just before the barn behind him exploded."

"Oh, this isn't good." She swallowed. "Did I... Did I kill all the vampires?"

In answer, some moved out of the surrounding woods. They crept into the open slowly, carefully, crouched low to the ground. Their yellow eyes glowed in the darkness. Without any light, she couldn't tell if the living vampires had been injured. She stiffened as they started to murmur quietly, hissing and slithering toward their fallen Master. Cary tried to move so she would be between Deacon and the vampires, but her muscles wobbled and it was more like an awkward lurch into Deacon's lap.

He grabbed her and held her in place. Her nerves screamed in pain, but she ignored it for now. They had bigger things to worry about.

The vampires gathered around Gabriel's body and head, sniffing, briefly reaching out to touch before jerking their hands back. Then, as one, they turned to face her.

Oh oh.

Cary prepared for the attack, hoping her powers would actually work since the vampires were intent on her and not necessarily the people around her. But none of the creatures moved. They remained crouched around Gabriel's body, staring at her with their yellow eyes, not moving even a little bit.

From behind the group, James stepped out from the darkness. Wherever he'd been, he looked like he'd missed out on all the destruction. There weren't even any bits of shattered barn in his hair or on his clothes. His pale skin glowed faintly in that vampire way, enough that Cary could see him more clearly than she could see anyone else.

She opened her mouth to say something, realized she didn't know what to say, and snapped her mouth shut again. Dizziness made her head spin. She realized with growing horror she was on the verge of passing out. Oh, she couldn't do that right now. Not right now.

She forced herself off Deacon's lap, hoping she could hold out just a little longer, even as darkness started creeping in at the edges of her vision.

"Well," James said, looking around at the wreckage. "Not exactly what I'd expected. But it got the job done."

She shook her head—a mistake as it made the dizziness worse—not sure she'd heard him right.

"Huh?" she asked eloquently.

"You don't look very good, Cary," James said. There was something...new in his tone. A power, a force that hadn't been there before. "You should rest," he continued. "I'll take care of this. We can discuss it later."

She wanted to argue with him. Or at least find out what he intended to do about the fact that she'd just killed the Master of Portland. But the darkness crawled over her vision. The last thing she sensed was her body dropping to one side.

And then she knew no more.

36

Cary shifted, sighed, and opened her eyes. Fred licked her cheek in a long, wet greeting, his doggie breath blowing warmly against her cheek. He wiggled against her and set his head onto her stomach. She looked up. Angie, Marianne, and Lucy leaned over her, staring into her face.

"This feels like déjà vu," she said. "I passed out?"

"Yes," Angie said.

"How long this time?"

"Six days," Marianne said. "Six. Days."

"You have to stop doing this to us," Lucy said, her little girl's voice high and sweet with her concern.

"Sorry." She assessed the mattress under her. Her own bed. Her own bedroom. "Where's Deacon?"

"Here," he said, moving into her view from behind where Lucy was hovering. "And they're right. You really have to stop doing this to us."

"Not my fault this time. Talk to the baby god." Her eyes widened and she sat up suddenly, forcing Fred's head off her stomach. He barked and readjusted so his chin rested on her leg. "The baby god? Elizabeth and Frank?"

"Everyone is safe and healthy," Angie said. "They took Elizabeth to a magical midwife to make sure the baby was okay. She's due in a few weeks."

"*Weeks*? Not months? So that wasn't our imagination. She did grow an extra two months in, what, a day? A few hours."

"Yup," Angie said. "Midwife said she's perfectly healthy. No signs that the sudden jumps in development hurt her. Or Elizabeth for that matter. They're back with their kids now, getting a room ready for the newcomer."

Cary let out a breath. "Oh, that's good. Mrs. Benson?"

"Safe," Angie said. "Jaxer took her home. She had no idea what her husband had been doing, or that the demon had been using her while she was unconscious to spy on this realm."

"Do we know how the demon and Mr. Benson found each other? What the demon was offering Mr. Benson?" Cary asked.

She adjusted herself on her bed. She was under a blanket, in her flannel pajama bottoms and a t-shirt, and her room was flooded with early morning light. At a glance, she spotted Buck and Pickles laying near her bedroom door, taking up guard positions on either side of the doorframe. She'd noticed them doing that more lately and wondered if they were as worried about her as her friends.

Marianne sat down on the foot of the bed, Angie to her left and Lucy on the right. Deacon remained standing next to where Lucy sat.

Angie absently scratched Fred's head as she explained. "Mrs. Benson isn't sure how her husband and the demon connected, but she did say that her husband always had an issue with her channeling gods. He hated beings that powerful. Said they were dangerous and she shouldn't interact with them."

"The demon really hated gods too," Cary murmured.

"That's probably what drew the two together," Angie said. "We don't know what the demon promised Mr. Benson. Can't know now."

"Can it get to Mrs. Benson again?" Cary asked. "She's vulnerable to it."

Angie exchanged a look with Deacon before answering. "Mrs.

Benson has... She's taken steps to end her ability to channel other-realm beings."

"What?" Cary asked slowly. "What exactly does that involve?"

"Some charms and spells and potions," Angie said vaguely. "It will take some time, but when she's through with all the rituals, she'll be deaf to the other realms."

"That doesn't sound... Right."

"Maybe not. But it was her choice. She was appalled at what had happened and felt responsible. She didn't want the demon to use her again." Angie shrugged. "I can't blame her for that."

Neither could Cary. It just seemed a shame the medium had to cut off a part of herself to avoid the demon.

"By the way, she's Ms. Cortez now," Angie said. "She's going back to her maiden name. Penelope Cortez."

"Penelope? I was wondering what her first name was," Cary said. After a few moments of silence, she said, "What happened to the Polrom acolytes?"

Marianne chuckled.

"What?"

Angie shrugged. "The cops picked them up wandering the back roads, talking about eagle-sized fireflies and dancing rainbows. It was obvious they were stoned out of their minds. The cops had them all carted off to various hospitals around the city."

"Jaxer disguised himself as a sexy nurse to go in and check on them," Marianne said. "Should have seen him. He pulled the illusion here in front of us. And she was one very pretty nurse he disguised himself as. I swear he picked that look just to tease me. As if the beauty of his normal look isn't tease enough."

Cary laughed. "So everyone recovered from the drugs?"

"Without a single memory about what had happened," Angie said. "None of them had a clue. Some of them aren't even from this coast."

"Well, Mr. Benson could teleport them, so that's not really surprising." Cary tried to pull up memories of the night of the fight. "He teleported differently to the way Frank did it," she said, mostly to herself. "The demon said like attracts like. It was referring to its ability to teleport, and I thought it was talking about Frank, but I suspect it meant Mr. Benson instead." And obviously teleporting wasn't the only thing they'd had in common, given they both hated gods. Like attracts like.

She frowned. "Still don't know why they couldn't budge me."

"Something to do with the baby god?" Angie ventured. "You absorb magic. You were soaking up god magic for a week while you were the surrogate. There was probably enough left behind that made you invulnerable to their ability to teleport."

"Except they could teleport Elizabeth carrying the baby god," Cary pointed out.

Angie shrugged. "Maybe you just are too stubborn to be teleported without your permission."

Cary huffed out a laugh. As good an explanation as any she supposed.

"Deacon and Jaxer told us about how you can absorb magic," Lucy said quietly.

"And that most people like you end up dead," Marianne said, also quietly. "How do you feel after exposure to all that god magic? And the demon power that got thrown at you."

Cary took a moment to assess how she felt. "Fine now. Good really. Rested. And hungry." She brightened. "Hey, I slept for six days. I can definitely eat pizza tonight. We're ordering pizza for dinner. Maybe lunch."

"No residual effects from the magic?" Angie asked.

"Not that I can tell. I feel like myself. But..." She shook her head. "I've always just felt like myself, and I never had a clue I was absorbing magic, so I'm not sure I'd know the difference."

"No doubt you blew it all out when you killed Mr. Benson and banished the demon," Angie said, "so you shouldn't have any issues."

"The baby god did that," Cary said. "She sent all that magic right on through me."

"That little girl is going to be one powerful being when she grows up," Angie commented.

"Yeah she is." Cary let out a breath at the thought. After another few minutes of silence, she cringed and asked, "The vampires?"

Killing the Master of Portland was not going to be good for her. It was, at the very least, going to complicate her life going forward, and she didn't want to think about it. But she had to face the blowback if she was going to deal with it.

All three of her girlfriends looked to Deacon. Cary narrowed her eyes at him. "What did you do?"

"Met with James to discuss the new arrangements," Deacon said matter-of-factly.

"You met with a vampire when I wasn't there with you?" She sat up straighter in bed. "What the hell were you thinking? Vampires love shifter blood. And the local hive is no doubt pissed off enough at me they wouldn't hesitate to eat you. You should have waited for me to wake up."

"No, I shouldn't have," Deacon said. "Not when your future safety was in question."

"My future safety is always in question," she grumbled.

"Don't remind me," he said. "Not now. Anyway, James acknowledges that he wouldn't want to start a war with my mother, so I wasn't in danger. We met during the day. In the open. And we established the new order of things."

"Which is?"

"James has taken over the hive," Deacon said.

"Ha! I knew he was a Master," Cary said, feeling vindicated. "Are they going to want some sort of, I don't know, restitution for me killing Gabriel?"

"No," Deacon said. "I get the feeling that was the outcome James was hoping for. He'd been looking for a way to take over the hive without having to fight Gabriel himself. James is…a diplomate more than a fighter."

Cary snorted. "A diplomate with a wicked set of teeth."

"A manipulator," Deacon said. "He'll make a good Master of Portland for that reason. He's better at arranging things than Gabriel ever was. Gabriel was all brute force, strength, and punishments. James intends to run the hive a little differently."

"And what does that mean to me?" Cary asked slowly, looking at Deacon sideways.

"They don't drink from the unwilling. They don't mess with you. And, occasionally, if James needs your help, you take his calls."

"You agreed that I'd help vampires?" Cary growled. "Without asking me first? I don't want to be James's pet any more than I wanted to be Gabriel's."

"Of course I didn't agree you'd help. Only that you'd take his call and hear him out. As a way to keep the peace, and to keep them from coming after you—since they know how to kill you now—I thought it was an acceptable compromise." His tone was neutral and quiet. That iceman tone he got when he was tamping down his emotions and holding himself under tight control.

She huffed. He was right. Given that the local vampires knew her weakness, the compromise was a good one. And she wouldn't have to do anything she didn't want to or thought was wrong. Just listen to James when he called. She could always hang up on him.

"If he asks me to kill his vampires for him or to punish them like I did Gabriel or some bullshit like that, I'm going to hang up on him," she said aloud. "I'm not a hired thug or vampire boogeyman. And I didn't technically kill Gabriel. The baby god did. Plus, my training doesn't extend to vampire hunter."

"I can teach you," Lucy said. "We can start on that training next."

Cary blinked and stared at Lucy. "You know how to kill vampires? You have training for that?"

"I read," Lucy said.

Cary stared a moment longer, looked away, looked back at Lucy. With a head shake, she focused on Deacon again.

His shoulders were stiff and his body language tight, but subtly. She wasn't sure the others would notice. He had that emotionless mask down over his expression now, so it was impossible to read what he was thinking.

After a few more moments of staring, she finally gave in with a begrudging exhale. "Fine," she said. "So long as he doesn't expect me to jump to do his bidding, it's a good compromise. Especially if it keeps the vampires off my back. Still, you should have waited for me. You didn't know he'd be too afraid of your mother not to eat you." She paused. "Although, it does prove he's got some sense. For a vampire."

Deacon's mouth ticked up at one corner, the iceman outer persona melting away. She narrowed her eyes. He'd been worried about her reaction to his meeting with James. That was the only reason he'd gone all emotionless and stern like that.

Was it strange she found that sweet?

LATER, AFTER HER FRIENDS HAD LEFT, AFTER JAXER HAD STOPPED IN TO annoy Deacon and make sure she was recovered, after the dogs had been run around the backyard, and after the Nags had paid a visit to ensure she was still alive and agreed to give her one more day off—so generous—Cary cuddled on the couch next to Deacon, giving him control of the remote so he could flip through TV stations.

Her tummy was full of pizza and chocolate chip cookie dough ice cream—because you could eat as much ice cream as you wanted after saving the world and then passing out and not eating for six days—and she was feeling warm and safe and a normal sort of tired.

"Do you have to work tomorrow?" she asked him as he settled on a superhero movie he knew she liked.

"Caitlin is giving me one more day off too," he said.

She chuckled at that. "You really have to stop dropping work every time my job gets weird. My job will always be weird."

He grunted a non-answer.

She shook her head. "Fine. But don't say I didn't try." She tucked tighter to his side and murmured, "I'm glad we'll have a day off together, though."

She grinned at his rumble of approval when she ran her hand up his thigh. They'd need some of their backup birth control because her doctors visit wasn't for another week. But there were plenty of condoms on hand.

"Are we going to ignore the aftereffects of you being pregnant and us finding out you can absorb magic?" he asked, though he sounded like he was only half paying attention to what he'd just asked.

Since her hand had crept higher, and her fingers were brushing against the inside of his leg now, she appreciated that his interest *might* be elsewhere. That was, after all, the point. But she did answer.

"We're going to ignore all of it for now. I'll have to figure out what to do about the magic absorption stuff later, after I've talked it over with the Nags, and probably Angie. And read more about it. But for now, just knowing it's a thing is enough." She let her fingers brush his cock, pleased when he groaned. "As for the rest... We'll talk about that when the time comes. Family and kids and all that are still a ways off for us."

His hand tightened on her shoulder when she cupped him, stroking him through his jeans.

"You're doing a great job of distracting me," he said, his voice all deep and growly and sexy.

"Good. We're agreed then? A conversation for later."

"Agreed." He groaned.

She grinned when he pulled her in for a kiss, letting go any worry for the future so she could thoroughly and completely enjoy her present.

He leaned back only long enough to say, "By the way, I had to agree to dinner at Trevor's house next week, or he was going to start investigating you. Saturday at six. Casual. Try to convince the Nags to leave you alone that night."

She sucked in a breath as he captured her mouth again.

Dinner with an inquisitive cop?

Oh boy.

THANK YOU

Thank you for continuing on this crazy journey with Cary and the gang. I hope you're enjoying Cary's adventures. For a sneak peek at Book 5 in the series, The Trouble with Magic and Faery Curses, keep reading!

If you're enjoying the series, you might also enjoy some of the short stories. Look for the stories of how Cary met all her friends (and some of her pets!) here https://books2read.com/rl/CaryMeetstheGang-Carousel. You can also read about Cary and Deacon's multiple attempts at their first date here https://books2read.com/rl/DateNights-GoneWrong. And coming soon, look out for the novella of Cary's first Jones family dinner as well as one of the earlier adventures for Cary and her girlfriends.

If you'd like to stay up to date on all my releases and news you can visit my website at https://www.katsimons.com, sign up to my monthly newsletter at http://eepurl.com/OxQQL (no more than monthly, I promise!), or you can follow my author page at your favorite vendor.

Thanks again for reading!

~Kat

THE TROUBLE WITH MAGIC AND FAERY CURSES

A CARY REDMOND NOVEL BOOK 5

EXCERPT

1

Cary considered the little brownie chattering at her. She couldn't understand a word it was saying, but it sounded very urgent. The high pitched, rapid fire rolling...language? Yeah, the little guy was definitely talking and those were words he was speaking. Accompanying gestures too. But...

Nope, none of it made the first bit of sense to her.

Behind her, another flash of light from the attacking hobgoblins lit up the air. She could just see the sparks in her peripheral vision. It wasn't often she found herself protecting one member of the Fae realm from another. They tended to keep this kind of fighting to Faery and out of her world. Which was really handy because the Fae were powerful, overwhelming, and occasionally batshit crazy.

Her faery mentor, Jaxer, would not argue with this assessment.

"I'm sorry, little guy," she said to the brownie, "but whatever language you're speaking, I don't. I can't understand a word you're saying."

More rapid-fire chittering and frantic hand gestures. Cary frowned. This was really frustrating. She knew whatever he was trying to say was important. His thin little brown body vibrated with urgency. His brown hair, short and raged, waved around his head with every movement. His sharp, angular features tightened with his own frustration. His brown eyes were huge and round, staring into hers as he spoke as if trying to force her to understand by sheer will. And she just knew if she listened to him long enough, she'd figure this out.

Problem was, she didn't think they had that kind of time.

She glanced back at the three hobgoblins arrayed in a half-circle behind her. They were all standing inside a clump of trees just off the road leading up the hill to the Rose Garden. The air had that crisp, freshness of predawn to it, with a hint of the flowers from the nearby garden faintly perfuming the air. But she could already feel the heat just at the edges. The early summer in Portland had been warm and sunny so far, boding well for the rest of the season, but this week the temperature had climbed into the nineties and didn't seem inclined to drop. And it was actually more humid than they normally got this time of year. Nothing like that one, and *only*, time she'd visited her sister in New York city in August—that had been grossly humid and she refused to visit in the summers after that trip—but still, muggy for Portland in summertime. She really hated muggy.

At least this early in the morning, before the sun was up, the area was quiet and no errant humans were driving by to interfere and give her one more person to protect.

The hobgoblins were huge creatures, easily three or four times her width and about twice her height. Their gray skin covered thick muscles beneath rough leather pants and jerkins. That leather was gonna feel miserable in another few hours when the heat really got going. The center hobgoblin, the one throwing jars of some sort of magical potion at her, had a long, hooked nose and shaggy greenish-brown hair. She kind of thought he might be the leader, but it was hard to tell. He was the one pulling magical Molotov cocktails out of the leather courier bag hanging at his hip. But none of them had said anything since she'd arrived, just started tossing those pretty green glass bottles at her and the brownie. So she couldn't be sure who was in charge.

The other two hobgoblins were not, outside of their size and being...you know, hobgoblins, particularly remarkable looking. They had some lumps and warts decorating their faces—typical species traits and given the arrangements could be considered handsome to other hobgoblins. She wasn't sure how to judge that, though. One was bald. The other had a long mane of black hair pulled back in a low tail. They both had muddy brown eyes. And at present, all they were doing was standing there staring at her and the brownie.

Hobgoblins, unlike their cousins the goblins, didn't tend to come into this realm much. According to Cary's reading, it was because they didn't like the smell. She'd also been under the impression they were supposed to be *smaller* than goblins on average. The one hobgoblin she'd encountered before this had been the same size as the brownie. Either she'd missed her guess on these guys and they were something different, or she just didn't know enough about hobgoblins.

Which, given the shear amount of stuff she'd been trying to learn over the last six and a half years, was entirely possible. There was a lot of stuff she didn't know nearly enough about.

She sighed and turned her back to them again to focus on the still frantically talking brownie.

Her bosses had sent her to intervene and save the little guy, waking her from a dead sleep to get her here in time. It was her job as a magical Protector to get between the good guys and the bad guys to keep the good guys safe. She even got paid for it. But typical of her bosses—who were also Fae, though members of a species native to North America—they hadn't explained *why* she needed to protect the brownie. Just that she was needed and needed fast.

She'd arrived just as the hobgoblins had stepped through a break in the fabric of reality that separated this realm from Faery and started throwing bottles. She'd skidded between them and the brownie just in time, only getting a little cut from the very first shattered glass. Her magic was purely defensive—and technically not even her own; she just channeled what her bosses had given her—so she couldn't really do anything to stop the hobgoblins from throwing the magic bottles. But she could stand in the way from now to the end of days and keep the brownie from getting hurt. A wonderful side effect of that was that she didn't get hurt either. At least, not much.

Okay, she couldn't be killed while she was protecting. She had actually racked up a substantial record of weird injuries over the years. But nothing deadly. Sometimes, especially when magic was involved, little things got through. And jumping in front of moving bullets was rarely fun. Still, she survived it all. She even had faster than normal healing thanks to her job, so the cut on her hand would be all better in another few minutes.

She could be killed, though. The trick for her was being in Protector mode, channeling that shielding magic that kept the good guys safe. If she was in the middle of doing her job as a walking, talking Kevlar vest, she could survive…well, just about anything as it turned out—though sometimes the worse for wear at the end. But when she wasn't in Protector mode, she was just an ordinary human, as vulnerable to bullets and magic potions as anyone.

She paused at that thought. Turns out she wasn't as ordinary as she'd previously thought. But that was an ongoing worry she didn't really have time to dwell on just then. The brownie's attempt at communicating had grown more frantic. There was something really important he needed to tell her.

"I am so sorry," she told the brownie, raising her hands in a helpless shrug. "I just can't understand what you're saying."

Damn, she wished Jaxer could be here to help.

Jaxer was a faery—no subspecies, but one of the highborn Fae—and he'd definitely be able to speak brownie. But as her mentor, he wasn't supposed to help her with anything this year. She was smack in the middle of her seventh year as a Protector and the Seventh Year was a test year. If she managed to survive it, she apparently came into her full powers, whatever that meant. She was much more focused on the "surviving it" goal.

"Is it the hobgoblins?" she asked. Maybe if they were patient, she could work this out. The brownie seemed to understand what she was saying even if she couldn't understand him.

The brownie nodded, his little head bouncing up and down rapidly. The gesture made his short crop of brown hair ripple.

"Okay. So it's something to do with the attackers." Another bottle shattered against her shields, spraying orange sparkles and green glass. "You know you're safe right now, right? They can't get through me to get to you."

He nodded again. Then started talking fast.

"Wait." She held up her hands. "Are they after you for a specific reason?"

He nodded, making a gesture she didn't understand.

"So not just a random attack on a random brownie?"

He shook his head. Then stomped his foot and put his hands on his hips.

"Hey, I'm trying here. And this is more information than I've previously gotten from all your talk that I can't understand. Be patient. We have time."

The brownie made a very pointed look at the sky, which was growing lighter as they spoke.

She sighed. "Yes, yes, the sun is coming up soon. I know. But if you'll be a little patient, we do still have time." More glass shattered and scattered around her. This time the sparkles were a bright white. They must be changing up the potions. "So, they're after you specifically. Did you say something rude?"

Head shake.

"Did you attack someone?"

Irritated head shake and another foot stop.

"Did you steal something?"

He shook his head. Then paused and nodded.

"That's less helpful. But a hint. You didn't but you did steal something?"

He nodded, jumping around enthusiastically. He said something she still didn't understand, and gestured at the hobgoblins.

"You stole from them?"

Emphatic—and again, irritated—head shake no.

"You stole from…someone they work for? Are they, like, guards or something?"

The brownie nodded and made a continue gesture with his little hand.

"They're guards, you stole something they were supposed to be protecting…?"

He nodded.

"From their boss?"

A rapid and enthusiastic series of words in his language.

"An actual object?" Since he'd said he both did and didn't steal something… "Or is this more like…information or a secret or something?"

The brownie did a jig and patted her on the hand. Then did another little dance, spinning in circles.

Okay. She'd hit on something there. "So you stole a secret of some kind? The hobgoblins are here to bring you back?"

Head shake.

"Kill you?"

Head nod.

"Wow. That must be some secret."

Emphatic head nod.

More glass and sparkles burst behind her. She ignored the hobgoblins. "And you stole it from someone powerful?"

Another nod.

"On purpose?"

The brownie made a face and looked away.

"So, not on purpose. You accidentally stumbled on the secret and now they want to kill you for it. Do I have the gist?"

He nodded and held his hands out to the side in a little helpless gesture that made her want to hug him. Poor little guy.

"Well, don't worry. I'll keep you safe."

She looked around, considering how she could get them back to her house—where hopefully she'd find a book in her secret attic with a Rosetta stone for brownie to English translation; she didn't remember having one, but that didn't mean she hadn't picked one up over the years—without putting him into her car.

Almost all the denizens of Faery had an allergy to iron, to one degree or another. The severity of allergic reaction depended on the species. Goblins had the least trouble with it. In fact, they kind of liked the stuff even though it gave some of them a burn. She wasn't sure if the same went for hobgoblins. Though cousins, the two species had quite a lot of differences.

Jaxer could handle iron better than any highborn Cary had heard of, but he still didn't climb into cars if he could avoid it because steel had high enough iron content to irritate. Jaxer was counting down until humans had fully developed plastic cars with no actual steel and iron involved—Cary wasn't hopeful this would happen in her lifetime. He managed to navigate the human world without going into anaphylactic shock or burning up or breaking out in a constant rash. But he still didn't much *like* iron, especially pure iron that wasn't part of an alloy.

As far as Cary could remember, brownies were very very susceptible to the iron allergy. Which meant even her home would be an uncomfortable place for the little guy. But she had a backyard with trees so he could hang out there and be okay. The problem was getting through the city and back to her house. They weren't exactly an easy walking distance.

If Deacon had been in town, she could have called him and had him just run the brownie back to her place. As a leopard shifter, he was fast enough to get the brownie there quickly, even in his human form, and at that speed, he blurred to human vision so no one would likely notice. But he was still in Eugene at a board meeting for the family business. And he wasn't due back until that afternoon.

That was another long and complicated bit of her life—having a leopard mate who hadn't been able to be away from her for very long until only just recently because otherwise he lost control of his leopard half, but who nonetheless had other things to do because he was on the board of directors of his family business which ran a bunch of animal rescue shelters around the country specializing in exotics. And she'd been really really upset that he couldn't work for so long because he *saved animals for a living.*

He was finally able to stay away from her for a few days at a time and not be super dangerous, so long as his mother was somewhere in the vicinity to help him control his leopard. He'd gone back to work full time last month, which she'd wanted to celebrate. He'd been pretty meh about the whole thing. And he definitely hadn't wanted to go away on this business trip. But she'd encouraged it. She loved having Deacon around and in her life, but frankly, the fact that she loved it so much scared the crap out of her. The fact that she felt his absence physically was equally disturbing. The mate business was new to her and because she wasn't a shifter it affected her differently than it did him, but she was still affected by it. In ways that made her distinctly uncomfortable sometimes.

Her reluctance to be away from him was one of the major "sometimes." Her inability to keep her hands off him…she minded that a lot less.

Without a handy shifter partner to do the running for her, she had to figure out a way to get the brownie away from the hobgoblins on her own, to somewhere safe, where she could translate his language. They needed to talk about this secret he'd discovered so she could figure out a way to keep him permanently safe.

More glass shattered around her as she considered the options. The number of bottles seemed to be increasing in frequency. Geez, how many magic potions did the hobgoblin have in that bag?

She glanced at him long enough to say, "You can stop now. You're wasting your magic."

The hobgoblin grunted and tossed another bottle at her.

She shook her head as it shattered a foot away, this time leaving a smear of rainbow color on the seemingly empty air where her shield resided. The color turned a deep purple black before sliding down to the ground where it sizzled in the dirt and grass like acid. That particular potion left a cloud of rotten eggs and piss stench in the air. Gross.

"Are you done yet?" she asked.

The hobgoblin with the bottles grunted something and turned to consult with his associates. She returned to her problem of where to take the brownie.

Her home was out of the question, at least in the immediate future. Too far and complicated. She needed to get somewhere nearby. Who did she know in this part of the city who might be able to translate brownie? Within walking distance? Who wouldn't be upset about her waking them up at this early hour?

She calculated where she was in her mental map of the town, and a perfect solution dropped onto it like a little red flashing location pin.

The Bookstore!

∽

Don't Miss
The Trouble with Magic and Faery Curses
Book 5 in the Cary Redmond series
Coming Soon!

BOOKS BY KAT SIMONS

THE CARY REDMOND SERIES

1 – The Trouble Black Cats and Demons

2 – The Trouble with Ghouls and Serial Killers

3 – The Trouble with Leopard Queens and Shifter Wars

4 – The Trouble with Baby Gods and Vampires

5 – The Trouble with Magic and Faery Curses COMING SOON

CARY REDMOND SHORT STORIES

When Cary Met Jaxer

When Cary Met Pickles

When Cary Met Angie

When Cary Met Lucy

When Cary Met Marianne

Cary and Deacon (Try to) Go On A Date

Date Night Take Two

Third Date's the Charm

TIGER SHIFTERS SERIES

1 – Once Upon a Tiger

2 – Along Came a Tiger

3 – Here There Be Tigers

4 – Her Tiger To Take

5 – To Tempt a Tiger

6 – Down Will Come Tiger

7 – To Catch a Tiger

8 – What a Tiger Wants

9 – Taming Her Tiger

Tiger Shifters Series Vol 1 (Books 1 - 3)

Tiger Shifters Series Vol 2 (Books 4 - 6)

ABOUT THE AUTHOR

Kat Simons earned her Ph.D. in animal behavior, working with animals as diverse as dolphins and deer. She brought her experience and knowledge of biology to her paranormal romance and urban fantasy fiction, where she delights in taking nature and turning it on its ear. Her Tiger Shifters series combines romance and the otherworldly with heart-pounding action adventure. Her latest urban fantasy romance series follows the adventures of Protector Cary Redmond as she tries to manage her personal life while saving the world. A lot.

After traveling the world, Kat now lives in New York City with her family. She is a stay-at-home mom and a full time writer.

For more on Kat and her future books:

Website: https://www.katsimons.com
Newsletter: http://eepurl.com/OxQQL